GAWAIN GREEN

A Fylde Family Mystery

Kate Laxen

Copyright © 2024 by Kate Laxen

All rights reserved.

No part of this book may be reproduced, or stored in a retrieval system, or transmitted in any form or by any means, electronic, mechanical, photocopying, recording or otherwise, without express permission of the publisher, apart from the use of short quotations in book reviews.

The story, all names, characters, and incidents portrayed in this production are fictitious. No identification with actual persons (living or deceased), places, buildings, and products is intended or should be inferred.

Cover: www.thecovercollection.com

ISBN 9798339530527

If thy brother wrongs thee, remember not so much his wrong-doing, but more than ever that he is thy brother.

Epictetus

Contents

1. Gawain..
2. Jacob...
3. Gawain...
4. Gawain...
5. Gawain...
6. Gawain...
7. Gawain...
8. Gawain...
9. Jacob...
10. Gawain...
11. Gawain...
12. Gawain...
13. Gawain...
14. Gawain...
15. Gawain...
16. Jacob...
17. Gawain...
18. Jacob...
19. Jacob...
20. Jacob...
21. Jacob...
22. Gawain...
23. Gawain...
24. Gawain...
25. Gawain...
26. Gawain...
27. Gawain...

28. Jacob ....
29. Gawain ....
30. Gawain ....
31. Gawain ....

1.Gawain

Hi, I'm Gawain, one of the doctors.

That's what I usually say when I pull the blue curtain to the side and make my entrance. But this time I only get as far as *hi*. The rest of the sentence collapses into a strangulated garble that doesn't make it past the back of my throat. I stand by the side of the bed and stare at the patient, then I glance down at my blurry reflection in the highly polished linoleum and I look up again. I repeat this process, twice, quickly, like a nodding dog. The second time, I screw my eyes shut and open them again. It doesn't make any difference. He's still here. I should have scrutinized his notes more closely before I breezed in. If I'd done that, I might have noticed his name and finding him of all people, here of all places, wouldn't have been such a god-awful shock.

I can't feel the floor through the soles of my trainers. This isn't all that uncommon for me. I have a tendency to float when I've been awake for longer than should be humanly possible. But it seems worse than usual this time. For a few seconds, I think I'm going to black out, although the colour flooding into my eyes is blue, not black. Most things are blue here, not just the curtains. The walls, the cupboard doors and my scrubs are blue, too, a deep sunlit, Californian sky kind of blue, like a seaside scene on the August page of a calendar or one of those paintings of swimming pools and boys by David Hockney. I suppose it's meant to provide a bit of cheer for the patients, a vague hint that things might improve for them. But the shade they've chosen is too vivid, and in any case, better times aren't necessarily on their way, are they? Particularly if you're lying flat on your back in this place.

My shift is nearly over, and until about ten seconds ago my plan was to deal with this final recipient of my expertise as quickly as possible, and then go home and sleep forever, or at least until I have to be back here again. But it's *him*. His long and lanky body is curled up on the bed, foetal style and he's cradling his head in his arms as though he thinks someone is about to strike him. Bony knees protrude through rents in his tattered jeans, and his hair, which used to be a very pale shade of blonde, is a dull and lightish mouse colour, thanks to what seems to be a coating of dust mixed with soil. Although he's facing me, I can't see his features properly because his elbows are in the way. But I know it's him.

Michaela, one of the nurses, is standing at the other side of the bed, throwing me significant looks for all she's worth. I get myself round there. His T-shirt has been removed, a hospital gown is draped loosely around his front, and he's been hooked up to the usual monitors.

As I get closer to him, I detect a faint hint of a shaming, unclean odour. Shaming for me, that is. I don't want to be this boy's doctor. I want to take him back to my flat, strip the rest of his clothes off him and throw them in a washing machine, and then run him a bath, fill it with bubbles and make him get in. And after that, when he doesn't stink like a landfill site anymore, I'd give him some of my clean clothes to wear, even though they'd be too small, and I'd address him by his name and ask him, *what the hell*?

I realise I need to get a grip and treat him like any other patient. I glance at the screen, which doesn't show anything particularly alarming. Then, I look at his back, which does, because it's covered in big blotches of dark red, clotted blood, matted with fibres in places, presumably from the shirt he was wearing. When I peer more closely I can see what look like a series of horizontal red stripes, but are actually lacerations, all approximately parallel to each other. At one end, none of them are much more than minor grazes and the shallower cuts have begun to scab over, but at the other end, where some of them wrap around his side, almost reaching his chest, they're alarmingly deep. I'll need to ring someone from the plastics team, so they can come and check the extent of the damage before we suture them. At a guess, I'd say these injuries are getting on for twenty-four hours old, or perhaps more than that. It would be useful to know for certain. We'll have to hope they haven't become infected in the time it's taken him to show up here. But they don't look infected and another quick glance up at the screen tells me his temperature is normal.

I allow myself a few seconds to stand back and assess his overall state. His sharp, white shoulder blades jut out like a trainee angel's, and I can see his ribs. I've spent a lot of time speculating about the way he might look now, but none of the images I've conjured up inside my head have ever come close to this. For one thing, he used to be much broader than me. He was a rugby player at school, whereas I was more of a sprinter, although sports were always much more his thing. Now I'd say he's about as slender as I am, and people never stop going on at me about not eating enough.

I walk back round to the other side of the bed and crouch down in front of him. The last time I saw him he was years away from shaving, but now his chin is covered in spiky stubble, not blonde like his hair, but gingery. It runs through my mind that maybe it isn't him at all, just someone who looks like him, an anonymous person I can treat, discharge and forget about. It wouldn't be the first time I've mistaken someone else for him. One time, a few years ago, I was sure a youth I'd spotted at Earl's Court tube station, leaning against the wall at the far end of the platform, in the shadows under the bridge was him, and then, more recently, I was convinced he was sitting a few rows up from me on a flight to Alicante. This could easily be another of those mis-identifications. And anyway, I thought he was in the US.

But when I look at his notes again, his name is written there, clear as anything, and the surname we share is quite unusual. Also, I can see little scar just above his right eye from the time I hit him with a plastic box of cup-cakes in the butler's pantry at school. The broken edge of the lid was sharper than I realised and caused more damage than I'd intended. I was a prefect then, and I'd given him a poem to memorise as a detention for something. I can't remember or even imagine now what on earth he could have done that was bad enough to merit a punishment like that. He failed to recite the poem back to me and then said he thought it was a load of bollocks, which annoyed me because it was *Here* by Philip Larkin. That wasn't why I clobbered him, though. I did that because two of his classmates were watching and I didn't want to show favouritism and risk him getting bullied because of it. Maybe I was showing off a bit, too, playing to the gallery, which was a habit of mine back then. Either way, I never meant to leave a mark.

My hand hovers a couple of centimetres above the top of his head and my fingers curl and then uncurl again as they fight the urge to ruffle his hair. His eyelids are crinkled, as if he's closing his eyes as tightly as he can, to make me think he's unconscious or sleeping. Patients often pretend to be more out of it than they really are, either because they can't face interacting with anyone or they don't like the harsh, exposing lights. I'm sure I'd do the same. I remove his arms from his face, gently slap his cheeks and tell him to wake up. I know my voice sounds harsh and possibly a bit bossy, but I really need to make sure he's capable of engaging with me. His skin feels clammy and cold, even though A&E is very warm, and he has purple-grey smudges under his eyes. Eventually, with what looks like great reluctance, his eyelids peel back just a little and then close again. This happens a few times, then his eyes stay open long enough for me to shine a light into them.

His pupils tell me he's pretty drugged up. He blinks a bit more and then fixes me with a measured, violet-blue gaze that's so familiar, so much a part of me, it kind of takes my breath away, and I watch as it slowly dawns on him that he's face to face with me, the last person he must have expected or wanted to encounter, ever, anywhere, under any circumstances. A tiny crease appears between his delicate, almost invisible eyebrows and the monitor above his head registers an increase in his heart rate.

If he could, he'd get up and leave, but he can hardly lift his head from his pillow, so he's stuck with me for now. I force myself to stay in doctor mode and I ask him loads of questions, to try and get a clearer picture of what's happened. What caused the cuts on his back, how long ago did they happen, how did he get here, how is his health in general? Then I move onto other, more personal questions. Where is he living? What about his asthma? Does he have an inhaler with him or doesn't he need one anymore? It feels incredibly intrusive and I hate myself for doing it. Any other doctor would ask the same or similar questions, but my need to know the answers goes beyond the merely professional. It's desperate and personal, selfish even. I'm gagging for him to tell me he's ok, despite the fact he's showed up here, thin and pale as a wraith, with his back all cut up, and also, on a more basic level, I want to hear his voice, because he hasn't spoken to me or communicated with me in any way whatsoever for more than eight years. Eight years, two weeks and four days, to be precise.

He ignores most of my questions. The only responses I get are a brief shake of the head when I ask him what he's taken, and the same again when I ask if he knew I'd be here.

'Okay,' I say, quietly, just like I would to any other patient. Then I add 'We'll get you sorted,' which I don't usually say, because, unlike most other doctors, I can't manage it without sounding melodramatic and patronising, and in any case, it's not always true.

His eyes flicker slightly, perhaps with relief that I'm not going to press him with even more questions, or maybe it's an involuntary reaction, an unconscious settling back into the remnants of his former relationship with me? I know I'm kidding myself about this latter possibility, but I'm desperate for it to be true, and all I want to do, now that I've managed to prevent my hands from touching his hair, is kiss him on the forehead. I used to do that all the time, and usually he stood there and let me. It embarrassed the hell out of him, particularly when I did it at school, but he rarely stopped me. And afterwards, if anyone was looking, he'd roll his eyes, smile and shake his head.

He needn't worry. Even I have the self-awareness to realise this isn't an appropriate time to reinstate the tradition. Instead, I stand up again and draw my scattered emotions into a tightly controlled ball for long enough to carry out a rapid, initial review of his condition and eliminate other potential issues, like broken bones or breathing and circulatory problems. Then I dash out of the cubicle and collect everything I need to draw blood from him. When I return and he sees what I'm going to do, he clamps his eyelids down again and presses his face into the bed. He hasn't grown out of his childhood terror of needles then. I don't apologise or warn him when I'm about to stick the needle in. I just get on with it as quickly as I can, and when his blood starts to glide smoothly and evenly out of the vein and into the capillary tubing I tell him it's nearly done. He doesn't respond.

Once the bloods have been dealt with, I come over all vague again. I've been here since yesterday morning, and although I've imbibed several Americanos and at least one flat white, the only thing I've eaten for at least twenty-four hours is a small chocolate biscuit. And in any case, given my relationship with this patient, I shouldn't really be dealing with him at all. Someone more senior needs to decide whether the police should be involved for one thing, and another doctor, any other physician who isn't me, might be able to get him to answer all the pertinent questions and then be in better position to help him.

I wander off to find someone. The Thomas the Tank Engine breakfast trolley trundles past on its way to the children's wards, grinning broadly and giving off a toasty, eggy aroma. Its appearance transforms the hospital from a night-time world to a morning one, and as if to confirm this, Bryan appears in the distance, striding down the corridor towards me, whistling and rattling his car keys in his pocket. His jowls wobbling as his feet strike the floor.

I hesitate for a few seconds. It *would* have to be him, the consultant who's been on my case big time since I started here, the one who gave me a massive telling off at the end of my first week, for coming across as *aloof* and *maybe a tad arrogant*, he said. *Fit in or fuck off* was the advice he offered me, like a sweary version of a fortune cookie. As I attempt to explain the situation, he nods his head and appraises me with his sad brown eyes. By the time I've finished, I can tell I've intrigued the bejesus out of him and he almost breaks into a run in his eagerness to get to Jacob's cubicle. Perhaps he's hoping this development will add a few more pieces to the Gawain-shaped puzzle he's tried and so far failed to put together.

'Hello Sebastian!' He booms as he pulls back the curtain.

'Jacob,' I say.

'Sebastian,' Jacob mutters.

Jacob is his middle name, but we always called him that. I have no idea why he wants to be addressed as Sebastian now. It feels like an affront, a random decision made just to get at me. Bryan strides across to look at Jacob's back, which Michaela has now cleaned up. He shakes his head slightly and then fishes his phone out of his trouser pocket and takes a few photos without asking for permission. I don't think my brother notices. I wonder whether he'd mind or not if he was aware of it. He probably would, very much. But all I do is watch in silence as Bryan completes this little task and then puts his phone back in his pocket.

'What happened?' Bryan asks, briskly, as though the idea that he might not get an answer hasn't even occurred to him.

Jacob doesn't respond, which makes me feel both better and worse at the same time. A long silence follows. Bryan probably hopes that Jacob will start to feel uncomfortable and volunteer more information. But he doesn't, so Bryan continues.

'Is there anything else you'd like us to know about?'

'Like what?' Jacob asks, his voice barely audible.

'Are you hurt you in any other way?'

He shakes his head.

'Do you want us to get the police involved?'

At this, Jacob drops off the side of the bed onto the floor and rapidly crawls towards the curtain. The wires glued to his chest peel themselves off one by one and dangle loosely from the monitoring equipment.

'Ok. No police then,' Bryan says lightly, as though it's all the same to him.

After we've hauled Jacob back onto the bed and connected him up again, Bryan looks over at me, clearly mystified, and who can blame him? I shrug my shoulders and shake my head slightly. My eyes are starting to sting. What did Bryan mean by *hurt you in any other way*? Jesus.

'Your shift ended when?' He shouts across the bed in my general direction. He doesn't give me time to respond, but speaks for me as though I've whispered the answer into his ear, like a glove puppet.

'Two hours ago? Go and sit over there. You be the relative. I'll be the doctor.'

I find a chair and position myself next to my brother, and I lean forward, with my elbows resting on the side of the bed and my head supported in my palms so my face is as close to his as I can get it. His eyes are open properly now, more or less, and his pupils are smaller and sharper. When his drug results come through we discover he's taken a common sleeping tablet, but not in a high enough dose to do any lasting harm, and its effects are clearly wearing off now.

Bryan's intervention seems to have brought about a slight alteration in the atmosphere and forced a narrow crack to open in the fragile barrier Jacob has constructed around himself. My brother meets my gaze properly for the first time, and we explore each other's faces, as though we're both reading almost forgotten, but familiar sets of instructions and trying to work out whether any of the details have changed or stayed the same. I can't tell what he's thinking. Is he genuinely horrified to find himself confronted by me or is he just confused? Or is he troubled by something deeper, something that goes way beyond the situation he's landed himself in right now? I sit and stare at him, noting his sharp cheekbones and his longish nose and wide mouth, which I also have, and his light eyes, fair hair and blond eyelashes, which are nothing like mine. I try to integrate this new, adult version of him with the thirteen year old I've carefully maintained inside my head for so long. I fail.

'You look awful,' he says, suddenly.

The huskiness, the sheer manliness of his voice gives me a jolt. And the way he pronounces *awful* sounds American.

'You don't look that great yourself.'

I can't think of anything else to say to him that isn't a question, and I want to bombard him with loads more of those: *why are you back in the UK, why has this happened, what the hell is going on, are you at uni, have you forgiven me, can we meet up sometime? Can I do anything to help? Please let me help.* But I keep all this inside my head and go for a safer option.

'Are you hungry?'

He nods. I smile, but he doesn't smile back. The boy version of Jacob was a notorious human dustbin. At school he could be relied upon to hoover up all the leftovers, even liver and onions, sago pudding and the brownish, liquid-based horror that inevitably appeared every Friday lunchtime, for no apparent reason, and was known by all of us in Cherry Tree House as *faecal vomit soup*. I dash off to the café and I buy him a cheese sandwich, a can of coke, not the sugar-free kind, because I reckon he needs all the energy he can get, and a bag of Doritos. On the way, I make a quick detour to my locker to pick up my wallet and my home clothes, plus a spare T-shirt for him. His own shirt was cut to remove it from him and is now propped against the wall at the back of the cubicle, a sandwich board of two semi-detached, blood-stiffened slices of material.

'Don't hurtle, Dr Fylde!' Bryan calls after me.

'He's always rushing around,' he says to Jacob.

'Yeah?' Jacob mumbles, as though he doesn't really care either way, but is prepared to take it for granted that I still do that.

I hurry because I'm scared they'll discharge him before I get back and he'll take the opportunity to disappear again without saying goodbye. But he's still here when I return, and I watch as he unwraps the sandwich and devours it rapidly.

Once the cleaning and suturing of his wounds is complete and he's been unplugged from the monitoring equipment, he pulls my T-shirt over his head and looks at me again.

'What have you done to your hair?' He asks in that American accent.

Michaela and Bryan look across at me. Bryan raises his eyebrows expectantly.

'It used to be longer and kind of curly,' Jacob explains in a sleepy monotone.

He manages to make it sound like a criticism, as though my corkscrew hair was yet another weapon deployed by me specifically to ruin his life. I run my hand over my head, absently. I've worn my hair cropped almost brutally short since the July before I went to medical school. Two days after I'd fallen out with my brother, to be more specific. He glares at me, eyes full of resentful curiosity. After all this time, does he really still wish I was six feet under or reduced to a shovelful of grit inside an urn on Aunty Susan's mantelpiece?

Pretty much, I'd say.

I quickly change out of my scrubs and into my own clothes in front of everyone. I don't care who sees what, not that there is an awful lot to see, but I don't want to leave Jacob alone for a single second in case he takes the opportunity to scarper.

When he's discharged and he scrambles down from the bed, I realise he's a good six or seven inches taller than me. Normal brothers who haven't seen each other for a while would probably marvel at this and maybe have a good laugh about it, particularly as I'm the eldest by five and a half years. But when we saunter off towards the exit together, neither of us even mentions it. I try to stay close to him, not touching, but near enough for us both to feel the electrostatic attraction between the hairs on our respective arms, the way we always did when we went anywhere together. But each time I close the distance between us he moves away again. It riles me and makes me decide not to let him wriggle off my hook. Not completely, at least not yet.

'How did you get here? I know you didn't come in by ambulance.'

'Someone drove me and left me in the waiting room.'

'Who?'

'Just someone. Nobody.'

His voice carries the slightest hint of a whine, now, like that of an overwrought child being badgered by a teacher or a parent.

'They left you in the waiting room, in the state you were in?'

He doesn't respond.

'Give me your phone, so I can put my number in it.'

'It's not mine. It'd be safer to write it on a piece of paper.'

'Safer?'

I regret saying this as soon as the words are out of my mouth, because his face closes up completely. He looks down at the floor and bites his lip. I rummage in a nearby wastepaper bin until I find a piece of cardboard from a discarded sandwich pack, and by very unusual piece of good fortune, I discover an ancient biro lurking messily in the bottom of my backpack. I scribble my number and address on one side of the wrapper and then I add my sister's details on the other. Then I give it to him. He glances at it briefly and shoves it into one of his back pockets.

'Keep in touch to let us know you're ok,' I say.

I might be off limits as far as he's concerned, but he didn't fall out with Amanda. He met up with her and spoke to her on the phone for years after he'd stopped speaking to me. He even went to stay with her in Edinburgh, where she did her medical training. Of course that was before he went to America for what was meant to be a gap year and disappeared off the radar completely.

'And if you're not ok, contact us and we'll come and get you.'

I try to make it sound as though this is a casual suggestion, a bit of a joke, Sir Gawain galloping to the rescue on his trusty steed, and all that. But in truth, I want him to ask for my help more than I want anything else in the entire world, and if he does call me, I'll drop everything. If I'm busy at work, I'll just walk out, even if I'm in Resus doing cardiac massage. I'll go anywhere, do anything, take any kind of risk.

'I don't usually have access to a phone. And even if I did I wouldn't...'

I cut him off because I don't want to hear him say I'd be the last person he would ring, even if he was about to be ritually slaughtered and everyone else in his contact list was unavailable.

'Well, anyway, you know where I work now and you've got my address,' I say.

"Sure," he says, politely.

I could be anyone, as far as he's concerned, I think. But then he looks me in the eye, very briefly, which surprises me and encourages me to stick my neck out a bit further.

'Do you want to come back to mine for a while?' I ask.

I might be wrong, but I think I catch him trying but failing to stop a shadow passing over his face. The look in his eyes is so sad and kind of lost it hits me like a punch in the stomach. Even so, unless I'm just projecting my own desires onto him, the possibility that he wishes he could come back with me, gives me something to cling on to. Briefly, I let myself imagine us spending a few hours together in my flat, Jacob eating the pizza I've ordered for him, watching films, catching up. He'd groan when he saw how untidy my place was and I'd open the windows and close the curtains to keep out the sun. If all he wanted to do was sleep, I'd sit and watch over him, for hours and hours if necessary.

'I need to make a call so they can come and get me,' he says.

I walk with him to the pick-up point in front of the main hospital building. When we reach the waiting area, he moves a few metres away from me, turns his back and puts the phone to his ear. I try to hear what he says to the person on the other end of the phone, but the noise of traffic on the dual carriageway that runs past the hospital grounds road is way too loud. When he returns, he seems agitated and he keeps looking up and down the access route that links the hospital foyer with the main road.

'You'd better go before they get here,' he says.

I step forward towards him so I can grab him by the back of his neck and pull him into a hug, but he realises what I have in mind and takes the same number of steps backwards, putting himself safely out of reach. I say *bye then* in a fake cheerful tone that sounds utterly ridiculous. He's looking down at his borrowed phone and doesn't respond, so I force myself to walk away.

Separating myself from him feels like swimming through concrete, but somehow I manage to get across the road and up the stairs to Level Two of the multi storey, from where I spy on him over the concrete wall. He stands there, shifting his weight from one foot to the other, until a clapped out old Ford Fiesta approaches and stops to let him get in. The driver is on my side, so I get a clear view of him. He looks older than both of us, in his late thirties, I'd say, and as pale and washed out as my brother, with long, colourless hair tied back in a pony tail and a sour, downturned mouth. Round his neck, he seems to be wearing one of those cowboy-type string ties. What a weirdo. I wouldn't be surprised if he turns up at A & E himself one day, if he hasn't already. If he does and he's allocated to me I'll find it difficult not to finish him off with a shot of insulin, just because he's allowed to drive my brother away, whereas I'm not.

As Jacob gets in the car, this bloke looks at him and says something I can't make out. Jacob settles in the passenger seat, but shuffles towards the door, as though he wants to put as much distance between himself and the driver as possible. Then he remembers his wounded back and leans forward and slightly sideways, with his face pressed against the window.

2. Jacob

When I get into the passenger seat, Ed looks me up and down. The car is suffocatingly hot and smells of his breath and the gum he's chewing to try and disguise it. Ed is the only one of them, apart from Ruth, who knows I went to the hospital.

'You okay?'

He scratches at a yellow spot on his chin. My South Carolina accent is starting to fade a little now we're back in the UK, but his is strong as ever.

'Fine.'

'What happened to your shirt?'

Ed doesn't miss much, particularly about me.

'It was stuck to my back. They had to cut it off.'

'Tell them you threw it away if they ask.'

'I know.'

'That one is way too short for you.'

I don't tell him it belongs to my brother, who has, in the years since I last saw him, managed to qualify as a doctor and just happens to be working in the nearest emergency department to the church. I hunch my shoulders and shift myself forward so my back doesn't come into contact with the seat, and I pull down the shade at the top of the windscreen to protect my eyes from the dazzling glare of the afternoon sun. Ed's right, the T-shirt *is* too short for me. I look down at my stomach and I gather some of the material in my hand and rub it between my thumb and my forefinger. I can't believe this item of clothing belongs to him. My actual brother. I imagine him running in it, sweating in it and sprawling in it on Aunty Susan's sofa, starfish-like, taking up all the available space, when sleep catches him unawares. I used to sit on him when he did that, and bounce up and down until he woke up and shifted himself along a bit so there was room for me, too. And I see him lifting up the front to wipe his forehead when he's hot. I do the same thing now, adding my own secretions to the mix. The T-shirt gives off the exotic tropical fruit smell of some fabric softener or other, but I can detect a trace of G's own individual aroma as well, peppery and subtle as a pheromone, so familiar after all this time, and so definitely there, embedded in the material. It almost makes me gasp to encounter it again.

Ed drives out of the hospital grounds and creeps forward onto the dual carriageway. The tinny car radio is playing a mawkish lament of a song from the nineties that always makes me want to slit my wrists. The traffic is nose to tail and we're stuck with all the other cars, buses and vans inching towards the roundabout in the petrol fumes and the heat. My stitches feel hot and itchy. I wonder if that consultant guy has sewn them too tightly. I bet he's too senior to for mundane tasks like suturing, except in situations like today, when his junior colleague loses the plot and the patient has injuries that are unusual. Maybe the stitches would feel looser if the nurse or G had put them in, although the idea of G doing anything like that is just mind boggling.

The traffic starts to move and the car jolts forward. My brain feels like a collection of clumpy fragments, tossing about inside my skull, like socks in a tumble drier. I might have to ask Ed to stop so I can puke in the gutter. I try closing my eyes, but violent circles swirl about and disorient me, as though I'm doing somersaults, so I open them again and try to hold my head rigidly against the headrest and arch my back away from the seat at the same time. I look in the rear view mirror to see if I can spot my brother behind us. I don't even know what car he drives, if he drives at all. The last time I saw him, he'd just left school, but he hadn't passed his driving test. When I was in the sixth form, they'd started this scheme where you could take lessons, and most of us learned to drive soon after our seventeenth birthdays. But G was long gone by then.

I'd never have let them take me to A & E if I'd known he'd be there. What were the chances? I knew he'd got into medical school, but I had no idea he'd gone all the way through the years of training and made it as a doctor. When I came back to Aunty Susan's at the end of that first summer holiday in South Carolina, he'd just gone off to King's in London, the room we shared was half empty and Aunty S was bouncing up and down as if there was someone hidden above her on the other side of the ceiling, pulling strings attached to her arms and legs.

'Straight A's, even in double maths. But it's not surprising, is it? Given that he was a scholarship boy and always so gifted.'

His astounding double maths marks were some of the highest in the country, apparently. We all, even Aunty Susan, knew why he'd done so well in *that* subject, but the way she went on about it, you'd think it had been entirely his own achievement. But then, G was always her favourite. Even when he'd done that truly awful thing and the only person who had the right to offer him absolution was me, she took his side. She said it was understandable he would do what he did, the poor mite, after all he'd been through, as though, out of the three of us siblings, he was the only one who'd been through it. When she finally stopped to draw breath, I told her I didn't want to hear anything else about G ever again.

I suppose being a doctor is another performative act for him. There he is, all swarthy and handsome in his blue scrubs, stethoscope draped round his neck, swanning into cubicles and leaning over patients with a concerned but professional expression plastered across his face, shouting instructions to the nurses like a dishy doctor in a hospital box set. I bet he's on a constant ego trip and everyone adores him, like they did at school. He must be drunk on the power it gives him. Just think, he's allowed to prescribe potentially dangerous drugs, make life changing decisions and do all sorts of things to people, like when he stuck that needle in my hand without any warning. He knows I hate needles. What a total bell end.

Aunty S struggled to accept my new attitude towards G. Before we fell out, G and I were glued together more or less. I honestly thought I'd started my life as a growth on his side, carved from his cells, and that I'd budded off from him as a fully formed entity, separate and distinct, but still part of him. His satellite. It was the same at boarding school. I couldn't cling to him physically in the same way there, obviously. Our overly intense connection was forced to transmute itself into something more subtle. But it was just as strong, a spectral rope nobody else could see.

It sounds lame, doesn't it? It *was* lame. My happiness and my ability to function were totally dependent on him. He was a drug and I was addicted, and when he betrayed me I had no choice but to go cold turkey and avoid him forever. Any kind of half-way house would have been unbearable. So I started going out to South Carolina, to stay with Mum at her church.

I need to stay calm. When I'm aggravated my can get triggered asthma, and I don't want that, because I haven't got an inhaler that works, just a lump of fabric in the style of a pincushion. Mum made it from an old skirt and stuffed it with herbs that are meant to clear your airways, according to an old book about plant lore she keeps in the kitchen.

Ed pulls up in the car park and turns the engine off. The old church and its vicarage or manse or whatever it is, bake quietly in the late afternoon sun, and there are no other vehicles. This place is rented. The longer term plan is to find somewhere more remote, like an old holiday camp or an abandoned farm, a place where nobody can watch and work out what's really going on.

Since we moved to the UK, On Mondays, since we moved to the UK, or rather moved back to the UK, because the church had an outpost here once before, a few years ago, Warren, who is my stepfather, and his brother Godwin have started going to meetings with elders from other communities in the UK Outreach Chapter of the church. I don't know where these weekly gatherings of Psychopaths Anonymous are held and I have no clue what goes on at them, but afterwards, they must go a pub or a bar somewhere, because they're always wasted when they get back. Mum goes out on Mondays, too, but not to the meetings. None of the women have senior roles at New Sunrise. But as the wife of the Chief Elder, she gets a generous allowance and they drop her off at the station, so she can catch a train to London or Basingstoke to do shopping and girly stuff. When she gets back, she's always loaded down with posh looking carrier bags, the kind made out of brightly coloured paper with thick string handles, and she often has different hair and nails, and a new make-over that covers any blemishes or bruising.

Yesterday, after the ritual was finished, Warren and Godwin carried me down to the basement and laid me on my bed. Mum snipped a few leaves from one of the aloe vera plants she keeps on the kitchen window sill and cut them in half so she could smear what she calls their healing juice onto my back. She told me to stop shaking because I was making the wounds bleed more, and when she'd finished, she said the lacerations would mend themselves. I could feel the trickle of the blood, wet and sticky, coursing down my back and soaking into the waistband of my jeans. The small amount of plant juice she managed to squeeze out of the leaves stung as sharply as if it had come from lemons, and was probably washed away by my own secretions before it could do any good. But Mum dabbed my back with kitchen towel and said I'd be fine. Then she hovered over me for a bit, murmured some sort of prayer about repentance, and gave me double my usual dose of sleeping tablets.

By the next morning, the blood had dried and my shirt, which I'd slept in because I was too zonked out to do anything more than crash on the top of my bed, was stuck to my back. I was still too hazy from the pills to care much about any of this, but Ruth, who is Warren's daughter and my girlfriend, kind of, said I might get sepsis. That made Ed go a bit twitchy. So once the others were out of the way, he drove me to the hospital and left me slumped on a chair in the waiting room. I think I must have slid onto the floor soon after that because I have a vague memory of footsteps running towards me and a sharp pain in my back when I got lifted up and put on a trolley.

I jump out of the car and run across the car park to the door at the side of the house before Ed can stop me. It's unlocked as usual, and I make my way into the kitchen-diner, which is empty. Ruth must still be in the church doing the sweeping and the brass polishing and all the other Monday chores. They will be taking her longer than usual because I'm not there to help. I leave the kitchen, dive through a narrow doorway halfway down the hall, click on a light and run down the stairs and across a shadowy floor, dodging several boxes of pamphlets offering handy information about how useful Jesus might be in a range of hypothetical and unrealistic situations. I reach the narrow space partitioned off from the rest of the basement, otherwise known as my room. I used to have a decent bedroom upstairs next to Ruth's, but now I have to be kept as far away from her as possible. My new room is more of a cell really, just wide enough for a single bed and a cupboard covered with peeling blue paint and decorated with ancient stickers with random words on them, like *groovy* and *freaky*. They won't shift no matter how much I try to scratch them off with my fingernails.

My room doesn't have a proper window, just a small glazed and reinforced rectangular gap fitted into the brickwork at the top of the wall. Right now, that's a good thing because it doesn't let the sun in, so the temperature is considerably cooler in here than outside. Exhausted and way more out of breath than I should be, I shut the door. G's T-shirt is starting to stick to me so I peel it off. I'm not sure what to do with it, but I can hear the shuffle and tap of Ed's metal toe caps, which means he's running down the stairs in his cowboy boots, so I have to decide quickly. I roll it up and shove it into my bed, between the mattress and the wooden base, then I grab one of my own T-shirts from the cupboard, a New Sunrise one in yellow, with a black cross emblazoned on the front, and I manage to push my head through the neck and cover my top half before he appears.

He opens the door, leans on one side of the door frame and holds his hand out. I still haven't quite managed to clear the memory of G's T-shirt from my mind, so for a second I think that's what he's after. But then I remember I've got his phone. I pull it out of my back pocket and hand it to him. He holds it in one hand and starts clicking and scrolling, looking down at the photos he took of me yesterday at the ritual and then up at today's version of me. He makes sure to take his time and I hear the slight increase in his breathing rate as he tries to hide the fact that he's getting himself all worked up. I roll onto my side so I'm facing the wall instead of Ed, and I pull my T-shirt down so it covers the gap where the skin of my lower back was exposed at the top of my jeans.

After taking me to hospital and driving me home again, he'll expect something in return. Poor Ed. He likes to think we have a kind of unspoken arrangement. He helps me out sometimes, like today, and I repay him. I never do though, or not in the way he'd like me to. Photos are all he's ever going to get from me. Despite my fall from grace, I'm still Pastor Warren's stepson, and Ed isn't all that much further up the pecking order than I am. He has to be mindful of that, and in any case, the others will be back soon. He contents himself with gazing at me for a bit. Then he slopes off.

I close my eyes and let my mind drift. Neither Ed nor Ruth will tell Mum about my trip to the hospital, and I'll have to keep the stitches hidden, because she'd pass the info onto Warren and then it will all kick off. She'll come down to my room at some point, though, to give me my next lot of sleeping tablets or whatever they are. Once upon a time, she might have asked me if I'm ok, and even brushed her fingers against my cheek. But these days, she hardly even looks at me, and when she does, her eyes, which are so similar to G's it gives me the creeps, are dead, like buttons sewn onto a soft toy. Her glance quickly strays away from my face and settles just to one side of my head, as though she can see some ghost or imaginary friend way more important than me, hovering behind my shoulder. To an outsider, I suppose her behaviour would seem weird. It *is* weird. I think my mother must be seriously deranged. But I totally get why she's afraid to engage with me now that I'm in so much trouble. Like the rest of us, she has plenty to be scared of.

It's all fine, though. Bad experiences don't really affect me anymore. I'm numb most of the time. Once I've swallowed the pills, I'll probably just hang for a while, waiting for nothing, hoping that for tonight at least, I'll be able to keep myself under the radar.

Then I'll sink into a slumber so deep I'll forget I ever had a brother.

3. Gawain

The Fiesta disappears round the bend in the service road. It has a dent in its rear bumper. Someone must have rammed it. I press my forehead against the concrete wall and wail silently. Good job I haven't brought my car to work because I don't think I'd be capable of driving it right now. When I've calmed down a bit, I go back down the stairs and walk along the footpath that winds like a zebra crossing version of the yellow brick road through the bottom level of the car park. The air is full of petrol fumes. I inhale them greedily. A single high pitched note reverberates inside my head, like some kind of alarm. At least I hope it's an internal thing. Maybe it's not. It's possible that I'm keening out loud at passers-by.

I reach the pavement by the side of the dual carriageway and I try and fail to spot the black Fiesta in the traffic edging slowly forwards towards the lights at the big roundabout. It must have already made it through to the other side, taking my brother God knows where. I'm filled with regret. If I hadn't hung about for so long in the car park, feeling sorry for myself, I might have caught another glimpse of my brother.

Today's been like one of those stories where the day starts just like any other and the main character has no idea something seismic is about to happen. How can that be possible? When you drop a stone into a calm pond, the ripples spread out equally in every direction, so why does an extraordinary event that plunges into your life from nowhere only impact on the future? Why don't its repercussions travel backwards in time as well as forwards and flag themselves up as omens or warnings?

But I don't really have the mental energy for such philosophical musings, and although I'm not hungry, I can sense my blood sugar levels have tanked. If I'm not careful, I'll black out, and if I do, there's a serious risk I might drop off the curb into the traffic, so I head for the supermarket at the other side of the roundabout. As I enter the building and pick up a basket, the air con gives me goose bumps. I look around to see what's on offer. I don't do mastication under any circumstances, so anything that might be crispy, chewy or need any kind of effort to be made by my teeth before being swallowed will not be going anywhere near my mouth under any circumstances. People often ask me why I only eat soft foods. My usual response is to roll my eyes and tell them to mind their own business. I'm bored to death with hearing that question and in any case, I have no idea why. There must be something to account for it, but whatever the reason, it has been locked away in the cess pit at back of my head for a very long time, along with all the other unprocessed psycho-crap I've never dealt with. Whatever the reason, I can't eat anything before it's been reduced to a mush or at least a semi-liquid paste. Food that offers any kind of resistance makes my teeth itch and I have to spit it out.

I'm a nightmare at dinner parties.

I pick out Greek style yoghurts, tins of spaghetti hoops and a toothpaste-like tube of processed cheese, taking care not to select the type that has those brittle, finger nail-sized fragments of something formerly known as ham in it. Then I see a sign promoting five-a-day, so I grab a couple of cartons of orange juice, making sure it's not the version with bits in it, which makes me gag, and a cheap bottle of red wine, because it's made from grapes and grapes are fruit. As I wander through the supermarket, dropping items into my basket, I make an attempt to shrug off the events of the day and I try to cobble together a mental construct in which my last patient was someone I used to know in another life, long ago, someone who it was interesting to bump into again, but who means nothing to me now.

I manage to keep this witless fantasy running in a half-hearted way until I've stumbled through the door to my flat and put my groceries away. Then I lie down on my sofa and close my eyes and the entire edifice breaks down into multiple fragments of self-deceit that flutter away from me like bits of litter in a breeze. The sofa is usually squishy and comfortable, but now it feels hard and uncompromising, as though it has judged me and changed its texture accordingly. I sit up and scan the room, looking for another source of comfort. My eyes fall on the small circular table I bought in a second hand shop. The pattern of the wood grain on its surface usually looks like an astonished but friendly face, but now its expression is one of shock mixed with disapproval. My cactus plant and whisky supplies sit on one side of this table, and on a shelf above it, I've stacked a small selection of books: everything by the Brontes, a volume Philip Larkin's poetry and Sir Gawain and the Green Knight. I can't manage without any of those for very long, and books are a big deal for me generally, because I don't do social media and I hardly ever watch TV. But leafing through any one of them now is completely beyond me.

The flat also has a tiny kitchen, together with a bedroom and a balcony that can be accessed from the living room through a sliding glass door. The balcony is the best part of the entire set-up, even if the view mostly consists of the car park and beyond that, the main line to Waterloo. On the other side of the rails, you can see a copse of tall trees, probably left over from a big garden or bit of woodland that was here before everything was concreted over. It provides a home for a colony of jackdaws or rooks, corvids of some kind. I'm not much of an ornithologist, so I don't know exactly what they are, but I like to sit outside at dusk and listen to them racketing about as they prepare to roost.

Or I did. My brain's so shaken up I don't actually know what I like or don't like anymore. I get up from the sofa and go into the kitchen. I pour a can of spaghetti hoops into a bowl, warm them up in the microwave, squirt a few swirls of cheese on the top and take them out onto the balcony with a glass of wine. I sit down at my little table and start to shovel the softened pasta into my mouth, taking care to swallow it quickly, before the little rings make contact with my teeth and make me gag. My plan is to get the food down my gullet, then sip the wine slowly and have a bit of a cry. Unfortunately, though, I've positioned myself so I'm facing the balcony next door, which, apart from a small gap at the front, is separated from mine by a thin barrier of decorated metal work in the form of a mesh with numerous circular holes in it of different sizes. The area occupied by the holes greatly exceeds that of the surrounding metal, so the barrier doesn't offer much in the way of privacy, and looking through these holes I can see that the other balcony is full of men, or more accurately, blokes. They've all got those bushy beards and that hair cut in the style universally adopted by white-van-men in the UK, long on top and shaved at the sides, and they all seem to be talking at once or laughing heartily and tipping their heads back as they neck beer from bottles.

I scurry back inside, hoping they haven't noticed me, and I close the curtains. Then I sink down and finish my dinner sitting cross legged on the living room floor. When I'm done, I drop the bowl into the kitchen sink with a clatter. But instead of feeling fortified, I get this sliding sensation as everything falls away from me, including the ability to maintain a standing position. This sensation is something I've experienced before. The contents of my head seem to drain downwards through my body and out of my feet onto the floor, forming a little puddle which quickly evaporates, taking with it everything that makes up my personality and my sense of who I am. I'm left empty, almost non-existent and weightless, too light for gravity to hold me down. I scan the room for something to grab onto, mentally or physically, either would do. The handles on the cupboards stare back at me, blankly. They don't care. Nor do the microwave door, the mess in the sink or anything else that catches my eye.

    I wonder what would happen if I went onto my balcony again, stuck my head round the metal divider and said something to the blokes, like *can you help me please, I seem to be floating away?* They wouldn't understand, but they might try to meet me half way, being a jovial, good natured and half pissed group of guys. Maybe they'd invite me round, pat me on the back and offer me a beer to take my mind of whatever it is that's bugging me. Perhaps they'd let me hang out with them on a regular basis and eventually I'd become as grounded and normal as they are. I might even end up shaving the lower half of my head.

    Who am I kidding? None of that would never happen. I'll always be disconnected from ordinary people, not just because I'm a weirdo, but because my past isn't like anyone else's. I'm the only person I know who was plucked away from somewhere he can't remember at the age of two and dropped into an Edwardian semi-detached house with a big garden by a busy road, occupied by a Dad I'd never seen before, an older sister I kind of half-remembered from somewhere, and an au pair. Don't get me wrong. My life story isn't a dark tale of abuse or anything like that. My Dad and my sister, Amanda, were nice, but as far as my two year old self was concerned, they were random strangers. I greatly preferred my real family and my other life, but I was wrenched away from it so suddenly I couldn't remember anything about it.

    I still can't.

    Amanda says she doesn't know where I lived before, although she has a hazy memory of being in the back of Dad's car when he came to fetch me from somewhere through a gate, down a tree-lined lane in the countryside. I was rigid with fury, apparently, screaming my head off so much she put her hand over my mouth and told me if I didn't stop, I'd turn blue and my eyes would pop out. She knew she'd been to this place before. She remembered collecting acorns under the trees in the lane, and putting them in a basket, and she isn't sure, but she thinks she knew she had a little brother somewhere else, but she never thought to wonder why he didn't live in her house. The other thing she couldn't shed any light on was why my mouth was bleeding when they came to fetch me, and why for ages afterwards, I could only eat yoghurt or ice cream.

Asking Dad was a pointless exercise. He never budged from a narrative in which I was a little gremlin who'd crawled out of the ditch at the end of the garden and sneaked into the house through the back door when nobody was looking. *That's where I found you,* he'd say, *sitting at the kitchen table covered in mud and pond weed, with snails in your hair!* Then he'd pick me up, hoist me onto his shoulders, jog down the garden at high speed and dangle me over the ditch in question, pretending to nearly drop me into the murky water over and over again. *Off you go, back to your own people* he'd growl, turning himself into Big Monster Dad. Usually, I'd shriek until he put me down on the grass. Then he'd roll me about and either bark like a dog or tickle me in the ribs and scrape his scratchy beard against my cheeks. I was always more or less hysterical by the time he'd finished, but never any the wiser about my origins. Eventually, when I kept on asking him, he started to become irritated, so I stopped. I thought he might be telling the truth about the gremlin part, though, because I was dark with permanently grubby skin that never seemed to get any lighter, however much I scrubbed it, whereas Amanda and Dad were fair.

I get up from the sofa and wander into the bathroom to stare into the mirror. When baby Jacob came along everything changed. Of course, we all adored him, but the big deal for me was that his face was really similar to mine. Despite our different colouring, he was definitely my brother. There could be no doubt about it, and his arrival gave me a legitimacy I'd not felt before. I look at my reflection now and mentally allow his blonde hair and fair skin to replace my darker counterparts and in my mind's eye, I cover my chin with his astonishing orange stubble. And there he is. It sounds like a major transformation, but it isn't at all. We're both there together, my brother and myself, superimposed on each other, our differences minor variations on the same theme. I stare at our shared reflection for a while, until I start to lose faith in it and end up only seeing my wretched self again, the tosser my brother hates so much. And I hate myself even more than he hates me.

So yeah, seeing him today was a hell of a shock. I managed to cope with it at the time just about, but now I'm flapping about like a bird at a complete loss about what to do, even in the next few seconds. The only thing I can think of is to run a bath almost to the top with water almost, but not quite hot enough to scald my skin. I've seen patients with dreadful injuries after immersing themselves in overheated bath water, and I don't want to be one of them. I pull my clothes off and sling them across the room, then I get in and sink down until my face is just above the surface. I take a deep breath, go under and stay submerged until my lungs are bursting. In the short space of time before I'm forced to come up for air, I face the facts. Fact one - for the last eight years I've accommodated the Jacob-sized hole in my life, and kept it safe and ready for him in the hope that one day, he'll return. I can accept that, nothing new there. But now I have to face Fact two - he's not thirteen anymore and I don't think the adult version of my brother will ever fit back into the space he left behind, which brings me to Fact 3 – I'll have to adapt the hole, bend it until it's the right shape for him to walk back into. I need to do whatever it takes to achieve this, anything at all, whatever the cost, otherwise I'll die.

The only trouble is, I have absolutely no clue how to go about it, and of course, he'd have to want it too.

4. Gawain

Next morning, I'm back on day shifts. I didn't sleep much last night, and the inside of my skull feels scratchy, as though it's been scoured with a scrubbing brush. I hope A&E will be rammed, then I'll be forced to focus on the patients and won't have time to think about what happened yesterday.

As soon as I step into the department, Bryan emerges from the doorway that leads to the CT scanner. He must have been lurking in the shadows like a shark, waiting for his favourite little tiddler to arrive.

'Am I late?' I ask him.

'Not at all,' he says, shaking his head emphatically as he ushers me into his corner and pushes me down by my shoulders into a chair.

He sits on the desk in front of me.

'Do you want to tell me what's going on or is it a big secret?'

'What do you mean?'

'Your brother.'

Oh God, really?

I look at him and swallow.

'I don't know what's going on. We fell out years ago, and I haven't spoken to him since. I didn't even know he was in England. Last I heard he was in America.'

'Ah,' he says.

He sounds sceptical. Does he think I'm lying?

'Do you have any other family?'

'I've got a sister and an aunt.'

'Have you told them?'

I shake my head.

'Don't you think you should?'

'I'll probably wait to tell my sister when I see her in person. Not sure about my aunt.'

He scrutinises me with his head slightly on one side. I don't want to discuss my brother or the rest of my family with anybody, let alone him, so I sit there pretending to myself that if I don't say anything else, he'll let me go. But he turns a computer monitor towards me and I'm made to look at magnified versions of the photographs he took yesterday of Jacob's back. The wounds are much harder to face up to now, when my attention isn't diverted by the fact that the rest of my brother is there as well.

'Someone's hit him pretty hard to do this amount of damage. With a whip or something similar, by the look of it,' Bryan says. His voice is quiet and casual. He might be talking about the weather.

I stare at the photos. Then he clicks them away to reveal a series of pictures from the internet, a mixture of drawings and photographs of a device that seems to consist of a hand grip with a shortish length of what looks like rope emerging from one end.

'The rope is stainless steel wire coated in plastic and at the other end of the handle, there's a glass breaker you can use to escape from a car should find yourself locked in without a key. A device with multiple purposes.'

I look at the pictures and read the short paragraph of information underneath. It says that the end of the whip travels much faster than the middle, so it delivers more force and pain. That would explain why Jacob's cuts were so deep at one end and shallow at the other.

'Is it legal?'

'Bit of a grey area, that. We should contact the police.'

'It might make things worse for him if we do.'

'I'll have to if it happens again. Or if anyone else turns up with the same injuries.'

I nod and clear my throat.

'Do you have any idea who might have done this to him?'

'He lives with my mother in a kind of church community. The pastor in charge is our stepfather. The church is a bit cultish, I think. I don't know much about them. I didn't realise they went in for this type of thing.'

It seems absurd to call Warren our stepfather. I've never thought of him in that way before. I've barely even spoken to the man. Bryan scrolls through the admission notes to see if Jacob provided any useful information. It turns out his address is there. I'm surprised. I doubt he would have offered up that crucial piece of information if he hadn't been half out of his mind on sleeping tablets. I'm equally astonished to discover he lives really close to the hospital, almost round the corner in fact, five minutes' drive away on a good day. Bryan lets me copy the details onto my phone.

I stand up and move towards the door.

'If you need to go now, we'll cover for you.'

They won't be able to do that when it gets properly busy. Patients will have to wait longer to be seen and the sum total of human suffering will be increased. I don't want to be responsible for that as well as everything else. And anyway, I can't just go there and get him, can I?

'I need to think before I do anything.'

Bryan looks unconvinced, but he doesn't say anything. As I get up to leave the IT corner, I realise I've been a bit taciturn, possibly even downright rude, to a man who has just gone out of his way to be helpful, so I turn back and thank him. He responds with a single, abrupt nod, and for the rest of the day, he keeps turning up and standing in the background, watching me work and probably waiting for me to screw up so he can step in, rescue the situation and send me home. But I make all the correct decisions as per usual. I'm civil to my colleagues, even the irritatingly stupid ones. I make sure I do everything by the book and I make a real effort to be kind and respectful without over-empathizing or trying to be the patient's best friend, like I used to do when I first qualified. Like I still do sometimes.

Being on my best behaviour is hard work, and when my shift finally ends, I'm shattered. I'm not going home, though. I have my car with me today, and after stopping off at the supermarket to buy a bottle of water and a set of three chocolate mousses in plastic pots with little spoons under their lids, I drive straight to the address in Jacob's notes. The traffic has died down, and it only takes me a few minutes to get there. His road is residential and fairly quiet, but just round the corner from the local high street. The house he claims to live sits on one side of a large car park. On the opposite is a large church constructed from red brick. The house is big, detached and looks well cared for. Tubs containing small olive trees stand on either side of the front door and all the windows have the same red blinds, which are closed at the moment, against the evening sun. The front door is heavy-looking and painted red to match the blinds, and sports a big brass knocker in the shape of a lion's head. I can see another door half way down the right hand side, also painted red. It opens directly onto the car park, and faces the main door of the church.

How would Jacob react if he saw me hanging about outside the house where he lives? He'd probably be appalled. If he asked me what I was doing or what I hoped to achieve, I wouldn't know what to say, except that I feel compelled to watch over the place.

It won't get dark for a while, so, in an effort to be invisible, I park a couple of car lengths away on the opposite side of the road. I put on a baseball cap and a pair of round, John Lennon-style sunglasses. It's not a bad disguise. I don't think anyone, except Jacob possibly, would recognise me, but the glasses make me look like a sex offender and the hat is way too hot. Beads of sweat creep down the back of my neck. I drink my water and eat one of the mousses just to get my blood sugar up to a reasonable level. Then I sit and watch.

Nobody emerges from either the house or the church, and no visitors turn up. As the daylight fades, lights come on behind some of the blinds and a strip of window low down on the wall casts a narrow segment of light onto the tarmac surface of the car park. The church itself remains in darkness. I try to guess which room belongs to Jacob, but the longer I sit here the harder I struggle to believe he's in there at all. He could easily have given the hospital a made-up address. But the road definitely exists and the house is clearly part of a complex that includes a church. At the front of the car park is large, brightly painted sign, with *New Sunrise* written on it in blue letters inside a yellow sun with rays emanating from it onto a blue background. Underneath, smaller letters exhort the reader to give his or her life to Jesus.

The church looks Victorian or Edwardian. It must have belonged to another denomination until its own particular branch of Christianity went out of fashion. And now the place is run by Pastor Warren, who seemed like a nice bloke with a face full of smiles and empathy as far as I can remember from the last time I saw him, which was years and years ago. Now, though, he seems to have turned into a person who thinks the lashing of sinners with a stainless steel tactical whip is an acceptable component of religious practice. People like him gradually change into their true selves as time progresses, I suppose, if nobody stops them.

He and Mum ran away together when Jacob was a newborn and I was five. She simply walked out of the hospital and left him there, alone. For a long time before that, Mum came and went, but mostly went. Sometimes, Amanda and I would hear her talking and laughing with Dad after we'd gone to bed. But she was never there when we went downstairs for breakfast the next morning. They behaved like lovers, not a married couple with two children. She kept a small selection of clothes and shoes in Dad's wardrobe. The shoes inspired Amanda to invent a brilliant game with a complicated scoring system that involved running, hopping or jumping up and down the stairs to the attic as quickly as we could in ballet pumps, high heels or the black patent sling backs, which were my favourites. When Mum left for good and took all her stuff with her, I think Amanda and I were more upset about the shoes than we were about her. And anyway, her final departure was completely eclipsed by Jacob's arrival, which happened at the same time.

    I'd been in hospital with appendicitis. Dad picked me up, spent ages saying farewell to all the nurses who'd inevitably fallen for him and drove me home in his big, flashy antique of a car. Once we were inside, he shouted for Amanda and ushered us both into his study.

    'Your mother's gone off to America with a vicar type person.' He was never one to mince words.

    'Like the one who does the carol service at Christmas?" Amanda asked.

    "Kind of.' He hesitated. 'No, not really, but it doesn't matter.'

    'Are you sad?' I wanted to know.

    'Er, yes a little bit, I suppose. But I'll be ok. Don't you worry about me.'

    'I don't want him to be sad,' I said to Amanda, after he'd gone dashing off in his car, back to the university where he worked. Although I was concerned about Dad, I was ecstatic about Mum's departure. For reasons I couldn't fathom, she terrified me. When she came to stay, I hid under my duvet and I was almost faint with relief when I woke up each time the following morning and Amanda, having sneaked downstairs to check, told me she'd gone again.

    'He won't be. He's got plenty of other girlfriends,' Amanda said. 'Let's have a look at your scar.'

    'Wow,' she said when I lifted up my jumper. She smeared ointment on it from a pot that had been on the window ledge in the bathroom for so long a crust had formed over its surface. While she was administering it she made loads of really gratifying comments about how long the wound was and how sore it looked. I basked in her attention like a heroic soldier returning from a war. Then I noticed she'd stopped and was puffing herself up like she always did when she had something important to say.

'Something really mega has happened,' she declared eventually, letting all the breath out of her lungs at the same time.

'Can it wait?'

I was starting to feel a bit weary and was thinking longingly about my bedroom and the books I'd missed when I was in hospital, particularly the one about the teddy bear who ran an umbrella hire business and was thrown into despair when there was a long dry spell.

'No way. You won't know what the noise is.'

'The noise?'

'It's *incredibly* loud.'

She grabbed my hand and pulled me up two flights of stairs into the largest of our two attic rooms.

Last time I was in there it had been full of junk, some of which was interesting, including an old rocking chair, a chamber pot and a pile of ancient copies of Women's Weekly, which had given us hours of entertainment. I listened while Amanda read out the mysterious questions on the problem pages, then we'd discuss the advice offered by a kindly looking, white haired lady called Mary Marryat. We were baffled by some of the terminology she used, including words like climax, which several of the letter writers were constantly striving towards, but failing to achieve. One day we looked the word up in the big dictionary in the study, but we were still mystified, so we asked Dad, who was drinking a cup of tea at the time. He spat his most recent mouthful onto the carpet and roared with laughter. I thought he was going to choke. When he'd recovered, he said it wasn't a problem he was familiar with, and left it at that, so we were still none the wiser.

All the magazines were gone now, as was the chamber pot, although the wooden cot was still there at the far end of the room under the sloping roof. It used to be a dull, uninteresting thing, full of burst cushions and moth eaten blankets, but now it had been given a new coat of white paint and was empty, apart from a tiny, pastel green bundle that seemed to be making snuffling noises. I ran to look at it through the bars.

Sticking out from the top of the bundle was a small turnip-shaped head in a green cotton hat, and two miniature fists curled up on either side of a little round face. It was so completely still and so very pale I wondered if it might be dead. It also crossed my mind that it was one of Amanda's dolls, a new one I hadn't seen before. I knew I shouldn't, but I couldn't resist pinching the knot at the top of its little cotton hat between my fingers and pulling it off so I could see its hair. It was blonder even than Dad's or Amanda's, almost white in fact. Suddenly, its face moved slightly to one side and turned bright red, and its whole body went rigid. I looked on in horror, wondering whether I'd set something in motion by taking its hat off. Then it grunted lengthily, as though it was trying to shift something heavy but couldn't quite manage it. After that, it seemed to relax again and its face turned back to a much more restful shade of pale pink, like the inside of a seashell. I touched one of little hands, and it unfurled like a flower and gripped my index finger.

Behind my back, Amanda was reciting everything she'd been told about the baby, in a monotone, as though she was ticking off items in a list.

'Dad says he's a marvellous little chap. His name Sebastian Jacob Fylde and he was born on the tenth of April. He's our brother, we have to call him Jacob and we mustn't touch him unless we've washed our hands first.'

I knew that last bit, about washing our hands, was Amanda's own addition to the list, but I regretted not doing it. The last place my finger had been was in the ointment coating my scar.

'Why is he our brother?'

'Because we all have the same Mum and Dad.'

'Why do we have to call him Jacob?'

'I heard Dad say on the phone to Aunty Susan that Mum got him put down as Sebastian Jacob. But now she's decided she doesn't want him and buggered off permanently, he doesn't belong to her anymore, just to us, and we have to call him by his middle name instead, which Dad prefers in any case.'

I pulled my finger out of his grasp and through the bars of the cot. Jacob's eyes snapped open and formed perfect little circles. His mouth did the same thing and a high pitched noise, as piercing as a dentist's drill emerged from it, crept up and down my spine and then spread into every corner of the room. But there was something familiar and amazing about him and about his pale eyes and his little nose, which was beaky, like mine, and I was smitten.

Darkness falls. I get out of my car and pace up and down. But there's no sign of Jacob or anyone else, and soon the lights in the house start to go off one by one, so I decide to put an end to my vigil. By the time I get back to my flat it's after eleven. I don't bother to shower. I just remove my trainers, jeans and socks and lie on the top of my bed in my T-shirt and underpants. I'm so exhausted I'm confident sleep will overtake me sooner rather than later, and it does for about ten minutes, but then I'm woken by uproarious laughter and the realisation that the guy next door has crammed all his mates onto his balcony again. They've clearly reached that stage of loud jollity that can only be achieved after sinking several pints with a selection of shots to spice them up. As far as these revellers are concerned, weekday nights are the perfect time to get bladdered and disturb everyone else in the block. I go onto my own balcony and stand there leaning on the front wall, looking over the edge, thinking that I might bloody well jump if that's the only way I'm going to get my brain to shut off.

I'm way too cowardly to complain, though. There must be eight or nine of them, all bigger than me, and I've worked out that the host is the buzzy one who jumps out of his chair at regular intervals as though it keeps giving him little electric shocks. He darts off inside and reappears with more bottles of lager or bowls of nuts, and he grins and laughs all the time, as though the whole thing is an enormous joke. One time he goes in and comes back out carefully transporting a birthday cake with lit candles onto the balcony table and they sing happy birthday to one of their company, the one they call Widger, in rich baritone voices. Then they applaud and cheer.

The balcony lights are dimmed at this time of night, but I can still see plenty. The buzzy guy has very dark hair and looks a bit like Heathcliff might if he had cheered up and been less of a misanthrope. I suspect he's ex-army, mainly because he's wearing a black T-shirt with a small union jack logo on it and capped sleeves that show off the muscle definition in his arms as well as the incredible art work that covers his biceps. There's something excessively enthusiastic and vivid about him that I can't quite put my finger on. Maybe it's the sharp contrast between his white teeth and his facial hair or the perfectly straight line where his beard ends and the hairless section of his face begins. No vague uncertainties or muted transitions for him.

I decide to try a bit of reverse psychology on myself. I fetch my small stash of weed from its hidey hole in my bookcase, behind the bulkiest of my clinical anatomy textbooks, and I sit down on one of my outdoor chairs and roll a very small joint. As I smoke it, I pretend that the very last thing I want to do is go to sleep, that what I really need is for them to keep me awake as long as possible. I close my eyes and follow the drift of their conversation as it meanders between different topics, like getting drunk in a various environments, running up steep hills and jumping into freezing water whilst carrying heavy backpacks and being shouted at by a crazed imbecile, or taking on ridiculously irresponsible challenges that mainly seem to involve what they call their *tackle*, which they've all at one time or another dangled into risky and unsuitable places for dangerous amounts of time, including the corner pockets of a pool table while a game is in progress and over the edge of a rock face during a hail blizzard in the Brecon Beacons. I've seen the consequences of this type of behaviour. The victims are usually pretty sombre once they realise what they've done to themselves. But this lot think it's all hilarious. Even I find myself smiling from time to time.

When I open my eyes again, I'm still sitting at the balcony table. My head is cushioned in my folded arms. It's nearly six in the morning and the only sounds are the occasional sparrow chirping from the shrubs in the car park, trains rushing towards Southampton or London, and the distant hum of the morning traffic starting to build on the motorway. As I get up and stretch my arms above my head, I notice a neatly folded foil package on the floor of the balcony close to the wall adjoining my neighbour's side, near the front where the mesh barrier is slightly lower. At first, I think it might be drugs, a large lump of resin, perhaps, that's fallen out of someone's pocket and somehow landed on my balcony. But it's way too big to be that. I go over, pick it up and peel off the foil to discover a slice of chocolate fudge cake decorated with little sugar violets. It looks home-made. I remove the sugar violets and flick them over the balcony rail one by one. No way are they going anywhere near my teeth. But I dip the rest of it into a cup of tea and suck down the resulting liquid mulch in a matter of seconds. The cake is rich and chocolatey, and its sweetness, as well as the unexpected kindness of the person who left it there for me, make me want to burst into tears.

5. Gawain

When I rock up on the Wednesday evening, I'm surprised to see that the church car park is full and there are no spaces to be had on the road outside. Must be a mid-week service or gathering, or whatever they call them. I have to park round the corner and walk back, which means I'm out in the open with nowhere to hide. I don my sunglasses and hat again and I lurk behind a small van on the opposite side of the street and spy on the church and the car park through its side windows.

When the service ends, a huge number of people pour out of the church. Older people and families with kids get into their cars and drive off and the rest of the congregation leaves on foot. Some of them cross to my side of the road, so I move away from the van and spy on them discretely whilst pretending to look at my phone. The ones I see up close are very young and they all seem to have the same slightly dazed but happy expression on their faces, as though they genuinely think themselves lucky to have been saved by Pastor Warren. At the same time, there's something slightly off about their eyes, as though they know deep down that being lost doesn't necessarily mean you should allow yourself to be found by an establishment like the Church of the New Sunrise, but they've let it happen anyway because it's better than spending night after night stuck in a rented room on their own. They remind me of the human flotsam that turns up in A & E late on Saturday nights or at the end of lonely bank holiday Mondays, the regulars who keep taking overdoses and are given cards providing contact details for the nearest branch of the Samaritans.

Once the place has emptied out, my mother appears in the doorway, all petite and glam, in a white dress with matching dangly earrings and high heels, similar to the sling backs I used to love so much. I haven't seen her since I was fifteen when she gate-crashed Dad's funeral, The shock of seeing her meant I had to stop to throw up outside an abandoned Little Chef with boarded up windows on the way home. Something similar is happening to me now. I'm not sure I'll be able to hang onto the yoghurt I ate on the way out of the hospital, and my heart is thumping violently. I wish I was brave enough to run up to her, spit at her like a cat and ask her what the hell she thinks she'd doing, letting my brother be whipped like that.

But I'm not, and it's lucky I don't, because shortly afterwards, Warren appears and stands next to her. His previously abundant ginger hair is much shorter now and has faded to a brindled salt and pepper colour. I thought I'd remembered how huge he is, but I hadn't quite. He must be at least six foot four and broad with it. When he and my mother have finished grinning at the departing celebrants, they start to walk across the car park, accompanied by an even larger version of Warren, a muscle bound meat head with a prissy, pursed up mouth almost lost in the middle of a slab-like face, and hair the exact same colour as Warren's, but sparse at the front and long at the back, making him look like an ex-member of a biker gang who got thrown out when they realised he was actually a species of ape. Although that's insulting to apes.

Soon afterwards, Jacob emerges from the church. This is the first time I've seen him since the hospital and it makes my heart pound even faster. The junkie bloke who picked him up from the hospital is close behind, strutting forward in cowboy boots with his hands in the front pockets of his jeans as though he's part of a line dancing team. He never takes his eyes off my brother, not even for a fraction of a second. By his side is a plumpish, fresh-faced girl about Jacob's age with long auburn hair tied back in a single plait. Ruth. I remember her. She was one of the reasons Jacob was always so keen to go and stay with Mum for weekends, after Dad died, back in the days before we had our falling out. They ran a different outpost in the UK at that time, somewhere in East Sussex. I was invited to stay with them too, but I never did. Eventually they disappeared back to the States again, and my brother started going out there in the summer holidays.

Jacob makes his way across the car park, head down and shoulders hunched. I wonder what they'd do if I ran over, grabbed his hand and tried to drag him away? Nothing good, and he wouldn't want to go with me in any case, so I remain where I am, safely hidden behind the van. Once they've all disappeared into the house through the side door, I walk round the corner to my car and drive back to my flat, my status as a scaredy cat and wretched failure of a brother confirmed once more. When I get home, my entire body is slick with sweat. It's very warm at the moment, and each day seems to be hotter and more humid than the previous one. I drink some water, strip all my clothes off, lie down on my bed, close my eyes and wait for oblivion.

But the bloke from next door is out on his balcony again, sitting, by the sound of it, about as close to my bedroom window as it's possible to get without actually climbing over the metal divider. I have some foam ear plugs in my bedside cabinet, but I don't want to use them in case Jacob rings, even though I know the chance of that happening is virtually zero. Beardy seems to be out there on his own this time, making calls to one person after another and addressing each of them in a slow, deliberate and very loud voice, accompanied by a lot of heavy sighing, as if he's trying to convey to them that he could become very angry, but he won't, not because they don't deserve it but because he's a patient kind of guy. I get the feeling that repeating the same words over and over again only to bang his head against almost identical brick walls of what he sees as crass stupidity is driving him demented. It would be so much better for his blood pressure if he just arranged a virtual meeting with them all at the same time. I wonder why he hasn't thought of this and I'm tempted to go out and suggest it to him. At the same time, I'll ask him why the hell he doesn't make these calls during normal working hours.

He continues shouting and bawling and occasionally laughing for so long that in the end I lose it completely and I leap out of bed, intending to scramble into some clothes and run out into my own outside space, so I can yell through the mesh and tell him to shut the fuck up. But it takes me forever to find my shorts. As often happens with my clothes and other items that belong to me, they've moved since I took them off, and now they're not on the floor by my bed, where I'm certain I left them, but in the middle of the living room floor. By the time I get out onto my balcony, his business calls have ended and he's engaged in a completely different kind of conversation, one where the person on the other end, who I can hear as clearly as if they're on speakerphone, interrupts him a lot and wants to know if he's alright and when he's coming home.

His tone is softer now and although he has his back to me, I can see through the mesh that he's sitting out there in a mid-length white, short-sleeved dressing gown, hairy legs on display, with his feet propped up on another chair. Sadly, he's wearing flip-flops, an item of footwear I can't abide under any circumstances, but his voice is soothing and my anger drains away as I listen to it. I go back to bed and as I let his voice ease me into a gentle slumber, I wonder about his accent. He must come from an area of Yorkshire much further west than the one where I used to live. A series of comforting images runs past my inner eye, mainly derived from a school trip to Bolton Abbey when I was ten: having a picnic by a wide river with stepping stones; dipping my egg sandwiches into a plastic cup of orange squash so I could suck them down; looking at endless lines of dry stone walls from the coach window; getting on a steam engine in an ancient railway station; and a scattered flock of tough-looking sheep with dainty black legs balancing delicately on a steep hillside. So restful. For once, I sleep well.

*

Somehow, I make it to Friday. I go to the church again both evenings, but nothing happens and I don't see anyone. I have the weekend off, but after what's happened with Jacob, I'm not sure I'll get through two whole days in my flat on my own, endlessly checking my phone, staring into the darkness until my eyes are as dry and itchy as if I've deposited teaspoons of sand into them, and making the odd half-hearted attempt to shovel tinned macaroni cheese and mashed baked beans down my throat. I could spend the entire time outside the church, but people might notice. On the other hand, I could text Cobblers and some of the other members of my posse of dormitory mates from school, the ones who still live nearby, and see if they want to meet up. But Cobblers is getting married soon and the rest of them are seriously paired up one way or another. The last thing I want to come across like a sad loser with nothing better to do than badger old friends and make them feel they have to change their weekend plans to accommodate me. So I decide to go and stay with my sister. She'll boss me around and feed me, which will be great.

And I need to tell her about Jacob.

Amanda trained and worked as a GP in Edinburgh, where she bought a big, gothic looking house with another GP called Duncan. I stayed with them a few times. Duncan was alright, or at least I thought he was. He introduced me to single malt whisky and made me kind of fall in love with Scotland. Then all of a sudden, Amanda moved back down here, alone. Now she works in a local health centre and she's sold her share in the Edinburgh house and bought a terraced cottage with a long narrow garden that backs onto a farmer's field.

'I've made soup,' she says when she opens the door.

Her darkish blonde hair, which is so glossy you can almost see your face in it is coming loose from a pony tail and she's wearing a flowery summer dress that almost reaches the floor. She tucks a couple of loose strands behind her ears and pads barefoot into her shady kitchen. I follow her, drop my backpack on the floor and reach into it to pull out the bottle of artisanal gin I bought on the way to her house. The gin is flavoured with something. Borage and lime I think. As I hand it to her she frowns a bit and bites her bottom lip. We don't look very alike on the whole, my sister and me, mainly because she takes after Dad, whereas I'm the image of Mum, but that lip biting thing is something I've caught myself doing on more than one occasion. I realise it has some kind of significance, but at the moment, I'm too preoccupied to wonder what it means. She plonks the bottle on the top of a stripped pine dresser. When she turns to face me again I've already started sifting through my mental vocabulary to find the best words to tell her about Jacob. I'm keen to start right away because the longer I stand here not saying anything, the more it will feel like I'm withholding information. And the more annoyed she'll be with me for not telling her immediately.

Amanda's eyebrows are darker than her hair and she can make herself looks quite severe when she frowns. She's doing that now, which means she's onto me. She knows something's up. She pulls out a chair at her kitchen table and manoeuvres me into it. Then she puts a couple of elegantly shaped tumblers onto the table and fetches a bottle of tonic water and one of sparkling mineral water from the fridge.

'Do you want lemon?'

I pick up the gin bottle and read the label again.

'It's already got lime in it, thanks.'

I pour myself a generous slug, add some tonic water, and start to do the same for her. But she shakes her head.

'I'll just have mineral water for now.'

This is unexpected. My sister's partial to a gin or two, particularly at the weekend. I raise my eyebrows then lower them again, just once, to convey that I'm surprised, but I'm not going to comment, yet. I do the eyebrow manoeuvre a lot. I find it really effective for prizing the truth out of patients, particularly the older ones who often try to make out they're not in much pain. It forces them to admit they could do with something, just to take the edge off, I sort something out for them and they feel better. Job done. Unfortunately, it irritates the hell out of most other people and puts them on the defensive. It has this effect on Amanda now, and she finds herself compelled to explain how dehydrated she is, in unnecessary detail.

I shelve my curiosity for the time being and focus on telling her about Jacob. She sits opposite me with her elbows on the table and her chin in her hands and she listens in silence while I recount everything, quite calmly for me, in forensic detail, from the moment I pulled back the cubicle curtain and saw Jacob lying there to the point when the cowboy-junkie guy drove up and took him away. When I show her the photos Bryan sent me of Jacob's back, she stares at them for ages. I wonder if she's going to cry, but she doesn't. When she's finished, she looks up at me again. I find myself wanting to defend myself and tell her it's not my fault, even though we both know Jacob's current predicament is totally down to me. If I hadn't done what I did, we wouldn't have fallen out and he wouldn't have gone running to our mother and her church.

Amanda isn't satisfied with my straightforward, linear account of the situation. She needs to mull it over and prod it from several different angles, and when she's finished doing that she has to experiment with a range of suggestions and explanations before she can even begin to sum it all up and come to a conclusion. She should have been a lawyer, not a doctor. I find her approach to the problem exhausting, but it's also strangely satisfying, because it brings out into the open all the stuff that's been whirring about in the back of my own mind, like a discordant and jangling guitar riff. Once her cross examination of the events and my role in them is complete, she stares into space for a few seconds, eyes darting from side to side as she continues to think it through.

I top up my glass, which is nearly empty. I had intended to sip my drink slowly, but somehow this hasn't happened. My mind starts to decouple a little as the alcohol kicks in and also due to relief that I'm no longer the only family member who knows about Jacob's current plight. I wait for Amanda to pass her final judgement. Eventually, I grow impatient.

'So what do we do?'

'I love how it's up to me to decide.'

'You're the eldest.'

'Shut up.' She unties her pony-tail and re-fastens her slippery hair into a bun which bobs about loosely on the top of her head. 'As I see it, we've got three options. They're all pretty crap, but…'

'What's option one, then?'

'We call the police and say we think The Church of the New Sunrise or their community or whatever the hell it is, has committed a criminal act. You never know. They might make an effort, seeing as we're both doctors. They'll probably make a few enquiries and go round there and have a word with them.'

'But Warren and the rest of them aren't going to put their hands up and say ok, it's a fair cop, are they?'

'We have photographic evidence and your consultant would back us up. And maybe Warren's already got form, or the church as a whole. Someone else might have made a complaint at another branch.'

'Hmm. Not sure. Option two?'

'We leave him be and hope he comes to his senses on his own. He's got our phone numbers and he knows we're not far away.'

'I can't see that happening. He's not himself. He was drugged up to the eyeballs when he first came in, remember. And he wasn't really right even after that had worn off.'

'Do you think he's been brainwashed?'

'I don't know. He seemed more cowed or scared than anything else, as though he's had to shut his true self away to survive. If you'd seen him you'd understand what I mean. It was in his body language. He was kind of huddled into himself and it was almost impossible to get him to engage in eye contact.'

'Really?'

'But that might have been because it was me. He must have been horrified when he realised I was the doctor looking after him. All he wanted was to bat me away. And even if he did leave the church, he wouldn't call me and he certainly wouldn't want to move in with me.'

'He could stay with me or Aunty Susan, and you gave him my number. Maybe he'll call me.'

'Dunno. Seems unlikely.'

'Why?'

'I don't know, Amanda. I just get the impression he's cut off from us to such an extent that, as far as he's concerned, we don't really exist anymore.'

That's not exactly what I mean. I know for sure I'm on his radar now that we've bumped into each other. And in any case, it was always me he was closest to. I'm pretty certain his anger towards me will keep me alive inside his head, if nothing else does. But I get the feeling he's forgotten about Amanda altogether. And as for Aunty Susan, he'd rather die than stay with her again. They never exactly hit it off.

'Also, he doesn't seem to have a phone of his own. The one he had with him in the hospital belonged to the cowboy-junkie bloke.'

'That's not a good sign, is it?'

I shake my head.

'Anyway,' she continues. 'Option three – we stage an intervention.'

'How the hell do we do that?'

'There must be a way. I'll Google it.'

'You mean we kidnap him and then keep him prisoner until we've de-programmed him persuaded him to move away from the dark side?'

'Kind of.'

'How far do you think we'd get – a smallish woman and her gaylord of a brother against a pair of psychopaths built like King Kong, a cowboy, an insane mother and an entire congregation of brainwashed zombies?'

'Maybe we could hire someone to help us from the dark web?'

'Like a hit man?'

'Or maybe a group of them. Is there such a thing? A hit gang? Or perhaps we could get some of his school mates together and go in mob handed.'

I know it's not funny, but a vision comes into my mind of his posh room-mates and member of his sports teams from school forming a posse and marching into the church, armed with cricket bats and pea shooters. I laugh in a hysterical, uncontrolled way, until my eyes water. I reach out for the gin bottle again, Amanda puts her hand on my arm.

'I'll warm up the soup,' she says.

She's made tomato, which is my favourite, and I suddenly find I can eat. She puts some sliced white bread on the table because she knows I can't swallow any other type and I take a knife, carefully cut the crusts off three pieces, spread butter on them and submerge them in the soup until they soften. Then I mash them up and eat them with a spoon. I focus on this to the exclusion of all else for a few minutes and when I've finished and put the spoon in the bowl, I notice how quiet it is. There's no sound at all apart from the ticking of the huge clock Amanda's put on the wall above the kitchen table. She's sitting really still, fiddling with the ends of her hair, which has now been freed from its bun. Not eating.

'Are you not hungry?'

'Not really.'

I manage to stop myself doing the eyebrow thing again. Once is enough for one evening. I don't want to get my sister's back up and anyway, I've had a lifetime of well-meaning but infuriating people asking me about my eating habits, in various sets of circumstances, so I'm not going to do that to her. But I register it as odd all the same. My sister likes her food under normal circumstances, and to be honest my brain hasn't stopped ticking away in the background since I arrived, trying to work out what's different about her.

*

I go down to the kitchen quite early the next morning to get some juice from the fridge. Last night we started watching a Danish crime box set, but I quickly sank into deep sleep mode on Amanda's sofa, then I woke up briefly, for just long enough to drag myself up to her spare bedroom. I take my juice outside onto the patio and sit on one of my sister's new wrought iron chairs, near two tubs of carefully coordinated pink, purple and white flowers. I don't know what they are. Flowers aren't my thing, but they're clearly popular with bees, and there's a row of other plants I *am* able to identify as tomatoes lined up against the white painted wall on the left. Beyond the patio, is a long, narrow and currently shady stretch of lawn. At the end of the garden is a with a cereal crop growing in it, ripening to a flat, pale gold in the late summer sun.

My sister appears, carrying a shiny metal bottle of water. Her face is the same shade of extreme whiteness as the wall behind the tomato plants, which makes me decide I can't sit here and say nothing.

'How far gone are you, then?'

Her eyes flash at me in indignation, which makes me want to laugh again. I lean back in my chair and watch as various expressions pass over her face as she tries to decide whether it's worth trying to deny it and then realises she can't be bothered. She sits down heavily and takes a sip of the water.

'Six weeks. Approximately.'

'Have you done a test?'

'I've done eight of the damn things. I keep hoping the previous one was wrong. It never is. Or it hasn't been, so far.'

Those are the easy questions. The rest are trickier, but I plough on because I need to know. She'd do the same if it was the other way round.

'How are you feeling?'

'Like shit, obviously, but that's a meant to be a good sign. If you want to keep the baby, I mean.'

"According to who?"

'The cleaning lady at the surgery, my friend, Tessa, who never felt sick once and then had a miscarriage at ten weeks, and that woman who answers the health questions in Baby Magazine.'

So much for the years of training it took to become a GP.

'What are you going to do?'

She doesn't answer because she has to get up and run off into the house. Her bathroom is downstairs and the window opens out onto the patio, so I can hear her retching. I wish I could stop it happening, partly because I'm a wonderful brother and I don't want my sister to suffer, but also because it's bad enough having to worry about Jacob without having to deal with this startling development, too. After about five minutes she reappears smelling of toothpaste, and she sits down, puts both feet on her chair and hugs her knees.

'I can't make my mind up. I thought I had it clear in my head that I was going to get it terminated. Every morning for the last two weeks I've intended to ring for an appointment, but instead I've just gone to work and carried on with my day as though nothing's happened.'

'You've never been great at making decisions.'

'That's so unfair. I just want to have a kid and be childless at the same time.'

I try to understand this dual state of mind and fail completely. I'm not sure whether that's because I'm not a woman or simply because I'm not Amanda. Luckily, I'm smart enough to realise suggesting either of these alternatives to my sister would be a mistake.'

'Maybe that means you want the baby but you're scared.'

She unfastens her ponytail, shakes her hair out and then pins it back from her face with two hair-slides. 'What if you learn how to raise your own kids by osmosis from your own mother? If that's how it works, how the hell could I do it without screwing up?'

'Debbie looked after us ok. You'll have absorbed childcare skills from her.'

Debbie was our live in nanny when we were small. We all thought she was wonderful, but Amanda was particularly close to her. After she'd left, when Dad decided, disastrously as it turned out, that we were old enough to look after ourselves, my sister was always round at the house where Debbie lived with her parents at the other side of the village.

She shrugs, puts her feet down and gets up from the chair. 'I'm going to shower and get dressed. There's some Ready Brek in the cupboard over the sink.'

I put together a large bowl of what turns out to be the chocolate flavoured variety, using up almost half the packet, and I carry it down to the end of the garden, where I sit cross legged on the lawn and look out at the field through the fence. The individual plants making up the cereal crop, which I think is barley, bend uniformly in the gentle breeze like a single entity. When Amanda reappears she seems a bit brighter and suggests we go for a walk. We pass through the gate at the end of her garden and follow a path that goes round the edge of the field and through a band of beech trees at the far end to a stretch of heathland that belongs to the army. You can walk there as long as red flags are not waving from the tops of the white poles that stand like sentries at regular intervals. When we emerge from the wood, the brightness is dazzling. We both narrow our eyes and I can't resist bending down to pick up bits of ordnance, even though there are signs telling you not to. I gather a little handful of brass bullet cases and rattle them in the front pocket of my shorts.

It's much easier to talk about difficult stuff with my sister we're walking along instead of sitting or standing face to face, so I embark on another, more intrusive line of questioning.

'Are you in contact with the father?'

I cringe, inwardly, as though I've just thrown a hand grenade at her and I'm waiting for her to throw it back at me.

'I bet you've been dying to ask that.'

I don't respond and we continue walking in silence, until one of her hair slides comes loose and falls to the ground. She bends to pick it up.

'There is no dad. Or at least I don't know who the dad is.'

'Out of how many?'

'Mind your own business.'

'Tell me.'

'Three. No, four.'

I'm so shocked I stop walking and turn to look at her.

'I wish I hadn't asked, now.'

'Christ, Gawain. It's not that big a deal. Just because you live the life of a monk, it doesn't mean everyone else has to.'

'But four, though. Bloody hell, Amanda.'

'I met two of them on Tinder and one at a nightclub in Guildford. I'm not planning to hook up with any of them again. The fourth is one of the partners at the surgery. I see him nearly every day, which is a shame. He's nice, but I wouldn't want to start a relationship with him.'

'You're winding me up!'

My sister isn't like this.

'I didn't even know the name of the nightclub one. Looking at the dates, it's most likely to be his.'

'You didn't conceive this child standing up in the bogs or against a wall round the back?'

'No. Well, not quite. It was a warm night and I didn't want to bring him back here, so we drove to that lay-by with the burger van on the dual carriageway, in separate cars, and walked into the woods.'

'The dogging lay-by?'

'Keep your voice down.'

'You went dogging!' I laugh. I can't help it.

She looks around to see if there's anyone about who might have heard, and she doesn't talk to me again for the rest of the walk. We spend the afternoon on sun loungers in her garden. I remain stationary on mine, basking in full sunlight in my Speedos, my skin turning toffee coloured as I half doze and half worry about Jacob and now Amanda, too. She keeps getting up and shoving her lounger into the little patch of shade that moves round the lawn as the day wears on. They're cumbersome, wooden objects and awkward to move. The first time, I offer to do it for her, but she ignores me, so each of the other times after that, I leave her to struggle with it on her own. At about four thirty I go and make some tea, in the way she likes it, using a proper teapot with cups and saucers, and I bring it out on a tray with a plate of custard creams fresh from the packet. I pour out the tea in a ridiculously camp way, channelling Charles Hawtry for all I'm worth. Eventually she smiles, despite herself.

'You're such a tit.'

She throws a custard cream at me. It bounces off my head. She picks up another one, breaks it in two and delicately nibbles away at the half that has the filling stuck to it.

'It's only like scratching an itch.'

'I get that. It's just that I struggle to reach beyond the restaurant stage.'

'How do you know? You never even try.'

'I have actually. I met someone I kind of liked a few weeks ago. But once we were back at his place, it all went horribly wrong. He moved towards me and I jumped back as though he'd pressed the end of a cigarette against my skin. Then I flung all my clothes back on again as quickly as I could, apologised profusely and left. The whole thing was mortifying. I could literally die when I think about it.'

'He can't have been the right person.'

'He was great. Nice looking, kind, educated. Brilliant sense of humour. He rang me later to ask if I was alright. If I can't get it on with someone like him, I don't think there's much hope for me.'

'You're still punishing yourself. You should talk to someone.'

'It wouldn't help Jacob, though, would it?'

She shakes her hair away from her face and frowns at me.

'Why does it have to help *him?*

6. Gawain

Three weeks have passed now since Jacob came into A&E and I've spent most of my evenings hanging about outside the church. I don't think anyone has spotted me yet, and I've become familiar with the New Sunrise routine. On Sunday mornings and Wednesday evenings they have services, which are always incredibly well attended, and on Tuesday and Thursday nights smaller groups of earnest looking types turn up at the front door of the house at seven thirty on the dot and are admitted by my mother or a smiling Warren. I don't know what they do, once they get inside, pray and read the Bible, I suppose. They always leave at exactly ten pm.

I've caught a few brief glimpses of Jacob walking to and from the church. I was kind of hoping he'd be sent on the occasional errand to the mini-supermarket round the corner for milk or something. Then I could pretend to be another customer and intercept him, ask him how it's going and kind of get him used to seeing me again. But that hasn't happened, and when he crosses the car park, he's always shadowed by Slab-Face or the cowboy, which makes me think they must keep him locked up the rest of the time. I can't bear to think about that for too long.

So yeah, by coming here every night, I've achieved nothing, apart from a mounting awareness of my own ineptitude. I'm a wimp, who loiters about behind vans or sits in his car, whining to himself and even crying from time to time into tissues from a box he keeps in the glove compartment. I'm not sure how much longer I can carry on like this. I'm not eating or sleeping, and at work, I've become a robot, just going through the motions. At the end of each shift I can't remember anything much about what I've been doing. Nobody's said anything, so I assume I haven't killed anybody and that I've behaved appropriately towards patients and colleagues. But I can't be certain.

As I wait for the Wednesday service to end, I think about New Sunrise. I've tried to do some research, but I haven't discovered much. Organisations like theirs tend to break-up, reform and change their name at regular intervals, apparently, often due allegations about child abuse or something similar. The only hint I've found of anything concerning is a single comment added to a forum about cults by a former member of the church in America. It hints obliquely at secret punishment rituals, but doesn't go into any detail about where they happen, who's involved or what they entail. The comment generates an entire thread of questions, but the writer doesn't reply. It's as though he's disappeared off the face of the earth or has been permanently silenced. When Jacob first started spending weekends with our mother, when Warren was in charge of an outreach group in East Sussex, they were called the Church of the Good Samaritan. After a couple of years, the mission in the UK ended abruptly, and they returned to the US and seemed to keep quiet for a while before starting afresh as New Sunrise. Nobody stopped them when they crawled back out into the daylight with their new name, and when the time was right, they decided to expand their mission into the UK again, with experienced and enthusiastic leaders like Warren.

    I find it hard to accept that my brother is a part of all this. He was always such a down to earth and sensible child. Sport was his passion in life, not religion. As far as I can remember, the only time either of us went to church was for Dad's funeral, which was when Jacob was ten and I was fifteen. We'd both been at boarding school for four years by then, living happily enough in Cherry Tree House and spending the school holidays at Aunty Susan's house, apart from the odd week here or there when Dad came down and rented a holiday cottages. We were all devastated when he died, but Jacob took it particularly badly.

    Dad was an academic and an author of international repute in the field of gender politics, the male equivalent of Germaine Greer, according to his fan base. He wrote a best seller that transformed his life and meant he spent a lot of time at book signings and conferences in glamorous places on the other side of the Atlantic, like Montreal or Seattle, or European cities, like Milan or Copenhagen. It also meant he couldn't look after us properly, so we moved down South to boarding school and Aunty Susan's. It was a wrench at first, but Dad came down as often as he could and he rented holiday cottages for us, usually by the sea or in the New Forest.

Mr Thompson, our house master, summoned me from a geography lesson. He wanted to tell me first, on my own. Dad was hit by a car outside a fish and chip shop in Bridlington of all places. I found it difficult to come to terms with, to say the least. My initial reaction was to make some awful, stupid joke about battered haddock and mushy peas mixed up with bits of Dad on the tarmac, then I ran to the window and stared out at the playing fields. Mr Thompson said I shouldn't use humour to try and make it go away, that it would be easier for me in the long run if I accepted I was upset and acted accordingly. But I was too worried about Jacob to cry.

He turned up in his football kit and was covered in mud from head to toe. When he was told, he inhaled sharply as though someone had dropped ice down his back and didn't speak for the next four and a half weeks, not a single word. He squashed himself against me so tightly and for such long periods of time that one side of his face was always pink. He didn't find his voice until the funeral was over and Dad was being lowered into the hole dug for him at the cemetery, when he fell to his knees and screamed and wailed, until I pulled him up and let him cover my face with snot and tears. I don't think that experience left him with the sense that religion would come to his aid in his hour of need.

Warren and my mother emerge from the church and position themselves in the doorway again, chatting and smiling to various members of the congregation as they file out. When the final stragglers have departed, Warren strides off towards the house and my mother struts after him in cork wedges. Slab-Face is next, followed by a long gap during which nothing happens. Dusk gets underway and a massive harvest moon slowly rises from behind the houses in the street that backs onto the church. I take off my sunglasses and I begin to wonder if I'd missed Jacob crossing the car park when I was researching New Sunrise on my phone or reminiscing about Dad. But a light comes on over the main door to the church and there he is, coming out with Ruth. They're chatting. She smiles at him and he smiles back. Then she reaches up and runs her hand over his hair backwards and forwards quickly, several times. I imagine she's saying something about how much it's grown in the last few weeks. When he came to A&E it was cropped very short, but now it's slightly longer and curling a bit at the ends, giving him a hint of the mop-top he used to have when he was a schoolboy.

Suddenly, their conversation seems to take a more serious turn, because they both stop smiling and step away from each other. The reason for this becomes clear when Cowboy-Junkie comes darting out of the church. He turns to lock the door. Then he catches up with them and puts one hand on Jacob's shoulder. He almost frog marches him over the car park towards the house, ignoring Ruth, who stands back and then follows them, head down and arms folded. As they get half way across the car park, Cowboy-Junkie suddenly puts his hands on the back of my brother's shoulders and shoves him so hard, Jacob falls to the ground. I'm not sure if that was his intention or if he just meant to propel him forward, and Jacob tripped.

Either way, he can't do that to my brother.

A black snake flicks and snaps its tail inside my head, and brightly lit shards and splinters of glass almost block my vision. While this is going on, I leap out of my car, cross the road and run over to them. Cowboy-Junkie stands there with his arms hanging loosely at his sides, looking down as Jacob tries to sit up. I push Cowboy-Junkie in the chest and yell at him to leave my brother alone. Then I reach down and try to link hands with my brother so I can pull him up. He doesn't put his hand up to meet mine and a fist zooms towards me from my left and makes contact with my cheekbone, just missing my eye. I fall to the ground and my hands scrape across the gravel. For a brief instant, I lie there stunned and then I feel Jacob's breath in my ear.

'Piss off, you total wanker,' he says in an urgent whisper.

Then he scrambles to his feet and steps away from me. Before I have the chance to put forward a rational argument against his proposal, I notice two pairs of boots close to my head. I look up to see Slab-Face and Warren looming over me. Cowboy Junkie is trying to do the same, except that he's scratching his head at the same time and looking a bit uncertain about everything. Warren and Slab-Face pull me up from the ground by my arms and drag me out of the car park. My feet scrape the ground beneath me and one of my ankles twists in the wrong direction. Cowboy-Junkie, who clearly wants to get in on the action, follows and keeps poking me in the ribs until he applies so much force the other two nearly drop me and Warren shouts at him to pack it in.

Next, Warren and Cowboy-Junkie stomp back to the house and I'm left alone with Slab-Face. He props me up against the external wall of a derelict factory building on the other side of the road, so close to my car that I'm taunted by the illusion of safety it presents. Slab-Face steps backwards a little so he can take aim and give me a hefty whack on my right temple with the back of his hand. I fall to the ground again and the black snake inside my head spins wildly. But it quickly slows down and I hear it whisper that snowflakes like me can't expect to come out on top in fist fights with ogres like him, that I couldn't win a fight against anyone, except perhaps a pensioner the other side of ninety or a very small midget, and that my best course of action would be to remain still, exactly where I am, on my side, with half of my face pressed against the gritty concrete, and pretend to be unconscious. Slab-Face steps back again, kicks me in the ribs and releases a gobbet of spit, which lands on my cheek. Then he spends a few seconds standing with his feet close to my head, snorting like a bull. I keep my eyes closed and steel myself to take another blow, but then I hear his footsteps fade away as he crosses the road again. When I'm sure he's gone, I crawl across the pavement and clamber into my car.

In what seems like an instant, I'm on the upstairs landing, outside the door to my flat. I unlock it, go in and slam it behind me so hard a massive echo reverberates through my living room and probably through the rest of the block. My memory has not retained any evidence that I've driven home. For all I know, I've left the car outside the church and staggered back on foot. Once inside, I don't bother to switch on any lights because my aim is to career rapidly across the living room to little table and my whisky stash. But I trip over one of the many scattered, random objects littering the small space between my sofa and the table, and I end up on my hands and knees. The offending item is a box containing a pair of ankle boots I sent off for ages ago and then lost interest in when the weather turned tropical. I pick the box up and hurl it away from me. It bounces heavily off the wall above the table and the lid falls off. Each boot crashes, one after the other, onto my two bottles of single malt. They tip over like skittles and one of them rolls off the table onto the laminate floor. A crack appears in its side, and some of its contents flow out and travel a short distance until they're soaked up by a small heap of dirty socks and underpants that instantly assumes a put-upon look, as though it thinks it was only a matter of time before something like this happened.

I crawl over to the broken bottle and carefully remove my four crystal lead glasses from the little table. I arrange them in a row on the floor in front of me. I can't bear the thought of wasting what's left of the whiskey, not because it cost a fortune, because of its associations with happy holidays in Scotland and the domestic harmony that once existed between my sister and Duncan. I divide it between the glasses, slowly and carefully, ending up with about three and a half fingers of peaty coloured liquid in each glass. Doing this calms me down a bit, and I settle myself on the floor with my back to the couch. My hand surrounds the first glass and warms the whisky up quickly so I can breathe in its aroma. Its smell is challenging, a bit like old mattresses dumped in ditches, surrounded by nettles or maybe thistles, but in a good way. My breath catches on the alcohol in the vapour. I try to sip the contents slowly, but in less than two minutes I've swallowed the lot. I get up and make my way over to my fridge to fetch a bottle of ginger ale. It's a travesty to dilute such a fine single malt, but it means I'll be able to gulp down the second glass even more quickly than the first.

Before sitting down again, I set up my Bluetooth system to blast shuffled tracks full of misery and rage across the room from my darkest, grungiest death metal playlist. It also includes a few classic rock ballads that suddenly slow down the tempo and catch me off guard because of the contrast they make with the angrier stuff. As it happens, one of the most mournful of these comes on first, a song about loss and grief that always hits me right in the gut. The shuffle option is meant to be random. It *is* random. But it feels oddly meaningful that this particular track gets picked first. I turn the volume as high as it will go, decide it's too loud and turn it back down a fraction. As I contemplate what I've just done and its potential consequences for Jacob, the music fills my head with a satisfying sense of misery and woe. I finish the whisky and ginger, then add some of the mixer to the third glass before making a start on that, too. I'm already fairly mellow and I start to feel oddly warm inside and not happy exactly, but vindicated, as though I've subjected my actions to an internal trial and the verdict has come out in my favour. I stopped dithering and actually did something. Yes, ok, it was a complete disaster, but at least it will have made Jacob realise I haven't forgotten about him, even if he thinks I'm a jerk.

Sleep pulls me into a downwards spiral or I sink into a stupor, I'm not sure which or for how long, but I get involved in what seems be an endless dream about being chased by a hidden enemy up and down tracks through darkly wooded hills whilst trying to control several wolf-like dogs on leads. I'm more exhilarated than frightened, and eventually, I let go of all the leads and the dogs scatter. Then I become one of them and I run and run and have the time of my life. It's possible that I howl, too.

When I open my eyes again, I'm still drunk as a skunk. The music has stopped and the main light in the centre of the ceiling has been switched on. At first I'm blinded and I have to force my eyes to stay open, but in the centre of all this brightness, there seems to be a tall black column standing a few inches in front of me. I close my eyes again. Perhaps I'm still dreaming and the wild dogs have met a giant puma or something. But when I look again I know for certain I'm awake. Slowly and reluctantly, I stare up at the dark monolith. It towers over me like a shadow figure, the grim reaper or a Gestapo officer in a dawn raid. I can't see its face. I'm not even sure it has one.

A strangled whimpering noises emerge from my mouth. I want to retreat from the thing, but I'm already sitting on the floor with my back against the sofa, so there's nowhere for me to go. Somehow, I manage to scramble to my feet, but the sofa catches me behind the knees and I lose my balance and fall backwards onto it in a sitting position. I fish my wallet out of my back pocket and try to hand it over, but the hooded phantom slowly shakes its head and says nothing, or I think that's what it does, so I drop my little leather bundle of credit cards and twenty pound notes onto one of the seats, in case it changes its mind. It directs its non- existent face downwards in my direction and shakes its head again. I look up at it and wait for death.

After a few more seconds of this ridiculous situation, my mental fog starts to clear and I notice the thing in my living room is wearing a kimono-like cotton dressing gown in black silk, with the hood up. My eyes are level with its crotch. All sorts of confused and not very funny kilt jokes and sporran-related innuendos flood my brain, probably because of the whisky, and I become convinced that the worst possible thing that could happen now would be for the dressing gown to swing open and for its owner not to be wearing anything underneath.

I scramble upwards until my feet are on the sofa and I'm sitting on its back. Then I drop down behind it and slide away until I make contact with the dividing wall between the living room and the kitchen. I will myself to sink into the brickwork, like Harry Potter on platform nine and three quarters. But the wall lets me down and remains solid, so all I can do is screw my eyes shut and transform myself into a little boy who hopes that if he can't see the scary thing, the scary thing can't see him. As I'm doing this, the scary thing clears its throat quietly and does a really good impersonation of an ordinary person who finds himself trapped in an awkward situation and doesn't know what to do or say.

My eyes snap open. From here I can see that there *is* a face inside the hood and it's staring at me, its gaze almost obscured by thick dark eyebrows beneath a wrinkled forehead. If there was a glowering competition and he were to take part in it, he'd be a dead cert for first prize.

As he scowls, he scrutinizes me, upwards from my feet to my head and then downwards again. He does this really slowly and deliberately, and then he does it again. Is he sizing me up? What will he do when he's worked out that, like most blokes, he's significantly bigger than me and that I probably don't weigh much more than a small girl? Will he get hold of me and fling me over his shoulder, so he can do what, exactly? Have his wicked way with me? Throw me down the stairs? I rapidly consider possible escape routes and come up with nothing at all, apart from the balcony door. Can I run over to it before he has time to get round to the back of the sofa and if so, will I have time to slide it open and jump off or climb over to next door and bang on my neighbour's window?

Hang on a minute. I look down at his feet. They're naked, apart from Japanese-style flip flops with bamboo soles, which are beyond ghastly, and I realise that this intruder, who is continuing to menace me with a thunderous look on his face to the extent that my insides are about to push themselves out through my belly button, is the man from next door.

He folds his arms.

'Hi,' I say in a thin, reedy voice.

'I did knock, but the music was so bloody loud you couldn't hear me.'

'Did you break the door down?'

I'm still backed away, as far from him as I can get, my hands splayed against the wall.

'It wasn't locked, mate.'

I must have slammed it so hard it bounced back, and the lock, which is knackered, to be fair, failed to catch. He removes his hood and continues to frown at me. I put my hands in the front pockets of my jeans and try to return his glare, but obviously I'm too puny to achieve much of an impact against someone like him. I notice his eyes are a very deep blue, and as they take me in, they make it very clear that their owner thinks I'm a total dickhead.

'Are you going to attack me?' I say, 'Because if you are, can you get on with it? The suspense is doing my head in.'

'I just came to ask you to turn the music down.'

He says this quietly and possibly menacingly, but that might just be my imagination.

I look at my watch. It's nearly two in the morning.

'I must have fallen asleep.'

'Well, don't do it again.' He turns to leave.

'I won't. Sorry. I'm not usually…'

He stops and looks back over his shoulder. 'Are you in some kind of trouble?'

'What makes you think that?'

'Nothing at all, Sunshine.' He stomps off towards the door, flip flops flapping as he dodges stray socks, plastic water bottles and empty carrier bags. I stumble after him, suddenly desperate to think of something to say that will make him turn round and look at me again.

Just as he reaches the door, I come up with something.

'I thought you were the grim reaper.'

It works. He stops and turns towards me. He clearly doesn't know what to say, but who would? I find myself half smiling at him, trying my best to make my face adopt an amused, self-mocking expression. In a minute I'll be raising my eyebrows and then lowering them again. Why am I behaving like this?

I know why. It's because he called me Sunshine. He doesn't smile back.

'Make sure you lock your door this time.' He says this so quietly I almost think I've imagined it.

When he's gone, I run to the full length mirror in the bathroom and look at myself. I wish I hadn't. My left cheekbone has a red mark running across it. Slab-Face must have been wearing a knuckle duster or a ring with a big stone in it because the skin is broken in a couple of places. My hair is sticking up in various directions in random clumps and the palms of both my hands are grazed and filthy. And most shameful of all, my shirt has a diagonal rip in it, exposing the nipple that I prefer to keep hidden, the one that's adorned, for sentimental and deeply private reasons, with a tiny silver charm. I look like a hot mess or a prize arse, or possibly both.

Well done, I say to my reflection. You should be so proud of yourself. Tonight has been an amazing success. In the space of a few hours, everything that hadn't quite gone to crap before has now safely arrived in Shitsville, and it's all your fault. First, you fail to rescue your brother from those people and probably make things a trillion times worse for him. While you're at it, you get your head kicked in because you're so feeble. Then, you end up wasted, sitting on the floor of your living room with the same song blaring out over and over again, and not only do you antagonise your neighbour, you make him think you're a rent boy. Next time he bakes a cake he won't be dropping a slice onto your balcony. In fact, you'll never be able to sit on your balcony again.

And when his mates come round they'll have something new to laugh about.

7. Gawain

I don't really care about the bruise on my cheekbone, nor am I all that bothered about the pain that shoots up one side of my back every time I move. It must be the area that took most of the impact when Slab-Face pushed me onto the ground in the car park. The ton of painkillers I've swallowed have reduced it to a dull ache, as long as I avoid twisting or bending, which is good, but I can't walk far without limping and I have this almost uncontrollable urge to hold my head at a slight angle. At work, just about everyone has something to say about my condition, patients and colleagues alike. At least I think they do. I keep going deaf in one ear for seconds at a time and then I have to decide whether to pretend I can hear and hope I'm not missing anything too important or keep saying pardon over and over again, like an idiot. It probably doesn't matter, because my mind is all over the place anyway, and each time someone asks me what happened, I come up with a different explanation, until in the end I can't remember what I've said to who.

When Bryan sees the state I'm in, he shoves me into a cubicle, gets his little torch out of his pocket and shines it into my eyes. Then he gets me to follow his finger as he moves it back and forth and interrogates me at the same time. I don't have the mental energy to fend him off with evasions, and when I've finished, he tells me to make a complaint to the police. I explain to him why I think this is a bad idea, and instead of arguing as I expect him to, he says okay several times and pats me on the shoulder. His kindness makes me tear up, but I manage to keep it together, just about, only because Bryan pretends not to notice and busies himself ordering a CT scan for me. For the rest of the day, which seems to go on forever, he hovers about nearby. Sometimes he disappears for a while, and then he returns and says something like *here you are* as though he's been looking for me and is delighted to have bumped into me again.

I stagger through the day, somehow. I treat patients and deal with the relevant admin, and I endlessly obsess about Jacob living with that bunch of thugs. But there is a flip side to all this mental anguish.

Worrying about my brother used to be the default setting for my brain, and it feels right to have him living inside my head again after such a long time. I was always the one who looked after him, even before Dad decided we were too old to keep Debbie on. After Dad died, I felt completely responsible for his welfare.

That was when it all started to go wrong for him. First, he shut himself off everyone and then he became obsessed with running. During lunch breaks and after school, he'd race around the outer perimeter of the grounds over and over again until it was time for afternoon lessons or lights out, or until Mr Thompson looked out of his study window and spotted him crossing the other side of the hockey pitches for the third or fourth time, and sent someone to bring him in.

One Thursday, he spent an entire lunch break running, even though it was bangers and mash with onion gravy, his favourite. When he came back in for afternoon lessons, he sat down in the art room and had a massive asthma attack. By the time I was sent for, his lips were turning blue and we all thought he was going to peg out before the ambulance arrived. I managed to make him sit up straight in hard chair and I got him to wrap his hands around my wrists and calm down enough to take a few deep breaths before the paramedics turned up. He stared at me with wild eyes, his defences temporarily lowered, but once his breathing had settled a bit, he became clam-like again. Later, when I tried to ask him what had caused the attack, he just closed his eyes and shook his head. The medics put it down to a combination of emotional stress and excessive exercise.

Soon after that he started spending weekends with Mum, and when he came back to school after these weekends he was different. He'd wander about the school, searching for me, and once he found me, it was clear something was wrong, but he didn't seem able to tell me what it was. I told him he didn't have to go and stay with Mum again if it wasn't working out, but he just shook his head. After a while, he always cheered up again, sort of, and a pattern started to form. He'd be quiet and reserved, but calm and generally okay-ish. Then he'd go and stay with Mum and be moody and impossible for a few days, before gradually reverting to his normal state again, when he'd focus on his rugby and cricket. And his running. I didn't like any of this one bit, and I tried my best to persuade him to stop going to East Sussex. He never listened, but at least I was around when he came back to school.

And now I've messed things up to such an extent that I'll never be there for him again. I can't even go back to the church and watch over him from a distance, because Slab-Face and the rest know who I am now. They're probably taking it in turns to look out for me, in case I turn up and try something else. What I really need to do is step back, make a proper plan and consider its potential consequences from all angles. Unfortunately, that's proving to be harder than it sounds and so far I haven't come up with a single glimmer of a strategy.

Despite all this brotherly angst, I manage to spare a thought for the bloke next door, and on the way home, I stop off at the supermarket to buy him a bottle of red wine. I try to find something a bit more decent than the cheap plonk from the bottom shelf. I tell myself I'm doing this to apologise for keeping him awake last night and definitely not for any other reason. But while I read labels on the backs of bottles and spend way too long agonising over what should be an uncomplicated decision, I hear faint yapping noises inside my head as my heavily repressed inner monkey, who knows all my secrets, pours scorn on my feeble attempts at self-deception.

The heat and humidity have now ratcheted themselves up to levels more suited to an expanse of equatorial rainforest than the Surrey-Hampshire border. By the time I get home and climb the stairs to the third floor, there are big wet patches on the back of my shirt and under my armpits, even though I showered and sprayed myself with half a can of deodorant at work before I left. The gloomy hallway outside the flats seems to have been filled with be a thick miasma that smells like minestrone soup. I hyperventilate as I walk along the landing and I start worrying about Jacob's asthma again. When he was in A&E he was wheezing slightly, but when I asked, he shrugged it off and said it wasn't a big deal.

I knock on my neighbour's door. After a painful hiatus that probably lasts only a few seconds, but seems much longer, he opens his door a couple of inches and looks down at me with his eyebrows clenched, as though he's trying out a new Heathcliff impersonation and would like to know what I think of it. It's pretty damn good, actually, apart from the fact that Heathcliff would never have worn a thigh length dressing gown in lime green. I wonder how many dressing gowns this bloke has. I don't even own *one*. Maybe it's an age thing?

As he stares at me, making me feel as awkward and exposed as a maggot squirming on a hook, I remind myself that in my job I spend most of my time interacting with one complete stranger after another, most of whom are less than happy to engage with me. But in those situations, I'm the one in control, and I can usually get patients to do my bidding without too much trouble, either because they know it's for their own good or they're too sick to object. Dressing-Gown-Man isn't my patient, and as I hold the wine out towards him, I realise he could do or say anything at all.

Ah well, I think. If he refuses to accept the bottle with good grace, I'll leave him to it. My front door is only about a metre away, a couple of jumps to my left. I put one hand in the front pocket of my trousers to check my keys are still there. With the other hand, I thrust the wine towards him.

'By way of apology for last night.'

I find myself doing that inane half-smile again. Yap, yap, yap goes the little monkey as it bounces from one side of my psyche to the other. I take a small step back and look up at him. The lines on his forehead are like those strips of plasticine you use to be able to buy at Toys R Us. He takes the wine, turns the bottle and spends an inordinate amount of time reading the label on the back, as though it has some hidden significance, and he'll reject my peace offering if he decides it isn't to his taste, if it has blackberry notes instead of plum, say, or contains too much tannin.

As I watch his wine connoisseur act, I grow increasingly irritated. Eventually, I decide he's being deliberately provocative, and if his perusal of the damn label takes much longer I really will walk off. Then I start to suspect he might be playing a game and if that's the case, I'm kind of up for it and curious to see how it's going to unfold.

Finally, he looks up and gives me a quick visual once over, like a bouncer at the door of a night club. Then he opens the door a tiny bit wider and stands back to let me in, still without saying a single word. I hesitate for a fraction of a second before squeezing through the narrow gap. My nose passes so close to his arm pits I can smell a warm and salty, but not unpleasant, aroma coming off him, mingled with hints of a male fragrance I've sniffed somewhere before, but can't identify. As I sidle past him, it suddenly occurs to me that he doesn't realise he's being ill mannered because he's on the autistic spectrum and has no awareness of personal space. But then I remember how neurotypical his behaviour is when he's on his balcony with his mates.

Nah, he's definitely winding me up.

The blinds that cover his sliding door are closed and it takes a few seconds for my eyes to adjust to the darkness. When I do, I see that his living space is bizarre and accidental looking, as though it wasn't meant to look like this, but has been the victim of a series of unpredicted furniture-related mishaps. Overall, the main room is grey in colour and minimalist, but this effect, which could be quite stylish, is ruined by the presence of odd bits of old fashioned and completely inappropriate items that look as though they've been dumped there from his nan's house.

He puts the wine bottle down heavily on a large, farmhouse kitchen-style table, fetches two large wine glasses from a starkly modernist wall cabinet with no discernible handles and decants most of the bottle into these two glasses, giving us a half pint of wine each, near enough. Then he crashes heavily into an old pink and white chair with black spindly legs that looks as though it was fashioned from a basket in the nineteen fifties and would suit Doris Day more than it suits him. I can't prevent myself from glancing briefly at the chair legs to see if any of them have snapped. None of them has, despite the fact he's bigger than me by some margin, which doesn't in itself make him huge in the general scheme of things, of course. It's more that he has a knack of seeming larger and heavier than he actually is for some reason.

'Cheers!'

His sudden and unexpected yell startles me so much my skin contracts. He holds his glass aloft as though we're about to embark on an evening of roistering. I do likewise, half expecting him to wish me a merry Christmas next, but silence thickens around us again. I swallow a couple of large mouthfuls of wine on an empty stomach and hop awkwardly from one foot to the other.

'Sit down for God's sake!'

This is a command, not a request and he sounds fairly put out, so I perch myself uneasily on the edge of a small metal stool next to the dining table, like a runner in the starting blocks, more than ready to spring up and get the hell out if things take the wrong turn. He crosses one neatly carved and hairy leg over the other and my mind makes a sickening lurch towards kilts again. I rapidly shift my gaze back to his face, but not before I notice his feet are hidden inside trainer socks, not exposed with his toes thonged into flip-flops, which is a gigantic improvement on yesterday. We sip our wine and cautiously eye each other up as though we're both standing at the bar in a club and have just noticed each other. His eyelashes are so thick and black it looks as though he's coated them with mascara onto them, but I doubt he's the type to do that. Gradually the glint in his eyes increases, until becomes too vivid and penetrating for me to deal with.

I lower my head and focus on my thighs. The space between us has become dense with something difficult to define. Perhaps it's full of questions we'd like to ask each other, but can't, either because it's way too early for that kind of thing or because the atmosphere he's created has made a rational exchange of information impossible.

In the end, the silence gets the better of me, so I decide to attempt some form of conversation, however blundering and stupid it sounds.

'Are you ill?' I ask him.

'What?'

'You're always in a dressing gown?'

My intonation goes up at the end of this sentence, making me sound both slightly Australian and very young compared to him. Loud, staccato gun-bursts of outraged, but delighted, laughter explode from his mouth, seemingly against his will. I've never heard a laugh quite like that.

'I've just been for a run. I was about to take a shower, until you knocked on my door.'

He raises his eyebrows as he says the last bit and lowers his voice to imply that I've done much more than knock on his door, which of course I have. I see that now.

I don't have time to wander very far down this particular avenue of self-observation, though, because he suddenly jumps up and unties the belt of his dressing gown in a series of sharp, rapid movements, as though he's a bit hyper. I manage to stay this side of panic, but I really want to go home now. At the very least I'd like to put my head in my hands so I don't have to look at him. But all I can do is gawp like a fool as he flings off the dressing gown and throws it over the back of his chair. When I see he's wearing running shorts and a red vest, I'm so limp with relief that he hasn't been perving at me whilst naked under a seriously dodgy outer garment, I almost fall off the stool.

He really *has* been for a run. There are sweat marks under his armpits and I notice for the first time the hair on his head is standing on end in little spikes, slick with moisture. It makes him look a bit like a dog that's just been for a swim in the local canal, one of those half-wild, scrappy looking mongrels that run away and refuse to come back once they've been let off the lead. But his physique is far from scrappy and his biceps are inked in various shades of black, grey and red. When I was at school, I once bunked off to Basingstoke and got two little navy blue dolphins inked onto the backs of my shoulder blades, but I've never seen anyone with tattoos as extensive as his. I'd love to inspect every inch of the work he's had done, slowly and carefully, and maybe track the way one image flows into the next with the tip of my index finger. Or perhaps with my tongue.

My God, what's wrong with me?

He flops into his chair again, heavily as a sack of cement dropped from a hole in the ceiling. I still kind of want to go home, but not quite as much as I did before. In fact, I think I've lost the ability to move now, apart from lifting the wine glass to my mouth. I think about cases in the news where the man that lives alone, the one nobody knows anything about, turns out to have lured a whole series of lonely boys like me into his home and done unspeakable things to them, either before or after killing them, and has gone on to dissolve their bodies in acid or drag them to a nearby cemetery and prop them up against gravestones. If he's one of those, it's probably too late for me to escape now. But this possibility doesn't worry me as much as perhaps it should, which is itself a little disturbing. I decide to be brave and look him in the eye without blinking, just for a short while, to see what happens.

'What are you looking at?' He asks, rudely. I notice his accent again. Green hills and soft rain. He leans forward in his chair and stares right back at me at me. I lean forward, too, narrowing the space between us to a few centimetres. His breath smells of pineapple and the floral notes of the wine we're drinking. I force myself not to smile.

'God knows.'

"What do you *think* you're looking at then?"

'It's difficult to say.' I have no idea. All I know is that I can't stop staring.

'Do you want to know what I see when I look at you?'

'Not really.'

'Yes, you do.'

"Go on, then."

'You're scared. And you're carrying a heavy burden. A kind of deep sadness. Deeper than you realise.'

What the hell? Is he some kind of clairvoyant or fortune teller? *A deep sadness*. Where did he get that from? It sounds like something from one of those dodgy self-help books or an online horoscope. Or maybe it's his way of telling me I'm a sad bastard. If so, I already know that, thanks very much. I look down sharply and discover he's holding both my hands between his. I seem to have missed the part where he took my glass and put it on the table. His grip is so tight I'm not sure I'd be able to pull away, even if I wanted to. I close my eyes.

'You did that last night,' he says.

'What?'

'Closed your eyes to stop me seeing you.'

I open them again and as I do so, I feel a flush rise up my face via my neck from two little points on either side of my collar bone. He watches and smiles as though I've changed my skin tone deliberately, just to entertain him.

'Would you mind opening a window?'

He lets go of my hands and gets up from the table. I'm relieved, but also a bit dismayed at how bereft I feel now that his hands are no longer in contact with mine. He strides over to the sliding door and pulls it open. The sun is lower in the sky now, so he pushes the curtains back too, and the room fills with a deep yellow glow interrupted by long bands of shadow cast by the trees on the other side of the railway line. Next, he disappears into what must be his kitchen and comes back with two pint glasses of iced water. I press my glass against my face and then knock half of the water back in one go. He watches intently, as though observing me is his favourite new activity. When I put my glass down on the table again, he picks up his and pours its contents over his head, the whole lot. It runs in little channels through his eyelashes, down his face and beard, onto his shoulders and inside his running vest, and leaves little shards of ice suspended in his hair. He shakes the water away from his eyes, reminding me of a dog again, and he grins at me.

His behaviour suddenly feels like an infection I have no resistance to, so I smile back, and I hand him my glass. He raises his eyebrows questioningly. I nod and his grin broadens even further, revealing two rows of neat little teeth. I expect him to just pour what's left in my glass over my head but he dashes off to the kitchen and fills the glass up again to make sure I get an entire pint. He tips it over me, towards the back of my head so that the water misses my face and eyes and instead flows down the back of my neck. My shoulders contract violently and most of the ice creeps down my shirt and gathers at my waist.

'I baptize you in the name of the father, the son and the holy ghost.'

'You have to do that three times for it to be valid,' I mutter between gasps. I stand up, wondering why the hell I just said that and I pull my shirt out of my trousers and jump around a bit to shake the ice out.

'Really?'

Gleefully, he gets behind me and I let him push me by the shoulders across the room and through the bathroom door, without even bothering to ask myself what he's planning to do next. When we get inside, he turns to face me.

Please call me Sunshine, I think.

8. Gawain

'Get your kit off, then!' He hollers.

'No!'

'No?' He pouts theatrically.

'No.'

Oh my God. Why am I here? I have no idea, but suddenly, I'm laughing so much my face is almost split in two and I can't stop. I don't think I've laughed like this for years and years.

'At least take your shoes and socks off.'

I do this quickly, and try not to look at my feet, because I despise them as much as I despise everyone else's feet, and the possibility that he might judge them with a similar harshness concerns me. Luckily, he doesn't even look at them. He never breaks eye contact with me, not even for a second, as he reaches behind me and inserts his hands into each of my rear trouser pockets, and pulls out my phone and my wallet. He spends a few seconds brazenly fondling my arse while he's at it, which makes me laugh even more. When he tries to put a hand in one of my front pockets, I step back quickly, because I don't want him to feel the effect he's having on me, although it must be obvious. He has to content himself with pulling my NHS lanyard over my head. He doesn't look at it, he just files it for safe keeping on the closed lid of the toilet with everything else he's collected from my person.

Next thing I know, he's bundling me into the shower almost fully clothed and stepping in behind me in his running gear. Cold water deluges over us in torrents. He turns me round to face him and pulls me close enough for our noses to touch and our arms and legs to interlock. He has to lean over a bit and I have to reach up slightly. I shift my position a little so I can press my face against the naked part of his chest above his running vest, because I suddenly need to extract as much warmth and comfort from him I can, but also because I don't want him to see my face, because I know my desperate neediness will be written all over it. He lets me get away with this for a few seconds, then he pulls back and starts to unbutton my shirt from the top. When he reaches the half way point, I put my hand over his to stop him. He looks hurt and perplexed about my inability to totally commit to getting naked in the shower with him. Then he focuses on my shirt again and pushes the material to one side, so he can inspect my nipple piercing, which he must have spotted last night.

'It's a tiny little fish.' He gently flicks it up and lets it drop down again, causing the skin underneath to quiver and harden. He keeps on doing it until I have to bite my lip to stop myself making a noise that might imply pleasure.

'Why do you only have one little fish?' He sounds as though he's talking to a small child.

'I lost the other one.'

'That's a shame.'

He bends to flick his tongue over the area he's been making the fish tap against and then gradually moves upwards, pressing his lips against my flesh until he reaches my neck and then my mouth, which he opens with his tongue. We wrap ourselves around each other again and we kiss under the icy spray. I'm slightly anxious about the feel of his tongue on my teeth, but it's not bad enough for me to make him stop. Water gets everywhere. It slides between our faces and our lips and it soaks our skin, our hair and the insides of our clothes until we're so chilled we've got the jitters.

'I don't even know your name,' I say when we've stepped out onto dry land again.

He throws me a towel.

'I don't know yours.'

He peels off his wet clothes in front of me and strides off naked into the living room to get his precious dressing gown. He clearly wants me to watch him, so I do. His body is tight and compact, but his muscles bulge more than mine ever will. I wonder how long he spends at the gym to keep himself in that sort of shape. I never go anywhere near physical exercise, apart from swimming and occasionally wandering off on long, aimless walks, and I haven't done either of those for months. I get away with it, sort of, because I'm so skinny, the few muscles I possess show up through my skin. But the thing I notice most about his body is his mysterious ink and the way it writhes and swirls in intertwining tendrils beyond his arms and across his chest and shoulders, narrowing to a point halfway down his back, like a pair of folded wings. He turns to face me again and I take my shirt off and wrap the towel around my shoulders. His eyes burn into me in a way that no eyes have done for a very long time.

Suddenly, he smiles at me in a different way. Not challenging or teasing this time, but conveying something else, simple benevolence perhaps or something deeper and a bit more difficult to define. Maybe by getting in the shower with him, I've passed a kind of test, and now he's happy to let me know he's a kinder, less quirky person than he's made himself out to be. This possibility disarms me to the extent that I'm almost completely undone by it. But I resist the urge to pull off the rest of my clothes and instead I smile, too, reflecting his benevolence back at him, trying to make him see that if he wishes me well, then I wish him the same.

I follow him into the living room. Water wicks down my trousers and drips onto his floor.

'Go get changed. Then come back.'

Obediently I make for the door.

'Shall I make coffee?'

I turn back to face him and I nod. He looks pleased and I sense a slight shift towards me in the delicate power dynamic that's flickering between us like a recently lit flame. It takes me about ten minutes to change, slick my hair down with gel, sling some dirty clothes in my washing machine and check my phone in case a miracle has happened and there's a message from Jacob. I don't pause for a single second to mull over the fact that this bloke with no name isn't part of my overall plan, that I've got other things to think about and the last thing I need is a distraction like him. All I want to do is to get back next door as quickly as possible and make him touch me and kiss me again, even if his tongue makes contact with my teeth.

We sit on his balcony, drink coffee and knock back shots of a noxious liqueur he says he brought back from a trip to Russia with his mates. It tastes a bit like tequila, but with undertones of those squishy pick-n-mix banana sweets. I make a mental note to drink mine slowly. I don't know how much alcohol it contains and the last thing I want is to end up wasted again. We're facing each other at opposite sides of the table, and he's leaning back in his chair and looking across at me, all serious and business like, as though he's conducting an interview. But the table is small and as soon as I sit down, our ankles touch. His dark hair is smoothed back and glossy with moisture and he's put on a pair of cut off denim shorts and a white sleeveless top.

He watches as I sip my coffee. It's pretty decent. I could drink gallons of it.

'Go on, then, posh boy,' he says. 'Tell me about yourself.'

Posh boy? I don't know how to respond to that accusation. I fold my arms and lean back in my chair, mirroring him. He surveys me for a moment. Then he leans forward and holds out his hand for me to shake.

'I'm Bart McGowan or Barty, if you prefer.'

Another smile fills my face without my permission.

'What's Bart short for? Not Bartholek?'

He doesn't have a clue why I said that, but then I knew he wouldn't.

'Bartosz. It's a family name. My great-grandad was Polish.'

I decide instantly that I prefer Bartosz to Bart or Barty. The combination of hard and soft sounds bounces satisfyingly off my tongue and the roof of my mouth as I say it out loud.

'Gawain Fylde.'

'What the fuck? Are you taking the piss?'

Bloody hell, how rude. It's not as though his name is John Smith or something.

'Do you want me to fetch my ID card?'

'No, I believe you, I suppose.'

'You suppose?'

'No. Not really. Go get it.'

He waves me off imperiously, and I have to traipse back to my flat again to fetch it because I left it there when I got changed. I hand it over to him. He takes so long to read the scant amount of information displayed on it that I start formulating a sarcastic question about whether or not he has learning difficulties.

'My mum wanted to call me Wayne, but my dad thought that was a bit common.'

I'm making this up. I have no idea what my parents did or didn't want to call me, if anything, before they settled on Gawain.

He laughs.

'You're a medic?'

I grin at him and nod.

'There's no need to look so bloody pleased with yourself about it.' He throws me a glance both saturnine and full of suspicion. 'You don't look anywhere near old enough.'

'Well I am. I've been qualified for a while now.'

'How old *are* you, then?'

'I'll be twenty-seven in September.'

'Twenty seven. Wow.'

'How old are *you* then?'

'Forty-one.'

Pretty old. Older than I thought, but I'm not going to tell him that.

'What do *you* do?'

'What do you think I do?'

'Something physical. Fitness instructor, PE teacher, football coach, bin man…"

My last guess at his occupation causes him to emit a series of amused chuntering sounds. He springs up and goes dashes the living room. I hear a drawer opening and then shutting again, and he comes back with a business card, which he hands to me. Turns out he's Divisional Director of Client Services for a wealth management company. He has several letters after his name that are completely different to the ones after mine and I'm pretty sure my Aunty Susan is one of their clients, which is why I recognise the name of the company. I think I've seen it written on pens left lying around at her house. It's not what I expected. It doesn't seem to fit somehow.

'So that big black Audi in the car park is yours, then?'

'Perk of the job.'

"You haven't always been in wealth management, though.'

'Have I not?'

Does he look a little uneasy now? Is there a little chink in his armour here, a small area that he doesn't want me to probe?

'You were something else.'

'Oh yes?'

'You were in the army.'

'Is it really that obvious?'

I nod and watch as he looks away and narrows his eyes slightly. It really is totally obvious. The tattoos, the intense camaraderie between him and his mates and the clipped, abrupt way he speaks. It all adds up. We have a contingent of military doctors and nurses at the hospital. They have a recognisable style. I'm pleased with myself for getting this right so quickly, but I try not to show it, because a faint shadow has fallen over his face. It makes me feel as though I've been cruel and prized this information out of him against his will. Unless he's just manipulating me to go down a particular emotional route.

Anway, he soon bounces back.

'I'm entitled to ask you another question, now,' he says.

'Go on, then.'

I try to make it sound as though I'm reluctant to continue with this interrogation, but in truth, I'm starting to bask in his attention and I'm longing for him to peel my layers back one by one. *Look - I'm under here* I want to say.

'Family? Mine are all in Yorkshire - my mum and my three sisters and the rest. My dad died when I was ten.'

He has no idea how blissfully straightforward that sounds, even the bit about his dad.

'Your turn.'

He looks at me expectantly.

'Do I have to?'

'If you don't, I'll be forced to grab you and suspend you over the edge of the balcony by your ankles.'

I'm so desperate for him to touch me again I shake my head. He plays along and comes round to my side of the table. He pulls me up by the waist, nearly knocking over my coffee and drags me to the front of the balcony. I yelp loudly and beg him to stop. Two women walking across the car park look up at us, so he pulls me back to my chair again. I'm not usually playful like this. It must be that dodgy tequila concoction. When I sit down again, he leans over me, clasps his hands in front of my chest and burrows his mouth into the side of my neck.

I take a deep breath.

'My dad died a long time ago, like yours, and I'm not on speaking terms with my mum.'

'What's she done?'

'It's complicated. She was never there very much when I was a kid, so I don't miss her or anything. I have a sister and an aunt, though.'

'And?'

'And what?'

"You're leaving something out. Or someone.'

'How the hell do you know that?'

'From the way you ended that last sentence. It sounded as though you were running up a flight of stairs, but when you were nearly at the top, you stopped.'

'Did it?'

'You know it did.'

'Do I?'

'Stop it, you little idiot. Just tell me.'

I'm suddenly appalled at the way he's holding me to account and not letting me get away with the little subterfuges I habitually adopt to keep my true self hidden from view. He's very good at it. I'm also pretty taken aback by the fact that he's inserted his tongue inside my left ear. But at the same time, I adore it, all of it, and I want to yield and let him prize me open completely. I have a feeling that in the end he'll make me tell him everything, even the bits I don't want anyone to know. Not for a while, maybe, but eventually.

'I've also got a younger brother, who I've lost.'

I this very quickly because I'm afraid if I don't, I'll lose my nerve. I've never discussed my brother with anyone who doesn't know him, apart from Bryan. Jacob is a topic that goes way too deep to be talked about with strangers. I press the end of a coffee spoon into the palm of my hand, making a dent, until Bartosz leans over me and takes it away.

'Who you've lost?'

'It's a long story. I wouldn't know where to start.'

'Start with his name.'

'Jacob.'

Naming him to this strange man instantly transforms Jacob into a creature with a new reality. It pulls him out of my past and into the present. It almost feels like a eureka moment. I realise sharing him with this new person might actually be a fresh start, unexpected and jarring, but welcome.

I'm over analysing again. I can't find the words I need to make Bartosz understand about my brother, so I fumble for my phone and I show him the selfie I took at the hospital. Jacob is leaning up on one elbow in his gown on what is clearly a hospital bed and I'm standing behind him, close but not touching. Neither of us is smiling and Jacob looks as though he can hardly keep his eyes open. I've stared at this photo so much over the last few weeks that the image has become fixed inside my head and I don't need to look at it to remember all the details. But showing it to Bartosz, makes me look at it in a different way, through his eyes. The expressions on our faces are inscrutable, like ones you sometimes see in old black and white pictures.

Bartosz frowns. 'Is he dead?'

'What? Oh my God. No! Why would you even think that?'

'You said he was lost. Is he sick, then?'

'No. Not at all. I mean, he's got asthma, and I don't think he eats enough, but he's ok.'

Bartosz releases a warm breath into the area at the back of my neck, above my shirt, either through relief or mystification. Or both.

'You look hot as hell in those scrubs.'

Or lust.

He steps back and moves his chair round so he's sitting next to me and he pulls me towards him as I scroll through my phone to find the photos of the scars on Jacob's back. I'd forgotten how much I love resting my head on another man's shoulder. He pours me more coffee and waits for me to compose myself so I can tell him, a virtual stranger, all about my brother.

'He's in a predicament,' I say.

I tell him some of it. I start in the middle, from the point when Jacob turned up at the hospital. Is that really the middle or is it closer to the end? Or is it the beginning of the end? It's too soon to say, but it's definitely a long way from the actual beginning, and I'm not going into all that, not yet anyway. I tell Bartosz about the Church of the New Sunrise, what they did to my brother and how he ended up in my A&E department, and then and I give him a potted summary of what happened next, the way I sat outside the church not knowing what to do until I lost the plot and made it all worse, and I finish by explaining that I'm completely at sea now, as is my brother. It all comes out in a kind of continuous blurt and Bartosz listens attentively, without interrupting. When I get to the end, the bit about yesterday evening, he turns to look directly at me and runs his index finger over the mark on my cheekbone. He does it so gently it's like being caressed by a blade of grass.

'I haven't told you it everything.'

'I know.'

*

'You need lime scale remover for that.'

My sister has turned up. She's spent the evening with her chums at the Green Dragon, which is close by.

I go into the bathroom and find her standing with her hands on her hips, looking into the depths of my toilet and tutting loudly at regular intervals. I've already had to listen to her going on about the hairs in the sink and the pile of clean laundry in the basket that wouldn't need to be ironed if I'd bothered to fold it up as soon as it came out of the drier. I never iron anything. I don't even own an iron.

I wish she'd gone straight home from the pub. I've only just got in from work, due to a major pile up on the motorway, the victims of which arrived in a series of ambulances about thirty minutes before my shift should have ended. And in any case, I was hoping to avoid seeing her at all until the bruise on my cheek has faded.

In order to avoid slapping her really hard, I need to eat something, so I leave her blathering on and on in the bathroom and I go into the kitchen. I pour the contents of a can of chicken soup into a bowl, tip a bag of roast chicken flavour crisps into it and set it to microwave for three minutes. While it's warming up she appears in the kitchen and looks at me properly for the first time since she arrived.

'Jesus. What have you done?'

I resign myself to telling her about Slab-Face and all the rest of it. She keeps interrupting me with exclamations of disbelief, not at their violence but at my stupidity for deciding to intervene.

'You're such a plonker,' she says when I've finished. 'Are you hurt anywhere else?'

'Why would I be?'

'You're moving oddly, as though you've done something to your back.'

'That can happen when you get a kicking from an oaf.'

'You realise you can't go there again?'

'I might give it a few days, wait until they've calmed down.'

'They won't do that. They'll be looking out for you now.'

'I know. That was a joke.'

'Funny.'

I fetch my food and we go onto the balcony. She sits and I stand leaning against the metal grid that separates my outside space from next door, shovelling my chicken dinner into my mouth. Hairs prickle on the back of my neck at the thought that Bartosz might be lurking behind me on his side of the mesh. But I can't hear him and there don't seem to be any lights on behind his curtains. I wonder where he's gone and who with. The events of yesterday evening fast forward through my mind making me shiver and flush at the same time.

'Have you only just got in?'

'Incident at Junction 4a.'

I sit down and put my bowl on the table. It lands with a clatter.

'Maybe I should go. I don't want to talk to you when you're in such a foul mood.'

I shrug and continue eating. The crisps have dissolved into the soup now, making a delicious, salty mess, an unhealthy, but tasty parody of a roast dinner.

'Is there any particular reason for your visit? Or are you just here to moan at me?'

'I thought you should know. I've decided.'

I stop eating and look at her.

'I'm not going to continue with it. I'm still within the limits for a medical abortion. Where you take the drugs.'

She sounds completely detached, as though she's talking about one of her patients.

'I know what a medical abortion is.'

'Of course you do. Sorry.'

'Are you sure?'

She nods.

'What if you regret it?'

'I won't.'

'It's a baby, Amanda.'

I get up and go inside. Amanda follows me and watches, arms folded, as I drop my dish into the sink, then fling myself on the sofa, where I lie on my back with my arms behind my head and my eyes closed.

"Not yet. It's just a collection of cells at the moment.'

'A collection of cells programmed to become a baby. If it gets the chance.'

'I didn't realise you were one of those pro-life fanatics, Gawain.'

'You know I'm not *that*. But it's a huge decision. It needs a lot of thought.'

'I've thought of nothing else for weeks.'

'But you'll be killing your own little boy or little girl. My niece or nephew.'

'That's not fair.'

'How can you be so detached about it? What's wrong with you?'

'I'm not having a child just because you fancy being an uncle.'

I want to slap her even more, now.

'If you don't want it, I'll have it.'

'Don't be stupid.'

'I'll adopt it.'

'Oh yes, that would really work. With your job and all the exams and studying you've still got to do, plus the fact that you have the emotional maturity of a ten year old and you're more or less clueless about normal life. You don't have any idea how people interact out there in the real world. You don't even watch TV.'

'I read books.'

She stops to draw breath and then continues. 'I can't even begin to imagine all the ways everything would go pear shaped with you as its main carer.'

'I know about babies. I took care of Jacob often enough.'

'And look what happened to him.'

I have this sensation as though a tide is receding inside my head, like water on a beach, revealing a little blue and red tug boat stranded in the mud with the word *hope* written on its side and wrecked beyond repair. She walks over to the door and opens it. I sit up and crane my neck round to look at her. A muscle contracts painfully in my injured back. 'I'll get Jacob back,' I say.

She gives me another look, a severe one, and leaves, shutting the door quietly behind her. I stay prone on the sofa and listen to the increasingly faint clicking of her heels as she walks off along the corridor and makes her way carefully down the stairs.

The next morning, remorse kicks in, and I ring her and offer to go over and be her support person when the cramps and the bleeding start. Then I suggest that if she doesn't want me there, she could go and stay with Aunty Susan. She laughs at that suggestion, but overall, her response is vague and non-committal.

And pretty ungrateful, if you ask me.

9. Jacob

My room has suddenly got very dark and the air feels zingy. I get up from my bed and switch on the light, which is only a dim bulb hanging from the ceiling, so it doesn't help much, and I have to lie down again quickly to stop myself from blacking out. Warren is punishing me because of my brother turning up like that, as though it was my fault. I'm confined to my room, apart from trips to the toilet at the top of the stairs, and I'm getting one meal per day, usually a couple of marmite sandwiches without butter, which Mum brings down in the evenings with my pills. Since G staged that intervention or whatever it was meant to be, they've increased the dose, so I've spent most of my time sleeping. When I'm not asleep I can't stop myself thinking, mostly about my brother and my Mum, going over and over things that happened years ago in another life.

The first time I met her, I had no clue who she was. We were still living at home with Dad then, and I was in the reception year at the local primary school. G was playing the part of a wizard in the end of term play and had stayed late for a rehearsal. I was meant to wait for him so we could walk home together, but I got bored hanging around on my own in the playground, so I set off on my own. All of a sudden she was there, in the street, crouching down in front of me, thrusting a parcel towards me, wrapped in bright paper decorated with little pink pigs and wishing me a happy birthday, although it would be six months before I turned five.

When I got home I unwrapped my present. It turned out to be a big metal excavator that could be dismantled with the help of the screwdriver that came with it. When G appeared, he was furious with me because I hadn't waited for him. I told him a lady had stopped me in the street, called me Sebastian and given me a birthday present and he ran off without saying another word. I heard him in the hall, on the phone to Dad, crying his eyes out.

Next thing, Dad arrived home earlier than usual. G had thrown up in the downstairs loo by then, and was in a state of mental collapse. Dad grabbed a roll of kitchen towel roll, tore off a piece and wiped

G's face. Then he tore off another piece and polished his glasses violently, as though he was angry with them for being dirty. After that, he knelt down by me on the floor asked me the same things about the lady and the man who was with her, over and over again, what they looked like, what they said, if they'd hurt me in any way, until I started crying. G ran up and put his arms round me, which I didn't want, seeing as he was the one who'd got me into trouble with Dad. I pulled his hair and pinched his arm.

Dad told me to go and play with my excavator in the garden, while he spoke to G in his study. I could hear him through the open window trying to calm G down. I didn't understand. Why was he all hysterical, just because someone had given me a present? Maybe he was upset because he didn't get one. But G didn't even like toy vehicles.

'I won't let her get anywhere near you again. Not ever,' I heard Dad say.

'Or Jacob?'

'She won't be going near any of you.'

He sounded very cross, which made me feel a bit scared.

After that, if G was late leaving school, I had to go and sit in the secretary's office and wait for him, and when we walked home together, he always held my hand really tight. I tried to ask him why he was so upset about Mum giving me a present. He said it was a kind of bad feeling he got, which he couldn't explain properly. I said I thought she was nice, but he just shook his head and his face crumpled as though he was going to start crying again, so I stopped talking about her.

I don't know what Dad did to prevent Mum from seeing us. Maybe he took out an injunction against her and Warren, or threatened them in some way. Or perhaps it was just that they went back to America. But whatever it was, years passed, and the next time I saw them was at Dad's funeral, when we'd been sent to boarding school. I hadn't noticed them in the church or at the burial, probably because I was too busy sobbing inside G's blazer. I kind of bumped into Mum accidentally at the wake, while I was piling sausage rolls, sandwiches and several portions of everything else, apart from the mushroom vol au vents, onto my plate. I was famished after the trauma of the burial and this was my second helping. I'd gone back to the buffet on my own. The others couldn't see me because they were all gathered at a table in a kind of alcove round a corner, close to the free bar. G had become seriously distracted by the selection of alcoholic drinks on offer, and once I'd cheered up and was eating again, he let me off the leash and focused on getting the bartender to give him a whisky. This was a challenge, because G was only fifteen and looked it, but he managed it in the end, probably by talking about Dad and playing the sympathy card. Unless it was because the bartender wasn't much older than my brother and couldn't care less who drank what. By the time we left, G had polished off two whisky and gingers, a rum and coke and a large bloody Mary, and Mr Thompson was annoyed with him.

Mum invited me to go and sit with her and Warren, so I did. They seemed really interested in me and my life and asked me loads of questions about school, my brother, Dad, Amanda and everything. They even brought up Aunty Susan, who Mum didn't seem keen on. I tried my best to answer them accurately and politely, and afterwards, Mum smiled at me, rested a hand on mine and said she was sorry to see how upset I'd been during the funeral and that maybe now Dad had gone from my life it would be nice for me to see a bit more of *her*. I thought how lovely she was, how dark and pretty and fragrant, and how miraculous it was to see her again, just after Dad had died, when I was feeling so sad.

I think that encounter set up a kind of yearning in me, like feeling hungry, but in the head instead of the stomach, and I couldn't understand why Dad and G wanted nothing to do with her when she was so nice.

Eventually Mr Thompson came looking for me.

'We're leaving,' he said, abruptly.

He didn't even look at Mum or Warren, let alone speak to them. Then he escorted me to the door, where G was waiting. Poor Mr Thompson. He'd driven us up North to the funeral and now he had to drive us all the way back again. Amanda was in her first year at Edinburgh then. We dropped her off at Hull Paragon, so she could catch her train back to Scotland via York. We'd only just reached the dual carriageway when we had to stop in a car park outside a boarded up Little Chef so G could vomit into a grate.

In the weeks after the funeral I had all these sensations dashing about and exploding inside my head and chest like little fireworks. I couldn't talk to anyone about them and the only way I could defuse them was by running. I ran and ran. Then I ran some more. I followed a particular circuit, past the front of the main school building and the front gardens of all the houses, which formed a wide, slow curve all the way round to the backs of the playing fields. Then I'd continue past the swimming pool, along the edge of the woods and back to the science block and the main building again.

One particularly foggy and damp lunchtime, I was approaching the swimming pool, when a pair of gigantic arms suddenly reached through a gap between two holly bushes at a point where the woodland at the edge of the hockey pitch was just a thin strip. The arms picked me up and dragged me through the band of trees to the lane. I screamed and attempted to struggle, but I knew nobody would see or hear or see me once I was on the other side of the shrubbery. The arms belonged to Warren and they put me down in front of someone standing by a car. It was Mum. She was wearing a fluffy white coat, white boots and a white bobble hat with silvery threads in it. Her hands were in her pockets and she smiled at me with her head on one side. They explained that they were living in England and were in the process of setting up an outpost of their church not very far away from the school.

'We'd love you to come and stay with us.'

'Now?'

Mum laughed.

'Not now, silly. After we've spoken to the school and made proper arrangements. Gawain and Amanda too, if they want.'

'Ok. That would be cool. Thank you very much.'

I smiled at her and nodded a few times, then I turned and ran back through the bushes as quickly as I could. Warren started to chase after me, but Mum told him to let me go. It was fine, I told myself. Dad had just died and Mum wanted to spend time with me. Where was the harm? But there must have been something, some little edge of uncertainty, a slight snagging in the smoothness of my assumption that Mum simply wanted to get to know me better. After all, to know my movements, they must have been watching the school for a while. They must have stood there before, on other days, making sure they were out of sight, as I ran past.

When I got back to the playground, Mr Thompson had already blown the whistle and the juniors were lining up to file into school for afternoon classes. My form were destined for the art studio. I joined the end of the line and tried to get my breath back as I waited for the person in front of me to start moving forward. After we'd walked into the wood-panelled studio, settled ourselves around the long table and stopped mucking about, Mr Meredith handed out boxes of pastels and sheets of black paper and told us to draw the person opposite. My breathing was already all over the place, and now it was getting to a point where drawing air into my lungs was like trying to suck treacle through a straw. I sat there with a pale yellow pastel crayon in my hand, staring at Joseph Sweeny on the other side of the table, who I was supposed to draw. I gazed vacantly at the drift of pale freckles sprinkled across his nose and cheekbones. I was rubbish at art and I knew I'd end up depicting his facial pigmentation as big brown dots, as though he was a dalmatian. Then Mr Meredith would tell me off.

But how could I draw anything when my hand was shaking so much and there was a heavy weight pressed against my chest? How could I behave normally, when not even fifteen minutes ago I'd almost been abducted by my mother and a huge man in the woods. If they'd grabbed me I wouldn't have been able to do anything. They could have thrown me into the car and done pretty much whatever they wanted with me. I told myself not to be so stupid. They hadn't abducted me, they'd just intercepted me because my mum wanted to see me. Because she's my mum and she misses me. But then, I thought, other parents don't get big men to grab their kids when they want to see them. They turn up for sports days and concerts or arrange to take them out on exeat weekends, like Dad used to. No, it definitely *was* out of order, the way Warren had suddenly appeared like that and just plucked me out of my normal life and deposited me in front of my mother. When I thought about it sitting there in the art room, I could hardly believe it had happened. But it definitely had, and now I couldn't breathe.

'There's something wrong with Fylde, Sir,' somebody shouted.

Mr Meredith came over to me, bent down and stuck his face close to mine. Then, quickly as anything, he pulled back my chair, hoisted me over his shoulder in a kind of fireman's lift and carried me out of the room. It must have looked hilarious, but nobody laughed. In Sick Bay, the nurse called an ambulance and sent for Mr Thompson and G. My brother sat with me while Mr Thompson went to look for my inhaler. I didn't know where it was, which shows how long it had been since I'd had problems with my asthma, and it took him ages to find it. Apparently it was under my bed in the middle of a tangle of lost socks, fluff, half chewed Pontefract cakes I'd bought from the village shop in a moment of curiosity, several multicoloured elastic bands rolled into a ball and my Spanish dictation book. By then, the ambulance had arrived and Gawain had managed to calm my breathing down a bit, using a trick he'd learnt when I was little and was going through a phase when I had a lot of asthma attacks.

They got my symptoms under control pretty quickly in A & E, but they said I had a chest infection and I ended up spending a night in the children's ward. I could breathe again, but I was a tearful wreck. I sat there, propped up on a pillow, trying to eat a trifle, which I really wanted because I'd missed lunch, my face wet with tears, ignoring every question and expression of concern G threw at me. They let him stay there with me for the entire night, curled up in a reclining chair, covered in a blanket by my bed, which was totally against the rules, because at fifteen, he was way too young. They must have made an exception because the only other people I would have wanted there were Mr Thompson, who had to get back to school because he was on night duty, or Dad, who was dead. I suppose they could have dragged in Aunty Susan, but they probably thought I'd have a relapse if she appeared.

My brother held my hand until I fell asleep. He knew it wasn't just a chest infection that had caused my asthma to flare up, and he kept on and on about it, asking me question after question. In the end I told him to stop because I wanted to go to sleep.

It was a mistake not to tell someone, in fact it was a huge, life changing error. I see that now. It didn't have to be G. I could have spoken to Mr Thompson or that shrink they brought in to talk to me, or the school doctor, who was really nice. But reticence has always been my style. The bigger the problem, the smaller the chance I'll ever mention it to anyone. And this was a big deal. G would have been seriously traumatized if he'd found out what Warren and Mum had done, and it would have caused a major kerfuffle at school. They might even have called the police. And I'd never have been allowed to go and stay with Mum.

One Saturday morning, a few weeks later, G and I were summoned to Mrs Hopgood's office. Mr Thompson was there too, and Aunty Susan. It turned out Mum and Warren had approached our Aunt. They were living in East Sussex now because Warren had become Lead Pastor of a new UK outpost of his church, which was known, in America, Mum said, for its good works. Aunty had already discussed the situation with the head and our form tutor, before we were even aware there was a situation to discuss, and they'd decided we should be allowed to make up our own minds. If we wanted to spend the occasional weekend with them, we could. If not, we didn't have to. No pressure.

As soon as Mrs Hopgood had finished explaining the situation, G made for the door.

'That's a no from you, then, Gawain?"

"Yes. Same for Jacob.'

He left the room and wasn't seen again until after lights out, because he bunked off, took a train to Portsmouth and spent the rest of the day hanging about at Gunwharf Keys, gazing at the sea and munching his way through a big bag of chocolate misshapes from the Cadbury's discount shop. When he reappeared he was given the bollocking of his life and suspended for five days. Aunty Susan was livid. She had to drive all the way back to school again that same evening to pick him up.

While he was out of the way, I decided I would like l go and stay with Mum and Warren. For a long time, it was only one weekend per term, and of the three of us, I was the only one who went. Mum would pick me up from school on the Saturday morning and drop me off again on the Sunday evening. The first weekend was alright. The community had moved into an enormous holiday camp and Ruth was given the job of showing me around. We had to do a few chores and turn up for meals and for church on Sunday mornings, but apart from that, we were free to roam where we liked.

The only odd thing was that when she picked me up from school, Mum always seemed really happy to see me. Then, gradually, over the next few hours, she'd sort of disappeared inside herself and when the time came for her to drive me back she'd barely speak to me at all. It was because I was boring, ordinary. Too quiet. Dull. A disappointment. Not sparkly and zany like G would have been. I'd have to work much harder to make her interested in me.

One weekend, someone told Warren they'd spotted me and Ruth fooling around inside one of the disused wooden chalets near the old mini golf course. We were both only eleven and we were mucking about playing hide and seek, not fooling around in the way they meant. We didn't even know what that meant. When Warren found us, I was helping Ruth clamber out of a built-in wardrobe in one of the chalet bedrooms. He went berserk and slapped Ruth across the face with one of his enormous meaty hands. She fell backwards onto the bed and when he pulled her up and started dragging her back to the house her nose was bleeding. I followed them, not knowing what else to do and I was made to stand and watch when she was beaten on the palm of her hand with a metal rod. She closed her eyes and kept her face blank. When he'd finished there was bruise, a thick purple line across her palm.

They didn't beat me then. They never did anything physical to me during those weekends. At first, I thought it was because I had a kind of special status as my mother's long lost son or because my behaviour was somehow more acceptable than Ruth's. But then I realised it was because their beatings left marks, and people at school would notice. For the same reason, when I went out to the US, later on, during the summer holidays, they would never beat me after the middle of August. Warren yelled at me at lot, though, in those early days. I was a trouble maker. I'd corrupted his daughter. I deserved to be horsewhipped, he said. I'd looked down at the floor so I didn't have to see the little bubbles of spittle forming at the edges of his lips. That Sunday, they dropped me off at school earlier than usual, and as I got out of the car, Mum handed me a leaflet. I shoved it in my blazer pocket and only looked at it later, after tea, when I was alone. It was full of lurid drawings, illustrating various sins of the flesh and the ways they could harm your spirit. I'd never heard of these sins, let alone attempted any of them, so I knew my spirit was safe. But the leaflet was a horrible thing. I tore it into a thousand pieces and chucked them away in the big food bin round the back of the school kitchens.

I waited for my brother to find me and ask how the weekend had gone. He hated me going to stay with them and he was usually hovering somewhere near the car park when I got back, wanting to make sure I was ok. I'd say I was fine, brush off his concern and tell him to stop hassling me. But that afternoon, one word from G and I'd probably have told him what had happened, that Warren was a brute and I was afraid of him, and that he often hit Mum, too, and sometimes she behaved like a mental patient. Then G would have made a huge fuss and sorted it all out for me. He'd have told Mr Thompson and maybe I'd never have gone back there again.

But G was nowhere to be seen and the moment passed. He didn't even turn up for Sunday tea, which was always an informal meal we made for ourselves, just toast and crumpets and mugs of cocoa. Pupils didn't have to be there for it. Some of them wouldn't be back from their weekends away yet or they'd doing something else, like piano practice or stuffing their faces with the contents of their tuck boxes in other parts of the building. A handful of the older students often sloped off to the woods to smoke weed, which was easy to get away with, despite being an offense punished by immediate expulsion, because there was only ever one teacher on duty on Sunday afternoons and evenings, and he or she couldn't be everywhere.

But it was odd for G not to be around. He continued not being around for hours and then, after lights out, he suddenly came charging up the stairs to the landing, where I was pacing in my pyjamas. He looked different, in a vague way I couldn't pin down, kind of blurry in the face. By then, I thought I'd more or less got my shit together, but when he asked me how the weekend had gone, I told him it had been great and started crying at the same time. He said I didn't have to go again if I didn't want to, but I changed the subject and asked him where he'd been all evening. He mumbled something about an extra maths tutorial that lasted longer than he'd expected because he couldn't get his head round differential equations. I knew he was lying, but I was preoccupied with my own problems, so I let it go.

After that, I went back to East Sussex loads more times before Warren and his acolytes were recalled to America, to establish another new community in South Carolina with a different name. I started spending the summer holidays out there. G I had fallen out by that time and while I was in the States, I got beaten, on a regular basis. Everyone under the age of twenty-one was thrashed one way or another, usually on the flats of our hands with a metal rod or across the backs of our thighs with a wooden paddle. The beatings on our hands hurt the most, but none of us ever put up any resistance because they'd just get someone to hold you down.

That last summer after my A'levels, when G was established at medical school and I'd become an expert at avoiding him, I really should have stayed in England. I could have got a job somewhere nearby and gone to uni in the September. If I'd done that, I'd be more than half way through my degree course by now. And I'd be safe, not trapped in a gap year that never ends. So many *ifs*. So many wrong moves. It's tough having all this regret whirling around inside my head. But I do have a couple of coping strategies. The first is hatred. It's the only strong emotion I feel these days, the only thing that keeps me going. When I recall, for the millionth time, all the different ways they've harmed me and other innocent people, I know, beyond all doubt, they're evil, and while I can't prevent a huge sense of betrayal from flooding my heart, my lungs and my brain, until it burns like some corrosive chemical, it's good to be completely sure I'm right and they're wrong.

My other coping strategy is the construction of lists. They're all works in progress and I kind of inhabit them, visualise what's in them, add detail and refine them by removing old items or including new ones. A lot are A to Z's: fruits, vegetables, cars, countries, capital cities, trees (impossible), boys' names, girls' names, parts of the male and female anatomy, all sorts of things. I also have lists about my former life: TV shows we used to watch in the common room at school, all the bedrooms I've ever slept in, cricket games I captained for the school, the types of sweets and chocolate sold in the school tuck shop, the players in the junior and senior rugby squads. I try and focus on these lists when I'm down here in my room for hours or even days at a time, with nothing else to do. I need to work very hard at them, because when I don't, my brother creeps back into my stupid, drug-befuddled head. He gets right in there beneath my skull and I lose the will to live.

I close my eyes. There's a sudden crack of thunder and it starts to rain.

10. Gawain

I'm pacing up and down on my balcony. This weekend, I worked a double shift, then did an extra night, covering for someone else, so I'm spaced out from lack of sleep again. My weather app says a storm is imminent. Greenish clouds have billowed up from nowhere and obscured the sun. The afternoon is hot, humid and generally unpleasant, but there's a dusty tension in the air that is making me twitchy with anticipation, as though something amazing is about to happen. I gaze across at the railway line at the trees on the other side and try to imagine the garden that once contained those trees. I conjure up a rose lawn, a tennis court and a picnic blanket spread over the grass beneath a huge elm. A couple of minutes ago, two gentlemen in straw boaters were lolling about on this blanket, dropping strawberries and bits of scone from a wicker hamper into each other's mouths. They were laughing quietly, not daring to really let rip in case someone heard them and wondered what was diverting them so much. Now, though, the darkening sky has made them scramble to their feet. One of them lights a pipe, and they stroll off, down a shingle path lined with lavender bushes, towards the house. A servant will come and take the blanket and the hamper inside.

   A tremendous thwack of thunder makes me cry out. About three seconds later the entire sky flashes white, then the rain begins, tentatively at first in scant, heavy drops that leave coin-sized circles on the balcony floor and release a wonderful smell of hot concrete. I stay out in the open and put my head back so some of the drops fall on my face and into my mouth, and I think about Jacob again and I wonder if he can hear the thunder, too. The rain rapidly intensifies into a deluge, so I close my mouth and put my head down again, which is when I notice Bartosz's Audi spin quickly into the car park and swerve abruptly into a parking space. I haven't seen him since shower gate, as I've started to call it, and I lean over my balcony rail and watch as he runs towards the building. Shortly afterwards, there's a pounding at my door. I open it, and there he is, leaning forward with one hand on the doorframe. From the neck down, he's debonair as hell, in a lightweight grey suit that's only a little bit wet, a pink tie and shiny black shoes. From the neck up it's another matter entirely.

'I'm having a heart attack. Can you ring for an ambulance? Or is it too late?' He pushes the words out abruptly between shallow breaths, and his forehead is glazed with a flat sheen of rainwater, mixed with sweat. More thunder begins in a rumble and builds up to a loud crack, as though a heavy object way up in the stratosphere has split into two parts.

'Shit!' He looks behind him and grabs my arm. I pull him in and shut the door.

The way he's behaving makes me want to laugh, although it's clear he's not joking. I make him take off his jacket and I push him gently onto the sofa. Then I remove his tie and undo the top button of his shirt. He looks up at me and in his eyes I see complete faith as though I'm some kind of shaman with the ability to draw life out of death. People are sometimes like that about doctors, even ones like me who apparently don't look old enough to be medically qualified.

'I don't *think* you're having a heart attack.'

He doesn't look convinced. So I sit next to him on the sofa and feel his pulse. Then I go and dig out my stethoscope, more to reassure him than for any other reason.

'Your heart's fine. It just needs to slow down a bit.'

'You sure?'

'Positive. The problems not here.' I put my hand on his chest. 'It's here.' I gently tap the side of his head.

'Yeah? How do I make it stop, then?'

He looks up at me and his face is still full of trust. If I recommend shoulder stands against the wall whilst chomping on raw carrots, that's what he'll go and do.

'Close your eyes, breathe in, count to five and breathe out again, and keep doing it, until I tell you to stop.'

He follows my instructions and I breathe in the same way to encourage him, like I used to with Jacob during his asthma attacks. I flatten my palm on his chest again and I feel his heart pounding away. Gradually it slows down. Then there's another huge bang from the skies. He almost falls off the sofa and we have to start again.

'Keep doing the breathing.'

I jump up and select some music to drown out the thunder, something powerful enough to command his attention, but melodic and calming at the same time, and I turn the volume up so it fills the room. Then I shut the curtains so he can't see the lightning, and I perch myself next to him again. He clutches at my hand and pulls it down so my palm is flat against his chest once more and closes his eyes. I talk to him about nothing much and he slowly gathers himself together. A good few minutes pass before he opens his eyes again, and when he does, he looks bewildered, as though he's forgotten the last twenty minutes and can't for the life of him work out how he ended up on my sofa.

'When did it start?'

'When did what start?'

'The heart attack feeling.'

'Oh right. On my way home from the office. I'd just had a meeting with my client from hell. He's a right bastard, can't accept anything I say at face value. You'd think I was trying to swindle him. Drives me mental. The traffic was shite. It took me forever to get across the roundabout and then there was that bloody big bang when I was driving into the car park. By the time I'd legged it up the stairs I'd got this really sharp pain in my chest.'

'If I hadn't been here, ringing for an ambulance would have been the right thing to do. Just in case.'

'What's wrong with me, then?'

'Nothing much. You had a panic attack, that's all. None of my business, but maybe it's something to do with being in the army?'

The expression on his face is suddenly so desolate I wonder if he'd have been happier if I'd diagnosed heart failure and said he was about to die. I put my hand on his forehead and brush a heavy lock of hair away from his face.

'You'll be fine,' I say, quietly.

We stare at each other. I can tell he's trying to convince himself I'm right, and that it's a struggle for him. We keep up this intense eye contact for ages, until I imagine myself turning into a tiny matchstick figure, tumbling into his eyes and spiralling as I sink deeper and deeper into their fathomless blue.

He coughs, rubs his eyes with his fists, and the spell is broken.

'You need to develop a strategy so you can deal with this if you feel it coming on again.'

'I've developed more strategies that you've had hot dinners.'

He shakes his head vigorously. I take that to mean he doesn't want to delve any further into the subject of stress-busting, so I don't pursue it. Instead, I let my fingers creep further into his hair and I marvel at its consistency. Each strand is as thick and straight as the bristles of a sweeping brush. It becomes another of the many things about him that make me smile.

'What's so bloody funny?'

'Nothing.'

'You're too far away.'

His breathing and the rest of him are back to normal now, more or less. I watch his features harden and his eyes flash as his customary alpha maleness reasserts itself. He's going to try and pretend the panic attack never happened.

'I'm right here.'

'Come and lie on top of me.'

'Doctors get struck off if they lie on top of their patients.'

'I'm not your patient.'

This is true and the invitation is too tempting to resist, so I scramble up and straddle myself over him, feeling awkward and clumsy, but not caring. He puts his arms round me and pulls me down so my head is resting on his chest. Then he places one hand in my hair and strokes my back with the other.

'Never mind,' he whispers and 'It's ok, don't worry,' as though I was the one who got myself into a state, not him.

I want to laugh and point this out, but I don't because it's been ages since anyone stroked my back and told me not to worry. The music's stopped, the thunder's faded away and the only sounds I can hear are the rain, which has eased to a gentle patter against the balcony window, and the distant swishing of car tyres on wet roads. It's kind of blissful.

'What did your dad do?' He asks.

'Why do you want to know that all of a sudden?'

'I want to know everything about you.'

'He was a university lecturer and he wrote books about gender equality.'

'Bloody hell.'

'That doesn't really explain much about him, though.'

'What do you mean?'

'He was an academic and an author, but at home he was loud and silly, a Dad with a capital D. And he was very popular with women. He always had at least one girlfriend on the go.'

'Your mum wasn't around, then?'

'Not after Jacob was born. And even before then, me and my sister didn't see much of her. She'd come and spend the night with Dad sometimes, but she'd and leave again in the morning before breakfast. Our parents behaved more like occasional lovers than a married couple.'

'That's bizarre.'

'I know. But I didn't want to have anything to do with her. I was terrified of her. I still am.'

'Why?'

'No idea. There's stuff I can't remember, from when I was tiny. It might be to do with that.'

'Did your dad about you?'

'No. But neither did I really. Or I wasn't sure. None of that started properly for me until after he died.'

'Ah, right. I always knew.'

'What did your dad do?'

'He was a supervisor at the local quarry. That's where he died. In an accident.'

I look up at him and then kiss the space between his collar bone and his Adam's apple.

'Was he a good dad?'

'Yeah. Why wouldn't he be?'

'Is your mum nice?'

'She's the best.'

'She doesn't like you living down here, does she?'

'How do you know?'

'I heard you talking to her on your balcony.'

'Little spy.'

'Why do you live so far away from home?'

I bounce up and down on his stomach.

'You're squashing me.'

He shifts me off his front. I settle myself in the narrow gap on between his body and the back of the sofa and I lean up on one elbow so I can brush the back of my hand over his beard. It's much softer than the hair on his head.

'You haven't answered my question.'

'Work. And some of my ex-army mates live around here.'

'I've heard them.'

'You would have.'

I know there's more to his move down South than work and mates, but I let it go. We've clearly come to an unspoken agreement after the trauma of his panic attack to keep things light and not probe each other too deeply for now. He doesn't want to get himself into a state again and I need to keep back from the edge of the abyss I nearly fall into every time I think about Jacob.

'Tell me something else about yourself,' I say.

'I'll tell you a proper secret. Something you'll be really interested in, seeing as you're a doctor.'

I look at him, wondering what on earth he's going to say. He gives me a sidelong glance and the expression on his face is devilish.

'Whatever it is, you seem mightily pleased about it.'

'I've got three testicles.'

'You haven't.

'I know my own bollocks.'

He beams at me proudly. I don't know what to think. Polyorchidism is a thing, but it's rare. I've never seen a case myself. What if he's not joking, but this putative third gonad is actually a lump, which he's googled and somehow managed to misdiagnose as the least likely thing it could possibly be?

'How long have you been aware of this third testicle?'

'I don't know. A while.'

'Tell me this is a wind up.'

He shakes his head. First he thinks he's having a heart attack and now he wants me to look at his balls. I'm deeply suspicious of his motives, but I can't be sure. He seems to be making light of it, but patients sometimes do that, even when they're worried sick.

'Seriously?'

He nods and narrows his eyes, as though he's challenging me to believe him. Then he unfastens the top button of his trousers and unzips his flies. Resigned, I slip back into doctor mode, clamber over him again and go back to balancing on the edge of the sofa. His eyes remain glued to my face as I move my fingers carefully over his scrotum and try to ignore the rest of what's on display, the bit of him I suspect he really wants me to see. The elephant in the room, as it were. Turns out he does only have the two, perfectly normal testicles. I zip him up quickly and fasten the button at the top his flies.

'You're such a liar.'

The look of dismayed outrage that briefly passes across his face makes me laugh out loud. Then he joins in.

'You have very gentle fingers,' he murmurs.

'Pack it in. And if you've got any other health issues go and see your GP.'

'I don't like my GP. I want you to be my doctor.'

'It doesn't work like that.'

His shirt is already half undone. I unfasten the rest of the buttons and follow the patterns on his chest with my index fingers. It's all very smooth. I wonder if he shaves to prevent hair growth from spoiling his art work. Soon my hand gravitates to a scar that runs vertically down one side of him from his armpit to just above his hip. I trail my finger up and down it over and over again. He flinches slightly, but I don't think it hurts, more that he doesn't want me to ask him what caused it.

'You're such a boy,' he says, as he slips two fingers under the waistband of my jeans and strokes my tiny appendix scar.

*

From that point onwards, we can't keep away from each other. For the rest of the week I'm on days, so we spend our evenings and nights together, but not at his place. I told him it feels like a storeroom at a furniture shop, because it's so empty and incomplete. When I asked him why his flat is so sparsely decked out, he acted all mysterious, so I've agreed to be puzzled for now and let him hang out in my cramped, but fully furnished little apartment instead.

He helps me tidy away all the crap littering the floor, but when I want to unpack my books and arrange them on the shelves he tells me not to bother. He helps himself to my single malt and he brings round loads of savoury nibbles, including some obscure peanut flavoured puffs he particularly likes and which are only obtainable from a Polish shop down a side street near the hospital. Of course, he's taken aback when I say I can't eat anything crispy. He offers to soften a few of them in his mouth and then pass them over to me, like a gorilla might do for its offspring.

'That's very kind, but no thanks,' I say and I drop a handful into a tomato cup-a-soup instead.

Then he wants me to list all the things I can and can't eat. I tell him I can't be arsed, so we make out on my sofa like teenagers who have to keep one eye on the door in case their parents walk into the room. So far I haven't let his hands rove very far over my body and never any lower than my appendix scar. He keeps trying to unbutton my jeans or pull down my tracksuit bottoms so he can explore new territory, and when I stop him he pouts at me. I explain to him that I need to go slow, that I've been celibate for a very long time, and deep down, I'm a very timid and shy person. But I'm sure he doesn't mind, not really. He loves this cat and mouse game we're playing, the way we stray close to the edge, but never quite jump off.

The spell of wet weather comes to an end, and it becomes bright again, but fresher and less humid, so we start going for long runs, down a footpath he likes that winds its way between a noisy dual carriageway and the tree-lined banks of a brook, in an area of edgeland, brash and urban on one side, but rustic and unchanged, probably for centuries, on the other. I imagine the gentlemen from the house over the railway line taking strolls along here, looking for lonely thickets where they would be completely unobserved. I wish we could stroll, too. Bartosz can jog long distances at a seriously brisk pace. Every so often, he stops to wait for me and watches, delighted, when I collapse, gasping and cursing at his feet.

One evening, we go for a wander around the big superstore, just down the road from our apartment block. He holds my hand as we dash across the dual carriageway and doesn't let go when we reach the interior of the store and the men's clothing section. The only other hand-holding relationship I've had was conducted in hiding, so I've never been openly *out* with anyone before. I keep my head down and avoid eye contact with other shoppers. But he doesn't care what people might or might not think when they see two men holding hands in a clothes shop. He tries on slim-fitting jeans in various shades of blue and black. I tell him I like the pale blue ones best, so he buys a pair, but there's nothing in the men's section skinny enough to fit me. I have to go to the boys' department to find things in my size.

'See - you're a nobbut a lad,' he says, eyes sparkling.

On the way out we go through the home section and I discover a load of bright red cushions that would be a perfect match for my sofa, which is grey. But he's not so keen.

'Don't waste money on things for your flat.'

'Why not?'

He doesn't answer. I don't buy them, but I secretly worry that I should have done and by not doing so, I'm letting him control me.

On the Thursday morning, when I'm spinning around trying to climb into my trousers and find everything I need for work at the same time, he sits up in bed and stretches. 'I won't be around tonight,' he announced.

I stop my whirling about to stare at him.

'On Thursday evenings I do a stint at the Samaritans.'

'All night?'

'Yep.'

I can imagine him being good that, listening, not interrupting or offering advice, noticing the gaps people tend to leave in their narratives, the silences that reveal the things about themselves they most want to hide. Not judging. Thinking about him in this way gives me that falling sensation again, as though I'm sliding downwards, struggling to get a foothold on a slope covered in loose shale. I'm afraid it might show in my face, so I turn away from him and carry on bustling about, getting ready for work, gathering up all the stuff that moved while I slept.

He climbs out of bed and walks with me to the door.

'What are your hours like this weekend?'

'I'm at work all day Friday. Then I'm free until six on Sunday evening.'

'Are you? That's good. Really good.'

'Why?'

'Pack an overnight bag tonight when you're on your own, feeling all lost and abandoned because I'm not here. Then when you get back on Friday evening, grab it and come and find me.'

'Where are we going?'

'You'll see.'

11. Gawain

Bartosz likes to drive fast. As soon as we get onto the motorway he puts his foot down hard on the gas and in seconds the Audi is doing almost ninety miles per hour. Either he hasn't noticed the signs about average speed cameras or he doesn't care about getting a ticket. I close my eyes and try not think about the carnage I've seen in A & E due to this type of craziness. I want to tell him to slow down, but I'm scared that might egg him on, make him go even faster. I still don't know where we're heading. When I got myself ready for this trip, I had no clue what to wear or what to bring. In the end, I decide to go for a shabby chic look, not too smart, but a bit different from usual, in case his plan is to take me to a party and parade me in front of his friends. So I'm wearing a baggy old dress shirt with fraying cuffs from a retro shop in Camden Market with red and black striped jeans, which are held up by a leather belt with a big buckle. The belt is a bit flamboyant, but if I don't wear it my trousers will end up around my ankles.

Bartosz chuckles when he sees me. Not the response I'd been hoping for.

'Do you want me to stand and deliver?' He asks me.

'Eh?'

'Don't worry. Ridicule is nothing to be scared of.'

I don't know what he's talking about, but I follow his advice and try not to let it worry me. This is quite easy to do, because I'm distracted, if not totally blown away, by the fact that he's turned himself green. His hair and beard are full of what looks like lime coloured powder, and his hands, arms and cheekbones are coated with streaks of what? Green paint? Woad? I hope he'll be able to wash it all off before Monday, when he has to see clients again. As far as clothes are concerned, he's wearing what look like army fatigues, including a T-shirt and camouflage trousers that are essentially green, too. If he squatted in the middle of the shrubs that line the car park, you wouldn't be able to see him.

As he drives, he sings loudly to the music he's put on. I don't know if he's doing this to avoid having to answer my questions about where we're going or if he's simply happy because it's Friday night and we're off on an adventure together. He loves the old stuff as much as the new, as long as it's heavy and metallic. The track playing now includes a fair amount of loud yodelling and he's giving it all he's got, but he can't quite hit the highest notes. It makes me want to tip my head back and howl.

Every time he changes gear his hand migrates briefly from the gear stick to my right thigh, but I think it's more of a friendly pat than a grope, to let me know he's excited about this outing and pleased I'm here. We only stay on the motorway for about ten minutes. Then he veers off at an exit, so quickly that the wheels on the driver's side briefly lose contact with the road. We join a wide and oddly empty dual carriageway for a short while before turning onto a B-road bordered by tall trees on both sides. If we'd continued going south on the motorway and left at the next junction or the one after that, we'd have been near my old boarding school, but coming off where we do, I have no idea where we are. There's not much here, apart from fields of yellow stubble, narrow strips of woodland, unkempt hedgerows and electricity pylons, and none of it is charmingly rural like the area around my school. It's another liminal space, like our riverside jogging route, a borderland of abandoned pastures, distant housing estates and occasional clusters of semi-industrialized farm buildings. A no man's land between the nearest urban development and the countryside proper.

Bartosz is still driving like a maniac, hurtling round every bend without any concern that there might be a cyclist or a tractor on the other side, or worse still, an animal of some sort. I grip the edge of the glove compartment with my left hand. As I do this, he suddenly leaves the road and slams on the brakes with a sickening lurch, bringing us to an abrupt halt. For an instant I really *do* think he's run into something and it must have happened so quickly I missed it. But then I notice an ancient wooden gate hidden in the shadows of the trees. Riveted to the top of the stone gatepost on the right hand side is a big wooden box with a slot for letters. He gets out, opens the gate, drives through and tells me to jump out and shut it. As usual, I obey him and I notice an ancient and tatty looking wooden sign on the gate with *Picardy* painted on it, in old fashioned, swirly gold and white cursive writing. If there is a house somewhere on the other side of this gate, you can't see it from here. Maybe it's derelict or was demolished years ago. I start to worry about what else might be here. What if it turns out to be one of those paintballing places? One of my school friends did that for his sixteenth birthday. I took a direct hit in my ribs almost as soon as battle commenced and scrambled into a ditch until the whole thing was over. It hurt like hell and I had a big purple bruise for weeks. No way am I putting myself through *that* again.

'Nearly there,' he says when I climb back into the car.

It still takes us a while to reach our destination, because the track is littered with potholes, some of which are the size of small lakes, so we have to drive slowly for the sake of the Audi's undercarriage. I can see nothing but trees and then more trees closing in on each side of us, and when I look back, the gate isn't visible anymore. Nordic death metal blasts out from the open windows of the car. I wish he'd turn it off. This feels like a place you should enter by stealth. So far, the lane has described a gradual curve to the right. Now it swings left, at almost a ninety degree angle, before levelling off alongside a clearing, bordered at the lane edge by a privet hedge more suited to a front garden in a suburban street than a forest clearing in the middle of nowhere. We go through a gap in this hedge into a gravelled forecourt and Bartosz switches off the engine. In front of us is a three storey detached house, with a new slate roof and sash windows. It looks Victorian or earlier and it would probably be attractive if it wasn't for the long, single story extension constructed from what looks like greyish concrete blocks, tacked incongruously onto its right hand side, as though a helicopter picked up an office block from an industrial estate in Basingstoke and dropped it here. There must be a party happening inside the house, then.

When we get out of the car, I hear the crunch of footsteps on the gravel behind me. I look round sharply, expecting to see someone walking into the garden, another party guest perhaps. But I can't see anyone. I stare through the gap in the hedge we just drove through, across the lane and into the band of trees on the other side, which seem to be beeches mainly, but also oaks and chestnuts, and evergreens, crowded together and darkening to black in the fading light. The footsteps stop and I strain my ears to pick up hints of voices and music, coming from the house. But all I can hear is a wood pigeon making that cooing noise that always seems to end abruptly, in mid-sentence. Bartosz takes a set of keys out of his pocket and rattles them as he strides off away from me towards the front door in his Doc Martens. It must have been his footsteps I heard, then, and I mistook their direction because I'm not familiar with the acoustics of the place.

I run to catch up with him. He opens the front door and slams it shut after we've stepped inside. The noise echoes through the house, waking up any ghosts that might be hidden away up the chimneys or huddled inside the corners of long forgotten rooms. The front door leads to a big square hallway with doors on each side, two at the front and two at the back. Directly in front of us, a staircase sweeps up to a galleried landing. The last of the light from the setting sun has gone from here and created a space full of shadows that seem to fall in unexpected places. I pick up a delicious aroma. Dust, mixed with fresh plaster and clean paint.

'Where's the party?'
'There isn't one.'
'Are we doing an urban exploration?'
'Nope.'
'Or a haunted house vigil?'
'I hope not.'
'Who lives here?'
'Me. Or I will be, once the wifi's connected.'
'Are you house sitting for someone?'
'Only for myself! I've been doing the place up for the past ten months. My mates have helped and I've had builders in to do the more structural work. The house was a bit of a ruin to start with, but it's coming along nicely now.'
'Is there electricity?'
'Yep. That's all done. Why?'
'Can we put some lights on?'
'Do we need to?'

Yes, we really do. Otherwise I might get so spooked I'll have to run out of here quickly before it gets completely dark outside, and make my way back to the gate and along the road to the dual carriageway. Then I'll either hitch a lift or ring for a cab to take me back to my not particularly imposing, but shadow-free little flat.

'I'll put them on in a minute,' he says softly, as though I'm a small child that needs to be mollified. Grasping two of my fingers, he leads me across the hall to a door at the back that opens onto much smaller and more modern, square shaped atrium, with two glass doors. One leads to the outside and the other leads into what must be the industrial unit tacked onto the side of the house.

'I bought the house off a company that sold cement and paving stones and what not. This was the storeroom.'

He opens the door. It leads into a long rectangular space with freshly painted white walls, wooden floors that have been treated and polished and uniform rows of windows on each side, covered with navy blinds. He pushes me in and flicks on a switch. Spotlights in the ceiling change the entire room from pink to blue via green and purple. I saunter past a pool table that can also be used for ping pong, he tells me, and a vintage football game on tapering brass legs. A huge screen is mounted on the wall at the far end, and a group of black leather sofas and chairs are arranged in front of it. Against the wall to the right, between the windows, is a double-fronted refrigerator with clear doors, like a retail display cabinet, filled with bottles of beer and cans of soft drinks. On the opposite side of the seating area, three electric guitars are suspended from the wall next to an arrangement of amps, pedals and other guitar accoutrements. One of the guitars is a Flying V.

'You're winding me up!'

He's smiles and bounces on his heels.

'You like?'

I nod.

'Thought you might.'

Encouraged by my reaction, he leads me back into the main part of the house and we climb the stairs. The first floor is high enough to catch the last of the setting sun, which casts a soft glow across the bare floorboards, making the landing seem slightly less eerie than the area below. At one end is another staircase, a narrower one that must lead up to the attics. A couple of treads are missing and the banister looks loose.

'How many bedrooms are there?'

'Seven. Four on this floor and three on the next.'

He points upwards and I look up, expecting Grace Poole to glide slowly into view as she makes her way down, unconcerned about the missing steps because she's hovering above them.

'You sound like an estate agent.'

My voice fades away at the end of this sentence as I realise the sardonic tone I was aiming for is inappropriate and unfair. He doesn't sound anything *like* an estate agent. He just sounds like what he is, a man who's been doing up a house and is really proud of the results. We wander in and out of the first floor bedrooms. Two of them are empty and decorated with ancient patterned wallpaper, now faded and blemished with large patches of moisture that seeped in, he says, before he got the damp course fixed. In one of these rooms, the wallpaper design is floral, but in the other it's a complex and interesting series of intersecting ellipses and circles. As I stare at it, I feel a strange jolting sensation as though the intertwining curves are a kind of code, a pattern carrying information that's important but too complicated for me to interpret. But then the entire house feels full of hidden messages.

'What are you doing?' Bartosz puts his arm around my shoulders as though he thinks I'm losing myself, which I am a little. He escorts me into the next bedroom, which is situated at the front of the house.

'This one's nearly finished. I thought it might make a decent guest room.'

I look through the doorway into a generous space with newly polished floorboards and freshly plastered walls, painted an eggshell blue. This could be Jacob's room, I accidentally think, and I swallow as the image comes into my head of my brother sprawled across a bed in here, thumbs clicking away at the phone I've just bought him. I quickly push the idea from my mind, because wild speculation like that is unbearable.

Bartosz leads me down the corridor to the final room on this floor, which is bigger than the previous one and dual aspect with large windows at the front and along one side. The walls have been painted a deep maroon and in the middle is a king sized double bed, with matching linen, flanked by a couple of bedside tables with lamps. Squatting in the far corner is a massive hulk of a wardrobe made from the kind of dark wood that seems to suck the light out of its immediate surroundings.

I slip my fingers out of his hand and walk past him to the front window. I rest my forehead against the glass. The car is sitting there with the passenger and driver's doors wide open, as though we'd leapt out and run away from it quickly because it was about to burst into flames. It occurs to me that someone is in the lane, hiding on the other side of the privet hedge. Can I see a crouching shadow through that patch on the left where the leaves are a slightly thinner? I really need to get a grip.

The pigeons have stopped their cooing. They must have settled in the tree tops for the night. Now there is no sound, just but an enormous, blank peace. It feels as though the house and its immediate surroundings don't exist in the present. Once you cross through the gap in the hedge, you arrive back in a quieter, more contemplative time, one where life isn't filled with the hum of passing cars and the insistent vibration of electronic devices.

Floorboards creak behind me and I realise Bartosz has left the room and is stomping down the stairs. Glad of the breathing space, I watch as he runs out to the car, opens the boot, gets out a couple of bright orange supermarket carrier bags, shuts and locks the doors and runs back in. His face is that of a man who has hatched a plan and is delighted to find that, so far at least, it's working out exactly as he hoped it would. I hear him singing under his breath and making rustling noises downstairs as he sorts out the food in what I assume must be the kitchen.

I check my phone. Nothing from Jacob. I know there's a signal, because a couple of other messages have come through. I can't identify the song Bartosz is singing and I'm vaguely troubled by this, in case, like the wallpaper it carries some kind of message that I really should be picking up. As dusk fades away, into inky blackness, I catch a drifting sense that tonight may be full of a significance missing from most other evenings. But perhaps everything seems weighted with meaning in this place, as though there are things you can see and things you can't, and it's hard to tell which of these you should worry about and which you should ignore. I shiver and wrap my arms around myself as though I've been caught in a blizzard without a coat.

When he runs up the stairs again, his step is much softer because he's taken his boots off. I'm still at the window. I turn towards him, this man who has painted himself green for me and brought me to this house with its strange atmosphere. This person I'm now alone with in the middle of nowhere.

'How come this belongs to you?'

'I had some money to invest and it was going cheap because it needed a lot of work.'

'What are you planning to do with it?'

'Live in it.'

'Isn't it a bit big for one person?'

'I won't be spending much time alone.'

Yet again, I don't understand what he means. I'm starting to find all this mystification a bit wearying, so I turn and face the window again and stare out into the darkness.

'Do you often bring people here?'

He laughs.

'*Do* you?'

'This is the first I've brought anyone here like *you*. I mean, my mates have been round a few times.'

'Are you sure?'

'I'm not a liar.'

'It's just, I'm not into casual hook ups.' I can't believe I'm making myself so open. This house has definitely cast some kind of spell on me.

He comes and stands next to me and puts his hands in his pockets. We both look out of the window, or rather, we stare at our reflections, which are now visible, thanks to the light he's just put on downstairs.

'Me neither. Not these days.'

'When was the last time for you?'

'Just over three years ago.'

"That's a long time.'

'I was with someone. We bought a house together and everything when I left the army. It wasn't far from my mum's. Thought we were well set up. But a month after we moved in he was diagnosed with pancreatic cancer.'

'Jesus. What was his name?'

'Mitchell.'

I think about Mitchell and a wave of sadness sweeps over me on his behalf, even though I never knew him.

'What about you?' Bartosz asks.

'I've only ever had one relationship. A secret one. It went on for more than three years, then everyone found out and it ended.'

'When was that?'

'More than eight years ago, now.'

'You must have been very young when it started, then.'

'Fifteen.'

'Fifteen?'

I nod at his blurry image in the window pane.

'Since then I've kept myself to myself.'

He turns to look at me.

'For eight years?'

'Yep. I've told you that already.'

'I thought you were having me on. Why would you stay celibate for so long?'

'The relationship I was in back then was a big deal and when it ended it was a disaster, and not just for me. After that I didn't feel like I deserved to be happy. I still feel like that, deep down. Some of the time, anyway. I don't know. It's complicated.'

I stop. I've revealed way more than I intended. I'm appalled and I wish I could take back what I've just said. I get another variant of that now familiar falling sensation, this time in a backwards direction into a large chasm. I can't see how, but he must be able to sense this, because he moves so he's standing right behind me and he wraps his arms around me.

'And now you don't know what you're getting into,' he whispers into my ear, as though it's a secret that must be kept from any of the house phantoms straining to hear our conversation.

'I think I'm starting to. Kind of.'

'You don't need to be afraid. Not of me.'

'I'm not afraid of you. I'm afraid of the consequences.'

'You don't need to worry about them, either.'

'How do you know?'

'Because I'll protect you.'

I am worried, though. Inside my head I can hear all the ghosts of the house muttering their reactions to his words, but I can't make out whether they agree or disagree with him. Perhaps they hold conflicting opinions and they're arguing it out. I lean back and press myself into him. His arms tighten around me and his mouth touches the back of my neck. After a few seconds I manage to turn myself round in his grasp so I can look into his eyes.

Years ago, I read somewhere that in order to fall for person you have to be able to see in them the child they once were, because it reveals something fundamental and really simple about them, something they can't hide. I can't remember where I read it. It might even be a song I've heard. But anyway, his inner child is shining out of him so brightly it almost blinds me. I can see it in his eyes and his smile, and also in the way he's acting cocky to compensate for the way he's taken a gamble and gone to all this trouble, decorating himself in green paint because he was mystified by a comment I made about his name and made the effort to google it.

Stuff it, I think. I'm done with all this prevaricating, fending him off all the time. What's the point? I wriggle away from him. I unbutton my shirt and shrug it off my shoulders onto the floor behind me as quickly as I can, before the fear creeps in again and makes me change my mind. And I maintain eye contact with him, although I'd much rather hide my face against his neck.

He doesn't say anything, but his eyes stop twinkling and he looks at me in a completely different way. His pupils are dilated and his expression is deadly serious. He lifts me up, something he can do without any effort, and I wrap my legs around his waist as he carries me over to the bed. We both smile and laugh as we pull each other's clothes off, quite roughly, I'm still anxious and embarrassed as hell, but a new sense of urgency is driving me forward, as though over the past few weeks I've slowly made my way the top a rollercoaster, and now I've finally reached the summit, I can't stop myself zooming down the other side. Once stripped, he pins me down by my arms and just looks at me for ages. At first I try to struggle out of his grip so I can cover myself, but he tells me to pack it in and holds me even more tightly, and I have no choice but to watch his eyes as they slowly take me in. Soon I think I can actually feel the touch of his gaze, the scratch of his eyelashes against my skin.

I think back to that first time with Will. When we got together, neither of us had a clue what we were doing. I was incredibly young. He was older than me, but not by much, and everything that passed between us was exploratory and cautious, a delicious process of trial and error.

With Bartosz, it isn't like that at all.

12. Gawain

Bartosz is flat on his back, fast asleep and handsome in a biblical way, like the picture of Samson after they'd cut his hair, in the book of stories from the old testament I used to have when I was a child. I've worn him out. Maybe in the future I should be more mindful of the fourteen year age difference between us. I'm not sure what I could have done to make him conserve his energy, though. He clearly likes to be in control. Is it ok that I adored the way he manhandled me and that I didn't even attempt to resist? Is it another aspect of my defective personality - an innate masochism or general feebleness of character that seeps out of my pores and encourages men to dominate me? Maybe it's him. Perhaps he was like that with Mitchell too. Either way, I don't care. He called me sunshine and at a couple of crucial moments, he paused and asked me if I wanted him to stop, which was polite of him, I thought. But that was the last thing I wanted, and now I'd like nothing more than to wake him up and beg him to start again. But he looks as though he needs his rest, and I need a bit of solo time to quietly absorb and perhaps even relish what just happened. I extricate myself from the duvet and pull my clothes back on as quietly as I can, so I don't wake him.

When I look out of the other bedroom window, the one along the side of the house, I notice an almost full moon has risen. The monochrome panorama includes a wide grassy area backed by a series of low and rather creepy outbuildings with little square windows and wooden doors painted in a pale, unidentifiable colour. I sneak out of the bedroom and click on light switches as I go, grateful to get a chance to explore on my own. Bartosz seems so keen, desperate almost, that I should love this house, and I'm not sure whether I do right now.

I climb tentatively up the stairs to the attic floor, taking care to avoid the gaps and not lean on the banister rail. Three unfinished, surprisingly large bedrooms open onto the narrow corridor. All of them are ensuite and their sloping ceilings contain skylights. An old rocking horse sits in the last of these rooms, a poor moth eaten creature with little holes on either side of its head, where its eyes once were. I bet it was here when Bartosz bought the house and couldn't bear to throw it away.

When I go down to the ground floor, I discover a big, open-plan kitchen, with a folding window the size of an entire wall that leads out into the back garden. I wish there were blinds at the window. Anyone could be out there looking in for all I know. Two of the walls are lined with sleek, modern kitchen units and Bartosz has had put a wood burning stove fitted into the other wall, with space for a couch to be put in front of it. I start to visualise other furniture I'd add, and the colours I'd paint the walls, even though interior design is something I've not contemplated before, never having had a place of my own.

At the front of the house sits a room I haven't seen yet. I click on the light and a naked bulb illuminates bare floorboards and what looks like a really old fireplace on one wall. Shelf brackets hang loosely from the walls and a filing cabinet crouches in one of the corners. It must have been the cement company's office. Again, I'm captivated by the notion that the rooms are thronged with spirits, layers and layers of them, and it occurs to me now that some of them may come from not from the past but from the future. Maybe older versions of Bartosz and myself are hovering around in here, together with Jacob perhaps and any children we might bring into the world. I wonder if there is a mental technique, something we've forgotten as we've become more sophisticated as a species, that would allow us to see these spectres and bring into focus the other, completely different world that lies hidden behind this one? Perhaps I could access it via that slight internal swerve of the eyeballs I use to wake myself from nightmares?

You'd never guess I've been trained to think scientifically, would you? This house has definitely cast a spell on me.

My reverie is shattered by the sound of Bartosz bounding down the stairs, shouting my name.

'Why did you leave me?' He booms.

The ghosts scuttle away to their various corners.

'You were asleep.'

'You should have woken me.'

He comes up to me and puts an arm around my shoulder, taking possession. His boy in his house. Then he escorts me back to the kitchen.

'Food,' he says.

Although he knows about my eating issues, I don't think he really believes in them, not wholeheartedly. I hope he hasn't brought anything you have to chew, like steak or salad, thinking that when I'm actually presented with it, I'll be able to shrug my shoulders, ditch my silly little affectation and eat it anyway. But he goes over to the enormous American-style fridge and gets out two packs of fresh ravioli, one filled with spicy sausage and the other with spinach and ricotta. He brandishes them at me.

'I got these.'

'As long as they're cooked properly, I'll eat either.'

'I wasn't expecting you to eat them raw.'

'I mean, if they're boiled so much that the filling leaks out and then the pasta is cut into small pieces so I don't have to chew it, I'll be fine.'

'Hmmm,' he says, and he starts to prepare the meal.

As he moves around the kitchen, filling pans with water and putting them on to boil, cutting French bread into tiny, crustless circles for my sake, and placing knives, forks and butter on the table, I notice we've become attached to each other by a short piece of invisible elastic that pulls us back into close proximity if one of us tries to move away. If neither of his hands is free to hold one of mine, I'm compelled to put an arm round his waist or just lean into him, pressing my face into his side or his back, as long as there is some form of direct physical contact between us. When he has an arm to spare he places it around my shoulder. I worry I'm the only one who feels this way, that I've suddenly become dependent on his constant presence, like a needy infant or small dog. As a test, I wrench myself away and walk over to the door, some three metres from where he's standing, and I lean against the door frame, looking out into the darkness, pretending to be interested in the construction of the hallway.

And there he is, behind me.

'Where do you think you're going?' He turns me round, nudges me back into the room and pulls me against him.

While he drains the pasta, which temporarily occupies both his hands, I try another, similar experiment. I stand behind him with my arms around his waist and my head pressed against his back, then I let go and take a few steps backwards. In an instant, he reaches round blindly with one hand. When he finds my arm he pulls it towards him and wraps it round his waist again.

When the pasta is cooked, we move our chairs as close as they will go and glue ourselves together. Once we've spread butter on our bread, we only use forks and our elbows don't compete for space because he's a leftie and I'm right handed. He feeds me small pieces of pasta and clumps of dislodged filling and watches to make sure I swallow them. We eat every last morsel and wash it down with bottles of Peroni. Then he pulls our chairs back and stares at me again in that new way. I feel both bashful and brazen at the same time, and we have to abandon our bowls on the kitchen table and rush upstairs again.

Afterwards, he's wide awake this time, and we're both occupying the same mental space. The moon has moved round and now it casts pale beams onto us through the side window. No more secrets it seems to be saying. I agree with the moon. I know Bartosz now. I don't know all that much *about* him, but then he doesn't know an awful lot about me, either. He doesn't even know how much there *is* to know about me. But still. I get him. I'm sure of him, and he's not controlling, not really.

'Do you always do that?' He asks after a while.

'Do what?'

'Keep really quiet, then scream like hell? I thought I'd injured you. If you did that in a hotel, the people in the next room would call the police.'

'Oh God, was I really that loud?'

I turn over and hide my face in my pillow. I never used to scream with Will. What's come over me?

'Don't hide.'

He pulls me round so I'm facing him again. Having all my layers peeled off one by one like this is painful, but also exhilarating.

'I was concentrating. Then I got to a point where I couldn't anymore and everything kind of imploded. Or exploded. Or both.'

He laughs a lot at this, and I can tell the mirth bubbling out of him contains triumph as well as amusement. Then he falls silent and I start to wonder if he's fallen sleep again. But he hasn't.

'We've done this the wrong way round,' he says.

'Have we? I thought this was how we both....'

'No, I mean we should have talked first.'

'Talked about what?'

The desire for sleep is starting to overwhelm me, drawing my limbs and my torso downwards into the depths of the big, soft bed. The last thing I want to do is talk, particularly if the topic of conversation is myself.

'You and Jacob. What's the deal with him? Why did you fall out?'

I fight my way back to the surface, prop myself up on my elbows and look at the moonlight on my pillow. Then I flop down again.

'Are you sure you want to know?'

'Yes.'

'What if it makes you hate me?'

"You'll have to leave, I'm afraid. But I'll drive you home, so don't worry.'

'That's good of you. I appreciate it.'

As he waits for me to gather my thoughts, he runs his fingers up and down my arm from my elbow to my shoulder and stares into my eyes without mercy. My brain works furiously as I try decide what to tell him and what to leave out. In the end, I tell him the entire sorry tale. The whole lot. Last time I started in the middle, but now I go right back to the beginning. It takes forever, and Bartosz listens without interrupting. He searches through my hair for the scars I tell him about, the ones Jacob gave me when he hit me on the side of the head with his tennis racquet. I squeeze my eyes shut. I don't care about the scars. I totally deserved them. But I can't bear to remember my brother's face when he sliced the racquet through the air in our bright, summery bedroom at Aunty Susan's and brought it down on my head, or the tears that pooled in his pale eyes and then coursed down his face.

Even in the moonlight Bartosz can make the scars out. He starts to fuss over them, as though I'm a baby or a favourite cat.

'Don't,' I say. 'I'm not entitled to sympathy.'

He ignores me and I lie there and tolerate him tapping my head and making sympathetic little tutting noises for a bit longer. Then I continue with my sorry tale.

'I lurked in my for two days, then I went to the barbers for a number one haircut, got brilliant A' level results I didn't deserve and went to medical school in London, where I kept my head down and worked my arse off.'

'Why did you shave your hair off?'

"It was long and curly. Kind of luxurious and self-indulgent. And I was vain about it, so chopping it off seemed the right thing to do. An act of penance or something.'

'You should grow it again.'

'Really? I don't know. It was quite high maintenance. Anyway, I focused on studying and exams. During the holidays, I'd only go back to Aunty Susan's if Jacob wasn't there, because if he *was* there, he'd lock himself in the bathroom and refuse to come out until I'd gone. Otherwise, I'd get the train to Scotland and stay with Amanda. But never stopped trying to contact Jacob, to try and make it up to him.'

Every word I tell him is weighted with huge significance for me, and dragging it all out into the open when it's been hidden from view for so long feels like pushing one boulder after another up a steep hill. When I'm done, I'm shattered and longing for sleep. I think he is, too, and I wouldn't blame him if he'd already nodded off, bored to death by my pathetic story, but each time I look at him his eyes are still skewering into mine.

'That's everything.' I clear my throat.

He cogitates for a while and I wait nervously for his verdict.

'You're too hard on yourself. I mean, you're not an innocent party in all this, obviously. But neither is your brother.'

'Surely you can see why he was so pissed off?'

'Yes, but keeping up a sense of grievance like that for eight years takes some doing. He must be a pig-headed bugger.'

'He's not. He's the sweetest, gentlest person on the planet.'

'Is he, though?'

"He's the type of person that gets taken advantage of because he's too reserved to say anything."

'Or too cowardly. Or is he one of those intense people who seem really nice, but once crossed take umbrage big time and can't let it go?'

'Maybe. Not the coward bit.'

'Ok. Sorry.'

'I'm too tired to talk anymore.'

'Shut up and go to sleep, then.'

He covers my shoulders with the duvet and I drift away. When I open my eyes again, I can see more of him, which means he can see more of me, too. The local sparrows are making their usual cheap-chirp-squeak-repeat sequence of noises. Somewhere in the distance I can also hear a dog barking and possibly a cockerel crowing. Maybe there's a farm. As I burrow further under the duvet, a familiar image I often see when I'm on the edge of sleep comes into my mind, of a black and white sheep dog running around in a yard dotted with rusty coloured hens, and a narrow rectangle of soil planted with sunflowers which look into the kitchen window instead of outwards towards the farmyard.

I'm dead to the world until two-thirty the following afternoon, when he wakes me. He tells he has run me a bath and he leads me to the bathroom. The sink, the loo and the bath are all bright green and the wall tiles surrounding them are black and shiny. The entire room gives off a worn and rather sad glamour and brings to mind a bygone age, the early fifties perhaps, a time populated by women in shape-defining swimsuits and men who smoke pipes and wear cravats. I can almost touch the excitement the owners of the house must have felt back then, when they took this bathroom-based stand against grey, post war austerity. The water is sumptuously hot and it fills the room with steam. Bartosz showered while I was still asleep, so he sits on the floor next to the bath with a towel wrapped round his waist and another one coiled, turban-like around his head. He looks like a genie summoned up in a puff of water vapour. I can see his reflection moving about in the tiles on the other side of the bath. Bartosz in stereo.

'I've been thinking about your brother.'

Not again. I'm really not in the mood.

'Alakazam. Izzy whizzy, let's get busy,' I say.

'Shush.'

He scoops out two bowls of bathwater and without warning, pours them over my head in quick succession, leaving me gasping and spluttering.

'You've got to stop fretting about him and do something. You can't let him stay in a place where people drug him up and whip him.'

'I know that. But what am I meant to do? He clearly doesn't want to leave and he hates me.'

'Of course he wants to leave, he just doesn't realise it. You need to extract him and if he's not happy about it you'll have to persuade him afterwards that he didn't want to be there. That'll be the hardest part.'

'Extract him? I'm not in the bloody SAS.'

'I'll help you.'

I look at the tattoos on his upper arms. None of them say anything like *who dares wins* and none of them seem to represent a particular regiment. Not that I'd know if they did. I haven't got the nerve to pursue it with him, but shit, though. I close my eyes and he anoints me with water again.

'You like pouring water over my head, don't you?'
'It's what you need. Absolution. Baptism and renewal.'
'It's nice of you to say so.'
'Not nice, just true.'
'Are you religious?'
'I was brought up catholic. We always went to mass on Sundays. I still go every so often.'
'Do you believe in it?'
'I like the ritual. If you hear it often enough and you already know the words before the priest says them, it feels like it means something. Particularly the communion part.'
'The repetition is comforting?'
'Kind of. But it's more than that. You should come with me sometime.'
'We could go tomorrow.'
'I can't tomorrow.'
'Ok.'
'Aren't you going to ask me why not?'
'Go on then. Why not?'
'Because tomorrow, Sunshine, I'm going to the morning service at the Church of the New Sunrise to see what they're all about.'

13. Gawain

I feel guilty about not keeping Amanda in the loop, so I ring her to say Bartosz is planning to attend this morning's church service. She turns up at my place less than fifteen minutes after we end the call.

'Who is this Bartosz?'

'He's my new person.'

'What's that supposed to mean?'

I've had enough of this line of questioning already. I really wish I hadn't called Bartosz my new person. It makes him sound like a robot I've ordered from a tech firm on the internet, or a little figure I've constructed from modelling clay and imbued with life in some kind of black magic ritual. What else could I have called him, though? Boyfriend? Soul mate? Love of my life? He could be all of those things, even the last one, but it's way too early for that kind of language.

My sister doesn't see it like that.

'As in boyfriend?'

'Er...'

"How long have you known him?"

'Not long.'

'Are you..?'

'No, Amanda. Of course not. We got together because we both like card games and scrabble. And monopoly. We're really excited because there's a beetle drive at St. Peter's Church Hall on Saturday afternoon.'

'But after all you said when you were round at mine.'

'Yeah, well. Famous last words and all that.'

'I hope you're being careful.'

'Says the person who went dogging and got knocked up.'

'If you're going to start going on about that again, I'm off.'

She stands up and grabs her handbag, a ghastly bunched up thing made from purplish leather that always reminds me of a uterus, and she makes for the door. But when she opens it she has to stand aside because Bartosz is there with his hand raised about to knock. He comes sweeping in, bringing with him the scent of rain and the outdoors and freshly washed linen. The room is rapidly filled by his loud voice, which seems to resonate off each of the four walls in turn. My sister follows him back into the room, as though he's generated an undertow and she can't prevent herself being pulled along by it.

I introduce him. He flicks on an emergency charm switch and actually bows as he shakes her hand. At first, I'm scared he's overdoing it and that my sister will think he's taking the piss, but she pushes her hair out of her face and furrows her eyebrows as she tries to pretend she's puzzled rather than impressed by him. Then he approaches me from behind and gives me a lingering kiss on the side of my neck before coming round and sitting down next to me on the sofa. The look on her face when he does that. No words in any language would be adequate to describe it. She tries to continue with her unfazed act as she settles herself in the armchair opposite, and I watch as she slowly takes him in, from tips of his brown Doc Martens right up to the top of his dusky head. Then she keeps shifting her gaze between him and me, as if she's trying to work out how on earth this pairing could possibly have come about. I bet she thinks I went cruising in Aldershot and found him all alone, nursing a pint in the corner of one of the pubs frequented by the military.

When I ask if Jacob was at the church, Bartosz nods, leans forward in his seat and clasps his hands together, in the manner of someone about to impart bad news.

'Just start at the beginning,' Amanda says, sensing that he's groping around a bit.

He looks at her gratefully.

'Ok. Well, I parked round the corner and walked the rest of the way. My car would have stood out and I thought it was best if nobody associated me with it, in case we decide to use it when we extract your brother.'

'Extract him?' Amanda says.

Bartosz and I both say yes at the same time as though we've been synchronised like stopwatches. But you can't hear my voice because his so loud it drowns mine out.

'When I got to the church door, there was this priest guy in a dog collar, a tall gingery bloke with freckles and an American accent.'

'Warren. Our stepfather,' my sister says.

'That's him. Pastor Brookes. He stood there smiling and welcoming everyone as they went in. He even hugged some of them. Then you had to pass a young girl with long, auburn hair tied up in a plait. She who looks a lot like him, but prettier. She was giving out copies of a newsletter.'

'Ruth,' Amanda adds. 'His daughter from before he got together with Mum.'

Bartosz pulls a crumpled piece of paper from his shirt pocket and hands it to her.

'The newsletter. Anyway, I went in. The old pews have been ripped out and replaced with rows of awful plastic chairs. There are other, more comfortable seats at the front, arranged at right angles to the congregation.'

When Bartosz is sure that my sister and I are both able to visualise the set up, he continues. 'I was going to sit at the back, but I hadn't bargained for how big the place is inside, and I realised I wouldn't see much unless I moved closer to the front. It filled up quickly. In the end it was rammed. Then your mother and Warren came in from a side door and sat on the chairs at the front, followed by Jacob, that Cowboy-Junkie bloke you were on about, Gawain, and the other fella, Slab-Face. I could tell it was him because his face really is like a big slab of pork. They all sat on one side. Your brother was sandwiched between the cowboy guy and your mother. Ruth sat on one of the chairs on the opposite side and then three young women with tambourines turned up and occupied the remaining seats.'

'How did my brother look? Was he ok?'

I jump to my feet and jiggle about.

'I'll get to that. Calm down, mate. Sit down, come on.'

He reaches out for my hand and pulls me down.

'The service passed in a bit of a blur because I was focused on your brother and the other people sitting in the seats at the front, trying to gauge their body language and their facial expressions, and how they interacted with each other. All that stuff.'

'And?'

'Gawain, stop interrupting,' Amanda says.

'The Ruth girl and Jacob kept exchanging glances during the service, but in a kind of undercover way. I'm not sure what that was all about. Jacob looked washed out, but that might be how he always looks because he's so fair, I don't know.'

'It isn't how he always looks. Or it didn't used to be,' I say.

'Right. Well, he was slouched in his chair through the entire service. Some of the time, when he wasn't looking at Ruth, he had his head down and his eyes closed.'

My sister looks across at Bartosz in quiet dismay. Me on the other hand, I want to run up to the wall between the living room and the kitchen and kick it so hard I make a hole in it.

Bartosz stops briefly and takes a breath.

'Next, they all did some happy-clappy singing and tambourine rattling. Although to me it sounded way more clappy than happy. Everybody jumped to their feet and swayed about. Then there were prayers and a couple of idiots stood up and started babbling.'

'Speaking in tongues?' Amanda asks.

'God knows. It sounded mental. After that, the priest did a eulogy type thing. He droned on for ages and I zoned in and out, but the tone of the whole thing was grim. The end time is coming because everyone is so sinful, blah blah. But luckily, the congregation have been specially chosen to prepare for this disaster and will survive it, as long as they obey Pastor Warren's special set of commandments. He read them out. There were more than ten and none of them were the same as the ones in the bible, although they were written a kind of oldy-worldy language to make them sound like they were. If you don't obey these rules you're screwed. Unless you go through this new forgiveness ceremony Pastor Warren has devised.'

'And get yourself whipped?' Amanda asks.

Bartosz looks across at her.

'He didn't actually spell it out. At that point, I glanced behind me to see how everyone else was reacting to this crap. I expected some of them to be laughing or even getting up and leaving, but they were all spellbound. It's hard to describe, but they all had same look in their eyes and the same goofy expression on their faces, as though they'd inhaled pixie dust or something. The other top dogs sitting at the front didn't react at all, apart from your brother, who started massaging his forehead as though he had a headache.'

'Or he was embarrassed,' I say. He used to massage his forehead a lot, usually when he was exasperated or perplexed by something I'd done or said and was wondering whether he should respond or just try and pull up a couple of floorboards and crawl under them.

'I'm going to get a drink of water.' Amanda starts to get out of the armchair. Her eyes are shiny like polished glass and Bartosz watches in alarm as I leap up and push her back down before she can stand up fully. I make her put her head between her knees and I sit on the arm of the chair with my hand on her back, to make sure she stays like that until she's ok again My sister faints sometimes. She always has. It's not that big a deal, but it looks alarming to people who aren't used to it. Without being prompted, Bartosz goes to my kitchen and comes back with a glass water. He opens the sliding door onto the balcony to let some air in.

'Is there anything else I can do?'

'She'll be fine in a minute.'

My sister resurfaces, sips some water and mutters something apologetic. Bartosz asks if we want him to go on. We both nod.

'There was a great rush of people standing up and saying halleluiah after that, followed by another bout of singing. Everyone was smiling and seemed uplifted. To me it was all, I don't know, way over the top, like musical theatre, Godspell or something. When it finished, Pastor Warren did another little speech about something he called the Country Fund. He wants people to pay into it so the church can buy a big plot of land in the countryside, to be used as a new home for the community. Then he invited everyone to tea or coffee in the little hall at the back.'

'Did you go for coffee?'

'Yep. It was really watery and the biscuits weren't up to much. They only had bourbons. I hate them.'

'Do you?'

I'm learning little facts about him all the time.

'Was Jacob there?' Amanda asks.

'He left the church after the service with Cowboy-Junkie and I didn't see him again.'

'Did Cowboy-Junkie come back?'

'He reappeared quite quickly and started doing stuff with the tea urn.'

"What kind of stuff?" I ask.

'Pouring water from it into cups. What else would he be doing with it?'

'I don't know. It's just that bloke, he makes the hairs on the back of my neck stand up.'

'I didn't speak to him, but I *did* speak to your mother.'

'No! I don't want to hear this.'

I put my hands over my ears and wonder how long it will be before I have to get up and rush to the bathroom.

'I know you don't, Sunshine, but this is exactly the sort of thing you need to start facing up to.'

His says this very slowly in his distinct, Yorkshire accent, and he gets up and bends over me so he can pull my hands away from my ears and settle them gently in my lap. My sister watches us both with a faintly bemused expression on her face. If it wasn't for Jacob's plight, she'd be enjoying this.

'I went up to her and said some bollocks about how good the service was, and I asked her if the church was a family affair. She said yes, her daughter in law and her son played active roles. She gestured vaguely over to where Ruth was standing and then she said her son was unwell, sadly, and had gone to lie down. It was bloody weird talking to her. She looks exactly like you Gawain, but twenty years older and wearing a dress.'

'Thanks.'

'But I couldn't fathom her out at all. She can hold a conversation and on the surface she's every bit the pastor's wife, but there's a kind of wall behind her eyes. I can't describe it. Sorry, I'm being very rude about your mother.'

'No worries,' Amanda says. 'The question is, what is on the other side of the wall? Something she wants to keep hidden or nothing at all?'

'Chaos?' I suggest.

'She does look weirdly like Gawain,' Amanda says.

Bartosz nods in agreement.

'How do *you* know? We haven't seen her since we were kids.'

'I went round there. After you'd come over and told me about Jacob.'

I jump out of my seat again.

'No you didn't!'

'I wanted to see him. Why shouldn't a sister be able to visit a brother who's just returned from America and is living close by? It's the kind of thing people in normal families do all the time. Or at least I think it is.'

'Why didn't you tell me?'

I manage to stop hopping about and I plonk myself down on the floor, close to my sister's chair.

'I couldn't face having to manage your reaction. You were being such a dick at the time.'

'Was I?'

'You know you were.'

'No I don't.'

My sister opens her mouth to answer, but Bartosz manages to divert her before our little squabble escalates into a major row. 'Do you mind if I ask what happened?'

'Warren answered the door and I asked him if my mother was in. When he realised who I was, he told me to take my shoes off and follow him down the hallway. I can understand about the shoes. Their carpets are ankle deep. But it made me feel as though I'd been carrying a gun for self-defence and they'd disarmed me before I'd even got inside.'

'God, Amanda.'

She ignores me.

'He led me into this fantastic open plan diner and food preparation area at the back of the house and positioned himself next to my mother, who was standing there as though she was part of an advert for a bespoke kitchen company. She was wearing a really smart sleeveless tunic dress type thing and her hair was perfectly white and cut into an expensive bob. She looked incredibly elegant and tasteful. And tiny. I stood there, with no shoes on, feeling overly large and hot and sticky, with my hair all over the place, as usual. Warren told Mum who I was, and she narrowed her eyes at me, which freaked me out big time, because you do the exact same thing. My first, stupid thought was that she was doing an impersonation of you to wind me up.'

'What did she say?'

'She smiled, kind of, and asked what she could do for me, as though the kitchen was a shop and I was a customer. If she was surprised or bothered or affected in any way at all about the fact that her daughter, who she hadn't seen for God knows how long, had morphed into an adult and suddenly appeared without warning in her house, she didn't show it.'

'Maybe she didn't realise who you were.'

'Warren told her when he brought me in.'

'Perhaps she was shocked by you turning up like that, and she was trying to hide it by acting neutral.'

'Are you taking her side now?'

'No. But it's possible. And anyway, Warren was breathing down her neck. She probably has to be careful how she reacts to things when he's there.'

'I get that. But still. I mean, I wasn't expecting to be welcomed like the prodigal daughter, but I thought I'd get *some* kind of reaction. Anyway, once I'd realised it was a waste of time trying to discuss anything with her, I said I'd like to see Jacob, please. She said he was sick. I asked what was wrong with him, but neither of them replied. Not a word. They didn't even try to make something up. So I said I'd still like to see him and that if they told me where his room was, I'd go and find it on my own.'

'What did they do?'

'Warren stepped forward until his chest was about two inches from my face and said that wouldn't be possible. Then someone else came into the room. The back-up, presumably. He must have been hiding round the corner and listening, a big bloke with some of Warren's features, but lacking his ability to construct coherent sentences.'

'Slab-face.'

'Sounds about right. He helped Warren escort me out. Literally. They took an elbow each and walked me to the door. It was awkward because I'd arrived in these complicated Roman style lace-up sandals and the laces had got all tangled, so it was ages before I managed to unravel them and get the damn things back on my feet. And all the time they both stood there, watching me in silence. Our mother stayed in the kitchen while this was going on. I could hear her singing to music on the radio, not giving a shit.'

'I can't believe they manhandled you like that. You should have told me you were going. I could have come with you or waited outside or something.'

'If they'd seen *you*, I'd never have made it through the front door. Anyway, don't worry. I won't be going again.'

I run out onto the balcony and watch an almost empty, London-bound train hurtle past the other side of the car park. I want to burst into tears, but I force myself to suck it up. Behind me I can hear Amanda trying to explain the thing about myself and my brother to Bartosz, how close we once were and all that. He already knows and I think he gets it, but he's listening to what she has to say, nevertheless. Good to hear it from another angle, I suppose. I turn round, go back into the living room and sit down next to Bartosz again. I'm dying to rest my head against his shoulder and make him put his arm round me. But he stands up.

'I'll go to the next service, the Wednesday evening one. You never know, I might get to speak to Jacob and get a sense of where he's at. If not, it's still a way of keeping an eye on him. Making sure he's still around.'

Then he stands up and disappears back to his own flat, saying he's got several meetings with clients tomorrow and the rest of the week is more or less the same, so he needs to iron some shirts. He's being tactful, letting us have some time alone, but all I want to do is trail after him on my hands and knees like a dog.

'I wonder what would happen Bartosz asked Jacob to leave with him,' I say, after he's gone.

'It would kick off big time. They're not normal, these people,' Amanda says.

'But why is he so important to them?'

'He's the son of the pastor's wife. Groups like that use the concept of family to persuade their followers that they're respectable and up front.'

'But the state he's in. How can that be a good look?'

'Chances are they think they can get him back to normal again, or their version of normal. Then he'll be the sinner who's repented. And at the moment, they can use him as a warning to the others.'

'Anyway, Bartosz is keeping an eye on him now.'

She nods. I notice she has some colour in her cheeks again now, and her eyes are back to normal. In fact, she looks pretty much like her usual self, and she hasn't had to run off once to throw up. Does this mean she's still pregnant and has got over the worst of the morning sickness? Or has she gone ahead with the termination? I decide to risk it and ask her. If the conversation goes pear-shaped, she'll just tell me to mind my own business and leave, slamming the door behind her. No biggie. Most of her visits end like that anyway.

But she jumps in first. 'Who exactly is this Bartosz?' She asks. 'And what sort of a name is that?'

'You've just seen who he is. His name is Polish, from his great grandfather."

'But where the hell has he sprung from? Did you go on one of the dating websites again, after everything you said?'

'He lives next door.'

'Oh, right.' She stops her inquisition for a few seconds to digest this simple fact. Then she continues. 'Does he have tattoos *every*where?'

'Nearly everywhere.'

'Why are you being so mysterious?'

'I'm not. Don't you like him?'

'I can see how you might find him attractive.'

'You think he's hot.'

'He's handsome, but he's so intense. And not a bit like you.'

'He is, though'

It's true. He loves football and most other sports, but I hate them all. I like to read, whereas he doesn't. And he left school at sixteen, while I'm still doing exams at twenty-seven. But beneath the surface, in some indefinable way, our minds, although not the same by any means, seem to have been constructed from similar raw materials. Perhaps we knew each other in a past life, or maybe it's just lust and a shared sense of humour.

'We've been spending the evenings together, except when I'm at work. And some Thursdays."

'What happens on Thursdays?'

'He does an all-nighter at the Samaritans.'

'So he's a good listener, you've told him about Jacob, and now he's decided he wants to help?'

'Yes.'

'But he hardly knows you. Why is he willing to give up his Sunday mornings and get involved in our sordid family affairs?'

'Because he adores me and wants me to have his babies.'

He did actually say this during a particularly amorous moment. I flush a little as I realise I've just confided this to my sister of all people.

'God, you two really are smitten with each other.'

'You make it sound like a major disaster.'

I wander over to the kitchen and ask her if she wants something to eat. She does, so I open a can of lentil soup, heat it up and pour it into two bowls, which I bring into the living room. My sister shovels it into her mouth as though she hasn't eaten since last Christmas.

'What does he do, then?'

'He's a kind of senior financial advisor type thing.'

'Really? He looks more like a boxing promoter or a drug baron. Or one of those delicately butch thespians.'

'Homophobic, Amanda."

'No it isn't. All I mean is, he seems quite virile, but sensitive.'

'Wow Amanda, stop digging. He works for that company Aunty Susan has funds invested with. It's not really his thing, though. His clients give him a lot of grief, but the money's ok, he says. Before that he was in the army.'

'That makes more sense, I suppose.'

'And he's doing up this huge house down the motorway, in the middle of nowhere.'

'How can he afford to do that?'

'Like I said, he's a financial advisor. And I think he's got plans for it, so it's an investment, kind of.'

'But houses round here cost a fortune, even if they're derelict, and the money he'll need to do it up will be like a bottomless pit. He must have another source of income.'

'Dunno. Who cares?'

'You need to ask him.'

'Do I?'

'Yes, you bloody well do. Pin him down a bit more. He might be a money launderer for all you know.'

'Really?'

'I just think it's a bit odd that he's got all this money and he's emerged from the woodwork all of a sudden wanting to be your knight in shining armour.'

'My green knight.'

'Gawain, listen to yourself.'

14. Gawain

I open the door. Bartosz rushes in, lifts me off the floor, pushes me down onto my bed and jumps on top of me without saying a word. I've just come to the end of a series of night shifts, and we haven't seen each other for a while. I spent the morning trying to sleep, but my circadian rhythm was having none of it, so I'm and wired and exhausted at the same time. He starts kissing me frantically, as though it's a matter of life and death. This is fine by me, but when I start tugging at his clothes, he detaches himself from me and leaps off the bed again. I lie there looking up at him, appalled. If I'd known he was going to do that, I'd have wrapped my legs and arms around him and clung onto him harder.

'The wifi's sorted,' he says, as he smooths down his hair and refastens his belt. 'Pack your things.'

'My things?'

'Have you got enough bags? I've got a couple of spare boxes.'

'What are you talking about?'

'You need bags for your belongings.'

'Why?'

'You're moving in with me.'

'Now?'

'Yes. Get a move on!'

'But what about Jacob?'

"What about him?"

'I don't want to be so far away from him. He's only round the corner here. Your place is miles away.'

'He's got your phone number. And anyway, I'm planning to keep going to the services. We won't be abandoning him.'

He kneels by the side of the bed and grabs my face in both hands.

'Please come and live with me in my amazing house,' he whispers.

'Isn't it a bit soon?'

'Yeah, it's way too soon. Obviously. Or obvs as you youngsters say. But we could be dead tomorrow. You know that as well as anyone.'

'But….'

'Don't you want to move in with me? If you stay here when I've gone we'll never see each other.'

'It's such a big step.'

'You've got that look in your eyes again.'

'What look?'

'That scared look. As though you're afraid of living your life. Or is it me? Are you frightened of me?'

He tries to make it sound as though he's joking, but with each word, his voice becomes slightly colder. Am I scared of him, deep down? If I am, I mustn't let him talk me into this. I wish I could take time out and call my sister for advice, in the bathroom perhaps, so he can't eavesdrop. No I don't. She'd tell me not to go live with him. Under any circumstances.

He watches me prevaricate for a bit. Then he stands up again.

'Ok. Let's do it like this. Bring what you need for a week. Then if you want to stay for another week, come back here and pick up your post and more of your stuff. If you don't want to stay any longer, you can move back here again. It's up to you.'

'Cohabitation with a rolling contract?'

'Kind of. Particularly the rolling.'

It sounds like a safer option to me. I stare at him as I mull it over. He stares back. His eyes suddenly seem bluer than ever.

'Ok,' I say, eventually.

'Good lad.'

He pats me on the top of my head and steps away. Job done. Recalcitrant child dealt with.

'Take your car, then you'll have it for work. Or if you need to escape. Which you won't.'

I watch from the bed as he strides out towards the door.

'See you there,' he says. 'I'll leave the gate open.'

At first, my state of interrupted tumescence is so painful I can hardly get off the bed, never mind put one leg in front of the other, but I force myself to focus and I fill my backpack and a holdall with clothes, three cans of deodorant, other toiletries, my little bag of medical equipment and the slim, plastic folder containing my life admin. Then I remove half a litre of full fat milk from the fridge and pour it down the sink, and that's it. Fifteen minutes, and my entire life is packed away.

By the time I pull up at the house, the afternoon is well underway. It poured with rain when I was on the motorway, and I had to take it slowly, because of the spray from other vehicles. The journey took long enough for my doubts to return big time, as though our relationship is a religion and in his absence, I lose my faith in it. The sun is shining now. Drops of moisture are suspended from leaves and blades of grass, making everything dazzle. I expect Bartosz to come rushing up to help with my stuff as soon as he hears my car pull into the drive. He must be listening out for me, surely? But there's no sign of him. I get out and lean against my car for a few seconds so I can stare up at the house. I wonder if the ghosts are shaking their heads at me from the blank, shadowy windows, muttering to each other that I've made a big mistake following Bartosz here on a whim like this. He was only teasing me, they say. He doesn't really want me to move in with him at all. It was a power thing. He just said it to see how I'd respond and now I've agreed, he's won a huge victory over me.

I walk to the front door, hoping he's left it unlocked, so I can creep quietly without any kind of fanfare. But he hasn't and I'm reluctant to break the silence by lifting the big knocker and letting it crash back down again, so I phone him to let him know I'm here. I hear his ringtone through the open window of the bedroom above me, quickly followed by his footsteps as he rushes down the stairs.

He opens the door.

'Stay there! Don't step over the threshold.'

I stand on the front step and watch as he runs towards my car and then back again with my bags. He puts them in the hall and then he approaches me with such eagerness I have to dig my heels into the gravel to stop myself taking a step back.

'Don't look so bloody terrified.'

He hugs me gently, as though I'm a sick child, which makes me start to relax a bit, but then he pulls me up into a kind of fireman's lift, and he carries me over the threshold and up the stairs to his, our bedroom. I scream and kick. But I laugh as well. He lays me down on the bed and puts his face close to mine.

'I thought you might change your mind after I'd gone.'

'I nearly did.'

'But you're here, so....'

'I'm here.'

He slides his finger under the waistband of my jeans and runs it back and forth over my appendix scar.

'Bartosz,' I say.

'Mmm?'

'I need to get acclimatized first.'

He removes his finger. I clamber off the bed, walk over to the side window and stare out at the overgrown lawn and the row of little outhouses. Even in the sunshine they look full of secrets, particularly the one on the far right, for some reason. He comes up behind me and turns me round so I'm facing him.

'You've been here before,' he says.

'But I hadn't moved in with you, then.'

'You're not moving in. You've come to stay for a week. Then maybe another week. And another one after that.'

I lean forward and put my head on his chest, but I keep my arms down by my sides, so I'm with him but not with him at the same time. He wraps his arms around me lightly, grasping his hands behind my back, so he's not really touching me either. I realise I'm waiting for him to say something to reassure me. Anything would do. But he stays silent.

I realise I've got myself into such a weird situation. I know all sorts of intimate details about his body and the quite astonishingly precise way he likes things to be done, but when it comes to Bartosz the man, his life so far, his personality and his current motivations, I'm not sure I know anything much. Even so, despite all the doubts and unknowns, that little piece of elastic is still tugging me towards him. If I'm honest, I don't ever want to be apart from him again. Not ever. In fact, right now I'd like nothing more than to dissolve inside him and disappear completely, become a spirit that haunts him, who can occasionally be seen in a certain light as a vague shadow, taking a timid glimpse at the outside world through his eyes.

'I hate being jerked around with,' I say eventually, my voice muffled against his shoulder.

He pulls back and cups my face in his hands. I can't translate the faint smile that's lighting up his features.

'You're so cute.'

'I'm not a child,' I say, instantly making myself sound like one.

'We're all children underneath.'

He kisses me on the forehead. I'm not getting through to him. He can't me as I really am, or rather, he only sees the part of me he wants to see. Sweet little Gawain. I rummage around inside my head for evidence that I'm a man, not a boy. The only thing I can come up with is my job. All the crises, the awful deaths and terrible life changing injuries I have to deal with every day, to say nothing of imparting bad news to relatives. I may only be a very junior doctor, but in the middle of the night, when everyone's flat out, I have to step up. In the early hours of Friday morning, for example, a teenager came in after a motorbike accident and went into cardiac arrest. We did everything we could to save him, but none of it worked, and I was the one who had to go into the relatives' room to tell his parents and much smaller brother that he was dead. The worst part, the thing I won't forget for a while, was the look on the little boy's face as he tried to take it in and be brave at the same time. But hey, it's part of the job. Afterwards, I didn't even go outside for a quick cry behind the bins. I went through a quick mental re-run of the way I'd spoken to the family, to reassure myself I hadn't made it worse for them because of something in my manner or the words I'd used. Then I manned up, did the paperwork and moved on to the next patient.

Does that make me an adult? Or does adopting a specific persona to get through the day just mean I'm a good actor, a boy pulling off a grown-up role? And when I'm not at work, do I even exist as a valid human being at all? I don't know. But at the very least, I can try to get explain to him about my job. It's all I've got.

'If you think I'm just a little man-child, you're wrong,' I say when I've finished.

He removes his hands from my face and puts them in his pockets. He stares down at the floorboards. I know he wants this conversation to end, but I haven't finished yet.

'And I've told you just about everything important about myself, but I know nothing about you.'

'Man-child,' he repeats. 'My little man-cub.'

We both laugh uneasily. He holds out his hand. I take it and he leads me down the stairs and out, through the front door. We walk along the track in the opposite direction to the road, still holding hands, but not talking. The breeze makes the leaves flutter and rattle against each other, as though they're chattering about us. Occasional rain droplets fall onto our hair and the air is filled with the scent of freshly moistened earth, which makes me realise summer will be over soon. The track follows a gradual bend until it comes to an abrupt end by a corrugated iron barn, painted black with a high roof and open sides, and surrounded by old hedges that have grown tall and straggly. There isn't much inside the barn, just a few old bales of hay, a clapped-out fridge lying on its side and a rusty bicycle frame. Bartosz sits on one of the bales and pulls me down next to him. Then he lets go of my hand and clears his throat.

'What do you want to know?'

'Everything important.'

He looks down at his knees. Then he shrugs and clears his throat again and scratches his head, making himself look vulnerable and caught out, as though I've pinned him down unfairly. It's making me feel a bit vexed with him, to be honest. But I'm not letting him off the hook. 'I'll ask you questions. You don't have to give me detailed answers, if you don't want to. But everything you say has to be true.'

'Right.' He doesn't sound very happy about it, but that's too bad.

'Did you like being a soldier?'

'I loved it. It was all I ever wanted to do. I joined straight after GCSEs when I was sixteen.'

'Why did you leave?'

'I was invalided out. An IED went off at the side of the road and I caught the edge of it. Two of my best mates were killed. Another lost both his legs. I was lucky.'

'Hence the scar.'

'I had to have my spleen removed and bits of my innards needed to be pushed back in and stitched back together.'

'That was enough for you to be invalided out?'

'Nope.'

'What else, then? PTSD?

He shrugs. I really want to pursue this line of questioning, but he won't look me in the eye and his scowl is so off-putting that I bottle it.

'What did you do next?'

'I settled back home and bought a small house near my mum's, with Mitchell, who you already know about. I wasn't bad at maths. I know it won't seem like much to you, with all your qualifications, but I got an A in my GCSE. And in Business Studies. So I became a financial advisor.'

'What did Mitchell do?'

'He was a manager at a big DIY chain.'

'And when he died you moved down here because of your ex-army mates?'

'They understand what it was like. Nobody else does. You had to be there. We're pretty tight and we help each other out. But it wasn't just that. The house wasn't the same without Mitchell. Even the town we lived in wasn't the same. All the pubs we used to go to. The hills where we used to run. It was all still there, but Mitchell wasn't. It did my head in. So when I was offered a promotion that involved moving down South, I went for it.'

'How can you afford this house and all the money you're spending on it?'

'Seriously?'

'My sister thinks you're a drug baron.'

He laughs, but in mirthless and possibly offended way, which is fair enough, really.

'I have a pension from the army, and my job, which helped me to get a decent mortgage rate. But mostly I've used money I inherited from Mitchell, which came from his grandad originally. He had a big house in a posh part of Leeds and a shed load of shares and fixed rate bonds. Mitchell left it all to me. It added up to a heck of a lot in the end when all the interest was taken into account. I was lucky, but I didn't feel like I'd earned it or deserved it, so I ploughed the whole lot into this place. To do some good, hopefully.'

'That's the second time you've said you were lucky. I think you've been incredibly unlucky.'

'Yeah, well. It's all relative.'

'So what's this good you want to do?'

'I'm going to set up a kind of refuge for army veterans who need a chance to get their shit together and all that. The house is peaceful and kind of in the middle of nowhere, but close enough to civilization to get people in to help, like therapists and stuff.'

'Wow, Bartosz.'

'Just two or three people at a time. They could use the bedrooms in the attic.'

'Yeah. I can see that working. It could be amazing.'

I'm glad he told me. I shuffle about on the hay bale and look at the ground, weighing it all up. Weighing him up and how he feels about me. He watches me.

'I don't see you as my plaything,' he says eventually. 'Well I do in a way, obviously. But you're much more than that.'

'Do you really want me here, sharing your house?'

'I wouldn't have asked you if I didn't.'

'Ok. One more thing.'

'Go on.'

'Why are you so keen to help with Jacob? You don't even know him.'

"Because you can't move forward unless you get him back and that means I can't either, now that we're involved with each other."

'Are we involved with each other?'

'I think so. Don't you?'

'I think we're entangled. Like two sub-atomic particles. The actions of one will always be linked with the actions of the other. Jacob and I are entangled too, in a different way. Even though we've lived completely separate lives for the past eight years.'

'Entangled. I like that.'

'And now you and Jacob are starting to become entangled, too.'

'He could move into Picardy, as well. If he wants to, while he gets himself together.'

Picardy, I think. What an evocative name. I googled it after the first time I came here. Some of the biggest battles of World War One were fought there. I imagine the grief some former owner must have felt to have given the house this name. Maybe it was to commemorate a lost son or brother. Perhaps that's why I keep picking up these waves of sadness when I'm here, particularly when the sun is low in the sky, casting long shadows over everything, like it's doing now. The going down of the sun.

I stand and pull him up by his hands. We walk back along the track, our faces illuminated by the rich, westering light. Suddenly, something I can't pin down, pushes away the sadness. I don't know what it is, a simple sense of warmth and wellbeing perhaps, because of the sun, or maybe even a faint glow of optimism. I don't get those very often.

I put my arm round his waist and rest my head against his shoulder as we walk.

'I've got loads of really bad habits. You'll be sick to death of me by the end of the week.'

'You don't say? Your slatternly ways will definitely wind me up. They already do.'

'You're really anal about tidiness.'

"I just like things to be in order. Whereas you leave a mess everywhere you go and you can never find anything.'

'I keep telling myself to do something about it, but it never happens.'

'It's really bad in the mornings when you're trying to get out of the door.'

'My stuff moves around in the night when I'm asleep.'

'It wouldn't do that if you squared things away properly.'

'I know.'

'Then there's your eating problem.'

'It's not a problem as such.'

"Gawain, when we got pizza delivered you scraped off the topping with a spoon and left the base.'

'It was too hard.'

'Why, though?'

'I hate it when people ask me that.'

'I'm not just people.'

'I don't know why. Something must have happened to my teeth, when I was tiny. I can't remember.'

'Do you ever go to the dentist?'

'God, no. Never. Cleaning them is hard enough, even with a soft brush. And flossing is a nightmare.'

'That's so odd. And for it to last such a long time.'

'I know it's a nuisance.'

'It's a proper pain in the arse. I love cooking. I do great steaks and barbecue food, but you won't be able to eat any of that.'

'Sometimes Aunty Susan makes casseroles and liquidizes them for me.'

'You can't liquidize burgers and sausages.'

'Whatever. Anyway, anyone would think you had no bad habits.'

'I don't.'

'You mutter in your sleep. Sometimes you sit up and say stuff.'

'What do I say?'

'I can never make out the words. You kind of ramble incoherently and sound angry, as though you're telling someone off, but you're frightened of them at the same time. After a bit, you lie down again and carry on sleeping as though nothing's happened.'

'You've never mentioned it before.'

'It's not a big deal. You always go back to sleep. But it'll freak me out more if you do it here.'

'Why?'

'Because of the ghosts.'

'Here we go.'

'You must be able to sense them?'

'Nope.'

When we get back to the house, the sun is shining into the porch, and the front door is warm to the touch. We go in, climb up the stairs and wander slowly along the landing into the bedroom. I start unpacking and manage to hang a few creased shirts and my leather jacket in the portion of the cavernous wardrobe allocated to me by its owner. But when I squat down and contemplate the rest of the stuff in my holdall, a thick grey cloud of weariness descends on me so rapidly I struggle to stop myself dropping onto the floor. I was already sleep deprived when Bartosz burst into my flat, and a wimp like me can only handle a certain amount of emotional intensity in one day. I've reached my limit.

I walk over to the bed and quickly strip off all my clothes. I drop my T-shirt on the floor and I step out of my jeans and underwear in a single move, leaving them kneeling stiffly on the floor, one garment inside the other. Then I stumble into bed, pull the covers up to my armpits, close my eyes and lie there with my arms down at my sides. Over by the wardrobe, Bartosz is verbalising the organisation of his socks into colour coordinated groups, as he places them in his half of the chest of drawers.

'Purple,' he declares happily, then 'blue'.

Beyond his voice, somewhere much further away, I can hear the sheepdog barking again. My mind returns to the farmyard and the hens, and this time an old lady with blonde hair tied back from her face walks into the scene and starts sweeping the yard with a big brush. Her benevolence washes over me and makes me feel peaceful. Then I think about Jacob and I try to beam some of my happy, sleepy vibes to him through the ether.

Eventually, Bartosz stops fetishing about with his socks and notices both my open holdall in the middle of the floor and the fact that I've gone to bed. He comes over and I half open my eyes to see him looking down at me, hands on hips. I can't summon up the energy to open my eyes properly, but I try to mumble an explanation.

'This is another of my bad habits. I go on and on for days with hardly any sleep, then I crash. I don't have any control over it.'

'Interesting it's happened now, when you're meant to be putting your clothes away.'

15. Gawain

'You've moved in with an ex-soldier covered in tattoos, fourteen years older than you, who you've only known for a matter of weeks, and you don't want me to worry?' My sister's voice is so loud I have to move the phone away from my ear.
'Yep. I thought I'd better tell you because if you turn up at my flat on your way home from the Green Witch or the Frog and Potatoes or wherever it is you hang out with your chums, I won't be there.'

I can't be bothered to justify myself or explain about the one week rolling trial period.

'You sound a bit weird. Are you sure you're ok? Has he bewitched you?'

'Pretty much.'

He has. Multiple times in his bed and in several other parts of the house, including the new couch in the kitchen, on top of the pool table in the man cave, which couldn't take it and now has one broken leg tied up with gaffer tape, and late last night, standing up against the wall by the front door. We'd just got back from the cinema in Basingstoke and couldn't wait any longer. The temptation to blurt all this out to my sister is so strong I have to pinch my arm.

'I think I should come round.'

'You can if you like. Bartosz has gone to New Sunrise again, for the Sunday service. Come for lunch.'

'Where *is* this house?'

'In the countryside. A few miles down the motorway.'

I give her the address and the non-motorway directions, which sound way more complicated than they actually are, a situation not helped by the fact that the house is strangely absent from all of the digital maps and doesn't seem to be recognised by anyone's sat nav either.

'Christ. I think I'll give it a miss today, if you don't mind. I've had a busy week.'

'No worries. Another time.'

'Just, you know. Be careful.'

'Bit late for that.'
'You're such an idiot. Anyway, I've got to go.'
'Amanda…'
'What?'
'How's things with you?'
'Alright, I guess. More or less.'
'Meaning?'
Meaning what have you done about the baby? Obviously.
'Look, I've got to go. Let me know what happens at the church.'
Her phone goes dead.

Living with Bartosz is going pretty well. We haven't had any major fallings out yet, apart from the other evening when he suddenly became incensed by my dirty socks and underpants, which, to be fair, were scattered all over the bedroom floor, rolled up into little balls. He had a right go at me about them, then opened the sash window, picked each ball up one by one with a set of wooden barbecue tongs and threw them all out onto the grass below. Then he handed me a plastic laundry basket and told me to go down and collect them all, and put them in the washing machine. He has no idea, but in revenge I've done away with his ghastly bamboo flip flops. I sank them to the bottom of the food waste canister under a mixed slop consisting mainly of spaghetti, fish heads and cabbage, and wheeled the whole lot down to the gate. The bin men have already taken them away with the rest of the rubbish.

I can't imagine what he'll do when he realises.

Also, we've ordered furniture for the big spare bedroom at the front, including a double bed, a storage unit and a window blind, also in blue with a smattering of grey. This will be the room we offer to Jacob if or when he leaves the church. The hope that this will happen gives me a burning sensation inside my chest, so I try not to dwell on it.

Bartosz is rapidly becoming a regular member of the New Sunrise congregation. He's listened to enough eulogies and skewed interpretations of various bits of the bible to know for certain he'll be going to hell, as will I and everyone else of our persuasion. Also, he's spoken to my brother. How amazing is that? Since that first time, Jacob hasn't been taken away at the end of the service. Instead, he's been allowed to mingle in the little hall and help out with the refreshments.

When Bartosz initiated contact to my brother, he was circulating with a plate of Rich Tea biscuits.

'At least they're not Bourbons this time. Not that these are much of an improvement.'

Jacob, who had been staring down at the plate looked up at him, his eyes suddenly round and wide open in astonishment or maybe amusement, Bartosz wasn't sure.

'Are you a custard cream man, then?'

'Not really. I prefer proper biscuits, like those German ones that have that thick ledge of chocolate round the outside.'

'I don't think they'd be within budget.' Jacob sort of smiled briefly, when he said that.

Then Bartosz went in for the kill. 'Do you buy into this crap? I mean. All those daft commandments.'

He spoke quietly and acted neutral, as though he was still talking about biscuits, but Jacob stepped back sharply. The plate tilted and three of the biscuits slid off onto the floor. Bartosz put his hand out and grabbed the plate before the rest of them tumbled off, too. They both crouched down to pick up the ones on the floor. Then, Bartosz looked over Jacob's shoulder and saw Cowboy-Junkie tapping his way towards them from the other side of the room.

'Your brother says *hi*,' Bartosz whispered.

This time, Jacob was better prepared. He made his face went completely blank. Then he took his plate and moved away to offer the biscuits to a trio of geeky looking teenagers.

After the next service, as soon as Jacob came into the room, he made a bee-line for Bartosz. He was carrying a plate of pink wafers this time, and they managed to speak for a bit longer. It was a weirdly disjointed conversation, Bartosz said, because they both had things they wanted to get across quickly before they were noticed and interrupted.

'Not chocolate, I'm afraid,' Jacob said.

'Never mind. One of these will do nicely.' Bartosz took a big bite out of the pink square. 'How's it going, mate?'

'Things have calmed down a bit. For now, anyway.'

'Good.'

'How do you know my brother?'

'We live together.'

'As in?'

'Yeah.'

'Oh. Right.'

'In a house a few miles down the motorway. With a spare room.'

Jacob didn't say anything to that.

'We'd like to get a phone to you, so you can contact us if you need to. Not sure how, though. I don't think it would be safe to hand one over in here.' Bartosz said the next time they were able to speak to each other.

'God, no,' Jacob said quickly. He thought for a few seconds. 'My room's in the basement. It's usually my job to lock the side door on the way out before the services start. I could forget, say on Wednesday night?'

'That might work.'

'I'm not promising I'll definitely get in touch, though. Me and my brother aren't, you know.'

'Fair enough. I know you have issues with Gawain. But he's frantic with worry about you. He wants you out of here. We both do. And your sister.'

Jacob blinked at Bartosz, as if he couldn't get his head round any of that.

'You can trust us. I used to be in the army. I was in Afghanistan.'

Bartosz said it felt a bit clunky throwing that titbit of information into the conversation apropos of nothing, but Cowboy-Junkie was watching, so time was limited. Bartosz and I had scripted an outline this conversation earlier. We agreed it would be worth slipping it in if possible, because Jacob had always been the type of boy who was interested in the army and warfare. At least he had been when he was thirteen. He used to be in the Combined Cadet Force at school. He loved taking part in drills and parades in his uniform, but he joined mainly because of the activities and the expeditions. He was never happier than when he was jumping backwards off a cliff into the sea or climbing a rock face in the pouring rain.

'Awesome,' my brother said vaguely.

We're filled with a new sense of urgency now, because Warren has announced that New Sunrise has put a deposit down on a tract of land belonging to a defunct outward bound centre in the Brecon Beacons. It looks as though the sale will go through quickly, because the church is a cash buyer. God knows where the money is coming from, but we'll need to act quickly if we want to get Jacob out. It will be much harder to keep in touch with him and achieve anything at all once he's hidden away in the Welsh countryside. This is why, the following, Wednesday evening, while Bartosz is in the church, I sneak into the manse or whatever they call it, through the side door, which has been left unlocked – thanks, Jacob, and I locate my brother's room in the basement. After standing there for a minute or two, looking around in horror at the dingy space they make him sleep in, I pull myself together and get the new mobile phone I've bought him out of my jacket pocket. At first, I can't decide where to put it. In the end, I hide it under the mattress. It turns out my navy T-shirt is there, too, all rolled up, so I put the phone inside it. Then I get the hell out and wait for Bartosz in his car. Before I went in, I created a WhatsApp group for Jacob, Bartosz, Amanda and myself and set the phone to ring at two am. I tried to make the ringtone just loud enough for him to be able to hear it, without alerting anyone else to its presence.

It must have been ok, because early the next morning, when I tumble out of bed and round up all the stuff I need for work, I hear an unfamiliar beep-beep and find that Jacob has posted a tentative message. All it says is *hi*, followed by a question mark. I want to say loads, but I just put *hi Jacob*, followed by a smiley face, and shortly afterwards Amanda does the same. Then I ask him how it's going. Later, I regret this because he doesn't reply and the question hangs uneasily in the air around my head for the rest of the day. Then, in the evening, quite late, Jacob posts again. He doesn't reply to my earlier question, he just asks *Where are you all?* He makes it sounds as though he's the only one who has turned up at some rendezvous point we'd all agreed on. We all reply, but after that, he goes mute again, and his silence haunts us for the rest of the week.

The following Sunday, Bartosz looks worried when he comes back from the church. 'Something's not right,' he says. 'One side of Jacob's face is all bruised. Looks bad.'

'Jesus. Did you speak to him?'
'Briefly. He came up to me. All he managed to say was Monday afternoons are best, because most of the others aren't on site then. I was going to try and make some kind of loose arrangement to pick him up, but before I could say anything, Cowboy-Junkie grabbed him by the shoulders and shoved him across the floor and out of the room.'
'Shit, Bartosz.'
'Don't panic. This is good news.'

'Is it?'

'Of course it is. He's decided to leave. That's a huge step. Does he like sausages?'

'What's that got to do with anything?'

'Tomorrow's the big day. We'll whip him out, no bother. Then I'll do a barbie in the evening to celebrate.'

16. Jacob

The tablets they gave me in America were better than the ones I get here. They made it kind of easy to shove all the bad stuff that was happening into to back of my mind. I'd be all spaced out most of the time, my mind at peace. I think the UK pills are just sleeping tablets, though, because that's all they do, make me sleep. And when I wake up, my head is throbbing and the fear is back. I'm permanently afraid, now.

They forced me to take a handful of the tablets about an hour before the whipping ritual, so at least I was partially out of it for that and for a while afterwards. But that wasn't why they gave me such a big dose. They only did that so I wouldn't struggle when they dragged me into the little hall and tied me to the post. They had that post put in specially. I bet the bloke who installed it thought New Sunrise was branching out into pole dancing. My mother always gives me the tablets. She counts them out, hands them over with a glass of water and watches as I put them in my mouth and swallow them down. Until recently, I haven't bothered to resist. Then, one time, I told her I wasn't going to take the tablets anymore. Mum shouted for help. Godwin and Warren came running in. Godwin held me down and my stepfather slapped my face until I opened my mouth.

But over the last week or so, I've worked out a way of pretending to swallow them. I act all compliant, but then I kind of hold the tablets under my tongue while I drink the water she gives me. It's quite tricky. The tablets are very small and can easily be dislodged by the water and get washed down my throat. But I'm getting better at it. Of course, this means I'm more alert than I used to be, and my anxiety levels are through the roof. I've gone from sleeping ten to fifteen hours a day to hardly sleeping at all, and I have this tremor that goes down my arms and into my hands, right down to the ends of my fingers. If it gets really violent, I have to ram my hands into my pockets so people won't notice.

Mum, Warren and Godwin have gone out, like they usually do on Mondays. Before she left Mum came into my room to give me my morning pills and impart some kind of message, just like she always does. She sat on my bed and patted the space next to her, but I didn't sit down. I stood over her with my arms folded and asked her what she wanted. Last week, it was detailed instructions about how to scrub the font with washing up liquid and a hard brush, but this time she wanted to talk about G. It was very important, she said, that I realised my brother is an evil influence and that I'm much safer here, away from him, in the caring arms of Jesus and the Church of the New Sunrise. I don't know why she suddenly started talking about *him*. She's never mentioned him before, even after he rushed into the car park and got carted off by Godwin. She rambled on about my brother for a very long time, so long the tablets started to dissolve under my tongue. After she'd gone I spat the crumbling white paste onto the concrete floor and ground it into a thousand pieces with my shoe.

So yeah, I'm wide awake today, which is a good thing, because I'm in the deepest of deep shit. Ed follows me everywhere. He's even set up a camp bed, outside my door. After last night's service, he decided to give me what he called a heads up. The elders have had a meeting about me. They've agreed I'm an escape risk, what with my brother sniffing around. And they're planning to tie me to the post and repeat the whipping ritual. I asked what I'd done this time, because I genuinely have no clue. I didn't try to go off with my brother. I told him to leave. But Ed just shrugged. He doesn't know what I've done, either. He just doesn't want to admit it. What a jerk.

The last whipping happened because they caught me with Ruth. Finally. They didn't realise the thing between us had been going on for years, since my first summer in South Carolina, when we were just fourteen. It was much easier to get away with it there. We had a lot more freedom, or at least I did, and there were more places to hide. In the afternoons, Ruth and I were allowed to go swimming together after we'd done our chores. We changed into our swimwear in an old wooden shack that had been abandoned between the marshes and the sea. At first we were very chaste. There were two separate rooms on the ground floor. She changed in the one at the front, and I used the one at the back. Then, one day, she came into my room and told me to drop the towel I was wrapping around myself. I did as I was told. I always did what Ruth told me to do back then. And that's how started, right there, on the scrubbed floor of an old hut with broken windows, with the constant swoosh of the ocean and cries of the sea birds in the background.

Ruth was the best thing in my life when I was in South Carolina. For a long time, I was crazily mad for her waist length, auburn hair and her creamy, freckled skin. She teased and ridiculed me, because that's how she is, but she still let me do whatever I liked to her. Her mockery never curbed my enthusiasm. In fact, it had the opposite effect. And later, when I was older and wiser and had grown disillusioned with her and just about everything else to do with New Sunrise, I started to regard sex with her as a sport. I've always been a good athlete and I guess I became as skilled at making love to Ruth as I was at playing football and cricket. In fact I got so good at it, I could often fuck the snarkiness right out of her. It gave me a kind of power over her, I guess. And each September when I flew back to England and school, I used these summers of passion to boost my ratings. The youngest Fylde boy, tall, blonde, great at sports and sexually experienced. That was me. Except it wasn't. Not really. The worldly, sophisticated British girls at school were nothing like Ruth. I couldn't even speak to them without stammering and blushing like a saddo.

It was much more difficult to keep things secret when we moved back to England. In South Caroline, the community occupied what amounted to an entire village, more or less, but in the UK, they only have the church and the house. And neither of us is allowed to leave the grounds, so we had to use either her room or mine. Ed's room was on the same floor, so I'm guessing he must have heard us and dobbed us in.

I was moved down to the basement and given a public beating a couple of days later. Ruth on the other hand was admonished in private. All she had to do was listen to an extended lecture about virtue and spend several hours reading specially selected passages from the bible.

The wounds from the last whipping haven't healed properly, yet, but being beaten again is the least of my worries. The thing that concerns me most is what they've got planned for me afterwards. They won't keep me here. That would make them look weak, as though they'd lost control of me. There was a guy in the South Carolina community called Ethan who questioned what they call *The Message* and got into loads of arguments with Warren and the other church elders about the scriptures and the way they were being used as justification for the physical punishments they were starting to mete out. It all came to a head when Ethan stood up one Sunday during the service and denounced Warren as a man of evil. Afterwards, he was escorted away and nobody ever saw him again. Later, the elders announced that he'd left due to a difference of opinion, but someone told me he was beaten unconscious and dumped in the sea. I didn't believe that at the time, but now I'm not so sure. It would have been easy enough to do. The ocean was so close and the beaches were practically deserted, particularly after dark. And they even had a boat they used for sea fishing. All they'd need to do would be to take it far enough out, weigh Ethan's body down with stones and nobody would ever know.

    So yeah, they'll get rid of me one way or another. Maybe they'll intoxicate me until I don't know what's going on and someone will dig out my passport from wherever they've hidden it and escort me back to one of the communities in America. Or perhaps they'll dispatch me here in the house, cart my body off in the back of a van and throw it in the Thames. Whatever they decide to do, it will be the end of me. I'll be deleted and no traces will be left for Bartosz or anyone else to find.

    And that's another thing. Last time, they invited all the men to go into the little hall to watch the punishment ritual. Now Bartosz will be among the spectators. The thought of him seeing them do that to me is beyond humiliating, much worse than the prospect of the physical pain. And what if he tries to stop them? The guy looks like he can handle himself, but there's only one of him and he's not Godwin-sized. Maybe they'd end up getting rid of him, too.

    So, another whipping? Nope. Not going to happen.

    When I spoke to Bartosz after the service yesterday and he saw the state of my face, he managed not to react, which must have been difficult, because his features are really open. You can always see what he's feeling, or at least I can. Not like the men of New Sunrise, who all have the cold, blank stare of a shark. I think Bartosz is one of those people who's never confused about what's right and what's wrong, like a reliable policeman in an old fashioned detective show. Talking to him makes me feel kind of comforted. Sometimes I wonder what it would be like if he gave me a hug. Then I despise myself for being so needy. We don't do physical affection here. We're taught that all touching, apart from the violent kind or sex between married couples is sinful. Anyway, I like the idea of living in Bartosz's house until I get my life together again. The only drawback is that my brother will be there too. But if G still behaves like a total dick, like he used to, maybe I could go back to our old room at Aunty Susan's or stay with Amanda.

I'm getting way ahead of myself here. I need to put concerns about my future living conditions and G's potential twattery firmly on the back burner and set my escape in motion before it's too late. Right now, I'm in the church, spraying the seats with disinfectant and wiping them with a towel. Ruth is around somewhere, doing other chores, and Ed is here, too. Clearly, his main task is to keep his eyes on me at all times. Even so, I managed to slip the phone in one of the front pockets of my jeans, while I was getting dressed. I removed it from G's T-shirt last night and hid it in my pyjama trousers, together with a prayer book, which is black like the phone and similar in size. When I got dressed, I held the phone under the prayer book and shoved them both into my jeans while I was pulling them up. So I've got the phone with me. But I'm not sure if I'll be able to use it.

I keep on draping the damp cloth across the seats, one by one, progressing slowly down each row. When I'm done, I have no idea how much time has passed. For all I know, it's taken ages and the others will be back soon. On the other hand, Ed might decide to march me back to my room in a minute. Then it will be game over, and by the end of the week, I'll be at the bottom of the Thames in concrete boots, or zonked out and lost in rural America. My hands start to shake more than ever and my mind jumps about all over the place. I need to come up with an exit strategy. Now. But all I can do is dither. If only Ed would stop staring at me. I feel like I'm going to vomit, even though I've eaten nothing since yesterday lunchtime.

Hang on. I could be onto something here.

I decide to go for it. I clamp my hand over my mouth and I run towards the back of the church. As I pass Ed, who is leaning against the altar, I mumble that I'm going to be sick, and I dive through the door at the back and charge across the little hall to the toilet in the far corner. I hear Ed's cowboy boots clip-clopping after me, but I manage to get the door locked before he can reach me, and I make loud coughing and barfing noises, to cover the sound my thumbs make as I tap at my phone. My hands are trembling so much I keep pressing down two keys at once and I have to start again, twice.

Eventually, I succeed in typing *now would be a good time.* Talk about understatement. I click the send arrow, shove the phone back in my pocket and flush the toilet.

I emerge and splash water over my face. Ed asks if I want to go and lie down. I shake my head and tell him I feel better now. I notice a sweeping brush leaning against the far wall, next to a mop and bucket, and say I'll tackle the floor. My phone is set to silent. If someone replies to my message and it buzzes or vibrates and Ed notices it when he's ogling my crotch, I'll be screwed, but I have no choice but to carry it with me. I shift the chairs to one side and start sweeping as slowly as I can get away with.

I have no clue how long it will take G or Bartosz to respond to my message, but once I've sent it, an unexpected, devil-may-care sense of bravado starts to unfurl inside my head. I'm definitely leaving, one way or another. The consequences can't be any worse than the fate they've got planned for me if I stay, can they? This amazing realization makes me want to laugh out loud, right here in the church, and then it sets off a cascade of other thoughts and concerns. Crazily, I start to worry about my clothes. I wonder if I should have put on my newish black jeans and purple hoodie, the ones I have to keep clean for services. Instead I've pulled on my usual thin grey tracksuit bottoms and matching sweat shirt. They must look hideous. I've worn the trousers so many times, the seat of the pants has become shiny and the top stinks of body odour even after it's been washed. I wish I could go back to the basement and change.

At the end of possibly the longest forty minutes of my life, my phone vibrates silently in my pocket. I glance up at Ed, as casually as I can manage.

'You feeling sick again?' He asks.

He hasn't noticed the phone, then.

'No. I was just going to fetch the mop, if that's ok. It's in the back.'

'Yo,' he says, like the fake cowboy tosser he truly is, and I dash off to the little hall again.

He turns on his heel, so he can follow me, but at that moment, Ruth asks him if he knows where the brass polish has gone, because she needs to do the candlesticks. He likes being asked questions, because he thinks it makes him look important when he knows the answers. He ambles over to her, and I know I've got a few minutes now, while he goes and looks in all the cupboards and fails to find the polish, which got used up in the last polishing session.

I stick the bucket under the big sink and turn the taps on full, dig out my phone and read the message. It's from G. He says he's stuck in traffic, but Bartosz is on his way, too, and I should go with whoever arrives first. *Run like hell and get into the first car that turns up*, he says. He can't resist sticking *love you* and a smiley face with little hearts flying out of it at the end of the message. It makes me tear up. For the last eight years, I've felt nothing but hatred towards him and an extreme irritation, like an electric shock thrumming through my body, every time I think about him.

But then he sends me a stupid emoji and I'm in bits.

I go back into the hall with the mop, and I try my best to hunker down and act as though cleaning the floor is the only thing on my mind. When there isn't a single smear of dirt remaining and I really can't justify continuing with this performance a second longer, there's still no sign of G or Bartosz. But I've passed a point of no return in my head now. No way am I going back into that basement again. Like ever. One way or another, I'm getting out of here. If neither of them turns up in the next few minutes, I'll make a run for it. It won't be a very fast run, but if I can get a head start, maybe Ed won't catch up with me until I've reached the road, and it'll be harder for him to rugby tackle me to the ground in a place where pedestrians and cars are constantly passing.

Ed and Ruth are still searching for the polish. Now they're emptying the cupboards near the door to the little hall, and an array of cardboard boxes, cleaning cloths and bottles of detergent is accumulating around their feet. The red light inside my head flicks to green. I walk quietly down the aisle towards the door, with the mop in my hand. If Ed notices, I'll tell him I'm going to swill the paving stones at the front of the church. But he doesn't even look up. Neither does Ruth. I turn the big metal handle. The main door to the church opens without a single creak. Thank you, God. For once. The car park is still empty, apart from Ed's Fiesta, tucked close to the wall of the house, and the road at the other side seems deserted. I step outside, still holding my mop. It was raining a while ago, and everything smells fresh and kind of renewed. I pause to take a deep breath. Walk, I tell myself. Don't look back. Put one foot in front of the other and get across the car park. When you reach the pavement, really go for it. Run as fast as you can, get yourself round that corner at the end of the road, find somewhere safe and contact G and Bartosz again, to tell them where you are.

But I've only gone a few paces when a big black Audi swerves through the entrance to the car park. Bartosz pulls up next to me, grins and leans across to open the passenger door. A blast of rock music almost knocks me over. Motorhead. Killed by Death. I haven't heard that for ages.

'Get in and hold on!'

'Hi,' I say as I jump in.

Before I've even managed to pull the door shut, he yanks the car around in a handbrake turn. Tyres screech against the gravel. He laughs and so do I.

Am I really out, and still in one piece? Is it really over? I can't quite believe it, not yet anyway. As soon as Bartosz has made this dramatic turn, a tatty old VW Golf drives into the car park and passes us as it approaches the church, where it does a similar manoeuvre and starts following us towards the exit. I turn in my seat so I'm facing backwards. My brother flashes his familiar, slow wide grin at me. Suddenly I'm back at school, coming into the dining room to find him strutting about on one of the tables, singing into a hockey stick, pretending to be Freddy Mercury or George Michael, making his friends and admirers scream with laughter. He was always doing stuff like that. I used to roll my eyes at him and hide myself away at the other end of the room, as far from him as I could get. I feel a bit like that again now, but in his scrubs, he looks like a bright blue angel of mercy and his face is full of what looks like genuine joy, because I've escaped and I'm safe and sound in Bartosz's car. I wish I could blank him, but my face won't let it happen and I smile back at him like I mean it. And just now, I do mean it.

The Audi purrs out of the car park and swings left along the road, in the direction of the roundabout that leads to the slip road onto the motorway. I hear a quiet beeping sound, reminding me to fasten my seatbelt. I'm still twisted round looking back at my brother, and inside my head I'm still trying really hard to adjust to the fact that I'm out. It's happened and here I am, in a car sitting next to Bartosz. I still feel uneasy. I don't trust my good fortune. It's ok, I tell myself. It's all fine. Ruth and Ed will have noticed my absence by now, but who cares? I'm heading towards the motorway and soon I'll be miles away, in a place they know nothing about.

Bartosz is still chuckling, and I notice for the first time that he's dressed for work and looking really suave in a charcoal grey suit and silver tie. It's mad because he's a stranger more or less, but I don't think I've ever felt as safe as I do now, sitting next to him in this speeding vehicle. He turns the music down a bit and behind us in the rear view mirror I watch as G slowly creeps forward between the two walls at the exit to the car park. The plan must be for us to drive to their house in convoy, I guess. Unless G is heading back to work, now he knows I'm safely out. I start wondering what their house is like and how long it'll take to get there. I turn in my seat so I'm looking behind me again, and I notice another car approaching the church from the opposite direction. It moves a bit closer and I realise it's Warren's Volvo. They're returning early from their day out, something they hardly ever do. If Bartosz and G hadn't arrived when they did I'd never have got away, and if I *had* decided to make a run for it on my own, I wouldn't even have got round the corner before they spotted me.

As I'm thinking this and congratulating myself on my good fortune, time suddenly slows down. Warren's car indicates left to turn into the church car park, and G moves further out, thinking he's ok to go. But instead of stopping until G exits, the Volvo suddenly leaps forward at high speed. I'm too far away to see who the driver is, but whoever it is, they must have slammed their foot on the gas until it hit the floor. The vehicle broadsides my brother's VW and of course, my brother, who, because of where he's sitting, takes the maximum impact. The bang is enormous and the VW is shoved over to one side against the wall of the exit, half hidden and half crushed by the bonnet of the other car.

Bartosz slams on his brakes and pulls up at the side of the road, then jumps out and rushes back to the car park exit. I follow. As he runs he dials 999 on his mobile. Ed and Ruth must have heard the impact because they are running towards the crash site from the church. Before the ambulances and police cars arrive, a seemingly endless gulf of time passes, during which Bartosz and I try to edge our way along the narrow gap between the wall and the smashed window on the passenger's side of G's car. Bartosz manages to wrench the door open just enough to reach inside. He grabs G's arm and starts pulling at it, as though he thinks he's going to be able to get the rest of G through the narrow space. I have to wrestle with him and shout at him to get him to stop and wait until the emergency services arrive. Eventually, he hears me, comes back to himself a little and steps away. He leans forward and rests his elbows on his knees.

I stare through the broken window at my brother lying there as though someone's pushed him over sideways. He's covered in shards of glass which have cut his scrubs into rags and pierced his skin in several places. Blood seeps from a gash on his head, through his hair, and starts to turn his face and neck red. But head wounds are often worse than they look, aren't they? They bleed a lot but they're not necessarily serious. I think I read that somewhere. His eyes are closed and I'm horrified at how small and fragile he looks. I want to pick him up and shake him.

Why are you asleep? I ask him silently. *You can't sleep here.*

17. Gawain

I run in circles round the farmyard in my navy blue wellies, and I chase hens and splash in puddles. Sometimes, I hold hands with one of the big boys and we go for a walk along the lane, where the sky goes on forever. Down the hill, across the fields, I can see a wide stretch of brown water straddled by a big bridge that seems to hang above it on long strings.

Nanny Flora says I'm the best thing since sliced bread. She loves me. Everybody loves me. The black and white sheep dog with its one blue and one brown eye grins and barks at me, its tongue lolling out between its teeth, and the two horses with their gleaming conker coloured coats toss their heads at me from their stable doors. Nanny Flora puts on her raincoat and headscarf, and she sweeps the yard, feeds the hens and mucks out the horses. Every so often she stops to make sure I'm not getting into trouble, and she tries to answer all my questions, even though I gabble them at her in an endless stream of baby words that make sense to me but not always to her. When they return from the fields for dinner or tea, one or other of the big boys might lift me up and carry me around on his shoulders making me laugh and kick my feet so much he tells me to stop or I'll fall off. Sometimes one of them puts me in the driving seat of the tractor and lets me turn the steering wheel.

On warm, dry days, the old man drags out one of the kitchen chairs and sits in the sunny corner by the sunflowers that are meant to face the yard, but stare through the window into the kitchen instead. He's called Pop, but he doesn't make noises like the ones that happen when you pour milk onto Rice Krispies. He sits there all day sometimes, and Mummy or Nanny Flora brings him cups of tea. Often he won't come in for his lunch, so they have to fetch that as well, in a plastic bowl, in case he drops it. He laughs when he sees me, and sometimes, when I whizz past him, he reaches out to try and stop me. I let him, and he lifts me up in the air, kisses me on each cheek and calls me names I don't understand. I giggle and Nanny Flora looks round and tells him to put me down before he drops me.

Sometimes, though, he cries, making great braying noises, like the donkeys in the paddock. The first time I hear him do this, I cry, too. Nanny says he's sad because he's not allowed to go roaming anymore. I understand that, because I like wandering too, and I never get far before someone comes and lifts me off my feet and takes me back to where they want me to be. So the next time he cries, instead of joining in I bring him little gifts to cheer him up: a pigeon's feather, a stone with a pink pattern on it or an empty beer bottle that turns the world browny-gold when you look through it.

My red plastic raincoat keeps me dry when the sunshine suddenly gives way to showers. Everyone shouts at me to come inside, but I run and hide in the barn with the rusty little bantams. They peck at my boots and I tell them off as I look for eggs among the hay bales. If I find any, I usually end up crushing them in my hands by mistake, then I wail because I don't like the feel of the gloop running between my fingers. Sometimes I climb the ladder to the ledge at the top of the barn and one of the big boys has to rush up after me and fetch me, because sooner or later I'll try to clamber down again, lose my footing and tumble to the bottom. It's a long way down and I'll break my neck, they say. The other thing I do when nobody's looking is race across the yard and round the corner of the house to the sheep field. If I'm quick, I can climb through the gap in the gate and drop down before they catch me. Then I try to dash as fast as I can across the cropped grass, crushing droppings that look like currants under my boots. I want to reach the hedge at the bottom and the wood behind it, but they always catch up with me before I can get there, and the sheep run away.

On days when the rain is set in and there's no chance it will give way to sunshine any time soon, I do my running inside, in and out of the kitchen and the living room, under tables and chairs, round the back of the sofa and best of all, up the stairs. I love stairs and I have to climb up them every time I see them. Sometimes I only get half way before Mummy or Nanny Flora stops me. But other times, I manage to get right to the top and I dash in and out of all the bedrooms, where I empty drawers and run my hands across the tops of bedside cabinets and dressing tables, sweeping ear rings, bottles of pills and abandoned glasses of water onto the floor. When Nanny Flora finds me she picks me up, carries me downstairs and says I'm a little scamp. She sits me on her knee at the kitchen table and I look up at her crinkly powdered face, gaze into her blue eyes and try to tell her she's my best person in the whole wide world. But it comes out all wrong, so I content myself with picking up almost empty tea cups and tipping them over so the dregs make beautiful little brown puddles for her on the pine surface.

If, on the other hand, Mummy is the one who finds me upstairs, she slaps me so hard she makes red handprints on my legs, and tells me I'm a pain in the arse. But sometimes she sits me on her knee, too, and she sings to me and strokes my hair, trying to make the sticky-uppy bit go flat. I quite like it at first, but soon I need to be on my way again, so I stretch my legs out and make them go hard, like the wooden skittles in the barn, and I arch my back so she has no choice but to let me slide onto the floor. Then I'm off, up the stairs again or opening drawers in the kitchen dresser, creating steps I can climb to reach the plates at the top.

All this fades away from time to time. Then I don't know where I am. I get the feeling I might have been a grown up once, but there was a big bang and I fell backwards into the past and became merged with a tiny boy who is in a magical place having the time of his life. My mind is like a children's colouring book. The line drawings are the experiences of the little boy, but the person who was once a man is colouring them in and adding nuance, even though he has no idea whether this place and these people are real or figments of his imagination. Neither version of me cares whether any of it is real or not, though. I'm happy here and I'm not going back to being an adult ever again, even if all this is only happening inside my head. When I get tired of all the hectic life of a toddler, I sink down into a tranquil, blue-green space at the bottom of a deep well, and I hibernate for a while. Unfortunately though, a kind of mental buoyancy keeps kicking in, and I drift up towards the surface. On the way up, bad memories lurk, and I'm forced to re-live events I'd rather forget, because they always lead to the day everything comes undone.

On the morning of that day, as soon as breakfast is over, Nanny Flora bundles Pop into the land rover and drives off down the track with him. He has to go to somewhere called the Stroke Clinic, which is at the hospital that looks like a big slab. You can see it from the farm. I'm not allowed to go with them, so they leave me with Mummy. I cry when Nanny Flora leaves, because, like I say, she's my best person and I like to know she's around somewhere, even if I wander off for a bit. Mummy drags me down from the kitchen window and carries me into the living room. She settles me on the floor in front of the TV and puts on a Rosie and Jim video. Then she sits in an armchair, lights a cigarette and opens a magazine. I stay kneeling in front of the screen until the opening music has finished and the man with the beard and glasses has said where they're all going and what they're going to do. They're planning to have a barbecue, but I don't know what that is. Anyway, I have to be off, so I get up and run over to the door. Mummy's shut it, so I holler and knock on it until she comes and picks me up, pinches me on the arm and places me in front of the TV again.

This time, I try really hard and I manage to sit still until the narrow boat has cruised all the way through a big, grey city. But by then I'm like fizzy lemonade inside a bottle that's been shaken up, so I run to the door again. I bang on it, thinking that maybe one of the big boys will hear me and let me out. But Mummy comes and picks me up again. I start whining, and she shakes me a bit. The she drops me onto the sofa next to her and tells me to pipe down because the racket I'm making goes right through her. She tries to hold me in place with one hand as she turns the pages of her magazine with the other, but I turn myself into a snake and I writhe and slither underneath her arm until I manage to slip away and run to the door again. I want to reach the handle, but I can't, so I try to make the door open by leaning on it. Mummy walks up behind me and opens the door. I fall through it onto the hall carpet, and she calls me a little bastard and shouts at me to bugger off if I can't do as I'm told. Then she goes back into the living room and shuts the door behind her.

Nobody else is around, and I don't know what to do with this unexpected freedom. I run into the kitchen and open all the cupboard doors, and I pull out tablecloths, napkins and oven gloves. Then I locate the crockery and throw dinner plates, bowls and serving dishes onto the stone floor, where some of them crack or smash into several pieces. The racket fills me with joy, and I decide to do the same with the best china, so I pull out the drawers of the dresser and I scramble up, right to the top. I've never managed to get as high as this before. When I reach the top, I wait for a while, giving someone, anyone, the chance to come and stop me, but nobody does, so I pick up the little duck-egg-blue cups and fling them down one by one. They break with an almost musical tinkling sound. I try to say smithereens, a word I've picked up somewhere, but it comes out wrong as usual. Frustrated with my inability to express myself, I reach for the big teapot, the one decorated with pictures of orange birds with long floaty tales. They always bring out on Sunday afternoons when everyone is sitting around the table. I need both hands to pick it up and I nearly drop it. But I'm super careful and in the end I manage to hold it over the edge of the dresser before I let go. As it falls in a perfect, vertical descent I clap my hands, and Mummy comes into the kitchen and screams. She'll murder me, she says, as she pulls me down from the dresser, drags me across the floor by my arm and throws me into the cupboard under the stairs.

The darkness in there fills my eyes, so I revert to my emergency default setting and scream my head off. But eventually, I notice some light creeping through narrow cracks in the door. This is a big space for a small boy and I've never been allowed in it before, so I start crawling about, exploring. I open umbrellas and empty shopping bags and I scrutinise a basket full of acorns and a collection of tins with lids I can't open, but which make rattling noises when you shake them. Next, I try on an old pair of slippers and walk up and down in them. After that, I start to feel hungry. I pick up the basket of acorns and suddenly think about Amanda, because I remember her collecting them one day when she was dropped off here for a visit. There were so many she ended up filling two baskets. She took one of them home with her, but left the other here for me. I pop one in my mouth and try to chew it, but it's hard. I suck it for a bit, but it doesn't get soft like Nanny Flora's toffees, so I spit it out. I cough and splutter, then everything stops.

Marco opens the door and lifts me up. I'm crying, but not much sound comes out, because my mouth is full of acorns. I mean, really full. They're crammed into all the available spaces, halfway up my nose down my throat, gagging me and threatening to block the entrance to my windpipe. Some of them are still sitting in the little cups and twigs that attached them to the tree field and the twigs are sticking into the insides of my cheeks and my gums, making my mouth hurt. My eyes water and snot pours out of my nose.

Marco carries me into the kitchen and lays me flat on the table. I try to get up, but he places a hand on my chest to hold me down, and he pokes all the acorns out with the fingers of his other hand, leaving an oily taste and a scratchy feeling in my mouth. When he lifts me onto the floor, I fasten my arms limpet-like around the beige nylon legs of Nanny Flora, who has just come through the kitchen door.

Pop is back too and is bending down and ruffling my hair. He keeps repeating the same thing over and over again. I know it's about me and about Mummy, but I don't understand all of it. Marco answers him using his other set of words, the ones that are curly at the edges, and then he turns to Nanny Flora and says he hopes I haven't swallowed any of the acorns. Mummy is nowhere to be seen and everyone keeps treading on bits of broken crockery, making it scrape against the floor tiles.

Marco picks me up and carries me out to the yard. A big, silver car is sitting there. He bundles me in and straps me down, next to Amanda, who is in her school uniform. She looks really grown up, apart from her messy pigtails, and she frowns at me, which makes me think of Heidi, the farm cat. I realise what's going on, and I scream and scream in my loudest voice, because of the sheep and the hens and the barn and Marco and the other big boys and Nanny Flora and Pop, but they all kiss me and say goodbye in happy voices, as though I'm going somewhere nice, just for a few hours.

Dad says *hello* in a jolly way, but his voice is loud and scary and the back of his neck is thick and pink and covered with gingery bristles. As he pulls away, my sister asks me what I've done *this time* and rolls her eyes. Then she tells me that if I don't stop screaming, I'll turn blue and my eyes will pop out. One of the boys, not Marco this time, holds the gate open for us and salutes grimly as we leave the yard. I look back and see Mummy staring at us from an upstairs window. The window's open and she's blowing cigarette smoke out of it, but she doesn't smile and she doesn't wave.

I try very hard to stay at the bottom of my deep, dark blue pool. But sometimes I see people up there at the surface, leaning over and looking in. I don't know who they are, but they want me to swim up to them and when I refuse, they do all they can to haul me up using chains of meaningless, whispered words. I make a huge effort not to listen, but sometimes they prize me out of the crack I'm hiding in and I drift upwards. Then I hang, like a mosquito larva, mostly submerged, but dangerously close to the surface. One of the people on the other side goes on at me for hours in a quiet voice with the sibilance of a snake. He wants to pull me out of the water completely, so he can dislocate his jaw, open his mouth wide and swallow me whole. For a while, I don't mind it too much, but then it becomes tiresome and I curl myself into a ball so I can sink down again, away from his murmurings. It takes a lot of effort to get back down, though. An unwelcome buoyancy always tries to pushes me in the opposite direction, until I grow desperate and think the sheep field and the white farmhouse will never come into view again.

Another time there's a soft, powdery fragrance and a female voice which forces me upwards because I need to say something important. It's about the fact that I'm a fish called a dory and I'm connected to a wizard, partly by name, sort of, and by something else I can't pin down. I quickly morph into a grown-up so I can make a proper statement about all this, and the voice that's pulled me out sounds surprised. I can't understand what she's saying. All I know is that she isn't Nanny Flora and she's not amused. By the time she's stopped speaking, I'm flapping horribly in the mud on the bank of the pool. I nearly suffocate, but I manage to cut myself loose just in time and I drift blissfully down again, deeper and deeper.

18. Jacob

Warren scrambles out through one of the rear doors of his car, more or less intact, and hugs himself as he walks slowly over to Ruth and Ed. He wasn't driving, then. The bonnet of the Volvo is crumpled against the driver's side of G's car. I try to peer through the windscreen, which is smashed into a mosaic of tiny fragments, hanging in place like a spider's web, rendering everything else invisible. I'd like to punch my fist through it and drag its occupants out by their throats. Particularly the driver.

When the emergency services arrive, Bartosz and I back away so they can access G. We position ourselves as close as we can to G's car, whereas Ruth, Ed and Warren stand over on the other side, nearer to the Volvo. Ruth and Ed both look across at me, trying to catch my eye, but I do my best to ignore them. Then, Ed carefully picks his way around the carnage and strides towards me, cocky as anything. He puts his hands on my shoulders, claiming me, and starts to escort me away from Bartosz, back to their side of the scenario. He doesn't realise I was in Bartosz's car before this happened. He thinks I came out of the church when I heard the crash and that I still belong with him and the others. Maybe he's right. Now this has happened to G, Bartosz won't have the headspace to think about me.

Ed starts to manoeuvre me towards the spot where Warren and Ruth are standing, and I let him. But Bartosz jumps forward, wrenches Ed's hands off me and punches him in the face so hard he falls to the ground. Then he grips my arm, drags me back to where I was before and positions me almost behind him, where nobody can get at me, he says. He doesn't let go of my arm until we go back into his car, not once. Ed stays flat on his back on the tarmac for ages, pretending to be hurt and waiting for someone to notice. I mentally urge the stupid fucker to get up before the police see him, but they don't even glance in his direction. Warren and Ruth don't notice him lying there either, and eventually, he scrambles to his feet, rubs his face and backs away from us as quickly as he can. From that point on, whenever I look over at him, which isn't very often, he's scowling at Bartosz. In other circumstances, it would be funny.

The paramedics take an age to extract G from his vehicle, but in the end they get him onto a stretcher and speed off with him in one of the ambulances. He looks like a broken doll, but the expression on his face is calm and untroubled, despite the blood, as though he thinks he's on his way to a better place. I ask if I can go with him in the ambulance. I might have issues with my brother and perhaps I only decided to leave New Sunrise because of Bartosz, but if these are going to be G's last few minutes on this earth, I need to spend them by his side. They won't let me anywhere near, though, and as they drive off, siren blaring, it occurs to me with a sick and sinking feeling that he's being taken back to his own workplace. If his colleagues have been wondering where he's got to and why he hasn't come back from his lunch break, they'll soon find out.

One of police officers asks if I saw what happened. I try my best to tell him, but it comes out all wrong and I end up bent over, hyperventilating, so he pats me on the shoulder and says later will be fine. He notices the bruising on my face. He must think I was involved in the accident, because he fetches a paramedic guy who scans my eyes with a torch and puts one of those metallic thermal covers around my shoulders. I tell him to piss off. I'm in shock, he says. I *really must* go and get myself checked out when we arrive at the hospital. Bartosz and I make our way there in his car. I ask him if he's ok to drive. He gives me a single, grim nod. I can't tell if he's in a similar state to me, but is pretending not to be or if he's better able to can cope with situations like this because of his military training or simply because he's tougher than me.

I throw off the blanket they've given me and chuck it in the back of the car. No way am I going to get myself admitted to A&E when we arrive the hospital. I'm not in shock, I'm just shocked. Who wouldn't be? I keep thinking about the last time I was at this hospital. I didn't want to speak to my brother and I wouldn't even look at him when he said goodbye. And now he's being rushed into A & E because he came to rescue me. I clasp my hands together to stop them trembling and I hold myself rigid as Bartosz bangs the steering wheel and cries out in frustration. Getting to the hospital and finding a parking space turns into a long, painfully drawn out nightmare from which there seems to be no end. We have to crawl through the traffic and queue before we even reach the car park, and then we're forced to drive around for ages between the two levels, waiting for a space to become available. Eventually, Bartosz manages to manoeuvre the Audi into a narrow rectangle partially blocked by a concrete pillar.

They escort us to the relatives' room. I expect to see Ruth, Warren and Ed inside, and I brace myself. I didn't notice them leaving the scene of the accident. They would need to call a cab, seeing as Ed's car is in the car park, the Volvo has been totalled and the exit is blocked by G's VW. But the room is empty, apart from several squishy chairs arranged around a long, low table with an ominous box of tissues on it. The walls are painted a soft orangey colour, coral or something, and there are couple of pictures of sailing ships drifting peacefully on a calm sea, one in bright sunshine and one in moonlight. I wonder whose idea it was to add these touches. Do they think it helps to look at ships when you're waiting to hear if your brother or your boyfriend is alive or dead?

Bartosz and I sit down next to each other. Almost immediately, the door opens again and Amanda walks in. My sister is much smaller than I expected her to be, and her hair is longer. Her face is the same though. Fierce and cat-like. I bet she's beyond angry with me for getting G into this situation. I stand up and boggle at her like a complete cretin whilst wondering if I should embrace her. Bartosz tries to pull up a chair for her opposite ours, but they're impossible to shift, so the three of us end up sitting in a row, like a set of dummies on one side of the table, Amanda and Bartosz at each end, with me in the middle. I decide to have a go at to explaining what happened, but I make an incoherent mess of it again. She scrutinises me carefully.

'He's tougher than he looks,' she says, when my ramblings fade away to nothing.

She sounds calm, but she's a rubbish liar, I'd forgotten that about her. What she really wants to say is *what the hell has he got himself into this time*? I'd forgotten that too, the tone in her voice, when G ends up in yet another scrape. She sounded exactly the same on the day G and I had our final, terrible argument. The day when everything between us shattered into a thousand pieces.

Bartosz watches us for a bit. Then he rests his elbows on the table and puts his head in his hands. This drives me wild. I want to shake him and scream at him, and tell him not to write G off so easily. He's still with us until someone tells us he isn't. And if he does turn out to be dead, please don't deny me a final few minutes of thinking he's still here. Then I feel sorry for him, and I wonder whether I should try and comfort him in some way, perhaps by patting his shoulder with my hand. But I can't touch him anymore than I can wrap my arms around my sister. I look at her again. She looks back at me but doesn't say anything.

When Bryan, the consultant who took over from G the day I came into A & E, walks in, I don't know whether minutes or several hours have passed. Amanda grabs my hand under the table. Bryan recognises me and says my name, and I somehow manage to cobble together the words required to introduce him to Amanda and Bartosz. I describe Bartosz as G's friend, but Bartosz corrects me. *Partner*, he says. Bryan shakes hands with each us in turn and sits down so he's facing us all. He looks drained and almost as shocked as we are. He sinks down into one of the excessively soft chairs opposite until his knees are almost level with his head.

'These bloody chairs,' he says, and he has to rectify the situation by pulling himself up into a standing position again.

Amanda and I watch him warily as we try to prepare ourselves for whatever he's about to say, but Bartosz keeps his gaze fixed on the table.

'We've tried to get him to open his eyes and talk to us, but he's having none of it, which isn't great. He's got some damage to his right shoulder and his ribs, and a lot of cuts and bruises, and he's lost some blood. But we're most concerned about the blow to his temple. We've done a CT scan and people from the neurology team has had a careful look at it. There's quite a bit of swelling and he's about to be taken up to surgery so they can assess the extent of the damage properly and do what they can to repair it. Then, all being well, he'll go to ICU.'

He stops and looks at each of us in turn. 'I'm not going to lie. They're not sure he'll get through the surgery and even if he does, it'll still be touch and go.'

I think that's what he says, anyway. It couldn't be much worse, apart from if G was already dead. I cling to the one positive fact. My brother is still alive, at least for now. I get all emotional inside my head, but I swallow a lot and don't let it show. A brief technical interchange full of medical jargon follows between Amanda and Bryan, but I can't understand any of it. Bartosz still has his head in his hands. He's really starting to annoy me now. I shake his arm and ask him if he heard what Bryan said. He nods.

'Can we see him?' I ask.

'Sure, in a minute. But I need to tell you about the other car.'

'Oh, right.'

I'd forgotten about the Volvo.

'Warren Brookes is your stepfather?"

I nod.

'He's ok. He's in minors at the moment. Just cuts and bruises. But your mother and Godwin Brookes were in the front. Godwin was killed outright and your mother's in a critical condition, I'm afraid. She suffered a serious head injury like Gawain and she also has a fractured pelvis, crushed ribs and a pneumothorax. Do you know what that is?'

It sounds like something to do with GCSE Biology and insects.

'I'll explain it to him,' Amanda says.

But when she tries, I tell her not to bother because I can't take it in, and in any case, worrying about Mum is beyond me. I've only got enough mental energy to try and keep one person alive with wishful thinking, and that person has to be G.

A nurse comes and escorts us to his cubicle. Loads of medical staff are in there, surrounding him, bustling about, adjusting machines they've wired him up to. None of us really knows what to do at first. They make us all stand on one side of the bed and they seem to recede into the background, apart from one nurse on the other side, who is delicately plucking bits of glass out of his skin. G still looks as though he's asleep and would wake up if one of us asked him to. His brow is slightly creased as though he's puzzled or worried about where he is and what's going on. I wish there was some way of telling him we're all here, that he's not alone. But he is alone, really. Or at least, he's not with us. He's in some other place, way out of reach.

Bartosz leans forward, brushes G's hair back from his forehead and then gets told off by one of the nurses for touching him. Chastened, he pulls his hand away quickly and holds it with his other hand as though it's the only way he can stop himself doing it again. As for me, I don't know what gesture I should make, or even if I want to make any gesture at all. In the end, I decide I need to touch him too, despite the reprimand meted out to Bartosz. When the nurse isn't looking, I let two of my fingers hover above G's upper arm and graze them against his skin. I'm surprised at how warm and alive he feels. But then he always used to radiate heat. When I was little I often had to squirm away from him because he made me feel like I was going to boil over. Now I'm suddenly filled with an irrational joy at this warmth and the familiar feel of his flesh under my hand. He might be in a coma. He might die soon. And I might hate him. But he feels the same as he always used to. And I know this sounds totally insane, but it's amazing to see him again, even under these circumstances.

The porter turns up and wheels his bed and his monitoring equipment into a big lift. A couple of the medical staff accompany him, and we follow them all up to another floor, along an echoing and shiny corridor, to the doors of the operating theatre. We stand and watch as the swing doors open and then close on him. This isn't a good moment. We look at the doors as though we think we'll be able to see through them if we stare hard enough. Then Bartosz turns and starts to walk down the corridor, and Amanda and I follow him, kind of blindly, because we don't know what else to do. He stops when he reaches a recess full of plastic chairs a few metres away and drops into one of them. Amanda and I do likewise. As soon as we're all sitting down, Bartosz gets up again, walks over to the opposite wall of the recess and stares at it with his back to us. Then Amanda jumps as though she's suddenly woken up from a deep sleep.

'I need to ring Aunty Susan.'

She starts tapping at her phone, but there's no signal, so she disappears through the swing doors that lead to the stairs.

'I should phone a few people, too,' Bartosz says, vaguely to the wall, after she's gone. 'I need to cancel my afternoon appointments and talk to my mum.' His voice breaks slightly when he mentions his mum.

'OK. See you in a bit,' I say.

He turns to face me. 'I'm not leaving you here on your own. He'd never forgive me if something happened to you *now*.'

The way he says *now* almost kills me. I want to apologise to him for getting us all into this situation, and I'd like to beg for his forgiveness, or at least ask him if he's angry with me. But it's not about me, it's about my brother and the gaping hole that will be left behind if the worst happens. I clench my fists and focus on the window in the wall opposite, to stop myself shaking. The window is ancient looking, opaque and surrounded by a rusty metal frame, very much like the one in the toilet in the little hall at the back of the church, where I checked my phone less than two hours ago, when G was ok. As my eyes follow the patterns on the glass, picking out the shapes of a small dog and a Christmas pudding with a sprig of holly sticking out of the top, I try my absolute hardest not to think about my brother, about how devastated Bartosz is and the fact all this has happened because of me. And how it would be so much easier to deal with if I hated G as much as I thought I did.

'He used to have much longer hair,' I say.

'I know. I've seen photographs,' Bartosz says.

Then he sits down next to me and all this stuff pours out of him, about taking G to his house for the first time and how it got serious between them really quickly. I tell him what G used to be like at school, what a performer he was and how popular, and that sometimes he got carried away and ended up going completely over the top. Bartosz says he's not like that at all now, he comes across as shy and reluctant until you get to know him, even a bit timid. I don't know what to make of that. Then we go on to discuss some of my brother's other foibles, his ridiculous eating habits, his almost pathological untidiness and the way he suddenly crashes out and falls asleep with no warning, wherever he is. We more or less manage to keep up the pretence that these things drive us insane, when really we'd both give anything to be irritated by any one of them again.

When Amanda returns, Bartosz disappears to make his calls. He's not away for long and when he gets back his cheeks are stained with tears that he doesn't even try to wipe away. I bet his mum was really sympathetic and kind, and made him cry even more than he was doing already. I've heard this can happen.

After an age, the surgeon comes out. He tells us they've removed a large clot, fixed a damaged blood vessel inside his skull and done various other things that make no sense to me. But the swelling is still considerable and the outcome remains uncertain. We catch a brief glimpse of him as he's wheeled to ICU. G is being kept sedated to minimise risk of more damage to his brain as the bruising settles down, and they've inserted a little tube into his skull to monitor his intracranial pressure or something.

We set up a makeshift camp on a row of chairs in the corridor outside ICU, and take it in turns to go in and see him. Bartosz goes first, then Amanda, then me.

When it's my turn, I have a kind of panic attack. I tell them I can't face it and I try to glue myself to my chair and plant the soles of my trainers firmly onto the floor. Bartosz says it isn't so bad. You just have to try and ignore the equipment. I shake my head. My brother needs me, he says. I can't *not* go in. He goes on and on. His voice is quiet and kindly, but insistent at the same time, and he makes it clear that if I don't get my sorry arse in there, he'll drag me through the door himself. So I wrench myself away from the safety zone I've established around my small, plastic chair and I walk into ICU. The area around his bed is brightly lit and noisy, more like a supermarket or a railway station than a place full of sick people who need to rest. It seems harsh and cruel and I want to cover his eyes with my hand. But he doesn't care. He's perfectly still, wired and tubed up all over the place, connected to various bits of kit and bags of fluids on stands, surrounded by beeping machines. You can't see all of his face because an endotracheal tube has been inserted into his mouth to help with his breathing, not because he can't breathe on his own necessarily, they're keen to tell us, but because he's unconscious, so he can't swallow and clear fluids away from his throat. More than anything, I hate the sight of the canula they've stuck in his hand and I wish I could do that part of it for him, let them slide the needle into my vein instead of his.

A thin blanket covers his body up to the level of his armpits. His narrow shoulders look cold, but when I lay my palm flat on one of them his skin feels as warm as it did before. A large, square portion of his hair has been shaved off and I can see two narrow, parallel scars on the side of his head, slightly raised and lighter than the rest of his skin. They look old. They can't have happened today. Almost idly, I wonder what caused them. Then I realise. Two wide swings of tennis racquet and two sweeping backhand strokes in quick succession. I remember his gasp after the first blow and my equally sharp intake of breath as I took aim to administer the second. And I remember how his face was wet with tears as he just stood there and told me to do it as many times as I wanted to, sacrificing himself but in doing so, taking centre stage as usual, or so I thought at the time. That made me even angrier. If Amanda hadn't rushed in and wrenched the racquet out of my hands, I'd have kept on hitting him with it. For how long, I don't know. Until he fell to the ground? Until he was unconscious or even dead? She hauled me away to her bedroom, pushed me onto her bed and sat on me until I'd calmed down.

I didn't calm down, not really. But I pretended to, and then I made this mental swerve that meant I stopped living in the same world as him. I terminated the contract that existed between us because it was too painful for me to be anywhere near him. And a few days later, I went out to America for the first time. The trip had already been planned, ages ago, of course, but the timing was perfect. He couldn't reach me out there, and I told myself South Carolina was a safe place for me, because he wasn't in it.

Those scars have been there for more than eight years and now he's in limbo, his body intubated, his breathing controlled and his mind either elsewhere or completely destroyed. Because of me. If I said any of this to Bartosz or Amanda, or even G if that was possible, I know they'd tell me to shut up and not to be so stupid, and that the blame lies with whoever was driving the Volvo.

But even if they're right, what if those two blows did some permanent damage and now that his head is injured again, what if they're the single factor that, all other things being equal, pushes him in the direction of death, when otherwise he might have survived?

19. Jacob

For the first twenty-four hours, none of us leaves the hospital. We hang out in the dreary camp we've made for ourselves, or we sit in the café downstairs, hugging cups of tea or coffee. I find it difficult to get any kind of fluid past the lump in my throat, but I'm cold all the time, as though some vital force inside me has been switched off and I need an external heat source to make myself function, so I appreciate the warmth it provides.

The nurses tell us take it in turns to sit by his bed and talk to him. It will stop him feeling lost and forgotten inside his own head, they say, and it might help him to regain consciousness. I don't believe them. I don't know what the others do when they're in there with him, but when it's my turn I just sit there in silence. One time, a nurse called Beth, comes up and rests her hand on my shoulder. I know she's trying to be kind, but the pressure of her hand through my sweatshirt is as painful as a scouring pad scraped over a patch of raw skin. It makes me scurry off to the toilets, where I sit for ages with the door locked. I watch my knees shake and I stare down at the shiny, blue floor tiles until Bartosz tracks me down and hammers on the door.

'Don't go off on your own,' he says when I come out.

He thinks Warren and Ed might be around somewhere. They're bound to visit my mother and they could easily come looking for me. I'm amazed he cares what happens to me now. But I guess he's thinking about G. Keeping me away from their grasp is what my brother would have wanted. Does want.

The next day, G's condition settles down a bit. They tell us he's no longer in any immediate danger, but he's still very sick and may only be stable because the meds and the machines are keeping his vital functions going. I watch him for a while and wonder if I can detect any signs of change his appearance, but apart from the dark stubble creeping across his jaw and the fuzz in the areas where they shaved his hair off, he looks exactly the same.

Amanda drives me to the police station so they can take a statement from me. The desk sergeant escorts me into a bleak little room and tells me to sit at a desk, as though I'm a suspect. Two police persons or whatever you call them come in and introduce themselves. PC Naylor is in uniform and not much older than me, but DS Warwick, a woman in plain clothes, has the look of someone who's been around the block more than once and whilst travelling around said block has seen it all several times. She reminds me of a chemistry teacher who hated me because test tubes and molecules were never my thing, and she looks as though she's going to tell me off for answering back as soon as I open my mouth. I wasn't planning to say much anyway, and the fact that she has a face like a slapped-arse makes me decide that I'll describe what happened outside the church and leave it at that.

Trouble is, I'm sleep-deprived, probably still in shock, and going cold turkey due to withdrawal from the drugs in a big way, so when they ask why Bartosz and G had come to rescue me, I can't summon the brainpower to filter my response and I end up telling them everything. It all splurges out of my mouth in a non-linear jumble, and by the time I've finished, I've described the church set up, their beliefs, the people involved and what they did to me. They both keep interrupting me with questions and they record it all. In the end, I think they manage to transform my wittering into a narrative that more or less adds up. It takes a while to reach that point, though, and when I describe the whipping ritual, I'm so exasperated by the mulish disbelief on both their faces that I take my top off and turn my back to them so they can see for themselves. This leads to an outbreak of head-scratching embarrassment and mumbled phone calls. Eventually DS Warwick leaves the room and PC Naylor sits there, gawping at me with his mouth open. I find this bloody rude and it pisses me off, but I'm too wiped out to object, so I lean back in my chair, stretch my legs out and close my eyes.

DS Warwick returns after a while and bustles me along a hallway and into small space that smells of disinfectant and contains a couch covered in oversized rectangles of tissue paper. Someone takes photographs of my back and then after a long wait, during which I sit on the couch and fidget until the tissue paper gets all crumpled, a bullet headed man marches in and says he's a doctor, but in a tone that implies he's not just a medic but is actually God's gift, both to his profession and the world. He waves his stethoscope in my general direction like an offensive weapon and tells me to remove the rest of my clothes. But I'm done with blind obedience now, so I just sit on the side of the couch and grit my teeth to stop them chattering. When he realises I'm not going to comply, he starts bandying around words like *abuse* in a voice full of unasked questions that sound more like accusations and talks pompously about forensic medical examinations and taking samples for use as evidence. I ask him what kind of samples he has in mind, but before he answers I realise exactly what kind and I shake my head, jump down from the couch and quickly reverse out of the door. Images of what they think Ed and the others might have subjected me to flood my mind and I almost laugh.

PC Naylor is waiting for me in the interrogation room. I'm not obliged to subject myself to this medical assessment if I don't want to, she says flatly, making it clear she's not bothered either way. I confirm that I won't be, and we carry on with the next part of the interview.

'You say this Godwin was driving?'

'He must have been. I wasn't the only one that saw Warren crawl out from the back, so it definitely wasn't him.'

'Did your mother not drive?'

'Not really. She hates driving.'

He leans forward and looks at me and then down at the desk several times and inflates his cheeks as though he's blowing up a balloon. I bet he's never had to deal with anything as screwed up as this before.

'What?' I ask eventually.

The balloon deflates. 'It's just that she was in the driving seat.'

"My mother?"

I realise this is possible. She could have been driving. Particularly if Godwin and Warren were more pissed than usual when they arrived at the station to pick her up. It wouldn't have been the first time.

'She could be charged with attempted murder.'

"My brother's not going to die."

'Oh no. Right. Of course not. Sorry.'

'Could it have been an accident?'

'Putting your food down on the gas and racing all the way down the road like that?'

'Maybe she thought he was a burglar.'

'We wondered about that, so we went and had a look. We got someone to sit down the road in one of our cars at the point where we think she started accelerating, and someone else sat in a car parked in the exit to the car park, where your brother was. Your mother would definitely have been able to tell it was him. Unless she was really short sighted, in which case she shouldn't have been driving without glasses.'

'She wasn't short sighted.'

'I'm sorry, mate.'

I shrug. It makes a sick kind of sense. The Volvo didn't speed forward like that on its own, and it's not really the sort of thing Godwin would do. Of course it was Mum. She tried to kill my brother, her son, because just at that moment, in her crazy world, it seemed the right thing to do. Because she knew he would take me away from her, because she was afraid of being left alone with Warren and the rest of them or because she's insane, psychotic, manic, loco, gaga, mental, a nut job, a nasty piece of work? Maybe all three. I go through all the predictable emotions, firstly disbelief, followed by denial, shock and then anger. But these feelings race through my head so quickly they hardly touch the sides, and here I am, already slamming into the final stop, complete acceptance, laced with disgust.

Amanda stands up when I emerge. She looks worried. More worried than I can handle right now.

'You were ages,' she says.

I know I should tell her what PC Naylor's just said about mum being the driver, but I don't. I need to process it again myself before I discuss it with anyone else, and in any case, G should probably be the first to know.

'They thought I'd been abused,' I tell her instead.

'You have been abused.'

'I mean, the other kind. They wanted to take loads of samples and make me leave my clothes behind.'

I realise I'm speaking in a shocked whisper that's more like a bark and almost as loud as my normal speaking voice.

She doesn't bat an eyelid. 'Have you been sexually abused?'

'No!'

'It's not your fault if you have. You should tell them.'

'For fuck's sake.'

'And you need to get some tests done. In case…'

'I don't need any tests, thank you very much. Why do you lot always want to poke and pry? Jesus. Anyway, I wouldn't let that doctor take samples from me even I had syphilis and he was the only doctor on the planet. I'd rather do it myself. There must be a YouTube video.'

'You smell, as well,' she says as we're walking out of the station.

'As well as what?'

'Never mind.'

'All my other clothes are in the house.'

'Well the ones you're wearing now belong in the bin. Or on a bonfire.'

'Ok, I'll take them off, then, and go round naked if that's what you prefer. It's all the same to me.'

She rolls her eyes, but she whisks me off to the nearest big shopping centre and buys me loads of stuff - puffer jacket, beanie hat, scarf, jeans, T-shirts, hoodies, underwear, joggers, pjs, trainers, some really great boots and a new pair of trainers. Then she says I need toiletries as a matter of urgency, for all our sakes, and we stock up on hair gel, deodorant and shaving stuff. She lets me choose everything myself and when I'm done she steps in and pays for it. Under any other circumstances it would be awesome.

'I'll pay you back when I get a job,' I say.

'No you won't. I can't remember the last time I bought you anything. All those missed birthdays and Christmases.'

She looks as though she might start to get upset. It's possible I might too, if I'm not careful, so I don't pursue it. I just thank her gruffly and then press my lips together. We go back to her cottage. We've decided I'm going to sleep here for now. She shows me the little spare room. I rush to the window and open it so I can stare out at the misty fields on the other side of the road and take in great lungfuls of fresh, damp air. I try everything on. When I come down, showered, groomed and fragrant in my new jeans and red hoodie, my hair scrunched up with gel, she's just sitting there on the sofa in her front room, in the dark. I sit down next to her. Even though she's eight years older than me and she's a GP and scary as hell, I feel protective towards her. I want to defend her against protect her against this awful situation, tell her everything will be ok. But I can't do that. Nobody can.

*

I wake from a ten hour sleep and remember today is G's birthday. He's twenty-eight and still totally out of it. I try not to let it bother me, and I do what I usually do these days when I wake up. I grab my phone to check for messages from the hospital or from Bartosz. I don't start breathing again until I'm certain there is nothing new in my in box.

When we get to his corridor, they won't let us see him because the ward round is happening and then after that, some checks and adjustments have to be done to the tech controlling his bodily functions and monitoring his reactions. We troop downstairs and gather around the table in the café yet again with our flat whites, and we nod at each other as we agree, with no actual evidence to back it up, that the fact he's survived another night is a really good sign.

Every day Bartosz looks a little bit more like a vagrant who has ambled into the hospital in the hope someone will take pity on him and buy him a cup of tea. He smells faintly of bins and sour milk, his beard has grown wild and wayward, and his eyes dart from side to side as though he thinks people are after him. If he wasn't with us the security staff would probably to escort him to the exit. Today, he's clearly even more upset than usual, and as we sit in silence around the table, he opens and shuts his mouth twice, without saying anything. Each time he does this, his entire beard shifts upwards slightly and then goes back down again, like a shovel.

'I ordered two alpacas for his birthday,' he finally manages to say. 'I got someone in to put up fencing and a little stable round the back, behind some trees, so you can't see it from the house.'

We both stare at him. I think this might be the saddest thing I've ever heard. I will him to stop going on about it. But he doesn't.

'I managed to stop him going round to that part of the garden all week so he wouldn't see it. They were supposed to be delivered today while he was at work and I was going to fasten these big blue bows to their collars before he got home. And I got fairy lights to wrap around the fencing.'

He scratches his head and looks at my sister and then at me.

'I've cancelled them,' he says, bleakly.

I don't know how Amanda feels about this, but the thought of alpacas being cancelled is too much for me and almost sends me running off to the toilets again. The video footage that Bartosz would have taken of G being led to the back of the garden blindfold, wondering what on earth is going on and then discovering the creatures all done up in their bows, runs through my mind as clearly as if it actually happened.

'Maybe you can get them delivered when he comes out of hospital?' I suggest.

'Yeah, maybe.'

'Why don't you go home and get some sleep?' Amanda says.

'I can't. What if? When I'm not here?'

He slumps down in his seat and one of his elbows slides into his coffee up and knocks it over. The cup was nearly full and its contents spread across the table and form a miniature Niagara Falls at the other side, which drips onto Amanda's legs. I rush off to get some paper towels and grab a moment to pull myself together at the same time. When I get back, Amanda and I use this incident to convince him he's all over the place and needs to go home for a bit.

We take it in turns to sit with G, while Bartosz is gone, but he doesn't stay away for long. When he returns, he smells a good deal fresher and his beard neatly trimmed. He's brought a bag packed with essentials and after that, he turns himself into a permanent fixture at the hospital, catching short fragments of sleep stretched out on the plastic chairs outside the ward when he can and washing and changing in the visitors' toilets. We bring him portions of casserole or lasagne and there's something valiant and touching in the way he acts grateful and tries his best to make himself eat big forkfuls while we watch, even though it's obvious he can barely swallow.

After ten days they decide to move G out of ICU to a corner at one end of the High Dependency Unit. It's not as glaring or hectic, and there's a bit more space, and curtains you can close, which makes it loads more private. The aim is to get him breathing unaided and gradually wean him off the medication. But nobody can say for sure when or even if this will happen. It's still possible he might not wake up at all and if he does, he might not be like he was before the accident. I've noticed the doctors here are big on telling it as is. They're so determined to avoid giving anyone false hope they show no mercy in what they say. I understand why, but it's hard to take sometimes and whenever a doctor comes to check on him or give us an update I want to put my hands over my ears.

Amazingly, though, once G's been moved, we adapt to the situation and get into a routine. Bartosz does the night shift, then Amanda drops me off at the hospital in the mornings before she goes to do her session at the Health Centre. I take over at the bedside and Bartosz goes to get a coffee and then stands outside for a while, making calls, running his life by remote control. After a few days of this, Amanda scares him into going home each morning to rest. She's as bad the hospital doctors when it comes to not mincing words.

'You're not too young to have a heart attack or a stroke,' she says. 'I've seen it all too often in people your age. And what use will you be to Gawain if you're paralysed down one side and can't string a sentence together?'

I've finally started talking to my brother. I feel less self-conscious doing it here in this quiet corner than I did the other ward. I usually end up chatting about when we were kids. It still feels really stupid, but I get used to it, and after a while I wonder if I can see some sort of response in his face, a faint twitch of his eyebrows. But I know I'm kidding myself, really.

At lunchtime, Amanda always reappears with my lunch: supermarket sandwiches or steak slices and sausage rolls from Greggs. She says I need fattening up. I usually leave the ward to eat. Bartosz is still worried Warren and Ed might be about somewhere, so I just walk cautiously to the end of the corridor and stare through a window I've discovered, with a view of a weird internal courtyard that somebody once tried to brighten up with a handful of garishly painted but now faded garden gnomes and a pot containing a big shrub that's totally desiccated and dead, but occupied by a pigeon's nest. Despite not wanting to bump into Ed and the rest, I take a risk and look in on Mum every so often. She is attached to a collection of wires and tubes similar if not identical to those connected to my brother. So far, she has always been alone. The first few times I go to see her, I feel sorry for her and angry with her at the same time, but now I don't feel anything much, apart from a mild, almost bored contempt.

At two on the dot, Aunty Susan sweeps in and sits with G for precisely an hour and thirty minutes, reading him passages from His Dark Materials or Harry Potter. I find a chair, hunch up inside my jacket and settle myself next to her, so I can listen, too. Sometimes I fall asleep for a while and wake up with my head propped against her shoulder. Then Amanda comes back with chocolate. I separate myself from Aunty Susan and she kisses G, leaving a lipstick mouth print on his cheek or forehead, which the Amanda removes later, with a wet wipe. For me this is the worst time of the day. I wish she'd stay and carry on reading forever, and seeing my brisk, unemotional Aunty kiss G like that, as though he's awake when he isn't, makes my throat ache. But I chomp on my Lion Bar or suck my way through my chocolate buttons and stare into space, waiting for the sugar hit to distract me.

When Aunty S has left the ward, Amanda takes over. She reads all sorts of things to him, from chunks of medical textbooks to gay, erotic fiction, which she seems to enjoy for some obscure reason. Hearing my sister calmly read out loud all these explicit sex scenes, describing men doing stuff to each other I'd never have imagined possible, using words I'd not heard before and can now never unknow, makes me want to jump out of the window. I didn't know about any of that stuff, despite sharing a dormitory with three other boys for years and years, and the fact I'm so shocked makes me hate myself for being a prude. I don't think I'm homophobic. That wasn't why I fell out with my brother.

Bryan often turns up at around this time, too. He goes on about G and what a fantastic doctor he is shaping up to be, tactfully taking care to use the present tense, and he tells me how worried G has been about me, that I need to put on weight and maybe take some supplements and get tested for anaemia. Please stop nagging me, I think. I'm eating as much as I can without throwing up. And anyway, it's none of your business.

At around five Bartosz returns for another night vigil. Amanda and I always offer to stay, but he wants to be alone with G, so we go back to her place. She cooks and I devour all of it greedily and kind of desperately, resisting the temptation to lick the plate clean, like a world war two soldier I once came across in a computer game, who'd just been released from a Japanese prisoner of war camp. I eat everything she puts in front of me. I'm not fussy, although I'm secretly disappointed if it's grilled fish without chips and totally gutted if it's salad. She usually nibbles her way through a much smaller portion of the same thing, then we load up the dishwasher, and if it's not raining, we wander down to the end of the garden and watch the bats swooping about in the twilight. After that, we sit in her living room. We've tried watching TV, but we haven't found anything that can hold our attention, so we talk on the dark instead. We seem to have a lot to say to each other, a lot of catching up to do, mainly about her life and what G's been up to in the last few years. Sometimes she tries to get me to talk about my life in the community, but I never want to do that. I tell her it doesn't matter now that I'm out.

She doesn't agree. 'You need talk to someone about it,' she says. 'Otherwise it will come back to bite you, probably when things are getting back to normal and you think you're over it.'

'I'm fine. I'm not even trembling anymore.'

I hold out my fingers to show her the jittering has stopped.

'What about your asthma? You didn't go to the appointment they made for you at the clinic when you were in A&E.'

'I couldn't. Anyway, it's nowhere near as bad as when I was at school.'

'Why don't I take you to my health centre. Then you can register with one of the other doctors.'

I shrug, but I let her. The GP I register with is a middle aged bloke. He asks me a load of questions, but he stops short of badgering me to death and he backs off completely when he realises I don't want to be touched. Come again, he says, if I need to. Or ask for a phone appointment. And he gives me a prescription for a new inhaler. Amanda looks at it and says she'd have prescribed something similar. I haven't needed to use it yet.

After we've been in our new routine for a few days, PC Naylor turns up at the hospital. Now that my head's cleared a bit I wish I hadn't made that statement. I'm not interested in getting anybody charged with anything. I just want to forget about it all and move on.

'We went round to the house, to bring them in for questioning,' he says. 'But nobody answered the door. Then we got a warrant to go inside and we found evidence that drawers and wardrobes had been emptied in a hurry, and there was a safe in the kitchen with its door left open. If there was money and passports in there, or other kinds of personal documentation, it's all gone now. Apart from these.'

He hands me my battered old school laptop and a bundle of paperwork in a clear plastic folder. My computer is still covered with Chelsea stickers and has my name printed across the lid in blue marker pen. I haven't seen it since I arrived in South Carolina after leaving school. I vaguely remember Mum telling me the community house in South Carolina had been burgled during the night while we were sleeping, and among the items taken was my laptop. I thought it had gone forever. Seeing it again is like bumping into an old friend I thought was dead. But I'm not going to get sentimental about it in front of PC Naylor.

I quickly rifle through the documents in the folder and find my passport, my A' level certificates and some correspondence from Durham University and from my head teacher, Mrs Hopgood, about their offer of a place to study Modern Languages and whether I was planning to take it up or not. I'm not sure I've seen any of this paperwork before. Aunty Susan or the school must have sent it all out to me in the States only for it to be intercepted before I could get my hands on it.

But wow. Here I am, a real person again, with an identity and a past and present backed up by solid documentary evidence. I can't get my head round it at the moment, though. After all that's happened and is still happening, who the hell is this Sebastian Jacob Fylde? And what is he going to do with himself *moving forward*, as they say? There is no moving forward, though. How can there be when I don't know whether my future contains a dead or a living brother. Or a permanently damaged one. Best to focus on the present for now.

'They've done a runner, then?'

'It seems they have.'

PC Naylor nods at me earnestly. I think he feels sorry for me and he's happy to bring me what he knows will be good news as far as I'm concerned.

'Right.'

'Also, we've had a couple of other complaints.'

'Really?'

'I'm not at liberty to go into detail, but two other people have come forward and made statements that corroborate yours.'

'From the same church?'

'One from your community and another from a branch in Lincolnshire.'

'Was the complaint from my church about me?'

'No. They did the same thing to someone else a few days after they did it to you.'

'Wow. I had no idea. Who was it?'

'I can't divulge that. They didn't go to A&E, but they've got exactly the same scars as you.'

I missed a few services afterwards. It must have happened then.

20. Jacob

They decide to remove G's breathing tube to see what happens. It turns out he can breathe unaided, and they tell us they're starting to reduce his level of sedation, but it might be a while before he wakes up properly. You'd think this would be a relief, but all it does is raise the stakes and ratchet up the tension. I've only coped so far because there's been no prospect of any real immediate change and I've become conditioned to living in a kind of stasis. I try to extinguish the tiny and unwelcome bit of hope that keeps trying to flicker into life inside my head. But it keeps flaring up again, even though G does nothing but sleep for the best part of another long week.

One morning, I decide I really must tell Amanda that Mum was driving the car that nearly killed him. She has just as much right to know as I do. I focus on her small, neat fingernails as she spreads lime marmalade onto a slice of unbuttered, wholemeal bread, and I fumble around for the right words. But she gets in first.

'I need to tell you something,' she says.

'What?'

'I'm sixteen weeks pregnant.'

Any possibility that I might have found a way to tell her about Mum and the car fizzles out like a firework in the rain. I've never known anyone who was pregnant before, apart from a handful of women at New Sunrise who I didn't have much to do with, and I have no clue what to say. The only thing I can think of is to ask how far gone she is, but she's already said that. I wish I could grab my phone and google *what do you say to your scary sister when she's just told you she's pregnant?*

'Jacob, are you there?'

I suddenly think of a question I would like an answer to.

'Does G know?'

'I told him I was going to have a termination.'

'I bet he wasn't happy.'

She shakes her head.

'But you didn't have one.'

'I *was* going to, but every day when I tried to dial the number to arrange it, I couldn't. Then I went for the twelve week scan and saw its heart beating. How I could I do something that would deliberately make it stop? First do no harm and all that. But I didn't tell Gawain I'd changed my mind.'

'Why not?'

'I don't know. Out of spite, I suppose. To get back at him. He'd tried to pressure me to keep it just because he fancied being an uncle. I didn't think it was fair of him. I was furious at the time.'

'I can imagine him doing that.'

'But really, he was genuinely pleased and excited for me as well as for himself and he couldn't hide how disappointed he was when I said what I was going to do.'

'You'd have told him eventually, wouldn't you? Or he'd have noticed. You didn't know he was going to end up in a coma.'

'Yes, but still.'

She gets up from the table and throws the remains of her toast in the bin. Then she stands in front of me, hands on hips and her eyes laser into mine.

'Anyway,' she says. 'What do *you* think about becoming an uncle? Do you have an opinion about it?'

She might as well ask me how I'd feel about going to live on the planet Neptune. Again I try my hardest, but I can't think of a single worthwhile thing to say.

'Dunno. Congratulations?'

'Brothers,' she mutters quietly as she clears away the breakfast things.

*

G finally starts to return from the dead during one of Aunty Susan's afternoon sessions, while she's reading a passage from Harry Potter about Dumbledore. G's eyes move suddenly start moving about beneath his closed lids. He smiles dreamily and then starts murmuring what sounds like the same few undecipherable words over and over again, in a scratchy voice. I press his buzzer. A nurse comes in, checks a few readings and says he's definitely starting to come round. I ring Bartosz, but by the time he arrives, G is inert again. He stays like that all night and for half of the following morning. I read to him from Gawain and the Green Knight. I even sing to him, but my brother's eyelids don't flicker and he doesn't move, not even by a fraction of a centimetre. In the end, exhausted by all this pointless self-mortification and exasperated by his refusal to respond, I slap his cheek and tell him to wake up. I keep doing it, my voice getting louder with each slap, until Bartosz appears and pulls me away.

'Sorry,' I say.

G's eyes snap open, but I'm not sure he's actually looking at me.

'I've got to get back,' he says in a whiny voice.

'Back where?'

'To the farm.'

'What farm?'

He doesn't answer and his eyes swivel about oddly, as though he's looking for someone or something. Then, he stares into the distance. From his downturned mouth you'd think he was a three year old, trying to be brave and not cry.

'Do you know who I am?' I ask him.

He acts as though he can't hear me and his hands fidget with the crease of the sheet, which is neatly folded against his chest.

The doctor performs all kinds of tests and asks him questions about himself and the world in general, the identity of the prime minister, the month and year we're in and things like that, he answers all of them correctly, apart from the month because he doesn't realise how much time had passed. Although nobody asks him to, he counts backwards from one hundred in sevens with perfect accuracy and little hesitation. The doctor concludes that G's cognitive abilities are intact, but when we talk to him, he acts as though we don't exist.

Lunch arrives, but the main course is pork spring rolls in crispy batter, so it's got no chance. I'm more optimistic about the little pot of trifle and the cup of tea that accompany it, though. Bartosz holds the cup to G's lips and he does take a few sips. But then he compresses his lips into a rigid line that won't let anything else through. He does the same when Bartosz offers him a spoonful of the trifle.

'You've got to eat something, Sunshine,' Bartosz says, but G just ignores him again and stares into space.

'How come the doctors think he's ok when he's behaving like a one year old?'

'He answered all their questions. And he counted backwards in sevens. I don't know about you, but I couldn't do that.'

'But he's not right, is he?"

'Give him a chance. I mean, look at him, sitting up and everything. It's a miracle.'

Amanda appears soon after lunch. She apologises for taking so long to get here. Something about fitting in extra patients at the end of her shift because another GP was off sick. As soon as he catches sight of her, G crumbles into a thousand pieces. He's always cried a lot and he's never been even slightly self-conscious about it. But this is way beyond anything I've ever seen him do before. He sobs, wails and gasps. Then he says he *really must* to get back the farm, that they'll be wondering where he is. My sister isn't fazed by any this. She puts an arm round his shoulder and talks to him in a baby voice. He's bound to feel weird after everything that's happened, she says. Just take a few deep breaths. There is no farm, she says. This drives him bananas.

Amanda might be may be ok about my brother's descent into infantilism, but it's all too much for me. When he starts screaming that there *is* a farm and he belongs there, not here, I run out of the room, hurtle down two flights of stairs and walk quickly through the foyer, past the restaurant and the little charity shop and through the sliding doors. I lean on the wall next to the main entrance of the hospital and I close my eyes.

My phone pings. It's PC Naylor. Fucking hell, not now. It pings again. I get a grip and take the call.

'They've scarpered,' he says, making it sound as though Warren, Ruth and Ed gave him the slip while he was pursuing them on a bicycle, blowing a whistle. 'They were on the 11 pm flight to Atlanta from Heathrow, on the night of the accident.'

'All three of them?'

'Warren and Ruth Brookes and Edwin Clifford.'

'So they'd already left when I came in to make my statement.'

'Yep. It's up to you if you want to take it any further. It'll be a lot trickier now they're out of the country. You'd have to hire a lawyer and start extradition proceedings.'

'God, no. I'm just glad they've gone.'

'I don't think they'll be back in a hurry. Their entire network of churches in the UK seems to have been shut down and they've all buggered off back to the States, the whole lot of them. None of them will get far if they try to enter the UK again.'

'Oh, right. Ok.'

Since the accident, I haven't had the mental energy to worry all that much about Warren, Ed and Godwin. I've kind of pushed all that to one side. But hearing that that they've gone makes my knees go weak. The part of me that's been holding everything together so tightly since the accident suddenly starts to work itself loose. I never cry if I can help it. I admit, I've come close a few times over the last few weeks, but I'm not going to start now. I chant this to myself and repeat it over and over again quickly like a mantra. Then I repeat it again more slowly, until the waves of emotion recede and I realise I'm standing talking to myself in full view of everyone going in and coming out of the hospital, dry eyed, but clinging to the wall like ivy, from the top of my head, via the palms of my hands to the backs of my calves.

Suddenly, Bartosz looms into view and leans over me, with one hand resting on the wall.

'What's going on here, then?' He asks.

I tell him the news. Without saying anything, he pulls me towards him with his other arm. Normally, I wouldn't allow this. I don't do close physical contact with men these days, even when I'm just about one hundred percent sure they mean me no harm. But I don't resist. As I squash my face into the side of his neck and inhale the comforting, citrusy tang of his deodorant, I desperately scramble around inside my head for my shit in order to get it back together again. When I do, I detach myself from him.

'She's managed to make him calm down,' he says as we go back into the hospital.

When we reach the ward, my brother is sitting there, red eyed and sniffing a bit, but quiet and staring into space, as per usual.

When we return to the hospital the following morning, G's sitting up in his bed again, not eating a bowl of what looks like porridge with golden syrup dissolving into it.

'Jacob's here,' Bartosz says.

I say hello, but my brother won't look at me. I smile at him as though I think everything is fine, but all I want to do is slap him again or force his mouth open so I can drip feed the porridge into it. In the end, I eat it myself.

Bartosz gives me a look.

'Well he didn't want it, did he?' I say.

They disconnect him from the remaining tubes and a nurse helps him to get out of bed and sit on a chair. He cooperates, kind of. Or rather, he goes totally passive and lets himself be moved around like an actor playing the role of a corpse. They say he needs to start getting mobile and we should encourage him to walk up and down. Together, Bartosz and I lift him from the chair. He doesn't weigh much, so this isn't too difficult. Getting him to walk is another matter, though. We manage to keep him vertical, but his feet dangle and flap loosely at the ends of his legs like flippers and refuse to engage properly with the floor. I just *know* he's doing it deliberately to wind us up and what patience I have soon crumbles away.

'For God's sake, come on, you stupid, dogmatic turd,' I say.

'He can't help it, Jacob,' Bartosz says. 'Let's have one more go. Try Gawain. Please.'

And this time, he does try. Or rather his feet relax into their customary way of doing things and place themselves flat on the floor. We get him to walk right down the length of the ward and back again, twice. Then we decide that's enough for now, for us if not for him, and we sit him on the chair again.

'Brilliant. Well done,' Bartosz says.

G stares at a point on the wall opposite. Yeah, well done, I think. An Oscar winning performance. Then he starts scratching his head so vigorously he's in danger of drawing blood. I grab his hands while Bartosz goes to fetch nail clippers from his overnight bag.

Another day of this odd half-recovery follows. Then they discharge him. Just like that. He's medically fit, according to their criteria. He can provide the name of the Chancellor of the Exchequer when asked, and he can eat, walk, piss and do everything else on his own, apart from behave like a normal human being. And in any case, they need his bed.

'But he's like one of the living dead,' I say to the doctor.

He smiles and shakes his head at me, as though he thinks I'm a bit of a joker, the zany younger brother. He sorts out a follow up appointment with the neurology consultant. Then his job is done.

As we gather G's things together, my brother sits in the chair by his bed, blank-faced. We have a hell of a job getting him dressed. It would have been easier to do it with him lying on the bed, but they've already come in to change the sheets and disinfect everything he might have touched or seeped fluids into. I don't think they're best pleased he's still occupying the chair. We try to get him to hurry up, but he doesn't offer any assistance and it takes three of us to push his legs into his underpants and his trousers. When we try to pull his T-shirt and a hoodie over his head and get his arms into his sleeves he transforms himself into an octopus, with multiple limbs flailing about all over the place.

Back at the house, we carry him into the kitchen and prop him up on the couch in front of the wood-burning stove, which Bartosz lights. Amanda keeps an eye on G, while Bartosz gives me a guided tour of the house, ending with my bedroom.

'Gawain chose the furniture and the blinds,' he says.

He sounds proud, of his house and this room, and also of G and his dedication to my wellbeing. The room is amazing, though. Too fantastic for me to put into words, particularly the big window which has a view of the land at the front of the house and the woodland on the other side of the lane.

At lunch, Bartosz puts a bowl of chicken soup in front of my brother. He prepared it from scratch, with actual chicken and fresh vegetables. Bartosz puts a spoon in his hand, but G lets his fingers go slack and the spoon drops onto the table. Then he does that sad little boy face again. Bartosz strides over to the sink, puts both hands on his head and stares out of the window. I move my chair close to G's and I butter some bread, break it into small pieces and drop them into the soup. Then I spoon up a tiny amount of bread and soup and gently tap the spoon against his lips. He opens his mouth and swallows what's on the spoon and we keep repeating the sequence until the bowl is empty.

'Well done, mate,' I say when he's finished.

'Pobbles,' he says quietly.

'That's right.'

Pobbles was the word Debbie used to describe the soft, mushy baby foods she used to prepare for him. Bread soaked in soup was one of his favourites.

We settle into another routine. G sits in the kitchen or in their incredible man cave, under a duvet, either staring into space or sleeping. Every so often he mutters something about the mysterious farm and complains he was taken away from it against his will.

Amanda comes over almost every day. She plays music to him and endless YouTube videos showing TV programmes from our childhood, to try and bring him back to us.

We take it in turns to help him get ready for bed. One night, he looks me in the eye so suddenly it makes me flinch.

'Jacob,' he says, quietly.

'That's me,' I say, attempting to match his emotional neutrality.

'These aren't my pyjamas.'

'Bartosz got them for you when you were in the hospital.'

'I wear scrubs at the hospital. Not pjs.'

'These are from when you were *in* the hospital.'

'In,' he says.

The next day, he looks at me a few times. He seems puzzled, as though he's sure he's met me before but can't quite remember where. In the afternoon, while I'm sitting with him by the stove in the man cave, he fidgets more than usual and stares at the view through the row of windows.

'What's out there?' I ask, not expecting an answer.

'The trees are in the wrong place. And what's happened to the hens?'

'There aren't any.'

'Are we in the barn? I want to go back into the house.'

'You're in the house.'

'Where's Nanny Flora, then?'

'Who?'

'My Nanny Flora. *Our* Nanny Flora.'

'I don't have a Nanny Flora.'

'You do.'

We go on and on like this for ages, back and forth, batting meaningless conversational ping pong balls to each other, until we both grow weary. He closes his eyes when the sunlight sinks so low it shine through one of the windows, directly onto his face. All of a sudden, it's nearly dark. I must have fallen asleep. Next to me, G's duvet sags limply on the sofa. I search all the rooms in the house. I even look under the beds and inside the wardrobes. When I come back downstairs again, I notice that the outside door in the vestibule between the main house and the extension is very slightly ajar. I open it fully and peer out into the gloom. I can't see much, but he doesn't seem to be in the garden, either.

'How long were you asleep?' Bartosz asks as he grabs his coat and his car keys.

'I don't know. Must have been at least an hour.'

'Has he taken his phone?'

"I think it was in his pocket."

When we dial his number, we can't hear it ringing in the house, and it isn't under one of the cushions or inside the cutlery drawer in the kitchen, the two places he usually puts it when it vibrates. Hopefully that means he's got it on him and we'll be able to get through to him eventually. Outside, it's dead quiet, apart from the distant hum of the motorway, and although the area immediately around the house is brightly lit by a series of motion sensitive security lights, it's very dark once you move beyond their range. We grab torches and search the garden again, including all the outhouses and the alpaca stables. No sign of him, so we jump into the car. First, we drive to the barn. We pull up in front of the black, skeletal structure and we jump out and shout his name. Nothing.

'What's that over there?' I ask. Through the bedraggled autumn trees you can see lights, some distance away, across a vast hedge-free field.

'Must be Motorway Services. I didn't know you could see them from here. I haven't been down here since the leaves started coming off the trees.'

'Do you think he might have seen them, and then made off towards them?'

'Why would he do that?'

'Well, there aren't any other lights. They kind of stand out. Maybe he thought it was his precious farm.'

Bartosz reverses the car slowly back down the track, past the house, towards the gate onto the main road. He drives slowly, with his headlights on full beam, and we look carefully along each side of the lane, shining our torches into the woods as we go. We've left the front door unlocked and the gate to the road wide open, in case he comes back while we're out.

As we speed off down the road, towards the motorway, I phone Amanda.

'Why did you fall asleep, you numpty?'

'I didn't do it on purpose.'

'He could be anywhere. He might have fallen in a ditch and be up to his knees in water. Or he could be wandering around on the motorway.'

It only take us a few minutes to get to the Services because Bartosz has discovered a local road a few minutes' drive away that leads to the back of the car park on the southbound side. You used to be able to get into the car park from this road and then take a short cut past the petrol station to the motorway. Bartosz parks the car in the small lay-by close to the barrier they put up to close this unofficial access point. We duck under it and Bartosz starts searching the southbound buildings area, while I run as fast as I can over the bridge to see if he's on the other side. As I'm careering down the steps, my phone rings and I try to look at it and run at the same time. I stumble, then trip down the rest of the stairs and land on my knees in the gravel. It's G. He's posted a message to the WhatsApp group he set up when I was still at New Sunrise.

'Where the hell are you?'

'Where the hell are *you*?' Bartosz replies quick as a flash.

'Outside Starbucks. What the actual fuck is going on?'

'Is that on the Southbound side?' I ask.

'Err, yeah. Where else would it be?'

I don't know, G. Up your arse, maybe.

'Don't move,' Bartosz types.

I hurtle up the steps again and back across the bridge. Bartosz and I both get there at the same time. G's sitting on the tarmac, leaning against the wall outside the drive-through Starbucks, holding his phone in one hand. His trainers and jogging pants are streaked with mud and his hair is slick with sweat. When he sees me approaching, he jumps up and run towards me. He holds my face between his hands and smiles broadly.

'I can't believe you're out. Are you ok? You look a bit pale.'

Then he notices Bartosz.

'What have we stopped here for, hun?'

Bartosz looks mystified.

'We haven't,' I say.

'What's happened to your jeans? Did you fall when you were leaving the church? I'm sorry I didn't get there sooner, I was stuck in traffic near the hospital.'

I look down at my new jeans. There are rips in both of the knees.

'I've got a First Aid kit in my car.' He looks over at the rows of parked cars under the dim lights.

'Only thing is, I've forgotten where I left it. Could it be on the northbound side? No, that wouldn't make sense.'

He stops his prattling for a couple of seconds and kisses me on the side of the head five times. I know because I'm too stunned to do anything other than stand there and count.

'How come it's so dark? It wasn't that late when we got to the church, was it? I know the traffic's bad, but still. I'll have to ring work. They'll be probably wondering where I am.'

He rambles on as we bundle him across the car park, through the pine trees and under the barrier, and once he's safely in the car, we call Amanda to tell her we've found him. Then we talk. It takes us a while to get through to him. The last thing he remembers is driving towards the exit of the church car park after Bartosz's Audi turned left and headed off. He thinks this all happened about twenty minutes ago and we've stopped at the motorway services on the way home to get food, because I'm hungry. In his head, Bartosz and I were queuing up for burgers and he'd nipped across to Starbucks to get a cappuccino. But he discovered he didn't have his wallet with him. He thought he must have left it in his car, but he couldn't work out where he'd parked, so he sat on the wet ground outside Starbucks and messaged us.

'Look at your phone,' Bartosz says. 'What's the date on it?'
'Ninth of November.'
'What was the date when Jacob asked us to go and fetch him?'
'Um, it was September, a Monday?'
'Exactly.'
'Your phone must be broken.'
'Jacob, show him yours.'
He looks at the date on my phone and shrugs.
'Feel the side of your face.'

I get hold of his hand his hand and place it on the side of his forehead near his hairline and make his fingers touch his new scar.

'Oh,' he says.

We explain everything. When we're finished, we ask him if he believes us. He nods. I look at him and try to imagine how it must feel to suddenly discover you've not only missed six weeks of your life, but you've also been in a coma and nearly died.

'I'm ok, then?' He asks.

'Yes. You're doing well.'

I feel sorry for him and I want to leave it there for now, let this part of the story sink in before we tell him anything else.

But Bartosz sees things differently.

'Your mother's in ICU.'

'Is she going to be alright?'

'They don't know yet.'

'Jesus.'

'And Godwin died at the scene, but Warren wasn't hurt.'

'Is he still at New Sunrise?'

'Nope. They've shut the place down and buggered off back to America."

G doesn't ask who was driving the car. He must think it was Godwin. I don't say anything. That will be my epitaph. *Jacob never said anything. Or nothing much. Particularly about important stuff.*

The drive to the house takes about seven minutes. G sits there next to me in the back, pulls me towards him and runs his hand over my hair in the wrong direction until my scalp hurts.

And by the time we're home he's completely assimilated everything we've told him.

21. Jacob

I thought I was getting over it, moving on. But suddenly, now the real G has reasserted himself and looks as though he's going to be ok, I've started having nightmares. When I wake up, I'm sitting upright in bed. My heart is pounding and sweat is pouring off me. At first, I think I'm back there, in that room in the basement, with Ed guarding the door. Living in a place where everyone hates me and anything could happen. Then I realise I can't see any light shining in through the rectangle at the top of the wall, and I remember. The darkness here is complete, but the silence feels kind of unstable, as though something was happening just outside my window and I've just missed it. I always get up, to look outside, but I never see anything. So I go back to bed, uncertain and uneasy, and I lay in my bed, exhausted, with all this stuff whirling about in my head, fighting against sleep, in case the dreams start again.

When the sun finally comes up, it shines through the gap in my curtains and forms a pale, yellow rectangle on the wall opposite my bed, like an unwanted painting. I call it the cold light of day. All I want is to stay here, in bed, hiding under the covers, like a vampire, waiting for it to get dark again. I actually tried to do that once, but G came bounding into my room without knocking, pulled the covers off my bed and exposed me clinging to the mattress like a limpet with no shell.

He still sleeps more than usual, and he struggles with his coordination a bit, but he's definitely G again, and the last few, terrible weeks, which traumatized the hell out of the rest of us, are a blank as far as he's concerned. He missed them and emerged on the other side unscathed.

I sling on the same clothes I was wearing yesterday. I don't bother to shower and I don't comb or gel my hair, even though I can smell an unwashed, sweetish scent, like sweaty toffee, coming from my scalp. As I make my way downstairs I hear my brother clattering around in the kitchen and singing to one of his playlists in a silly falsetto voice. The kitchen is filled with the same watery sunlight as my room and G is alternating between chopping fruit and whisking eggs.

'Where's Bartosz?'

'Cardiff. Gone to see a couple of clients. Won't be back till late.

This is the first time I've been alone in the house with my brother since he came back to himself.

'Hey!' He skips to me and kisses me on the forehead, like he always does now when he first sees me in the morning. He has to stand on his tip toes and kind of drag my face down towards his.

'Hi,' I say, quietly.

I sit down, rest my elbows on the table and prop up my face with my hands. I try my best not to look miserable because he'll be on me like a ton of bricks if he detects any sign of weakness, asking if I'm ok, what he can do to help and all that. And he's so incredibly happy. Clichés rattle through my head. Don't be a spectre at his feast. Don't rain on his parade.

'What do you want for breakfast?' He asks.

Don't piss on his cornflakes.

He leans against the kitchen top with his arms folded and eyebrows raised, waiting for me to answer. I'm not even remotely hungry.

'I'm having scrambled eggs and a raspberry and wheatgrass smoothie?'

'Eggs. Not the other thing. Thanks.'

We sit opposite each other and eat, the silence between us partially, but not completely, filled by his bouncy music. I think it's synth-pop, but I'm a bit out of the loop when it comes to music genres. He squeezes tomato ketchup all over his eggs and then spoons them delicately into his mouth. He doesn't bother with toast because he'd have to suck it, which would take all day, probably.

With the help of a mug of coffee, I manage to wash my eggs down past the pebble sized blockage that seems to have formed in my throat, and when we've finished, I start to get up.

'Sit down for a minute.'

He moves his plate away and leans forward. His elbows rest on the table, mirroring mine.

'Tell me how you're getting on,' he says.

'You sound like a doctor.' I stare down at my plate.

'I *am* a doctor.'

'Not my doctor.'

'Look at me.'

I lift my head up to see exactly what I expect to see - his caramel eyes burning into mine.

'Everything's fine with you, is it?'

'Yes, thanks.'

'Jacob?'

'What?'

'Everything can't be fine.'

This is what the new G's like. It was so much easier when he was on another planet, controllable, not really seeing me. But now he won't leave me alone. It makes me feel as though I've been dropped into a slightly different version of reality. Not a parallel universe exactly, but a world that flips between something I recognise and something I don't.

'I'm great.'

'There's no point pretending. Not with me.'

'I'm not pretending anything.'

'You don't look great.'

'Is that a medical diagnosis?'

'Kind of. We're trained to read body language, spot symptoms people try hide.'

'Are you? Ooh, that's clever. Well done.'

'You're boiling and raging inside. And screaming for help. I can see it.'

'I'm so *not*.'

'You're forgetting, Jacob. I know you. Inside and out.'

'No you don't. You don't have a bloody clue. I'm not thirteen anymore. A lot's happened since then.'

'Nah. You're still you. And you'll to talk to me eventually.' He smiles, picks up the remote and turns the music off. 'One thing,' he says. 'Tell me one thing that's happening in the world of Jacob. Then I'll leave you alone. Until tomorrow. Then you can tell me something else. One thing per day. How does that sound?'

There's a short silence after this. It feels like part of his performance, particularly when he terminates it with a sigh. 'Look - I'm sorry for what happened,' he says.

I stare at him.

'I'm sorry for what I did.'

I can't believe he thinks it's ok to bring it up like this, so casually. As though it was nothing.

'Breathe, Jacob.'

'You fucked up my life, but all you have to do is say sorry and everything will be fine?'

'I know I did that. It broke my heart. Still does. But you're back now. We can sort it all out. If we keep talking to each other.'

He ratchets up the soulfulness in his eyes and they beam across the table at me on full power, as though he's sent out a micro-sized drone which will burrow into my skin, enter my brain and break me down. Then he smiles at me with such self-assurance that I hate him even more than I did before. He's rescued me, with a lot of help from his devoted, muscle-bound boyfriend. He's even given me a home. And now he's turned on his charm and tossed a glib apology in my direction, one that cost him no effort at all. That's all it takes, folks. Little bro is back on side again.

Except that I'm not. I want to hit him over the head with the frying pan he used for the eggs, and wipe that fake, self-deprecating expression off his face.

I stomp back upstairs and I mooch about in my room for the rest of the day. The next morning and the one after that, the rectangle of cold yellow light appears on my wall again and when G repeats his request to tell him one thing, I do. I tell him to bore off and mind his own business.

*

Bartosz drives G to his appointment with the neurologist. G guilt trips me into coming along, too, because he thinks we should both go and see Mum afterwards. The appointment doesn't go very well. G thinks he's ready to go back to work, but the consultant says he mustn't even think about doing that until after Christmas, at least. We sit in awkward silence next to each other by Mum's bed for about twenty minutes. G seems genuinely taken aback when he sees her, whereas to me, she seems even less real than she did the last time I saw her, more shrivelled up doll than human being, and my head feels like an empty bag when I rummage around inside it for a sense of loss or even just a little bit of sadness. The only sensation I come up with is fear that she'll wake up one day and recover, only to be charged with attempted murder. Then G will find out she was driving and that I knew, but didn't tell him.

I wonder if I should tell him now. There'll never be a better opportunity. But he puts his head in his hands.

'Are you crying?'

He nods and I change my mind. The chances of him finding out any other way must be just about zero. Nobody knows apart from me and the police, and looking at the state of Mum, she's never going to recover and stand trial.

'You're mental,' I say.

He shakes his head and grabs a handful of tissues on a cabinet by Mum's bed. Then he gets grip in a *look at me, I'm sad* kind of way. When we get up to leave, a nurse approaches and asks who we are. She wasn't part of the team who looked after G. When I tell her we're the patient's sons, the words sound strange, almost as though I'm lying. The nurse must wonder why we haven't visited more often. But it turns out she's preoccupied by something else.

'We've been trying to contact her next of kin, but we haven't got an address.'

'Warren's gone back to America.'

'Warren?'

'Her husband.'

She gets something up on her computer screen.

'According to this she's not married. Where it says next of kin they've put *brother*.'

'Brother?'

I realise I'm sounding a bit rude. It's not the nurse's fault they've abandoned my mother without even leaving their names.

'Aldo Valdini. Do you have his contact details?'

'I didn't even know she had a brother,' I say.

'Neither did I. Although I think there was a Marco,' G says.

'What? Since when?'

'I don't know. From when I was in hospital? No, that can't be right. I don't know.'

Bartosz picks us up and we head off to the supermarket to buy alcohol and party food. They've invited a few people round, some of G's old crowd from school, the ones that still live close enough, and Bartosz's army buddies. And a few of my old school friends, if I want. But I don't want. My mates are all progressing with their lives now, nearly finished at university, planning their next moves. Me on the other hand, I've been a slave in a closed religious community since I left school. Now I'm living the life of a gooseberry in my brother's house, and as far as moves are concerned, I don't have any.

Bartosz pushes the trolley and G chucks in sausages, burgers and chicken drumsticks.

'All that crap Warren preached about sex out of wedlock and he wasn't even married to your mother,' he says.

'And then at the slightest hint of trouble, he disappears back to America and leaves her here on her own.'

'It was a bit more than a hint of trouble, Gawain. What with the crash and all. And what they did to Jacob.'

He murmurs this really quietly and casually, as he reads the ingredients label on a multi-pack of beef flavoured crisps, realises they contain onion powder, which he avoids, and puts them back on the shelf.

'Can you stop talking about me as though I'm not here?'

They exchange a look, then stare at me. Both of them. I notice that several other shoppers have moved away and are giving us sideways glances as they pretend to browse the items on the shelves.

'What the fuck is the matter with you?' My brother whispers.

I'm not sure exactly what happens next inside my head. Everything goes a deep red colour for a second as my brain tries to re-set itself, but fails and instead tells me to pick up a large jar of something close to hand and hurl it at G, which I do. The jar bounces off his shoulder onto the floor, where it shatters, releasing chunks of tomato, an orange liquid and a vinegary smell. It looks like salsa, but it could just as easily be mango pickle. Bartosz marches up to me.

'I'll take him back to the car,' he says to G.

He leaves the trolley with my brother. Then he gets hold of me and frog marches me to the exit in front of all the other customers, with one arm bent behind my back, as though he's a security guard and I've been caught shop lifting. I struggle, but he's stronger than me. He pushes me into the front passenger seat, holding the top of my head, like the police do, and he gets in at the other side so we're sitting next to each other. I can't describe how it makes me feel, being manoeuvred about like this by Bartosz of all people. I thought he was my friend and now he's behaving like the men at New Sunrise.

'You and me need to have a talk,' he says.

22. Gawain

When we get home from the supermarket, Jacob jumps out of the car and stomps off. I go into the utility room, pull my shirt off my shoulder and look at myself in the big mirror. There's a red mark where the jar hit me and it hurts when I prod it. I know it's a trivial injury, nowhere near bad enough to require medical attention, but when you've been hit by a car, any kind of onslaught, particularly when it's deliberate, makes you feel fragile as glass. I leave Bartosz to put the shopping away and I walk down to the barn, so I can sit on one of the hay bales and have a good mope about everything. I cry for a bit, then I hear a rustling noise coming from the hedge behind me and I can't work out what's causing it, so I run back to the house.

Bartosz is still in the kitchen, humming to himself and sorting stuff out for tonight.

'Did Jacob help you put the shopping away?' I ask him.
'No, he just went up to his room.'
'What are we going to do with him?'
'Leave it to me,' he says.
'What's that supposed to mean?'
'You'll see.'
'You're making me uneasy.'
'Too bad. Suck it up, Sunshine.'

I can tell from his voice that he's annoyed, but trying not to show it. And it's not just Jacob he's hacked off with, but me as well.

I do make an effort to suck it up, though, and so does Bartosz. The weather is dry, if a little chilly, so we string fairy lights around the gazebo at the back of the kitchen, shovel coal in the chiminea, light up the barbecue, and we dish up the meat with jacket potatoes, focaccia and salad. Cobblers and his fiancée turn up, as do three other members of my close circle of school friends with their partners, and Bartosz's balcony companions. My posh mates and his army buddies get on unexpectedly well and before long, we're laughing riotously. We drink copious amounts of wine, lager and shots and we sit outside until it gets too cold. Then we go in and huddle around the stove in the kitchen, and I tell them about my accident. My experience of it exists on two levels now. Underneath, I still feel that vulnerability, but on the surface, the entire episode is transforming itself into a damn good story. The only downside to the evening is Jacob's non-appearance. We tell everyone he's ill, but it must seem odd to them that he doesn't even pop down to say hello. His absence seems slightly off to us, too, and it casts a faint shadow over everything.

The next day Bartosz and I have finished breakfast by the time Jacob comes downstairs. Pale and shadowy eyed, he grunts at us, helps himself to two Weetabix and sits down at the table. Bartosz gets up and moves to the sink and I stay where I am and stare at him, trying to think of something to say.

'Did we keep you awake last night?' I ask him.

'Nope,' he says without looking up.

End of conversation. I stay sitting at the table and watch him as he struggles to swallow his breakfast and tries to act as though nothing's wrong. Outside, the grass and the roofs of the outhouses are white with frost and there's a chilly draught blowing in through the window over the sink, but Jacob's wearing a T-shirt and shorts and the skin on his arms looks white and cold. I'm dying to tell him to put something warmer on. I try to think of something else to say, but before I decide what it's going to be, Bartosz strides up to the table and slams his hand down on it. The pepper pot tips over and Jacob jumps and drops his spoon. It clatters onto the floor. 'Right my lovely! Living room. Now,' he says. He puts his arms under Jacob's shoulders and lifts him out of his chair.

'I haven't loaded the dishwasher,' I hear my brother say faintly as they disappear out of the room. That's meant to be his job, although he rarely does it.

'Gawain can do that,' Bartosz says.

It takes me a while. When I've finished, I sit down at the kitchen table again. I bite off all my fingernails and leave anxious little crescents all over its varnished surface.

I hope Bartosz isn't too hard on him. What if he makes things worse? He doesn't have brothers. He can't possibly understand Jacob or the way the two of us interact. What happens on the surface between us is merely a symptom.

The ticking of the kitchen clock is the only thing that breaks the silence. It sounds ominous, like a slow and measured countdown towards an as yet undeclared catastrophe. Thirty minutes crawl by. I text Bartosz to ask him if everything's ok, but nothing comes through on my phone, apart from an E-mail from a pharmaceutical company promoting a new drug for some obscure paediatric condition I've heard of but will probably never encounter. I fetch my laptop and log onto a site that lets me access medical journals, as though my intention to do a bit of catching up is genuine. Then I stretch my arms above my head and yawn.

Another thirty minutes creep by. I can't sit here any longer, like a lemon, not knowing what's going on. I put my trainers on and go outside, though the sliding door that leads to the patio, and I creep around the back of the house towards the windows along the side of the extension. This is very difficult to do this quietly because the ground is littered with leaves that make loud crunching sounds when I tread on them. Luckily the blinds are all open on this side, although the windows are slightly obscured by vegetation that has got a bit out of control. I peer through it into the window closest to the TV area at the far end of the room. Jacob is sitting in front of it, cross legged on the floor holding his head in his hands.

Bartosz is sitting on one of the armchairs and leaning forward towards him. Jacob occasionally brushes his sleeve across his eyes, but Bartosz carries on talking to him as though everything is ok. I want to climb through the window and push Bartosz out of the way so I can take over. But then, as though he's read my mind, Bartosz hands my brother a box of tissues and comes and sits in front of him on the floor. Jacob kind of leans into him and Bartosz puts his arms round him and rocks him backwards and forwards. I'm spellbound and deeply moved at the way Bartosz has managed to shatter my brother's reserve to such an extent that my brother is letting himself be hugged like that.

I'm at a loss about what to do next, and pretty upset, too. I wander around the garden for a bit. The air is bitterly cold and the grass is brittle with ice on top, but spongy and damp underneath. Moisture soaks through the tops of my trainers and into my socks. Behind some trees, right at the back of the garden, I discover a new building. At least I don't think it was here before. The wood used in its construction smells clean and sharp, as though it was part of a pine forest in Norway until very recently. It looks like a stable and is surrounded by a little yard, enclosed inside a fence. Why don't I know about this? Maybe I do, but my head injury has made me forget. If that's the case, what else have I forgotten? What if all my medical training has slipped away too? Mentally I thrash about until I settle on something to test myself on. I opt for the bones, tendons and ligaments of the foot and ankle. I can see them all in my mind's eye and I still know all their names and how they connect. Next I go on to the valves and chambers of the heart and the most common ways in which they can malfunction. All there. What about the more obscure human metabolic disorders? How many inherited chromosomal disorders can I remember and name? Several, it turns out. Well that's a relief.

I'm just about to wade into virology, an area I find a bit sketchy and slightly implausible, when Bartosz interrupts my musings with a text.

We're done. Bring coffee.

I rush back to the kitchen, grind some of the really strong Italian beans we keep for special occasions and make a big cafetiere of the stuff. Then I put it on a tray with cups, saucers, milk and a plate of chocolate Hob Nobs, and I rattle my way into the man cave with it.

'Yay, I didn't drop it!' I say, turning my entrance into a bit of a performance. 'If tray-carrying was a coordination test at the neurology clinic I'd be back at work by now.' I put the tray down on a table. 'Phew, it's hot in here.'

It really is, and on top of that the air feels feverish and frantic, although that might be me. They're both still sitting on the floor, still cross legged, but next to each other now, facing the stove and staring at its flames, and Jacob isn't leaning into Bartosz anymore. I deposit the tray on the table and make a production out of pouring the coffee. Neither of them responds to my attempt at lightening the mood. I settle myself on the floor opposite them both.

'Are you ok?' I ask my brother.

His eyes fill with tears again and he hides his face in his palms. I lean forward to rest my forehead against his and put my arms around him so I can rock him backwards and forwards, like Bartosz was doing when I spied on them through the window. But he picks up on my intention and quickly shuffles backwards until he's out of reach.

'You need to back off completely. Stop pawing him like a dog and treating him like a child,' Bartosz says later, when we're tucked up in bed.

'Pawing him? Is that what he thinks I'm doing?'

'He's uncomfortable with physical contact.'

'He doesn't seem to mind it with you.'

'Yes, but I'm slowly with him and giving him time to get used to me. You've just assumed he's still the same as he was eight years ago and that you have the right to say and do whatever you want to him.'

'But he's my baby brother.'

'He's not a kid anymore, and since you were last together, he's gone through a ton of crap. And you must have changed loads in the last eight years, too. I bet he hardly recognises you. You both need to start again and get to know each other as you are now. And even then, you might decide you don't like each other very much. You may never get back to the way you once were.'

The next few days are beyond awkward. I try really hard to follow Bartosz's advice. I avoid touching my brother and I try to speak to him in a more detached and respectful manner. Instead of making assumptions about his feelings and preferences, or anything else to do with him, I ask him polite questions. But I feel like an actor, half-heartedly uttering strings of badly written words, and every time I say something to him, he looks at me, puzzled and kind of caught on the hop, as though we're actors in a play and he doesn't know what to say because he's forgotten his lines.

Eventually, we both get the hang of it. Kind of. We treat each other with extreme courtesy and we never fight or even argue, which is great, but it makes him seem strange and unfamiliar. In fact, he starts to creep me out a bit with his level stare and his careful, measured words. I look at this fully grown man and search his face for vestiges of the boy he used to be. Is he still my brother, or has his psyche been permanently damaged? Seclusion and ill-treatment in a sinister religious community with a bunch of crazed religious oddballs isn't going to do a lot for person's emotional development, is it?

23. Gawain

Last night, we went to bed at around midnight and I fell asleep quite quickly for me. But an hour or so later, I was wide awake again, and my head was filled with the echo of a noise. I couldn't identify it or even be sure it had happened at all, but I was left with a kind of vague impression I'd heard glass breaking and the suspicion that someone was trying to break into one of the outhouses. I went over to the window, pushed up the sash and peered out. I couldn't see anyone, but there I was aware of a faint but constant wall of sound hovering at the border between my imagination and actual sensory perception. It could have been the rustling of leaves; there are so many trees around this house. But it could just as easily have been whispering voices. This thought freaked me out so much I pulled the sash down again. It descended too quickly, with a jarring, nails-on-blackboard screech that ended in a crash loud enough to wake the dead.

Bartosz never appreciates being dislodged from sleep. He sat up in bed, looked around and put his hands in his hair as though the room had just been invaded by enemy forces. When his eyes settled on me, he looked more annoyed than relieved.

'What in heaven's name are you doing?'

'I thought I heard glass breaking and people whispering.'

He groaned, theatrically in my opinion, got up very slowly, ran a hand through the row of dressing gowns hanging from pegs on the door of the en-suite, selected his green velvet one, put it on and muttered to himself as he strolled casually over to the window and looked out. 'Nothing,' he said in a resigned and martyrish voice, as though this wasn't the first time I'd woken him up to look out of windows.

When I wake again it's morning. When I reach out for Bartosz, he isn't here. I sit up and wait until the dizziness subsides and I try my best to shake off the thing that seems to be clinging to my back, a little imp called *Doom* with sharp little fingernails that nip at my skin. Then I get out of bed and pull on the first items of clothing I can find, which turn out to be my Lycra running shorts and a Leeds United hoodie belonging to Bartosz, which reaches almost down to my knees. I put the hood up and my head starts to feel a bit more protected. I glance through the window towards the outhouses again. Did I really think people were out there, talking? Through the other window, I spot Bartosz outside in the mist, chopping wood for the stoves. I go downstairs, grab a yoghurt, put my lace up boots on without stopping to tie them and shuffle out, peeling off the foil top as I go, in a feat of coordination I wouldn't have been able to manage even a week ago. I rest my yoghurt and spoon in the long grass, so I can approach Bartosz from behind, press my head into the top of his back and wrap my arms around his waist. He flinches, removes my arms and turns to face me.

'Jesus Christ.'

"What?"

'It's not the greatest idea in the world to sneak up behind someone who's holding an axe.'

'Particularly not when they're as wired as you are.'

I put my arms round his waist again, from the front this time, and I reach up and press my face into the side of his neck.

'Go and sit over there and eat your yoghurt.'

'Where's Jacob?'

'In the porch. I'm chopping. He's stacking.'

They operate as a team these days. I do as I'm told and I watch as he starts wielding his axe again. When Jacob emerges from the porch, he frowns at me and nods, as though I'm the guy who has come to read the meter. I finish my yoghurt and Bartosz continues to ignore me, so I wander off into the house again. Before the accident, I used to sleep through the night. But now, I'm wakeful and restless, and Bartosz is in a mood with me about it. Part of the problem is the naps I've got into the habit of having during the day. It needs to stop. Sometimes I even go back to sleep in the mornings, not long after I've risen. But today, I've decided that is *not* going to happen. I position myself out of the way, in the man cave, with one of my textbooks. I read and then start writing notes on my laptop. It goes quite well for a while, but then Jacob and Bartosz appear and start playing table tennis. Their loud joviality and the repetitive *pock* of the ball as it hits the table shatter my concentration. I could move to the kitchen, but I know this table tennis game is a prelude to lunch, which means they'll be in that room too, shortly, clattering and banging about. I take my laptop and books up to the bedroom and curl myself up on the bed, where I won't be disturbed. Within minutes, I'm fast asleep. I sleep for so long, I miss lunch.

As a consequence, I'm here again, wide awake in the darkness, and I'm every bit as restless and on edge as I was last night. Except that this time, I'm already awake when the noises start. It definitely sounds like glass shattering, but it seems come from the lane rather than the outhouses. It doesn't last long, but then I hear someone moving about close to the house.

I get up quietly, pull on my joggers and a sweatshirt and sneak downstairs. The door that leads into the garden from the utility room is slightly ajar. I know for a fact that it was locked last night, because I saw Bartosz do it before we went to bed. Shaken, I jump back into the relative safety of the kitchen. Should I fetch him? Hell, no. I'd rather venture outside into the darkness and face whatever's out there on my own than deal with the consequences of my boyfriend's wrath. I stand on the doorstep, switch on the torch and scan the area in front of me. Almost immediately, I catch a glimpse of movement just to the right of the row of outhouses, a flicker of something white that appears and quickly vanishes again. Brave as anything, I make my way towards the outhouses.

My torch provides a narrow and next to useless cone of light that allows me to see my feet as I step across the lawn, but not much else. When I get to the end of the last outhouse, I put my left hand out, feel the brick wall and follow it round to the back. As soon as I turn the corner, my feet come into contact with something soft. I trip over it and end up flat on my face in the wet grass. I scramble up again, but I drop my torch. It switches itself off and as I'm flailing about trying to find it, my hand touches a long, cold arm. I scream and pull my fingers away quickly. The arm retreats from me with equal rapidity.

'Get off me,' my brother shouts.

His voice is hoarse, more like a bark. In the almost completely black depths of what I realise now is a totally moonless night, my eyes start to adjust and I can make out his blonde hair and his upper body. He's wearing sweat pants on his bottom half and a white, sleeveless top on his upper half. God knows why he isn't wearing anything else. It's freezing out here. The skin of his shoulders and arms is almost translucent and as easy to make out in the darkness as a high vis jacket would be. He's squatting on his haunches and he seems to be out of breath.

'Why are you following me?' He gasps.

'I'm not. I didn't even know you were out here.'

'Liar. You heard me shutting the back door.'

'I didn't actually, because you left it open,' I say, triumphantly, not caring one bit that I sound like a kid in a playground.

'Oh right. I didn't mean to. Sorry,' he says sarcastically.

'Why you out here?'

'I thought I heard something moving around'

'Behind the outhouses?'

'No, not really. I don't know where it was coming from. The main reason I'm round here is because I was hiding from you.'

'Why, you total bastard?'

'I didn't realise it was you.'

'What did you think it was.'

'Dunno.'

I'm conflicted by this: pleased that someone else has heard exactly what I heard and overjoyed that my brother agrees with me about something for once. But at the same time, I'm appalled because I can no longer tell myself I imagined it.

My brother is wheezing. You can hear the tightness in his chest. Without thinking, I go over to him and grasp him under his arms to pull him into a more upright position.

'Get your filthy hands off me!'

He shoves me away with such force, I fall backwards again, into the nettles. The back of my neck begins to itch.

Jacob's decision to use the word *filthy* is calculated. He's throwing down a gauntlet, He knows how much of a trigger that word is for me. It stemmed from Dad saying I was a gremlin that emerged from a ditch. Jacob, Amanda and Dad were so blonde and fair skinned, compared to me, I really did feel like a changeling a lot of the time, a dirty little boy. I ended up with a permanent insecurity about hygiene issues that is still so severe I spend half my life in the shower or the bath, and I get through almost two cans of deodorant every single week. My brother used to be sympathetic and patient with me about my cleanliness problem. He was always ready to reassure me that I looked as clean as everyone else and he said the only odour that ever wafted towards him from me was deodorant or some male fragrance product or other. I used to ask for those as birthday or Christmas presents.

I bounce back up from the ground, push him against the wall of the outhouse and slap him hard across the face. 'You shit. You miserable little shit,' I growl.

All the careful civility of the last few days goes out of the window. It feels wonderful, like a drug, and I want more. I swing my arm back to slap him again, but he's ready for me this time and he grabs my wrist and pulls it down to my side. He does the same to my other wrist and digs his fingers in as he twists me round and slams me against the wall. The back of my head scrapes against the rough brickwork and he presses his forehead against mine.

'You think you're so fucking awesome don't you? Dr Gawain, with your hot boyfriend and your big house and your fabulous career and every damn fucking thing going your way.'

'It's not my fault you attached yourself to bunch of psychopaths.'

He lets go of one wrist to thump me in the stomach, then he grabs it again.

'It *is* your fault. You know it is, you vile little cunt.'

'I've said I'm sorry. And I nearly got myself killed trying to rescue you. What more do you want from me?'

'You never have shown up if you'd known *that* was going to happen. And as for being sorry, you have no bloody idea. Dad was right about you. You're minging. It's no wonder Mum...'

'Mum what?'

He doesn't answer. His face is distorted with rage and his eyes burn unshed tears. Without letting go of my wrists, he steps back very slightly. He's going to headbutt me. Jesus. He's way more unhinged than I thought.

But now isn't the time to carry out a mental health assessment. I realise I can move my left leg. Jacob is too enraged to notice when I slowly bend it upwards. And it comes as a complete surprise to him when I slam my knee into his balls. He yells and falls backwards. I jump on top of him and jam the same knee into his crotch for a second time. I wait for him to push me off, but he doesn't. Because he can't breathe. Serves him right.

I sit on his stomach and get hold of his right hand. I bend his thumb back as far as it will go. He lets out a loud groan.

'That's for saying I'm dirty.'

'Filthy,' he gasps.

I grab his index finger and bent it back. 'That's for refusing to forgive me for what I did, even when you knew I was genuinely sorry.'

I do the same to each of his other fingers, one by one. With each finger, I drag up some grievance from our past to justify the pain I'm administering. The items I come up with are serious to start with, but they become increasingly lame, with each successive digit. Nevertheless, the gratification I get from the moans and whines he hurls at me never diminishes.

I finish with his right hand and grab his left thumb. I'm just about to start on more recent grievances, ones that have arisen in the last few weeks. But when I stare down and watch him as he yells and begs for mercy, I realise there's an element of the theatrical in his voice. His anger is genuine, as is mine, but soon one will cancel out the other. I love the noises he's making and I appreciate and respect him for the effort he's putting into them. Similarly, I know he secretly adores the way I'm bouncing up and down on his stomach, restricting and then releasing his already laboured breathing.

This is a ritual fight between blood brothers who are satisfying a shared urge. The whole thing is amazing, or awesome, as Jacob would say if he could speak, and I realise how very, very lucky I am to have a brother who knows the worst possible thing anyone could ever say to me, the thing that pushes all my buttons at the same time. I can't imagine how I've managed to exist for the last eight years without having him on hand to torment and insult me in such an intimate and personal way.

In a minute, I'll get off him. Then we might wrestle and roll about in the long grass for a bit. After that, we'll stop and go inside.

Unfortunately, Bartosz chooses this particular moment to appear. He's wearing his least favourite dressing gown, the red velvet one with the three quarter length sleeves, which is a bad sign, and he's blind to the subtleties of this *brother* thing that's just flared up between Jacob and me. All he sees is me sitting on Jacob, pushing his fingers back and squashing him while he struggles to breathe. He pulls me up, away from my brother. This frustrates the hell out of me because I wasn't quite finished.

I sink my teeth into the flesh of Bartosz's lower arm. I'm fully aware this is a step too far, but I'm in such a state of frenzied passion I don't care.

'You vicious little bitch!' Bartosz grunts. He wraps his arms round me from behind and drags me backwards. I shout at him to get off me and I wriggle like hell, but his hold on me becomes increasingly vice-like until I can't move my arms or my legs or any other part of my body.

'I'm not letting go until you calm down.'

'I can't.'

He puts one hand over my mouth and looks at his watch.

'If you move or speak again, I'll restrain you for another thirty seconds.'

My brother props himself up on his elbows and laughs.

'It's not bloody funny,' Bartosz says.

*

The following night, I know I won't be able to sleep, so I go and sit in the man-cave and start half watching a documentary about cannibalism, with the volume turned down low so I don't miss anything kicking off outside. Soon, Jacob joins me. I haven't seen him since last night. I think he stayed in his room most of the day. In the light from the TV screen, his skin tone is a pale, slightly luminous green, like a tasteful Halloween mask. I decide not to mention it.

'This is gross,' he says.

'Grim.'

'Do you ever get half eaten patients in your A&E?'

I'm just about to respond to this piss-take of a question with the scorn it deserves, when Jacob suddenly leaps out of his chair and dashes to one of the windows facing the front of the house. He pushes up the blind up and stares into the darkness. I join him.

'It's like a whole load of stuff is going on out there, but you can't hear it or see it.'

'I think you need to speak to someone, Jacob. Not Bartosz. This kind of thing drives him bonkers. Someone better qualified.'

'Like a shrink?'

'Yeah.'

He turns to face me and hold out his hand. 'Let me introduce myself. I'm Kettle. I believe you're known as Pot?'

'Shut up.'

I start thinking about what I should say next to add fuel to this enjoyable little contretemps and maybe build it up into a full-blown slanging match, but I'm forced to put it on hold, because a car suddenly shoots across the gap in the hedge from left to right in the direction of the barn, followed quickly by the sound of tyres squealing and an enormous, glass-shattering crash. There shouldn't be any cars out there. The lane, and the land it runs through belongs to the house and the gate is always locked at night. We put trainers on, grab torches from the ledge by the back door and leg it out of the house as quickly as we can. We make it through the gap in the hedge and half way down the track towards the barn before we both have to slow down to walking pace. Rapid movement still makes me dizzy and Jacob's asthma is bugging him again.

When we finally make it past the bend and reach the point where the barn comes into view, there is no sign of any car.

'This is so uncanny valley,' Jacob says.

'It must have crashed through the barn and gone into the field.'

We walk on, straining our ears and wave our torches about in the darkness that surrounds us, but we see nothing and hear even less. We reach the barn and inspect the hedges that surround three of its open sides. They are all intact.

'I don't get this,' I say. 'It must have gone somewhere.'

We turn away from the barn and start walking back along the lane towards the house. Just after the bend, we hear the screech of tyres behind us and car headlights cast shadows of us silhouettes of us onto the ground by our feet. We both jump backwards to get out of its way and end up in the ditch, which is full of brambles. By the time we've pulled ourselves free of the long, prickly tendrils and got ourselves onto the lane again, the car has screeched back round the big right-angled curve. It sounds as though it's hurtling towards the gate. We can't see anything, but we hear it squeal to a halt, followed by the same crashing sounds that came from the direction of the barn, although this time I think I hear a heavy metallic crunch, too, and a man shouting.

We head to the gate, staying close to the side of the track so we can jump out of the way if the car comes back again. But when we get there, all the noise has stopped. There is no car and no sign of anything unusual: no skid marks, no broken glass and no sheared off pieces of metal. The gate is intact and securely locked. The only way to open it is via a keypad or the control panel in the kitchen. Jacob clambers over and walks a few metres down the road. He shines his phone about, first in one direction and then the other.

'Nothing,' he shouts.

His voice is quickly swallowed up by the surrounding silence. He climbs back over the gate and drops down onto his knees. Then he looks at me for a couple of seconds with wild eyes. As I watch and wonder what on earth he's about to do or say, he throws up all over the grass. I go and stand close to him, and my hands move forward to push his hair away from his forehead and stroke his back, but I manage to stop myself.

'Better out than in,' I say instead, in Aunty Susan's voice.

He laughs and puke sprays out of his nose. Once he's completely certain he has nothing more to add to the splat he's deposited by the gate, we move away from it, lower ourselves down onto a log further back up the lane and discuss what has just happened.

I'm desperate to find a rational explanation. 'The car must have been further away than we thought,' I say. 'There's a lot of winding lanes round here, going through the middle of all these woods, and sound travels differently at night.'

'But we both saw it.'

'Maybe we dazzled ourselves with our own torches?'

'Like this?'

Jacob shines his torch in my face and waves it around. Then he turns it on himself and does a selection of grimaces and impersonations, of teachers from school and Aunty Susan. His performance diverts and entertains us both for a while, but then he goes really serious and looks at me.

'The thing is, G, it sounded exactly the same as the crash outside the church. The revving up of the car engine, the squeal of the brakes, the glass breaking and that heavy crunch when the bonnet crumpled against the side of your VW. It was the same. Like a kind of delayed echo.'

He must be more feverish than I thought.

'Is that really what you think or are you winding me up?'

'I know for sure that's what it was.'

'But you can't possibly remember the exact sounds from the crash.'

'I'll never be able to erase them from my mind.'

I decide to humour him.

'Ok, say you're right. What do you think would've happened if we hadn't got out of the way when it came towards us?'

'It would have passed straight through us, as though it wasn't really there. It *wasn't* really there. It was a trick of time, an event from past that returned and superimposed itself on the present. Like that horse and carriage that goes past the church near where Borley Rectory used to be.'

'Haunting by vehicle.'

'Yeah. Kind of.'

'Why, though?'

'The crash was a big deal for us both, obviously. The memory of it will always be somewhere in the back of our minds, and we haven't even begun to process it yet.'

'I can't remember any of it.'

'It'll be in there, tucked away in a dark recess somewhere.'

We slowly make our way back to the house. When we get there our plan is to go straight inside to bed.

But the night isn't done with us yet.

24. Gawain

'Something's not right,' Jacob says as we walk back through the gap in the hedge.

His voice is calm and quiet, and extremely eerie. I think of the phrase *chilled to the bone*. That's how he's making me feel. I look at him and follow his gaze, which is directed towards the outhouses. The door to the one on the far right is open, and light from inside is spilling out onto the grass. Jacob starts to cross the lawn towards the open door. I don't want to go anywhere near it, but I can't let Jacob handle this on his own, so I force myself to follow him.

When he gets there, the door suddenly slams shut and the light goes off. We both leap back.

'Is it windy enough for that to happen?' I ask, trying to sound casual, as though I'm asking a rational question about a regular occurrence.

'I don't know. But even if it was, the light couldn't switch itself on and off on its own. Could it?'

'There might be an electrical fault.'

'Nah, someone's in there.'

Jacob steps forward, pulls the door wide open and shouts *hello?*

It's difficult to describe what happens next. A maelstrom of noise seems to leaps out at us from the little room. It sounds a bit like the wings of an enormous bird flapping against the walls, and also as though someone or something in soft shoes is shuffling about and making dull thuds as it bashes into stuff.

He shuts the door again, quickly.

'Maybe it's an owl?' I suggest.

'Wearing gigantic slippers?'

This particular outhouse is empty at the moment. Bartosz has cleared it out to make space for a hot tub. But right now, it sounds as though the space inside is cluttered with all sorts of stuff and the thing inside is crashing into it and knocking everything over.

'I don't know what it is,' Jacob says. 'But I think it wants to get out.'

He steps forward and opens the door again. The light has gone off, so we can't see what's inside, but we hear what sounds like a big creature fluttering and flapping about and frantically rocking from side to side.

Then the sound stops, and a tremor enters my chest, passes straight through my heart and departs through my back.

'Did you feel that?' Jacob asks.

He goes back into the outhouse and switches the light on. A single bulb illuminates the space. The walls are painted freshly painted in a calm eggshell blue and the room is completely empty. Quickly, he switches the light off again and shuts the door.

'It's gone,' he says in a weirdly quiet voice.

'It must have been an animal.'

He shakes his head. Then he does it again and again, with increasing rapidity, as though he's building up to a three hundred and sixty degree swivel, exorcist-style. If he does that, I'll die.

'Stop it,' I say.

'What?'

'Shaking your head like that.'

'Sorry. It's just. I get it now.'

I don't know what scares me most at the moment, the thing that just happened in the outhouse or the look on my brother's face.

'It was Mum,' he says.

Jesus.

'What the hell?'

'It was Mum. I don't want her going through me like that.'

'It was a big bird.'

'Like the one on Sesame Street?'

'Not Big Bird, you melt. An owl maybe, or a red kite. Or an eagle that's escaped from somewhere. It didn't go *through* us as such, it went near us as it flew away and we felt its wings vibrating or something, because it was so big.'

I take a risk and tentatively pat his arm. He lets me, but only for a few seconds. When he realises, he pulls away and stares down at the place the area where my hand made contact, as though my fingers have burnt his skin.

'I don't want her anywhere near me.'

Jacob's been incredibly courageous tonight. I'd never have had the guts to go back into the outhouse like he did just then. But now he sounds like a little boy.

'She wouldn't hurt us,' I say.

'She might. Anyway, I thought you said it was a bird.'

'It was.'

'What if it was her, though?'

'None of this is real. Something's messing with our heads.'

'Yeah, Mum is. She was dreaming about us and trying to make contact. I think she's been trying to do that for a while.'

He shakes his arms and stamps his feet as though he's cold. But what he's really doing is trying to cast off the strangeness.

'You're not thinking straight,' I say. 'Anyway, it's gone now.'

I'm not sure it has entirely, but I'm hopeful that saying it out loud will cast the thing into oblivion, once and for all. And anyway, I desperately want to sound like the confident reassuring big brother I used to be once, long ago. He looks at me and nods. I think he wants me to be that, too, just at this moment.

After that, everything really does feel normal again, and we're just two blokes, standing outside, shivering, in the early hours of a cold, winter morning. When we get back into the kitchen he says he's starving. He's lost that alabaster look and I know I should remind him it's not long since he threw up and suggest he sticks to dry toast or plain biscuits, but like he says, I'm not his doctor, and although I'm still his big brother, he's a grown man now, and he's entitled to decide for himself if he wants to risk puking again. I rummage around in the fridge and find a big supermarket raspberry trifle in a plastic bowl. Between us, we wolf the whole lot down. I watch him, my long lost brother, the front of his T-shirt rancid with vomit where he used it to wipe his face, shovelling whipped cream and cold custard into his mouth as though he's scared someone will snatch it away. I know he doesn't feel the same way about me. I accept that. I don't blame him.

But I'd die for him. Anytime. In fact, if he asked me to drown myself right now by face-diving into the remains of the trifle, I'd do it.

*

Next morning, a muffled buzzing sound drags me from a deep sleep. I sit up and notice my phone flashing underneath the wardrobe. God knows how it got there. I drop from the bed onto the floor and slide across to it, but it stops just before I reach it. When I see it's a missed call from one of the hospital numbers, I assume it's about my next neurology appointment, and I almost decide to leave it for now and go back to sleep. Instead, I press the recall button. After a few rings, a female voice answers. It's Clare, one of the nurses from ICU.

'Hi Clare' I say, all breezily.

'Hi Gawain.'

I pick up the edge in her voice and I know exactly what she's going to tell me.

'I'm not really meant to be ringing you like this,' she says. 'Seeing as to you're not listed as the next of kin. At least you won't be saddled with the admin, though.'

'It's all down to the brother?'

'Aldo Valdini. He's making arrangements for her to be transported up to Yorkshire.'

I pause, in an attempt to take all this in. Then I realise it will take way more than a few seconds. 'What was the time of death?'

'Three twenty-four.'

After terminating the call, I sit on the floor for a while, pulling bits of fluff out of the carpet, waiting for the news to sink in and wondering whether I'll cry when it does. Nothing happens, so I go and look in on my brother. He's lying face down on his bed, fast asleep. I hate the idea of waking him, so I head downstairs to tell Bartosz. He's in the room at the front of the house, which he uses as study, doing things with numbers on his lap top. A mug of coffee is going cold by his left hand. I put my arms round his shoulders and press my face into the back of his neck. I know this will annoy him while he's trying to focus on work, particularly in his current mood, but I need to smell his hair and his skin.

'See any ghosts last night?' He asks in a distant voice from spreadsheet land.

'Plenty. But I've just had a phone call from the hospital.'

That gets his attention. He turns to look at me.

'Have you told Jacob?'

'Not yet. I don't want to wake him."

'You must.'

'Can you do it?' I don't know what to say.'

'Jesus Christ, Gawain. He's your brother, not mine. Man up for once in your life.'

I turn away quickly in an attempt to hide the fact that my eyes have now filled with tears, but he notices and his voice softens.

'Tell him to come down and sit in the living room. I'll move my work stuff onto the ping pong table so I can hover in the background. Keep an eye on you.'

I know Bartosz is right. I should be the one to tell my brother, but it seems horribly cruel disturbing him with such bad news when he's so deeply asleep, and I'm scared he might find a way to blame the messenger, seeing as it's me. I sit on his bed and shake his shoulders, gently. He turns onto his back, bewildered, but after he's rubbed his eyes and focused his gaze onto my face, I don't need to say anything. I had no idea at all how he would react to this news. He could be relieved or devastated or anything in between for all I know. He gives me a searching look as though he's wondering the same about me.

'Bartosz says don't stay up here on your own. Unless you want to go back to sleep.'

'I won't be able to sleep now.'

Eventually, he appears, freshly showered, in clean clothes, and flops down next to me on the sofa. Bartosz comes over, puts his hands on Jacob's shoulders and then lifts one hand and presses his palm down on the top of Jacob's wet hair as though he's giving him a blessing. It's a peculiarly manly gesture that I've not seen before. It hits just the right note, but I can't help feeling a bit aggrieved that he doesn't do the same thing to me. He disappears and returns with mugs of sweet tea. Then he relocates to the ping pong table with his laptop and his calculations, and fades into the background so he can watch over us from a tactful distance. Rays of cold sunlight cross the room and Jacob rests his head against the sofa and screws his eyes shut. I ask him if he wants me to close the blinds. He shakes his head.

'Now we definitely know what last night was about,' he says.

'The car?'

'It was a re-run of the accident, which killed her in the end, as it turns out. And the noises in the outhouse were her soul trying to escape.'

'Why would her soul be trapped in Bartosz's outhouse?'

'It wasn't. Not literally. It was trying to escape from her body. The outhouse was where the whole thing was staged, because we were close by. She wanted to say farewell to us and that she was sorry for everything. She had to do that before she could move on.'

He delivers this interpretation of last night's events in a matter-of-fact voice, as though it's a satisfactory end to his dealings with his mother and he's as ready to move on as she supposedly is.

'Jacob, for God's sake.'

'What's your explanation, then, smart-arse?'

'Like I said last night, the car must have been further away than we thought. The sound of the crash travelled an unusually long way because of atmospheric conditions or something. And the noises coming from the outhouse were animals or birds.'

'It's called retrocognitive dissonance, what you're doing. People often backtrack after they've witnessed strange phenomena. They find excuses to explain it all away. Particularly scientists like you. You congratulate yourselves on being so rational and clued up with your left-brain way of thinking but you know sod all about anything.'

'Whereas people like you make stuff up because it's more interesting than the truth.'

'It *is* the truth.'

I wonder if Bartosz will come and stop us squabbling, in case it escalates. I look round and see he's sitting bolt upright, listening to our conversation.

'Did you make a note of the time when the outhouse thing happened?' He asks.

Jacob nods. 'It was about half past three when it all stopped.'

'And Claire said your Mum died at what time?'

'Three twenty-six,' I say.

'There you go then. It was Mum. Case closed.'

'There's something wrong with the electrics in the outhouses,' Bartosz says. 'I keep meaning to get someone in to have a look.'

He's not overly impressed by Jacob's interpretation of events, then, despite egging him on by asking about the time of death. If I was the one favouring the supernatural version of events, he'd tell me to pack it in, that it was all coincidence, that I should grow up and stop letting myself get carried away.

Jacob sighs. 'Her last thoughts were about us, and at the point of death she wanted us to know she was sorry for being such a crap mother. She couldn't leave until she'd communicated that to us.'

'You can't possibly believe that.'

'Can't I? Ok. Thanks for telling me. I won't, then.'

When Amanda pulls into the drive after morning surgery, she finds us both outside exploring the outhouse again, opening and slamming the door and jumping up and down inside to see if we can get the light to come on. It remains resolutely in the off position. Amanda pushes herself between us and puts an arm round each of our waists.

'How are we, boys?'

'Yeah. Fine, I think,' Jacob says.

'How are you?' I ask my sister.

'All the time you were in hospital, Gawain, and I was coming in every day, I never once went to see her. And she was only upstairs. I'd be a hypocrite if I got upset now she's dead, wouldn't I?'

'That doesn't matter.' Jacob says. 'She was still your mother. You can be sad if you want to.'

'I'm not feeling anything, right now. I'm not sad, not grieving. Not happy she's dead. Not bothered either way.'

This bluntness is so typical of my sister and so reassuring it makes me laugh, but something twists in my gut and my laughter threatens to turn into something else. Jacob gives me a sharp, sideways glance and I clamp my lips together.

We go in and sit in the man cave again. Bartosz joins us. We drink tea and wolf down the cheese sandwiches, sausage rolls, crisps and red velvet cake he conjures up for us.

'Carbs for the shock,' he says. 'And for the babby,' he adds, looking at Amanda.

I dip some cake in my tea. It falls to bits and I spend ages scooping it up with a teaspoon. Gives me something to do while I struggle with the fact that my siblings seem totally fine about the death of our mother.

Three days later, I get an E-mail from Aldo Valdini. Claire must have passed on my details. Aldo has sent us an invitation to our mother's funeral and wake in East Yorkshire. The funeral is at a catholic church in the village where we lived before Aunty Susan came and whisked us away, and the wake is somewhere called White Farm.

I phone Amanda. She comes over again.

'That must be where me and Dad went to bring you home with us. Where I got the acorns.'

Something snags at my memory, and I try very hard to pin it down, but it slips away again.

'We should go,' she adds. 'Apart from anything else, I want to meet this Aldo Valdini. I didn't realise we had Italian relatives.'

'Me neither.' But as soon as I've said this, faint echoes of words spoken in a strange dialect start to bubble up from the deepest, darkest parts of my memory. I understood what some of them meant, once. And I knew the people who spoke them as well as I knew myself.'

'You look a bit Italian,' Jacob says, looking at me. 'As did Mum.'

'Is that meant to be an insult?'

'What the hell? Why would it be an insult? What's wrong with looking a bit Italian?'

'Nothing.'

'What are you going on about, then?'

'Just the way you said it. As though you think I'm a wierdo. Anyway, you have the same nose as me. Maybe it's an Italian nose.'

'Great. Who cares?'

'Boys!' Amanda shouts.

'I'm definitely up for going,' Jacob says.

'But what if they're all, you know. Like Mum?' I ask.

'I've had an idea about that,' Amanda says. 'Why don't we go up there, anyway, for a holiday? I've got leave to take and you're not going back to work for nearly another month, Gawain. All we have to do is show our faces at the church. If we get bad vibes and they make us feel uncomfortable or unwelcome, or it quickly becomes obvious they're all stark raving bonkers, we can sneak out. We don't have to go to the wake. The rest of the time, we can do what we like. Chill, go swimming, have little outings to places like Bridlington.

'Not Bridlington,' Jacob says.

'Scarborough, then.'

'Or Filey,' I add, remembering an outing with Dad when we had apple pie with whipped cream at a café on a caravan site, after walking along the Brigg. The pastry was so soft it melted in my mouth without needing to be chewed.

'I've already found somewhere for us to stay.' Amanda forwards us a link to a holiday park consisting of luxury wooden lodges surrounded by trees, with a lake and a swimming pool and spa complex under a dome.

'Looks awesome,' Jacob says.

25. Gawain

Amanda books a chalet for us at the holiday park, and things settle down a bit in the run up to the funeral.

Then Bartosz dumps me.

We're basking in what I think is a warm and happy post coital glow. But he rolls over onto his back and stares at the ceiling. 'You've been through a tough time, but now you're just about over it,' he says flatly.

I turn onto my side and prop myself up on my elbows to look at him. But he won't meet my gaze.

'True. And?'

'You'll be wanting to move on, now you're ok again more or less and you've got Jacob back.'

'What do you mean, move on?'

'You're still young. You've got so much ahead of you. Why waste your life on a clapped out old soldier like me?'

'Clapped out?' I almost laugh.

Then I understand.

'You're dumping me.'

'I'm just saying, if *you* want to end things, now would be a good time.'

'If *I* want to end things? You're hitting me with the *it's not you it's me* bollocks? When really, as far as you're concerned, I've turned out to be nothing but a stupid little twink, and you want rid of me?'

'That's not what I'm saying at all.'

'That's what it sounds like to me?'

'It's not that. I just want to give you the opportunity to take time out and re-think everything. If you decide you want to leave, it would be best to do it now, before we get too entrenched.'

'We're already entrenched aren't we?'

He shrugs.

'Don't you feel entrenched?'

He doesn't reply.

'Bartosz?'

'It's just, I don't know. It all happened so quickly, and you hadn't been with anyone else for such a long time. And the way you've been carrying on lately, all this ghost stuff and this bad blood between you and Jacob, it makes me think you've still got a fair bit of growing up to do. You don't really know what you want yet, particularly when it comes to me.'

I try to digest what he's just said. I don't much like the way it sits in my stomach.

'And you've got Jacob back now,' he repeats.

'Jacob's my brother, not your replacement, and anyway, I haven't got him back. If he belongs to anyone, which he doesn't, it's *you*. He barely tolerates *me*.'

'That's down to you.'

'What does *that* mean?'

'It means stop behaving like a little kid and get to grips with what you've done to him.'

'I've been trying to do that.'

'No you haven't. All you've done is caper about with him in the middle of the night, as though you're in an episode of Scooby Doo, egging him on with his crazy ideas about ghosts and all that. He's been through a lot. He isn't over it yet. It will take a while. Right now, he needs stability and support, not a playmate. You've got to settle yourself down and talk to him properly. Listen to what he has to say, then bloody well apologise and get him to see that you mean it.'

'Right. Thanks very much for the advice.'

I get out of bed, find my clothes, pull them on as quickly as possible, grab what possessions I can find at such short notice and stuff them into a holdall. Then I call a cab.

When I try to leave the bedroom, Bartosz blocks the exit.

'You've misunderstood me. Completely.'

'I'm not stupid, Bartosz. You want to break up with me. End of.'

'That's not what I said. Come on, don't leave like this. It's past midnight.'

He grabs me by the shoulders and his blue eyes bore into mine. After a few seconds I can't bear it and I have to look down at the floor.

He regroups. 'Ok. Let me put it another way. You've got two days before you go up North for the funeral. While you're there, have a good think about what you want. And sort things out with your brother.'

He stands to let me pass and follows me downstairs. We sit across the kitchen table from each other waiting for my cab to arrive. I worry that the driver won't be able to find the turning and I get up and use the keypad on the wall to open the gate remotely. When I sit down again I think back to that first time we sat in this kitchen together. Neither of us could find a seating position that brought us sufficiently close to each other. I still want to merge with him like that. I'd do it now if he'd let me, if he wasn't frowning at me across a big void.

'Look at it as a trial separation,' he says.

'I don't need a fortnight away from you to make up my mind.'

'You might start seeing things differently when you're away from here. Particularly if you patch things up with Jacob.'

'I won't.'

'You might. And we shouldn't contact each other, either.'

'Why not?'

'It'll give you a chance to clear your head.'

'And get myself into a state of mind where I can accept that you don't want to be with me?'

'Gawain, have you heard anything I've said?'

I can't speak to him anymore. I can't even bear to be in the same room as him. Without saying another word and without looking at him again, I get up and unlock the kitchen door. I walk down to the gate in the darkness, dragging my holdall behind me, so I can wait for the cab on the road. But when it arrives and we drive off, I feel as though I'm being physically ripped away from Bartosz against my will. I have to grip the edge of the glove compartment to stop myself opening the door, jumping out of the moving car and running back to Picardy. I've got keys. I could let myself in, go upstairs and climb back into bed and say *can't we talk about this some more?* Make him change his mind. Beg him, if necessary.

My flat smells like a place nobody would ever want as their home, an unwelcoming mixture of plastic, damp and black mould. A lone plant, a housewarming gift from Amanda, sits on my table drying out and waiting for death in its cheerful little pink pot. I go to the kitchen and fill a glass with water to pour onto its parched soil. Then I sift quickly and numbly through all the mail that's accumulated on the floor, throwing most of it back down again without really looking at it, until I get to a letter from the police.

It says they won't be prosecuting my mother for attempted murder now she's dead. They use more official language than that, obviously, but still. What a stupid letter. Do the dead sometimes get prosecuted, then? But that's not the point. My mother was driving the car that accelerated into me. My mother tried to kill me. Or rather, my mother nearly *did* kill me. I wonder if anyone else apart from the police know about this. They must have told Jacob when he went to make his statement about the crash. And I bet he relayed the information to Bartosz in one of their sessions. But neither of them told me. They preferred to let me think it was Slab-Face.

I remember the litre bottle of Polish vodka I left in the kitchen cupboard when I moved in with Bartosz. I take it to bed with me. My duvet feels damp and tacky, but I wrap it around me and spend the rest of the night sitting up, huddled over the bottle. Every mouthful makes my eyes water and my salivary glands shrink. I doze lightly from time to time, but I'm never under for long. I'm scared that if I sleep too deeply, I'll think I'm with Bartosz when I wake up and I won't be able to bear the shock when I realise I'm alone in my flat.

In the morning, most of the vodka is gone, and my phone suddenly starts jumping all over the bedside cabinet as it fills up with messages from Jacob, who was asleep when I left the house. Then a few from Amanda start to appear. But there's nothing from the only person I really want to engage with. He meant what he said about zero contact, then. I turn my phone off so I don't have to listen to it pinging and vibrating.

I walk over to the balcony window and look out. Rain is pouring down and the clump of trees on the other side of the railway lines looks like a set of gibbets now the leaves have gone. The two gentlemen will be sequestered away in the library of the big house now, with a fire blazing in the grate.

I can hear the distant hum of traffic on the motorway. The southbound cars will soon be passing the petrol station you can see from the barn, a mere jog across a muddy field from Bartosz. Closer to the window, a robin is singing. It goes on and on, in long warbling bursts, piercing my brain like an avian pneumatic drill. It makes me realise it will be Christmas soon. I was *so* looking forward to spending it with Bartosz and Jacob, getting a huge tree for the hallway, inviting loads of people round, deciding what gifts to buy.

I can't go on like this.

I have to bring it all to a close, as soon as possible, preferably before I sober up. But how? None of the obvious options appeal. Then I remember the small convection heater I bought to heat the flat quickly when the central heating had broken down. I plug its extension lead into a socket in the living room, take the heater into the bathroom, put it on the floor, run a hot bath and get in. Then I realise I don't want to be found naked, so I get out again and rummage around in my bag until I find my Lycra running shorts. Once I'm submerged again, I pick up the convection heater from the bathroom floor, switch it on and hold it up to my face.

It purrs warm air at me and blows my hair back from my forehead. I think about the blank emptiness I've fought so hard all my life to avoid falling into. Is death the ultimate emptiness, or is there another world beyond ours, and will people I know be there, like Dad or even Mum? I don't really care. I just want to terminate this particular existence. I remember that song Bartosz is so fond of, and I decide that no, I don't fear the reaper. Not one bit. I'm much more afraid of waking up to another morning of being me again, the person who came from nowhere, who nobody wants, stuck on his own in this miserable flat, with that heavy grey sky hanging outside the windows, already gathering itself together for another endless night, even though the day has barely begun.

'Piss off world. Glad to be going.'

I raise my arms to plunge the heater into the water and inhale deeply, thinking this will be the last breath I ever take.

But an image comes into my head of the electricity zig-zagging through the bathwater to my body in a series of electric blue waves, and it terrifies me so much that I scream, drop the heater on the floor and jump out of the bath. I sit across from it on the soggy mat and let its warm air caress my face and my shoulders. Gradually, as the constant, parching heat makes the bathwater evaporate from my upper half, leaving my skin smooth and dry, I start to think that if I hole up here in my flat and remain constantly enveloped in this tropical atmosphere, I'll be ok. Maybe I should nip out to the local DIY superstore and buy a couple more heaters, in case this one breaks down. I could pick up a few more bottles of vodka at the same time. I listen to its whirring and focus on the way the sound undulates, becoming louder and then softer and then louder again, as though it has some kind of agency and its main aim in life is to sooth me. This could be a new type of therapeutic intervention. Next time I have to treat a patient who's taken an overdose, I could suggest they buy a fan heater instead. Just try it, I'll say. You'll be amazed.

I have no idea how long I sit on my damp bath mat, basking in endless waves of thermal convection and listening to their song before I suddenly become aware of other sounds, muffled thuds, irregular and jarring, coming from somewhere beyond the constant thrum of the heater.

At first I ignore them, but they don't stop.

'Are you in there?'

I stagger to my feet and wander vaguely across the living room floor towards the door. I become instantly cold as soon as I move out of the heater's range, but I can still hear its steady hum behind me. I keep stopping to listen to it, so it takes me a while to reach the door. On the other side, my brother repeats my name over and over again.

'Why are you calling me Gawain?'

'It's your name.'

'You usually call me G, or dickhead. Or wanker. Or Tosspot.'

'Whatever. Can you let me in?'

'Nope.'

I sway from side to side and watch the door knob vibrate as he tries to turn it.

'Ok then. I'm going to dial 999,' Jacob yells.

'Cool.'

'But first I'm ringing Amanda.'

I open the door. He strides in, pulling behind him two suitcases on wheels. He has two dark suits, with matching shirts and sober ties, wrapped in clear plastic, draped over one arm. My brother looks as though he's arrived at what he thought was a five star hotel, only to find he's accidentally booked himself into a seriously dodgy hostel occupied by a small madman in wet shorts. He kicks his way through the pile of mail I didn't get round to reading after I'd found the letter from the police, and as he surveys the state of the place and of me, his height and thinness, and the way his eyes and mouth form almost perfect circles, transform him into a human exclamation mark. An upside down one. He doesn't need words.

'You should think about becoming a mime artist,' I say.

He gives me a funny look, and I watch as he drops the cases, lays the suits across one arm of the sofa, and follows my damp footprints across the floor, into to the bathroom. He comes running out again, carrying the convector above his head. 'You supreme, fucking tosser!' He shouts as he searches for the socket. When he finds it, he switches off the convector and unplugs the extension lead from the wall. He holds the heater at arm's length, as though it's a dangerous animal that might bite him if he isn't careful.

'How did you get here?'

'Bartosz gave me a lift.'

I dash over to the balcony door, open it and scoot outside to try and catch a glimpse of him sitting outside in his car, not caring how pathetic it makes me look. Jacob follows me and chucks the fan heater over the balcony wall. At first I think it's going to miss the cars parked closest to the flats, but it bounces off the laurel hedge at the side of the building and crashes into the hood of a red mini with a white top and union jacks on the backs of its wing mirrors.

'That's my heater!' I grab hold of the front of his puffer jacket and start trying to push him towards the door of the flat. 'Go fetch it!'

Jacob stands his ground. 'Not doing that. Not now. Not ever. And Bartosz left as soon as he'd dropped me off. He didn't want you to see him.'

I collapse onto the living room floor in front of the sofa. My brother stands over me and scratches his head.

I start to feel a bit sorry for him.

'I need to let Bartosz and Amanda know you're ok,' he says eventually. 'Obviously, you're in a right state, but I'll gloss over that. Don't move.'

He marches off into the bedroom and shuts the door.

I can hear his voice, through the closed door, but not what he's saying. Not that I care. Right now, I'm more worried about the heater. I hope it still works. Maybe I could sneak out and get it while Jacob's in the bedroom? But I'm only wearing a pair of wet shorts and I don't think I'm capable of finding clothes and getting dressed at the moment.

It doesn't take him long to make his phone calls, and then he's back, staring down at me, again, with his hands on his hips. I look up at him but I have to stop because he's shaking his head so much it makes me dizzy. After a while, he marches off into the bathroom and reappears with a large towel, which he drops onto the top of my head.

I rub my hair and my eyes with the towel and then wrap it around my shoulders. Next I pull my soggy shorts off and throw them across the room. We both watch as they stick to the wall opposite and slowly sink to the floor like a half cooked pancake.

'Now you know I'm ok, you can leave,' I say.

'In what sense are you ok, exactly?'

'I'm fine.'

'Knock it off, bro.' He sounds really American when he says that. It still happens sometimes, even now, after he's been back in the UK for several months. I think it might be a sign that he's really angry, but it makes me want to laugh. What's wrong with me?

'I'm meant to be dead in the bath.'

'Exactly. I'm not going anywhere.'

'You can't move in with me. There's not enough room.'

'Shut up. I don't mean permanently. There's been a change of plan. Amanda's picking us both up from here the day after tomorrow.'

'Why's she doing that?'

'Our trip. The funeral – you haven't forgotten, have you?'

'I've had other things on my mind. Anyway, I'm not going. She tried to kill me. Mum, I mean. Not Amanda. She can sod off and go to her own funeral. On her own. Without me.'

I say this with a bit of a flourish, as though I think I'm being clever, but I must be sobering up a bit, in a relative sense, because I've suddenly become aware that I'm slurring my words. He crouches down in front of me.

'Who told you?'

'It was on the floor.' I wave vaguely in the direction of the front door. 'Letter from the police. They're not doing attempted murder on her now. She's dead, so she wouldn't be able to make it. Unless they dig her up and usher her into the courtroom propped up in a wheelie bin.'

'Shit, G.'

'You knew, didn't you?'

'I was going to tell you. I kept trying to, but it never seemed like the right time, and in the end I decided it might be best if you didn't know.'

'Who else?'

'Knows?'

'Yeah.'

'Nobody. The police told me when I made my statement. I never said anything about it to anyone else.'

'Not even Bartosz?'

'Nope. If I wasn't going tell you, it seemed wrong to tell anyone else.'

'Oh.' I hesitate for a moment to digest this unexpected piece of information. 'Why didn't you want *me* to know?'

He sits down next to me on the floor and taps me on the knee, just like he used to when he was half my size, to make me pay attention.

'I didn't want her to do that thing to you. Or rather I didn't want you to know she was doing it.'

'Thing?'

'That thing she does. Did. Where she acts like you're her son and she couldn't love you more, but then the next chance she has, she behaves as though you're her worst enemy and screws you over completely. She did it to me loads and I forgave her over and over again. It messes with your head in the end.'

'I'm gonna be sick.' I start crawling away. Jacob gets in front of me, grabs me under the arms and slides me along the floor face down, towards the bathroom like a human mop. He moves quickly, but I still don't make it. Some of my vomit ends up on his trainers.

'Sorry. Cleaning stuff's in the kitchen.'

I crawl back to the sofa and drop down onto the carpet in front of it again, and I wrap the towel around my head and shoulders so it covers my face. When he's finished sponging and cursing, Jacob comes back to sit next to me. We stay like this for ages, not speaking. I rest my head on his shoulder. He doesn't push me away, but he doesn't put his arm around me or tap me on the knee again.

I begin the grim process of sobering up.

'Anyway, Mum's history now. Other things are more important,' my brother says eventually.

'Like Bartosz dumping me?'

'Like the way you totally failed to get what he was saying.'

'He's spoken to you about it, then? I don't know why I'm surprised. You two are such best-bosomy palsy-walsies these days.'

He doesn't respond to this, so I continue. 'I'm not grown up enough for him, apparently.'

'You're not grown up enough for anyone.'

'I try to be, but it always goes wrong.'

'Oh my days. Get the violins out.'

'Even without the grown up thing, he's had enough of me. I'm not really real, in the same way as other people. You must have noticed.'

'What are you talking about?'

'I'm not like them.'

'Who?'

'Other people.'

'No, you're way more stupid.'

'Thanks.'

'Look, Bartosz is just scared he trapped you into something while you were vulnerable. He wants you to think about things. He told you that, didn't he?'

'He was ditching me and trying to soften the blow.'

'He really wasn't. He was trying to give you a way out. He's gutted you left the way you did. Heartbroken. God knows why, but he is. When I went down this morning, he was sitting at the kitchen table, crying his eyes out. It was sad, man. He said he'd been there all night.'

'Oh God. Jesus. This is a disaster. Christ almighty. Bollocks.'

'Shut up. Eventually, I got him to calm down and we had what people call a *conversation*. That's a thing where you exchange information and accept what each other is saying without going off on one.'

'How come you can both do that with each other, but not with me?'

'Good question. Look, G – do you love him?'

'I hate that word.'

'So you don't love him?'

'That's not what I said.'

'And there we have it. You love him to the moon and back. But you can't bring yourself to tell him. You can't even bring yourself to admit it to me.'

'They're just words.'

'But sometimes they have to be said.'

'People say stuff like too often. You should hear some of the relatives in A&E. They don't mean it. They just enjoy the drama of it all.'

'Of course they mean it. You're such a coward. And Bartosz always treats you as though you're made of glass. He lets you get away with loads of stuff. He can't stop himself, and you let him. I can see that's the way things fall naturally between you. It's your default setting as a couple, kind of, and that's ok up to a point, but beyond that point, it's not fair on him. He doesn't have an equal partner who supports him. He has someone who acts like a child or an adult with special needs. It's lonely for him. Can't you see that?'

'But he makes it difficult for me to be anything else. Like the other day, when he pulled me off you and held me so I couldn't move.'

'And you bit him.'

'He called me a vicious little bitch.'

'That's not the best example of what I mean. But he loved it when you did that.'

'Really? I left tooth marks."

'But you kind of showed your true self. You should do more of that. Reset your relationship and flip things around a bit. Surprise him.'

'Bite him?'

'No, you numpty. Just, I don't know - put yourself out there for him. Do some of the decision making. Take a few risks.'

'Like how?'

'Like literally. Boss him about a bit.' Jacob hesitates. 'And I bet he's always the one who, I mean, I bet you've never....'

'Never what?'

'I don't know how you say it. In words. In fact, forget it. I don't know what I'm talking about.'

I peep out from my towel and watch as pink blotches start to appear on Jacob's neck and then joint together and move upwards until his entire face his scarlet. I suddenly realise what he's trying to say. My cheeks flush, too. But credit where credit's due. He's putting himself out there to say this and he's not doing it for a cheap laugh, but because it's his take on the situation and he reckons it needs to be said.

I smile. I can't help it. 'When did you get to be so wise?' I ask him.

'I'm not wise. I'm just wiser than you, which isn't difficult. Anyway, I'm done with telling you what to do. It's not really any of my business.'

He jumps to his feet and scans the room.

'This place is beyond a hot mess. And the state of you, sitting there with a towel over your head and your junk on display like a little heap of squashed chipolatas.'

I look down and see what he means. The state of me.

'Where's your clothes?'

I point to my bag which is still hunched despondently near the front door as though it's expecting a good kicking. In fact I think I might have given it a good kicking at some point over the last twenty four hours.

'Get dried and find something to wear, then go to bed. I'll stick the rest of your stuff in the wash.'

I lurch across the floor to my bag, and I dig out pyjama bottoms and a T-shirt and go to bed and lie there listening to the buzz and swish of the washing machine and Jacob bustling about, tidying, sorting and singing to the music he's put on. He brings me a bottle of water and puts the plastic bowl from the kitchen sink on the floor by the bed, just in case.

After that, he keeps coming in to check on me. He always wants to me to show him my hands in case I've got some means of doing away with myself hidden under the duvet. But I haven't. It was only a few hours ago, but already, I can't remember, let alone feel the exact combination of emotions that led me, or almost led me, to electrocute myself in the bath.

It's all become kind of hypothetical now because my brother's here and he's chased the worst of it away.

26. Gawain

Next morning Jacob comes bouncing into my bedroom.
'Are you back, G?'
'My life's gone to shit, but apart from that, yep. I'm back.'
'You need to pack it in with the self-pity.'
'Are you still angry with me?'
'Livid. Seriously, imagine if I'd arrived a few seconds later.'
'I was just sitting there with my lovely heater, which you destroyed.'
'Not funny.'
'Sorry.'
'That sounded genuine. As per usual.'

He pulls up the window blind and light floods the room. I realise he's wearing nothing but a pair of bright turquoise boxer briefs.

'I've thought of a way you can start making it up to me,' he says. 'It'll help you get through today, as well.' He parades up and down in front of me, like a model on a catwalk. Intrigued, despite my wretchedness, I prop myself up against a pillow and watch. He doesn't seem to be prancing about and camping it up, just walking back and forth, and each time he reaches the full length mirror attached to the wall by the side of the bed, he pauses, turns slightly to one side and scrutinises his reflection.

'Are you coming on to me?' I ask him.

His stares at me in horror, then collapses onto the bed at my feet and shrieks with laughter.

'I don't know what's funniest,' he says. 'The idea that I'd come on to you or that I'd do it by walking up and down in front of you in my underpants.'

'Well you certainly caught my attention.'
'Sorry bro. You're not my type. And we're related.'
He gets up and looks at himself in the mirror again.
'I'm way too skinny, aren't I?'
'Too skinny for what?'

He doesn't answer. He's actually pretty hot, in my opinion, with his lean athletic body and the thin line of uber-blonde hair that trails down from his belly button and loses itself inside his underwear. He might well be my type if he wasn't my brother. But I'm not planning to say any of that, or even think it again.

'You've got a bit of definition around your pecs and your abs. Not a huge amount, but some, if the light falls on you in the right way.'

He eyes the bits I've just mentioned, carefully, from various angles.

'I'm not very buff am I?'

'Not very.'

'Does it matter? You've always been a weedy little runt. It's never stopped you.'

'Of course it doesn't matter. What's wrong with you?'

'And the scars?'

'You can hardly see them now. And they've still got plenty more fading to do.'

He half turns his back to the mirror and lifts his arm up so he can look at them.

'It's just…'

He seems genuinely worried.

'Go on.'

'At this tropical dome thing, in the holiday park, will I have to run from the changing rooms and jump into the water before anyone sees me? Can I get away with hanging around by the pool on the sun beds or in the jacuzzi without people pointing and laughing at me?'

'What people are you thinking of?'

'Girls.'

'Girls?'

'Females. You must have heard of them. Amanda's one. At least I think she is.'

'Oh. Right. I don't know. You'll probably be fine. Some girls like skinny guys.'

He looks so downcast I'm forced to relent.

'I'm winding you up. You're totally hot to trot.'

He continues to assess his body, then he grins at himself in an exaggerated way, showing all his teeth.

'Don't do that to girls. In fact, don't do it to anyone. Unless you actually want to look like a chimpanzee. Or a bonobo.'

'In America everyone has perfect teeth.' He beats his chest, purses his lips to make monkey noises, then pulls the covers off me. 'Get up, we're going shopping!'

'Are we?'

'I need stuff for our trip.'

'Like what?'

'Swimming trunks for a start. And shorts. I can't go poncing up and down the edge of the pool in my underpants.'

This is true, and I have no desire to witness the spectacle again, so I suggest we walk to the big M & S, which is just up the road. But Jacob says their clothes are for granddads and saddos like me, so we end up taking the train into Reading. We go in and out of just about every outlet in the entire town centre, and if he finds something he likes the look of, he has to try it on. I sit on chairs outside, and in one particularly pretentious establishment, I loll about a chaise longue, biting my nails as I agonise about Bartosz. Jacob does manage to distract me a bit, though. Each time he puts on a new item he shouts for me to come into the changing room and offer my opinion. Most times I say he looks great, and I mean it. But he always disagrees with me, and it soon becomes clear he thinks one of his arse cheeks is bigger than the other. I try to reassure him that isn't the case, but he's having none of it, and in one place we argue about it in increasingly loud voices, until other blokes in the changing room start casting discrete glances at his bum to see what we're talking about. I threaten to go and buy a tape measure so I can do an accurate comparison of his globes. He tells me to never use the word *globes* again. Like ever. It's too gay even for most gay people, he says. Then, one of the other guys in the changing room approaches him and tells him he thinks he's got a very nice, evenly distributed tush. Jacob looks horrified, but thanks him politely. After that, he never mentions it again.

The morning passes in this vein, as does most of the afternoon. I follow my brother around in neutral mostly, not happy exactly, but not in too much pain either, and if I'm honest, I'm getting a huge buzz out of buying him stuff. I'm not a millionaire. Junior doctors don't earn as much as people think, and splashing all this cash will make a significant dent my bank balance. But it feels like I'm righting a wrong, or at least chipping away at the surface of the harm I've done to him.

We end up in a tapas bar down a quiet alleyway. As soon as we've found a table and ordered our food Jacob jumps up again.

'I promised Bartosz I'd contact him every day at around five to tell him how you're getting on - what you're doing and all that.'

He goes outside and it's a good ten minutes before he returns and forces me to eat patatas bravas, and peppers marinated in garlic. I find I'm quite hungry and I can get most of it down my throat if I mash it up so my teeth don't have to get involved in the process. We concentrate on the food until it's all gone. Then I take a deep breath and ask him if Bartosz is ok.

'Yes, but that's not the point. I'm meant to tell him about you, not the other way round.'

'What did you say?'

'I said you're a bit shaky but I'm keeping you busy and I've managed to make you smile three times.'

My brother has counted how many times I've smiled. My eyes fill with tears.

'For God's sake, G. People will see.'

I wipe my eyes with my napkin. It's one of those flimsy, thin ones and it falls to bits instantly. Little balls of damp paper stick to my cheeks. I have to pick each one of them off separately with the remnants of my fingernails.

'You didn't tell him about yesterday?'

'I told him you were too full of vodka to answer your phone and left it at that.;

When we get home, Jacob struts his stuff again, but in his new apparel this time, not his boxer briefs, whilst I clap my hands and occasionally hoot. Then he folds it all up neatly and packs it into his holdall, ready for our trip. After that, we lounge about watching TV and talking. By nine, he's starving again, so I order him a large pizza with stuffed crusts and extra salami. I think back to the day he appeared in A&E and I had that fantasy about taking him back to my flat and looking after him. I realise it's come true, sort of, except that I'm the one who needs to be watched over, not him.

A game show comes on. The contestants, who are suspended in the air on wires, attempt to biff shuttlecocks into a series of different sized nets. Then they have to answer the same number of general knowledge or logic questions as the number of shuttlecocks they manage to net. The difficulty of the questions is inversely proportional to the size of the nets.

'I don't get the point of this,' Jacob says after a while.

'I do, but it's so ridiculous it's not worth explaining. Unless you mean philosophically, in which case, I agree.'

He turns his head to look at me.

'It must be incredible to be as brainy as you are, with your five A grades and your medical career.'

'I'm supposed to be gifted.'

'Gifted at being a twat.'

'What did you get? Remind me?'

'A's in Psychology, Spanish and German and B's in Biology and Critical Thinking. Not as good as *your* grades. Obviously.'

'Not far off. And I only got a D in Critical Thinking. I approached the questions from the wrong angle.'

'You would.'

'Have you any idea what you're going to do next?'

'Psychology with Neuroscience at King's. If they'll have me. I managed to get my application in just before the deadline. Mrs Hopgood helped me with my personal statement.'

'I had no idea. When did all that happen?'

'No, well.'

'I wasn't paying attention, was I?'

He shrugs.

I turn the TV off. 'Look - can I ask you about other stuff? You've probably told Bartosz everything, but he's big on confidentiality. I don't know anything much about all that.'

'What do you want to know?'

'Why did you stay in the States after your gap year finished?'

'It's difficult to explain and anyway, it's kind of embarrassing because it's so lame.'

'This is me you're talking to. I've got a PhD in feebleness.'

He takes a swig from his can of orange Fanta and sighs. 'Ok. In my head, there are two versions, the one I kind of remember and the one that really happened. The first version is all blurry, but talking to Bartosz has helped me pick through it and get it straight.'

'Go on.'

'So, when my gap was meant to be ending and I was getting ready to go back to the UK and take up my uni place, Mum and Warren sat me down in the community office and did a big number on me. They begged and pleaded with me to stay in South Carolina. Mum cried and Warren said a load of stuff about God's plan for me, and how it didn't involve me going back to the UK. I insisted I had to go and start uni and I promised I'd come back the following summer. But they must have known I was lying about that, and I'd probably seen too much by then. Mum slid a load of prospectuses for US colleges towards me across the table. They were all obscure religious institutions, not places I'd ever choose. I said as much, which was a big mistake because Warren whacked me across the side of my head with the back of his hand, and that same week, I had a really bad asthma attack. It was a shock, because I hadn't had one for ages. They didn't rush me to the nearest ER. They liked to think they were self-sufficient when it came to medical problems.'

'Either that, or your health insurance had expired.'

"Yeah, maybe. I didn't think of that. They called this doctor who was part of the church community, and he prescribed pills. He said they were to help my airways stay clear, but they made me feel woozy and separate from everyone else, as though I was the only zombie in a computer game. It's difficult to explain, but my mojo, or whatever it is you need to conduct your life, vanished completely. I had no control over anything.'

'When you came into A&E you were full of sleeping tablets.'

'The pills they fed me in the US were different. And by then, I didn't have my laptop. Mum and Warren told me the church house had been burgled and it had been stolen. Long before that, Godwin stamped on my phone and they wouldn't let me use their PCs or cell phones, so I couldn't contact anyone, and I couldn't run away. My passport wasn't where I left it, nor was my return plane ticket, and I had no money of my own because they'd emptied my bank accounts.'

'You were a prisoner.'

'I see that now. But I didn't at the time. I took my pills and accepted everything they threw at me, praise one minute and character assassination the next. I did as I was told, and I gradually became more and more, not brainwashed exactly, but acclimatized to their way of doing things. Even when we came back to England, I couldn't break away from it. We were living in a town, close to a railway station and there were loads of times when I could have walked out. But I didn't. I just couldn't see clearly enough anymore to realise how dangerous things were for me. I suppose I started to wake up a bit when Bartosz sought me out after the church services. But even then, I wasn't seeing things as they really were. I mean, I left and all that, but I didn't realise properly until after you were out of your coma and on the mend.'

'Was that why you got so upset when you had that first counselling session with Bartosz?'

'All this emotion I didn't even know was there just poured out. I finally allowed myself to acknowledge how lost and terrified I'd been the whole time. It was never right, even when I first started spending weekends with them in West Sussex, just after Dad died.'

'You should have said something.'

'I wish I had.'

He splays out his right hand and squeezes it with his other hand at the points where his fingers meet his palm. 'They have these metal rods. I don't know where they get them from, but they're exactly right for the job they're meant to do, which is to hit you on the hand in a way that causes maximum pain. All the kids in the church get beaten, for all sorts of stupid reasons. It hurts like shit and you end up humiliated too, because they like to gather an audience together and make a thing of it. Like they did for the whipping. They hit you on your right hand if you're right handed and on the other way round if you're left handed.'

Without thinking I grab hold of his right hand and gently manipulate various parts of it, to try and work out whether there is any permanent damage. Then I remember the night when I pulled his fingers backwards one by one. I let go of his hand again.

'It's ok most of the time. If I've got a virus or the weather's wet or something it aches a bit. I'm not sure I could play cricket now.'

'I bet you could. You need to get it checked, though.'

'That's not the worst part.' He looks down at his hand again. 'After your twenty-first birthday, you become an adult and they stop. But then you're expected to do it to the other kids. They give you lessons and teach you how to make it really hurt, as if you don't know how to do that already.'

'Did you do it?'

'I had no choice. To little children, who'd only just turned five, girls and boys I taught in scripture classes, kids who knew me and maybe even liked me. Of course, some of the other adults were really into it, the ones who were on a power trip. But even if you were normal and hated doing it, you had to act like you meant it. If they caught you doing it too gently, the kid would get a proper thrashing from someone more brutal. Sometimes they were sent away afterwards, and you'd never see them again. And even if they were allowed to stay, nobody was allowed to speak to them to them for weeks or even months. That's how they operate at New Sunrise. They force you to do so much bad stuff, in the end you feel disgusting and degraded. I don't know if souls exist, but if they do, mine's got a stain on it that I'll never be able to wipe away.'

'I had no idea.'

'Even if you had, you couldn't have done anything.'

'I'd have flown out to bring you back.'

'Would you, though?'

'In a heartbeat.'

He looks me in the eye for the first time since we started this conversation. I can't tell whether he believes me or if he thinks I'm bullshitting. Then he looks down and squeezes his damaged hand again.

'Like I said, I knew they were sketchy, right from the start. I only went because of Mum.'

'One time, you were really upset, but you wouldn't say why.'

'I remember. I got back around tea-time. I looked for you but you were nowhere to be seen. Because you'd been with Mr Thompson.'

'And when you found out about me and Will, you were pushed towards New Sunrise even more?'

'Yeah well, I felt so screwed over by you both, I thought spending time with Mum was the right thing to do. It felt like the only thing I *could* do. I wasn't prepared to spend the entire summer holidays with you at Aunty Susan's.'

'I was devastated. I don't suppose it helps for you to know, but it ruined everything for me. Not just splitting up with Will. I mean yes, I was gutted about that, but I got over that eventually. I never got over falling out with you, though.'

'You should have told me. I didn't even realise you were gay.'

'You were only ten when it started. I didn't think you'd understand. Then as time went on, I couldn't see a way to bring it up without seriously upsetting you.'

'At least I'd have been in the loop and it wouldn't have been such a shock when all that crap appeared on Facebook. *Your brother's a gaylord with Mr Thompson. Gawain takes it up the arse for Cherry Tree.* Three whole years and I'd known nothing about it. How could I have been so blind? The hours you must have spent in his apartment, in the same building as my dormitory, fucking each other stupid and I never realised.'

'We were very careful.'

'You must have been. And all those times you went off for the day during the holidays, from Aunty Susan's. Meeting up with Cobblers and the rest of your mates from school, you said. I'm such a muppet.'

'Will used to park a couple of streets away, so nobody would see him.'

'Did the rest of your dorm know?'

'Only Cobblers.'

'You must have told so many lies.'

I think back to those cringeworthy photos on Facebook. Will flat on his back at Newlands Corner, his unmistakable, reddish hair spiking upwards behind one of my shoulders, and me sitting on top of him, feeding him chips. We'd hidden ourselves away in a narrow rectangle of grass between some trees, miles from the path. We never imagined for one minute that Matt Westerham from Jacob's year was in the area on a camping trip with the scouts and would walk right past us. He was a photography nerd and had a massive camera slung round his neck with a state of the art telephoto lens. We were busted big time, and so was Jacob, by default. Within minutes it was all over social media and everyone knew, even my sister, who had left three years before. And by the evening, Will, who'd never been anything other than honest and open until he met me, had admitted everything to Mrs Hopgood. He was sacked on the spot. I never saw him again.

Poor Jacob. He doesn't even seem angry about any of it, just resigned and hurt, and worst of all, he's clearly decided to use his trusting nature back then as another weapon to beat himself up with.

'Were you ever going to tell me?'

'Of course I was. I hadn't bargained for Matt Westerham showing up like that. And after that you wouldn't even speak to me, so I never got the chance to explain or make things right between us.'

'Matt rang me later the same day. He was shocked, not that you were gay, but because you were so underhand about it. You were the king of the upper sixth. All those girls who had crushes on you and all those boys in the lower school who looked up to you. He thought you deserved to be exposed like that. But he hadn't thought about the impact it would have on me. When he saw all the grief I was getting on social media, he felt really bad.'

'Jesus.'

'I don't think you realise what it was like, G, even now. Mr Thompson was a big deal to me, particularly after Dad died. And all the time he was secretly screwing you. Then, when it finally became public knowledge, school was over and done with for you. It was me who had to go back and face the consequences.'

'You think it was all my fault?'

'I *know* it was your fault. Mr Thompson would never have initiated anything like that. You must have gone after him and refused to leave him alone until he caved in.'

'I did pursue him a bit. But not until he'd got me all fired up. When I was sick outside that Little Chef on the way back from Dad's funeral he ran his hand up and down my back in a really slow and deliberate way and grazed his fingers against the bones in my spine. It was way more than just a kindly pat on the back. It changed everything. Before that, I was clueless. I thought I liked girls, but at the same time I was secretly bored by them, too. I was mightily confused. He shone a light on all that.'

"Honestly, G. You make it sound as if you had no control over any of it. Surely you could have taken the gay thing on board without chasing after our housemaster.'

'I only puked outside the Little Chef in the first place because Will told me about Mum turning up at the wake and you going to join them as though that was a perfectly normal thing to do.'

'And that gave you an excuse to chase after our housemaster and seduce him?'

'It wasn't as simple as that.'

'Will wrote to me, to apologise.'

'So did I."

'He was genuinely sorry.'

'So was I.'

'I don't think you were. You just wanted was absolution to make yourself feel better. You had no idea what you'd done. You still don't, not really. I had no family, apart from Aunty Susan who thought the sun shone out of all your orifices and Amanda, who was living her best life in Scotland. The only person left for me was Mum.'

His face closes up, hiding any emotions he might be feeling, and the reconciliation I thought we were moving towards, slips out of my grasp.

27. Gawain

We don't park directly outside the church. Instead, we find a space along a wide avenue just round the corner. We made the trip up north yesterday. Amanda did the first hundred miles or so, then Jacob took over. He soon got used to the general flow of the motorway and before long he was changing lanes like a pro. By the time we reached the M62, Amanda had stopped nagging him and my eyes were open again, taking in the amazingly flat landscape flying past on either side of us. Sadly, though, he let himself down when we arrived at the holiday park, where he underestimated the length of the car and reversed it into the concrete wall outside our chalet. Amanda nearly gave birth on the spot, Jacob got really antsy and I couldn't stop laughing, which infuriated them both.

So no car park today. Imagine if he'd hit a vehicle that belonged to a long lost relative? *Hi, so you're our cousin? Sorry about your car.*

We're way too early. Once Jacob has managed to align the vehicle with the pavement, more or less, after spending an age backing up and going forwards again, then mounting the kerb and complaining that Amanda's car is so long it's ridiculous, we give him a sarcastic round of applause and go for a wander around some of our old haunts. We stare through the railings at our old primary school, then we make our way back to our old house, the three-storey, semi-detached Edwardian villa, where Amanda, Jacob and I lived until we were fourteen, six and eleven. I look up at the window of the room I shared with Jacob, and remember waving to Dad from it before he got into his car to drive to Manchester Airport. By the time he got back, all the kerfuffle had happened and we'd been taken away by Aunty Susan. He'd be in his sixties now. I wonder how different everything would have been if he hadn't died. Will and I probably wouldn't have become a thing, and Jacob would never have got involved with Mum and New Sunrise. Also, I wonder how Dad would have reacted when he found out I was gay. It matters to me that he'd have been ok with it, but at the same time, standing here now, it feels as though Dad and everything that took place behind the door of this house was part of someone else's reality, not mine.

We return to the avenue where we left the car. Several vehicles pass us as we walk in the direction of the church. Jacob pulls the sleeves of his suit jackets down over his cuffs and glances around self-consciously. He has no idea how striking he looks in his charcoal grey suit, which contrasts dramatically with his blonde hair. My suit is darker than his, almost black. We wanted to get matching outfits, but Amanda reminded us we were going to a funeral, not a wedding, and Jacob was planning to wear a pair of dark glasses, until she pointed out he was a mourner, not an extra in a mafia movie.

I feel sick. I was fine when we were standing outside our old house, but suddenly I'm that little urchin again, the one who was transplanted here, to this village from somewhere unknown, the boy who isn't the same as everyone else and doesn't really belong anywhere. And God knows what I look like walking down the road with my siblings. Suspicious might be the most accurate word, a short, darkish-looking bloke, hovering alongside a taller, fairer man and woman, using them for cover as he makes occasional dashes down driveways to steal Amazon parcels from doorsteps.

At least I'm clean. I spent so long in the shower this morning, Jacob started banging on the door, and I'm almost one hundred percent certain the only aroma emanating from my person is the expensive sandalwood fragrance Amanda gave me for my birthday. Maybe it's a bit too much, though, for an occasion like this? I don't want to make an exhibition of myself in the church, because I'm wearing an inappropriate and overpowering scent. I stop walking and windmill my wrists about frantically to make some of it evaporate.

'Is there a wasp?' Amanda asks.

My sister is wearing a purple velvet coat over a lime green dress, a floppy hat with a big purple flower sewn on at the front to match the coat and spiky-heeled black boots that go up to her knees. She can't quite fasten the coat because of the little bump, which is visible through the soft fabric of her dress. She looks kind of sweet, which is new for her. I'm not going to tell her that, though.

'You look really nice,' I say, instead.

She furrows her eyebrows and wrinkles her forehead uncertainly in a movement that seems to travel from one side of her face to the other, like a small Mexican wave.

'Yeah, you look amazing,' Jacob adds, and she has to do it all over again.

'Come on, then,' she says once she's recovered.

I don't move. 'Nobody's seen us yet. We could get back in the car and leave. They won't even know we've been here.'

'Not going to happen,' Jacob says. 'Not when we've come all this way. And anyway, I'm looking forward to it.'

He marches ahead of us both. He's been looking forward to his mother's funeral. How does that work? I remember what he was like at Dad's funeral, how he tried to hide in my blazer and then had that spectacular graveside meltdown. Somewhere along the way, he's changed so much he's not even fazed by his mother's death. I hang back with my hands in my pockets. Eventually they both stop and turn round to look at me.

'You two go ahead,' I say. 'I'll stay in the car. Jacob, throw me the keys.'

'Nope," Jacob says. 'Not doing that. No way.' He smiles and raises and lowers his eyebrows.

'You total bastard. Ok. I don't need the keys. I'll go for another walk. There used to be a park somewhere around here. I think I can remember how to get to it. There might be a café. I could get a latte or an Americano.'

Amanda addresses me slowly, enunciating every word, as though I might not understand what she's saying, because I'm only three years old. 'All we have to do,' she says, 'is go into the church and sit down in a quiet corner at the back. If we feel uncomfortable and nobody speaks to us, we'll slope off quietly and drive to the seaside, like I said, and get fish and chips.'

'If you're a really good boy, I'll buy you a bucket and spade and some of those little paper flags so you can make sandcastles,' Jacob says.

I want to take a run at him and kick him hard on his shins several times with the tips of my highly polished shoes. That would wipe the smirk from his face. But my brother and sister stride off again, arm in arm, so I thrust my hands into my trouser pockets and follow them reluctantly, trying my best to hide behind them.

When we turn the corner, the church looms up in front of us, a big beige building with no windows, slightly monolithic, like the palace of a great leader from a gloomy metropolis in a sci-fi movie. The hearse is parked up outside, together with a matching black car for the chief mourners. A few soberly dressed strangers are milling around and a small handful of children are run up and down a path at one side of the church and shriek until a plumpish woman tells them to pipe down, herds them up and escorts them into the church.

We stand in a row and watch as the funeral attendants open the back of the hearse, revealing the coffin. It's a plain, wicker casket with a simple spray of white roses on the top. I'd forgotten how jarring it is when you first see the coffin at a funeral and the deceased status of the person inside shifts from theoretical possibility to cold fact. That's my mother in there, I think to myself. She tried to kill me. She stood by while they tortured my brother. But I don't want her to be dead. Or do I?

And then, in the space of about three seconds, the World turns upside down, completely and forever.

I'm just about to tell my siblings, I'm not joking. I really am going bottle it. And I've decided that once I've said it I won't wait for their reaction, I'll just turn and retreat round the corner quickly, before they can stop me, and I'll find a café somewhere and slope back to the car in about forty-five minutes.

But footsteps are running towards me from the direction of the church. At first I think some catastrophe has happened, that the church is on fire or something, and people are trying to get away. When shift my gaze away from the coffin I notice three men speeding towards us. And instead of turning away and making a quick exit, I find myself striding forward to meet them at such a brisk pace, I overtake my siblings and leave them behind. One of the men moves faster than the other two and reaches me first. He must be the youngest, possibly around the same age as Bartosz, I'd say, and his hair is still dark, like mine. And curly, again like mine. And his face is like mine, too, particularly his eyes and the way he peers at me as though he's short sighted. I peer back. His arms open and he embraces me tightly. We separate, but he still holds onto my wrists.

'Marco,' he says, in an insistent tone, implying that surely I must remember *him*.

Do I? I think I'm starting to. His face and his voice, and even his touch are utterly familiar.

'Gawain,' I say.

'I know that! I'd know you anywhere.'

He smiles and caresses my cheek with the flat of his palm, as though he needs to check that I'm real. The other two men have greyer hair and are slightly older. When they catch up with Marco, they take it in turns to wrap their arms around me, and they all laugh as though they've never witnessed anything as miraculous and amusing as my appearance here, in front of this church, at this particular time. I laugh, too, and they take turns to hold my hand in both of theirs and say my name over and over again, as though they can't believe I'm here. We're the same height, the four of us, and so alike, I feel as though I'm looking at a range of different versions of my future self.

'There's loads of them,' I hear Jacob say behind me. 'Are they clones, or what?'

I think it comes out at a higher volume that he intended and it sounds rather rude, but the three men laugh again and let go of me so they can hug Jacob and kiss Amanda. The eldest, Aldo, has a closely cropped beard and thinning hair, and the middle one, Enzo, has my corkscrew curls, only his are white. They introduced themselves. Aldo, Enzo and Marco are our uncles, our mother's brothers.

Who knew? Well, me as it happens. At least I did once, long ago. As I stand and look at Marco, it all starts to come back to me, and I marvel at how I could ever have forgotten any of it.

He rests his hand on my arm. 'Talk properly later, at the wake?'

I nod.

He steps away and Aldo takes his place.

'We thought you three should walk behind the coffin into the church. We've reserved seats for you at the front. Is that okay? Afterwards, the *do* is at the farm. We didn't want to hire a hall just for us lot. Give me your numbers and I'll send you the address.'

They all speak with the same strong, East Yorkshire accent. The one I used when I first learned to speak, when I wasn't using words from their dialect. The *farm*, I think. We're going back to it. I'm going back to it. I shake my head in disbelief. Aldo notices and steps forward again. He puts a hand on the back of my neck and pulls me towards him so he can plant a big wet kiss on my forehead. Now I know where this gesture comes from. I've done the same to Jacob more times than I can remember. I've done it to school friends, too, and, more recently, to Bartosz. They all crowd around me again. Enzo and Marco take an arm each and escort me towards the church. Aldo walks ahead.

The priest greets us and our uncles melt away. Amanda, Jacob and I follow the coffin down the aisle. We don't know any of the other people here, but we, the estranged children of the deceased, are the main mourners, the main supporting stars in Mum's final show. There's an unfamiliar smell, which I assume is incense, and music cascades over us like a thick mist. The entire effect is cloying and laden with emotion. To me the organ music sounds syrupy and overly sentimental, yet at the same time I get a sense that a darker, more complex message lies hidden beneath its surface. But then, this is a catholic church. It's not like the school chapel with its plain benches, its row of teachers at the front belting out the hymns whilst trying to pretend they're not embarrassed as hell, and its traditional organ voluntaries, painstakingly stumbled through by sixth formers hoping for university music scholarships.

As we sidle into the pew on our right, Amanda first, then Jacob, then me, the weight of the occasion really starts to bear down on me. I'm a small boy again. I reach for Jacob's hand, my fingers spread apart, as though he's still a small boy, too. Then I remember we're both grown men and I curl my hands up and stick them in my jacket pocket.

The priest gets the ball rolling and everyone crosses themselves, apart from us. They all seem to know what to do and how to respond when the priest says various sets of words. We try our best to keep up, and we manage to stand, sit and kneel with only a fraction of a second's delay compared to the rest of the congregation. When the singing starts, we don't join in. I was in the school choir, first as a treble, then when my voice broke, as a tenor, but I don't know these modern-sounding Catholic hymns and I find it difficult to anticipate where the slightly quirky melodies will go next.

Aldo goes to the front and gives a eulogy about our mother. I don't hear the first bit because a baby somewhere close behind me sets up a sudden howl, as though someone's stuck a pin into its leg, and there's a noisy bout of apologetic shuffling as it gets carted off outside. The part I do hear is sensitively worded, but truthful and unsentimental. It must have taken him ages to work out what to say and get the tone so right. It moves me to think that he's made such an effort for my mother. Perhaps she deserves this tribute. Maybe I've underestimated her, and I should made more of an effort, gone to stay with her when Jacob went.

A lump forms in my throat, but after I've swallowed twice, it's almost gone. We have to stand for the communion part of the mass. I think back to what Bartosz said about how this ritual grows in meaning when you've heard it so often you know the words off by heart, and I ponder about the transubstantiation that's supposed to take place. As I watch the priest, I visualise Jesus as a tiny concentrated force, like an illuminated jelly baby, a yellow one, full of concentrated sunlight, flying in through one of the windows, splitting into two parts and combining with the bread in the priest's hands and then with the wine in the silver goblet. I'm not trying to be glib or clever. I think it's wonderful that Bartosz believes something like this actually happens. His ability to accept miracles as facts suddenly makes him seem extraordinary, a much bigger and braver person than me, because he's prepared to take a leap of faith, whereas all I can do when faced with the numinous is invent facetious metaphors involving confectionery.

So far, I've managed to stand here, with my mother's coffin right in front of me, so close I can smell the fragrance of the lilies resting on the top, and I've kept my emotions more or less in check. I was completely thrown when I first saw the wicker casket, like I said, and I've struggled to swallow a couple of times. But I'm pretty sure I'm going to get through the entire ordeal without breaking down. Once everyone has gone up for communion and the final hymn has been sung, it will be over.

A woman's voice rises up from somewhere at the back and the sound swells until it reaches the very top of the vaulted ceiling. Later I google it and discover it's the Latin prayer version of Schubert's Ave Maria. Everyone apart from Jacob, Amanda and I starts the process of getting up, sidling out of the pews and walking up to the altar.

I'm not really grieving for my mother. How could I be? Surely my sorrow is on a level with the generic type of sadness people feel when a popular character dies in a movie? But when this singing starts, a mass of emotions slams into me from an unknown place. My startled brain struggles to sift through them all and find words to describe and categorise them, so I can take the sting out of them all and regain my equilibrium. I manage to pluck some abstract nouns and phrases from the general mish mash, and then I wish I hadn't, because they're way too powerful for me to deal with. But it's too late. They're here, in the front of my mind and they're not going anywhere. Humility is first, followed by truth and abandonment of self and maybe even love. Yes definitely love. That word again. The one I can never say. And Jacob. His name is in there, too, hanging there quietly and modestly in the background, but he's the adhesive. He's the one who makes the rest of it stick together and form a shape I recognise.

I glance at him to see if he's as upset as I am. I can see the flames from the alter candles reflected in his pale eyes as he watches the priest. His face is perfectly tranquil.

Everyone files past us and makes for the altar in an orderly line. The priest and his two helpers or whatever you call them mutter *body of Christ* over and over again as they offer the bread and wine and the communicants respond with *amen*. Bartosz would be going up for communion if he were here. Then he'd sit down beside me again, our thighs would touch and I'd feel involved in this ritual, if only vicariously.

When they come back from receiving the bread and the wine, most of the communicants drop kneel and bow their heads. I decide to do the same. I rest my head on the little shelf in front of me, and I think about the words the priest said about not being worthy. I know they always say that, but it felt as though he was talking about me. I'm definitely not worthy. Even my mother knew that. And my sweet, good natured brother has paid the worst possible price for my unworthiness. How can I ever make it up to him? And what words do I need to say for us both to be healed?

I tell myself to get a grip and not be so bloody melodramatic, but it's too late. I've plunged head first into a soupy darkness, a black hole full of uncontrollable feelings. When the bread and wine have been distributed and the woman has stopped singing, the final hymn finishes me off completely. The words are romantic and sentimental, something about the spirit of God being in the clear running water. But the hymn is also earnest, pure and sincere. And brave. I've not been any of these things for a long time. I've always been clever and funny and I've relied on my ability to switch on my natural charisma and manipulate everyone around me, making them all dance to my glittery tune whenever I've felt like it. And I've sailed through loads of exams and become a person able to act like a doctor in a hospital for hours at a time. But who am I really? When was the last time my true self had the guts to put in an appearance?

And how much harm have I done to my precious brother, who is a much better human being than I'll ever be and has endured and seen through this act of mine since he was a baby?

28. Jacob

As soon as that woman starts singing I know G's going to lose it. When the mass is over, I pull him up and let him lean against me. Keeping him in a vertical position is a struggle, though. As the bearers get ready to carry the coffin out, he sinks down onto the pew, covers his face with his hands and sobs. I sit down again put my arm around his shoulder and try to reason with him, but none of the words I mumble under my breath have any impact at all. I don't think he can even hear me saying them.

Amanda pushes past us.

'You stay with him. I'll wait for you outside and mingle. If anyone asks, I'll say he's a bit upset.' She looks down at G and shakes her head as though she can't believe he's being such a plonker. Then she seems to think again and she scratches the top of his head, through his curls. 'It *is* our mother's funeral, I suppose,' she says.

'G's taking one for the team,' I say, and I jiggle his shoulders a bit with my arm, but he doesn't respond.

At first you can't hear him much because the organ is belting out something by Bach, which I recognise it from services in the school chapel. But once everyone else has exited the church, the music stops, and G's wailing is the only thing you *can* hear. I glance about and search for a clue about what the hell I'm meant to do with him. Nothing jumps out at me apart from the depressing series of paintings bolted to the walls depicting Jesus struggling to carry his cross and encountering one disaster after another. We didn't have those at New Sunrise. Just as well. They'd probably have given the elders a whole new set of ideas about how to torment us.

Eventually, I notice a heavy, gothic-looking door over to our right. Perhaps if I get him outside into the fresh air, away from this heavy atmosphere, he might come to his senses. I drag him across the stone flags. The door is unlocked and leads to a dark, narrow passageway between the church and another, more modern building, which opens out into a tiny lawn at the back of the church. On one side, the lawn is overlooked by a big window in the modern building, which is decorated with tissue paper flowers in bright pink and purple.

I prop my brother up against the back of the church and place one hand on his chest to hold him there. I tell him to take a few deep breaths. Surely he'll stop now. He can't have cared *this* much about our mother. He never even saw her, for God's sake. I was the one who spent most of the last three years living in the same house as her.

He sinks down onto his haunches and starts making groaning sounds, like an animal in terrible pain. It reminds me of the New Year's Eve when Wilson, Aunty Susan's sausage dog, had a fit after he'd managed to pull an entire box of crackers and an almost complete wheel of Stilton onto the floor in the kitchen and more or less scoff the lot while we were outside watching the fireworks. Aunty took him to the emergency vet the next day, and he had to be put down. The hopelessness we all felt as we stood there and watched him rolling around on the kitchen floor like a little, stumpy-legged barrel, is exactly the same sensation as I'm feeling now. I literally have no idea what to do or why this is happening. Is it because of the knock on his head or is he having a nervous breakdown?

In the end, I kneel down, take his face in my hands and make him look at me.

'G, nothing can be this bad.'

He looks at me and inhales deeply as though he's trying to stop, and for a second I think he will, but then he starts again. I look around for inspiration again, like I did in the church. A row of three very small faces are watching us from the window with the tissue paper flowers. Their mouths are open. There must be a playgroup going on in there.

'You're upsetting those children,' I say, although they look more fascinated than traumatized.

He squints at them for a few seconds, then he stops groaning and starts making a mewling sound that's slightly quieter and higher in pitch. I wonder if I should slap him across the face, but the children would see that as well, and in any case, my brother may be as annoying as hell, but it turns out I don't want to hurt him, not really. A woman appears behind the kids and stares out at us as though she's thinking about calling the police. She ushers them away from the window and G gets onto his hands and knees and starts crawling about in the gravel and the patchy grass, whining, like a little brown bear who's been beaten and forced to wear a suit.

Oh my God. One minute he's a sausage dog and the next minute he's a bear. I'm not sure I can cope with the pathos much longer. I wonder if it would be ok to leave him here for a couple of minutes while I go and fetch Amanda.

'Do something to make me stop,' he mutters.

'Like what?'

'I don't know. Find a plank of wood or a brick and hit me over the head with it.'

'I'm not going to do that, am I?'

'It's what I deserve.'

I almost laugh when he says this, but he carries on with the horrible whining sound, and I stomp about, getting into really serious panic mode, until I scrape my calf against a tap emerging from the church wall right next to where I'm standing. Beneath the tap is a collection of cracked and abandoned glass vases piled up in a grate. Without hesitating, I pick one up, fill it with water and chuck it over his head. He gasps and stares at me through red rimmed eyes. Tears mixed with water from the vase course in channels down his face, and a trail of greenery, algae I think it is, drapes itself over one side of his head.

But he stops making that noise.

'I didn't know what to do,' I say.

'I'm so sorry.'

'It's ok. I didn't think you cared about Mum as much as this, though.'

'No, I mean I'm sorry for everything. I've been such a shit brother. I've ruined your life.'

'Have you? I thought I'd turned a corner, but what do I know?'

'*Nearly* ruined it, then. I don't expect you to forgive me or anything like that. I just want you to know that I'm truly sorry now. I wasn't before.'

'I know you weren't. It was kind of obvious.'

'I didn't really get it. I thought I did.'

'You always think you get everything, G.'

'I get *this*. I can feel it in my gut.'

'Ok, well thanks. I forgive you. Can we move on now? Amanda's waiting for us at the front.'

257

'Not yet. There's things I need to say.'

'Please don't. You'll only embarrass yourself. And me.'

'I have to, though.'

His voice goes really high pitched as though he's worked really hard to crank himself up to a kind of sublime, prize-winning level of hysteria, and he doesn't want to let go of it now after all the effort it took him to get there. It freaks me out big time and I'm scared he'll start crying again, because I've run out of ideas for making him stop. I clamp my mouth shut and brace myself to hear whatever it is he's so desperate to say.

'After we had that argument and you went to America, everything was different. I never saw Will again. His life was ruined, too.'

'No it wasn't. He went to live in France. He got married in the end. Started breeding ostriches and opened a gite with a big carp pond in front of it. He's got four kids now.'

'How do you know all that?'

'We've kept in touch.'

'Wow.' He screws his eyes up at me as he digests this new nugget of information. After a few seconds, he carries on. 'Anyway, I cut my hair short, went to medical school and worked my arse off. And I never looked for anyone else to replace Will. I was done with all that. I kept my head down and lived the life of a hermit, more or less. Until I met Bartosz, which was an accident. The point I'm trying to make, is that what I did to you, it didn't just break your heart. It broke mine too.'

I'm making it sound as though he's calmed down and is speaking normally now. But he isn't. He's talking very quickly, throwing his words down in rapid little deposits between whimpers and gasps. pull a strand of aquatic greenery out of his hair.

'You look like some sort of pond life.'

He half smiles. Progress of sorts. My heart rate slows down a bit. 'And anyway, I'm sorry, too,' I find myself saying.

'What for?'

'For hitting you with the tennis racquet and giving you those scars. I hate that they're so visible. After the crash, I was terrified I'd caused a permanent injury that might affect your chances of surviving. And I'm sorry for not speaking to you for eight years. If I hadn't been so stubborn and incapable of opening up, we'd have sorted it out ages ago.'

I pull him towards me and we hug. I let him cry into my shirt until it's as wet with snot and tears as his was after Dad's funeral. Gradually, he starts to calms down. Then he pulls away and holds me at arm's length. 'You know what we were talking about in my flat?'

'We talked about a lot of things.'

'Love.'

'Er, ok?'

'I'm going to say it. But only once. I love you. I love you just as much as I love Bartosz. In a different way, obviously. But just as much. Maybe more.'

'Thanks. Good to know.'

'I really, really love you, Jacob.'

'I thought you were only going to say it once.'

'It's not as hard to say as I thought it would be. I love you. I love you. I love you. Do you believe me?'

'I do. You can stop saying it now, if you like.'

'Do you love me?'

'Of course I do, you stupid cockwomble. But can you shut up about it now? And never mention it again? Like ever?'

He jumps up and opens his arms wide, Christ-like, as though he's giving me a blessing. I wonder what the hell he's going to say or do next, but he just steps forward again and pulls at the front of my shirt until he has sufficient material gathered in one hand to wipe his face and blow his nose again. After that, he seems ok, more or less. Unlike my shirt.

The burial is in a windswept cemetery on the outskirts of the village. I don't think it's the same place as the one where Dad is buried. It seems smaller and has more trees. We take it in turns to throw single red roses into the grave, and when we start to disperse, Marco walks up to us. He looks at my brother, who is still weeping, but in a controlled way.

'Let me have him,' he says, as though my brother is a difficult baby and we all have to take turns in looking after him. He fumbles in his pocket and finds a handful of tissues, gives them to G and they stride off together, his arm replacing mine around G's shoulder. Amanda and I follow them. I expect them to climb into one of the funeral cars. But they go straight past the line of vehicles and disappear along a footpath that leads to the other side of a nasty little chapel, with boarded up windows and mysterious pink and lime-green graffiti on one side. I feel a surge of resentment towards this uncle of ours and I wonder where he's taking G. I'll need to keep an eye on my brother from now on, make sure he's ok, that he stays this side of sanity. I don't really want to leave him yet. I'm not ready to move on. If I get into King's, perhaps I could carry on living at Picardy and commute into London for lectures and tutorials.

I want to wait for G, but Amanda says he'll be ok with Marco, so we set off to the farmhouse. I miss the turning and we have to drive several miles down a narrow road, trying to ignore the satnav woman, who sounds increasingly outraged each time she asks us to do a U-turn. The countryside we're driving through is lonely and wide open with big skies. I find a space wide enough to turn the car round safely and when we reach the entrance to the yard, Aldo is pacing up and down, waiting for us. We have to dodge a handful small hen-type creatures, shaped like footballs, with killer expressions on their faces and ferocious little beaks.

'Guinea fowl,' Aldo says. 'They won't leave anyone alone, and they make a right racket. Better than any guard dog.'

When we enter the big kitchen, we see that G is already ensconced at one end of a long table, with the uncles and an older cousin, who Aldo introduces as Podge. The little group of men, or group of little men, have already taken their jackets off, loosened their ties and rolled up their sleeves, and they're talking loudly and glugging red wine from the kind of reinforced glass beakers we used to put toothbrushes in at school. On the table in front of them is a stack of photo albums. My brother keeps laughing and shaking his head and at one point I think I see him grab a handful of crisps from a bowl and shove them all into his mouth at the same time. But later, I decide I must have imagined that. Every so often there's a sudden burst of loud laughter from their direction, as though they're a team, a tribe who share a sense of humour that nobody else could possibly understand. Podge gets up and goes to fetch another bottle of wine and one of lemonade. Before he sits down again, he palm of his hand against the side of my brother's arm.

As for me, it turns out I have cousins: Marco's children, Josh and Hannah, and Aldo's youngest, Gabriella. How awesome is that? They pounce on me as soon as we've been properly introduced to everybody, thrust a bottle of cider in my direction and ask me tons of questions. I think it must be a test, to find out whether I'm an ok person or a complete bell end. I think I qualify as ok, because they usher me out of the farmhouse kitchen and across the yard to a barn. A handful of guinea fowl take the opportunity to dash through with us while the door is open, and instead of shooing them out, Josh opens the door wider to let the stragglers in, because they panic and kick up a fuss, he says, if they get separated. Once inside, they dash about en mass, gobbling and cackling, and I act as though I don't notice when they start pecking at my shoes.

    Josh and Hannah are tall and fair, and look a bit like me, whereas Gabriella is small and dark, like G and the uncles. They don't use this barn for animals anymore, apart from the guinea fowl and four enormous white geese who cast wary glances at their small, speckled counterparts, through milky blue eyes. My cousins hang out here when they're home from uni. They've put in a couple of electric heaters, a bit of old carpet and a collection of battered leather armchairs, and Josh has set up a dartboard, a baseball hoop, some second hand gaming equipment and a couple of speakers. It's beyond cool. I know I've only just met them, but they seem okay, and they have these amazing East Yorkshire accent, which is so familiar I begin to think I must have the same speech patterns embedded deep inside me, like the first rings that form inside a tiny sapling before it grows into a tree. I've never heard Mum talk like that. Even though she grew up here, she always sounded more American than anything else. But I think G did, when we were both really little.

    Josh and Hannah say they knew they had cousins down south, because our grandmother used to talk about us sometimes, particularly about G, but they didn't know where we lived or what we were doing. Despite their friendliness, I'm still a bit cautious at first. Or at least, I try to be. Bartosz has warned me to be careful who I trust in the future, because I can't afford to let myself get exploited again. But we work our way through a crate of cider and platefuls of food we bring over from the house, and we play games on Josh's play station, and they seem so genuinely interested in me I end up telling them almost everything about myself, including about New Sunrise. I wasn't planning to, partly because Mum doesn't come out of it very well and she's their aunt. But I decide I can't be bothered to bottle up all my crap up anymore. If people aren't happy about it, that's their problem, not mine. It's not as though I'm inventing any of it. And it's not my fault I had such a shitty mother. When Josh gives me a clean T-shirt to replace my stained dress shirt,

I even show them my faded scars. They're appalled, but fascinated too, and seem totally on my side.

Late in the evening, Amanda texts me from the main house to say we're leaving. I go back to the kitchen. G's still in a huddle with the uncles. I wrap an arm around his neck as though I'm going to strangle him and I rough up his hair. He laughs and rests his hand on my wrists. The uncles laugh, too. I look at the empty bottles of wine on the table and the shot glasses and I realise they're all pretty wasted. Tomorrow, we've been invited to Marco's for dinner. He lives with his wife and my cousins in a bungalow at the other side of the sheep field, and he works the farm with Aldo, who lives in the main farmhouse. A couple of days later we're driving over to Enzo's place in York, where he lives with his partner, Greg. Then we've been invited back to the farm for lunch with Aldo and the rest of them next Sunday, I think. I can't remember exactly when we're doing what, to be honest, but Amanda will know. And my cousins say they're holding a big party in the barn on New Year's Eve and it would be great if I could come up for it.

Later, when we're back at the holiday park, I realise I've completely forgotten to phone Bartosz. It's too late now, and I'm too full of cider to say anything coherent, so I cobble together an apologetic few words and I send a photo I took of G sitting with the uncles. I follow it up with a selfie of me with Josh and Hannah. When Bartosz replies he doesn't mention the photo of G, but he says Josh, Hannah and I look more like siblings than cousins. I respond instantly with a smiley face.

29. Gawain

I'm sitting on a metal bench at the railway station, shrouded in freezing fog. I can see the vague outline of a row of terraced houses behind the opposite platform, but the mist gives the impression that the place is in the middle of nowhere. I know the station is close to the big, wide river you get such a good view of from the farm, but you can't see it from here. Also, according to Marco, the site of the camp where my grandfather was imprisoned during the war is just down the road. After the burial, Marco took me to see his grave, and my grandmother's, which is next to it. While we were there, he showed me a small black and white snapshot of them both that he keeps in his wallet. My grandfather is sitting on his chair outside, close to the kitchen door and my grandmother is standing behind him with her hands on his shoulders. You can tell they're staring into the sun because they're both squinting, and he's clearly much older than her. But there's someone else in the photo, a tiny boy in dungarees and a stripy T-shirt. He's sitting on the old man's lap and he has a big grin on his face. And he's peering at the camera, not just because of the sun but because that's what he does.

My grandmother only died seven and a half months ago. She was in her mid-nineties and she fell and broke her hip, but was still completely lucid. She got pneumonia, and when she was dying, she talked about me and how she'd have given anything to see me again. They tried to find me, but they didn't know where to look. I'm not surprised really. I don't do social media, so I haven't left many virtual traces of myself out there. I told Marco I'd have given anything to see her, too. Then he gave me the lowdown on the rest of the family, *my* family. Eventually, he got to the cousins, the eldest of whom is Podge, Aldo's son. So named because he's even skinnier than the rest of us, if that's possible.

'I think I remember him. He used to follow me around the farmyard with a notebook and pen, and report back when I did something naughty.'

'It was a good job he did because once you started walking you were a right handful. We'd only to turn our backs for a second and you'd be dashing across the sheep field or you'd be half way down the lane dragging one of the guinea fowl behind you in a plastic bag.'

'I climbed on the dresser, didn't I? And I threw the big tea pot and all the little egg cups onto the floor.'

'They'd been in the family for generations.'

We walked back towards the area near the little chapel, where all the cars had been parked. Most of them had left. It was coming back to me, in fragments. I needed to join it all together, to make it form a proper narrative.

'Where does the name Valdini come from?'

'Your grandad was an Italian prisoner of war. There were loads of them round here. They were let out during the day to work on the farms. He was sent to ours. It belonged to your grandmother's parents back then. He was older than her by a good few years.'

'He used to cry, didn't he?'

'He'd had a stroke by the time you turned up, and he was a bit of a wanderer by nature, so he hated being stuck at home. Before the stroke, he'd disappear after breakfast and you wouldn't see him again until tea time. He did the milking, before he set off, but our mother did most of the other work on the farm. We helped as much as we could, of course, after school and in the holidays.'

'Where did he go?'

'Usually, he just roamed the lanes around the farm. He had his favourite spots in the fields and the woods, where he liked to sit and stare or have a little kip, if it was warm enough. But sometimes he'd hitch a lift and end up in all sorts of places. One of us would have to go and fetch him. Often it was Driffield or Beverley, which weren't too bad, but once he managed to get to all the way to Spurn Point, which was a right pain. Later on, he took up with a fancy woman, a retired teacher called Geraldine. She lived in one of those big semis down Priory Road, as you go out of the other side of the village. I've no idea what she saw in Dad, but we all blamed her when he had his first stroke. It was too much for him at his age, all that carrying on.' He laughs. It's clearly all water under the bridge now.

'I used to wander off, too. My dad had to come and find me.'

'Your mother was the same. When she was a kid she was always disappearing down some footpath or other, and when she was a teenager she used to run off to the village and hang about on the green, drinking and mucking about with lads. She could never stick with your dad for long, either. I don't know why she was like that, but that's how you ended up with us. You were only a few days old. She more or less handed you over to your grandmother.'

'Maybe she didn't like babies. She vanished completely when Jacob was born.'

'I remember. She said she'd had enough of your Dad and she went off with that Warren chap.'

'There was something wrong with her, wasn't there?'

Marco sighed. 'Sometimes she seemed normal but I think that was an act she'd learned by copying other people. I don't think she was ever right. Not really. I don't know what went on inside her head. Nobody did.'

'Was she the reason I was taken away from the farm?'

'Your granddad had an appointment at the stroke clinic at Hull Royal and your grandma had to drive him there. She couldn't very well take you with her, so she left you with your mother. She wasn't happy about it, but she thought you'd both cope for a couple of hours.'

'And when she got back, I was locked in the cupboard under the stairs and my mouth was full of acorns?'

'Not acorns. And you were in the yard, not the cupboard. Your mouth was full of gravel. There was a pile of it by the back door. Your mum said she'd shovelled it in with a spoon to shut you up. It was everywhere - down your throat and up your nose. We thought you were going to choke. I got it all out in the end, but it was sharp and the inside of your mouth was cut to ribbons. We decided it would be best to get you away from her for a while, so we rang your Dad. He came the same afternoon. We thought he'd bring you back once everything had calmed down. But your Dad had other ideas.'

It's all fine. I don't care what my mother did to me, because those early pages in the book of my life, the ones that used to be a complete blank, are now filled, not just with vague sketches and dreamlike images, but with detailed drawings. Every line is clearly marked and each space accurately shaded, and knowing is much better than not knowing, no matter how awful some of it is. I don't suppose anyone would ever ask me anything about the toddler version of me, apart from Bartosz perhaps. But if they did, I could answer all their questions now. Suppose, for example, someone asked me how old I was I started walking, what my first word was and what I liked to eat best when I was a toddler? I wouldn't have had a clue before, but now I'd be able to look them in the eye and say eleven months, Marco and fish fingers.

I waded through the piles of photo albums they stacked in front of me, and as I gradually remembered my early life, Aldo, Enzo and Marco started asking me questions about me as I am now. It felt like group therapy. In the end, I we reached a point where they knew the twenty-seven year old version of me as well as they'd known the two year old. They were gobsmacked to hear I'd become a doctor and even more dumbfounded when they discovered Amanda was one too. They all stood up to shake me by the hand, then they went and did the same to a bemused Amanda. Aldo said he was so proud he could burst. Then, inevitably, they all started asking me to diagnose their aches and pains, and as each of them described their own particular problems and I got them to stand up and bend over or roll up their trouser leg, or whatever was required, the others mocked and heckled.

When I'd had a few glasses of wine, I plucked up the courage to discuss Bartosz with them and the way we'd left things. Be honest with him, they said. Just explain how you feel. Be courageous. Life's way too short to be anything else.

I still feel a bit nervous about that. In fact I'm bricking it, if I'm honest. But I'm a completely different person to the one who walked out of Bartosz's house that night just over two weeks ago. I was a ghost then, an approximation of a person. Now that I know my origins, I cast proper shadows in sunlight, I'm firmly tethered to the ground and when I stamp my feet, there's the slightest hint of a vibration.

Our holiday has come to an end. Amanda and Jacob dropped me off at the station before hitting the M62 and heading home. The Leeds train doesn't arrive for another twenty minutes, and the fog is starting to cling to my clothes, so I decide to go and sit in the waiting room. There isn't much here - no toilets and no café, just a screen informing travellers whether their train is on its way or has been cancelled. This screen and the accompanying public address system have just caused serious consternation to most of the waiting passengers, by announcing that the previously soon-to-arrive King's Cross train has dropped off the face of the earth, due to the presence of cows on the line near Peterborough. The erstwhile London passengers are all standing on the platform next to their suitcases on wheels, tapping at their phones as they try to restructure their journeys.

My train arrives on time, but it ends up rammed, because one option for the London passengers is to get on and change at Leeds, so I have to stand. After a lot of tedious stopping and starting, some of it at stations, but mostly in the middle of desolate looking fields of yellow grass and thistles, the suffocatingly overheated train finally pulls into Leeds and we all shuffle out and inhale great lungfuls of cold air. I look at the departure boards for a connection to Skipton. There should be two trains every hour, but I soon discover that there are none at the moment, due to a police incident at Crossflatts.

Okay, never mind. I'm not in a hurry. I survey the various food outlets, and try to decide what to have. In the end, I opt for a vegan sausage roll and a passion fruit smoothie, but then I decide to splash out and I buy not only cheese puffs, but a box of Maltesers as well. I've never been able to eat either of these without skewering them onto forks and dipping them into cups of soup or tea, but they can't be worse than a mouthful of gravel. And I survived when I allowed a mouthful of crisps to come into contact with my teeth at the wake for a few seconds, before I panicked and glugged them down, sharp edges and all, with an entire glass of Chianti.

I find a metal seat in front of the departure screens, open the cheese puffs and put one in my mouth. I suck it until it goes soft. Then I swallow it. It tastes ok, but I'm not really getting the benefit of the texture, and squashing bits of extruded corn between my tongue and the roof of my mouth isn't exactly pleasant, so I bite the next one in two and crunch half of it between my teeth. I wait. Nothing bad happens. I put a whole one in and my teeth work overtime as they chomp it into little pieces. I munch my triumphant way through the rest of the packet, perhaps making more noise than you might expect to hear from people already acclimatized to Wotsits, and I put the Maltesers in my backpack for later.

The Skipton trains don't start again until mid-afternoon, and it's nearly four before we pull into the station at the town known as the Gateway to the Dales. The air smells damp and soft with a hint of the kind of smoke you get from coal fires. I soon give up trying to fathom out the bus timetable on my phone. In any case, the bus station doesn't appear to be anywhere near the exit from the railway station, or if it is, I'm unable to see it for some reason. There are taxis, though, so I jump into one. It takes us through the town, past the entrance to a castle, of all things, and along a road called The Bailey. We soon turn off onto another road that runs into a depression, passes a few fields and then rapidly emerges into the first of two villages that are attached to each other and have similar names. Bartosz's mum lives in one of these villages, and he's been staying with her for the past week, according to Jacob.

Bartosz's childhood home is at the end of a raised stone terrace. You have to climb up a small flight of steps to reach it and the road beneath is very narrow. I wonder where the residents park their cars. I can't see his Audi anywhere. The frontage of his mum's house is slightly wider than that of the adjoining houses, and the front door has a stained glass window depicting a pastoral scene with a vivid green tree and two creamy sheep. A table lamp in the window of the front room casts a warm apricot glow over the over a portion of the neatly mown front lawn.

As soon as I'm sure it's the right house, the new, bolder version of me fades away. I grip the wrought iron gate with one hand, to stop myself floating into the air, and I glance at my watch. If I call another taxi now, I'll be back in Skipton before six and I should reach Leeds before it's too late and pick up a London train. Too late. A woman is waving and smiling at me from the window of the front room. I wave and smile back. Next thing she's opening the door and running down the garden path in furry pink slippers.

'Hello!'

She sounds as though she's been looking out for me on and off all afternoon, hoping I'd turn up, and now that I have, she's thrilled. She can't have known I was coming, can she? I haven't told anyone where I was going or why, apart from Jacob and Amanda. And the uncles. And Podge. Ok, that's six people. But they've all been sworn to secrecy and none of them even know Bartosz's mum, let alone her phone number.

'Come in!'

I follow her down the path. When I get inside I hear myself say *I'm Gawain*, and I nearly add *one of the doctors*. How mortifying that would have been. A flush spreads across my cheeks at the thought of it.

'I thought you might be,' she says, a hint of irony in her voice.

She looks just like you'd expect Bartosz's mum to look, but I can't quite pin down how or why exactly. She doesn't have his blue eyes or his saturnine frown or his sweeping-brush hair, and she's smaller and much softer round the edges. One of the mysteries of heredity, I guess. After pulling me inside she kisses me on both cheeks as though she already knows me quite well. I bet she does. Bartosz is pretty close to his mum. She probably knows every last, shameful detail.

The hall is warm. On the way in, I notice a collection of colourful glass horses from that island near Venice. They're standing about on a little shelf over the radiator as though they've stopped in mid-trot so they can listen to our conversation. As I move further down the hall I hear a gentle clinking sound and realise I've swept several of them onto the carpet with my backpack.

'Oh, no! I'm so sorry!' I bend down and pick them all up. Luckily none of them are broken. I try to put them all back on the shelf, trying to make sure each one stands on its four delicate legs and doesn't topple over, but my hands are trembling and most of them end up on their sides. She takes them from me one by one and laughs quietly.

'Bartosz has gone for a run,' she says. 'He was feeling a bit caged in. Would you like a cup of tea or maybe you'd like to go after him? He's only just set off.'

I'd quite like to chat to her for a while, get her take on the situation between Bartosz and me. But now I'm here, I'm desperate to see him.

'Do you think I should go after him?'

'I'm sure he won't mind.'

She sounds pretty convinced.

'Which way did he go?'

'Up the crags.'

We walk down the garden path again, until rising land comes into view behind the house. She points to a straggling row of big rocks on top of the looming hillside. Then she points to an area much lower down, close to the house.

'See that field?'

I nod.

'If you follow the little footpath straight across it to the other side, you'll come to a track that curves round a small reservoir with a boating club. Then it leads directly up to the top.'

'Ok. Got it. Thanks."

'Do you want to leave your bag here?'

I thank her and she smiles again as I hand her my backpack. I've got the most important thing on me, nestling in its little square box in the side pocket of my leather jacket. I set off at a run. Good job I'm wearing decent boots with soles that have some grip because the path across the field is slippery as hell. The drizzle is relentless and my hair, which has grown out a lot since the accident, is turning into a kind of holder for hundreds of drops of moisture. I can see some of them in front of my eyes, hanging off my fringe like decorations on a miniature Christmas tree. I find the track, follow it round the reservoir and as I start the almost vertical ascent, I spot Bartosz ahead of me in the distance. I can tell it's him by his gait, which is bow legged, as though he's spent most of his life on a horse. I had a go at him once about increasing his vitamin D intake, but he got shirty and said the shape of his legs was both genetic and none of my business.

Unfortunately he's wearing his grey long sleeved T-shirt, not his red one, and his black leggings, so I can only just make him out through the murk. I shout his name, but my voice is deadened, either by the direction of the wind or the acoustics of the place, and he doesn't look round.

30. Gawain

I try to sprint up the hill, to match his pace, but I'm still operating at a very low fitness level. Soon, I'm out of breath. Climbing twenty steps then stopping for a count of ten seems to work, but it takes me ages to reach the first of the crags, and by the time I get there, Bartosz has vanished into the mist. As I move forward, more and more of these dramatic rocks pop up in front of me. If he comes back the same way, we'll probably collide with each other any second, but if he decides to use a different route for his descent, I'll have to keep chasing him. I might not catch up with him until after he's back home. They'll wonder where I am, and start talking about sending out a search party. When they find me, his mum will be all kind and sympathetic, and I'll feel like a prize imbecile.

Nobody else is about, probably because most sane people don't run or walk in places like this when it's starting to get dark. I walk along the desolate brow of the hill, dodging boulders and boggy areas. As I pass each crag, I half expect to find Bartosz standing on the top, in Heathcliff mode, frowning moodily and majestically into the distance, his hair and beard blowing back from his face in the wind.

When I do finally spot him again, he's a miniature action man receding into the distance, jogging away from me downhill along a narrow track that cuts through an area of rough moorland. I locate the beginning of the track and pursue him. I make faster progress going down than I did going up, but I'm terrified of tripping over a stone and falling flat on my face. I get to a point where I think I'm gaining on him a little, but all of a sudden he disappears again, which puzzles me because I can see all the way down to the bottom of the fell from where I am.

When I get closer, I realise the path turns sharp right round the bottom corner of an enclosure of pine trees within a dry stone wall. And there he is, a couple of metres in front of me, sitting on a bench, staring moodily, not at the distance but at his running shoe, which he's taken off and is trying to clean by swiping it across the grass at his feet. I know why. Just before you get to the bench you have to dodge a cow pat, a large, moist browny-green splodge, almost divided into two halves by the print of his trainer. I take a step back round the corner so I'm out of his line of vision again.

I don't think he spotted me, but I half expect to hear his voice any minute. *What the bloody hell are you doing behind that wall? Come out here where I can see you, lad.* He doesn't call me lad very often, to be fair. But he might do here, on his home turf. What he actually says is *bollocks*, followed by *shit* with a short gap in-between. The Gods are on my side for once. Time to prepare, quickly, before he gets his running shoe back on and sets off again. I shrug off my leather jacket. Underneath I'm wearing my best sage green shirt. Even though I start shivering as soon as my jacket comes off, I roll up my sleeves to somewhere just above my elbows, and I undo a couple more buttons to reveal the toffee coloured tan I managed to accrue over the summer and which hasn't completely faded yet. I wish I could squirt some deodorant onto my armpits, but the can is back at the house, in my bag, and anyway the spraying noise might alert him to my presence before I'm ready. Mind you, he won't smell all that sweet himself at the moment either, particularly after treading in a cow pat. I run a hand through my hair. I don't have a hairbrush or any gel on me to tame my corkscrews. I imagine I look pretty wild or maybe, with a bit of luck, wildly pretty.

Time to stop dithering. I check again to make sure the box hasn't fallen out of my pocket. Then I close my eyes for a brief couple of seconds as I get my swagger on, and I turn the corner and stride towards him, carrying my jacket over my shoulder, my other hand tucked casually into one of the front pockets of my jeans. I smile. But he doesn't even look up, so I end up standing there unobserved, right in front of him, with a bird's eye view of the sweat pouring down the back of his neck into his T-shirt.

'Alright?' He says quietly. He heard me, then, but he thinks I'm another runner or a walker passing by on my way down the hill. He thinks I'm going to respond with a similar greeting and disappear off towards the village. Instead I sit down at the far end of the bench, which isn't much more than a horizontal plank. Even then, he doesn't change his position, so I move along until I'm really close to him, much closer than an unknown person would sit, so close that our hips are touching.

'Hi,' I say, quietly.

He leaps off the bench, steps back a couple of metres and stares at me, with his feet apart and his hands on his head. Then he sits himself down in the wet grass. At first I think he's winding me up, acting shocked for a laugh. In a minute, he'll get up, make some irony-laden comment about me of all people turning up here and we'll launch ourselves at each other. I sit on the bench and smile at him. Silence surround us. There isn't a single sound. No birds singing, no sheep bleating and no traffic noise from distant roads. It feels as though we're inside some kind of soundproof pod, sequestered from the rest of the world, waiting to be abducted by extraterrestrials.

Then he comes to his senses. If he could vaporise people by scowling at them or skewering them with his eyes, I'd be gone in an instant. My smile fades. I put my jacket back on and zip up the pocket containing the box.

'What the bloody hell are you doing here?'

'Your mum told me where you'd gone. I've been trying to catch up with you for ages.'

'You could've texted me.'

'I wanted to surprise you.'

'You did that alright.'

'I didn't mean to trigger you.'

'You didn't trigger anything.' He follows this statement with a series of muttered curses.

Little orange lights, streetlights I suppose, are twinkling down below us in the valley, and I don't know about him, but the cold is starting to seep into my bones. I get onto my feet and offer him a hand to pull him up, but he ignores it and gets up under his own steam. Then he slips and ends up on his arse again, which makes him even tetchier than he was before.

It takes us ages to negotiate the path down the hill in the dark and we don't say a single word to each other. The further we go, the more exhausted I feel, and I start to lag behind. He stands and waits, but with his head turned away from me, staring at the path ahead and jiggling one leg, as though he's barely able to tolerate the delay. When we finally reach his mum's house, she's nowhere to be seen, and it feels less warm and welcoming than it did before.

Bartosz fires a series of clipped, need-to-know sentences at me. 'My mum goes line dancing in Gargrave on Friday nights. I'm off upstairs for a shower. You can have one after me, if you want. Leave your jacket and boots in the hall.'

He puts a hand on my back and shoves me into a dark room at the back of the house. He tells me to stay there until he comes down again. I find a light switch and see that I'm in a big living space with one of those enormous corner seating units at one end and a dining table at the other. On the wall above the table is a poster-sized and very glossy photograph of a boy with spiky black hair, who must be about ten years old, wearing a Leeds United shirt and surrounded by three older girls. It looks like a professional picture. They must have had it done specially, in a studio. Nobody ever took a picture like that of me and my siblings.

I settle myself on the sofa and dig out my phone. There's a message from Jacob.

'You there yet?'

'Yes, but he's behaving like a knob.'

'He'll come round.'

'You think?'

'I think.'

Bartosz take ages in the shower. When he finally reappears, his hair is shiny and slicked back from his face, and he's put on his black tracksuit, the one with the logo of his regiment embroidered discretely across the top of his right sleeve. His brow is still furrowed, and overall he looks as though he's going to a fancy dress party dressed as an angry aquatic mammal, a walrus, perhaps. When he passes me on the way to what must be the kitchen, I smile up at him from the sofa. He manages to achieve eye contact with me, but instead of returning my smile, he scratches the back of his neck and looks away again. After clattering about in the kitchen for several minutes, he reappears, wearing oven gloves and carrying a big covered dish, which he slams down on the table. Then he goes back into the kitchen again and returns to sling plates and cutlery in the same general direction.

'Chicken casserole, if you want any. My mum made it. You should be able to eat it if you mash it up a bit. I'm not bloody liquidizing it for you.'

I go and sit at the table.

'That's my chair.'

I get up and move to another chair, and he spins a plate towards me across the table like a frisbee.

'Is there anything to drink?'

'Whaddayawant?'

The way he slurs all the words together makes me burst out laughing, and once I start I can't stop. He stomps off into the kitchen again and comes back with two glasses of water.

'I can't believe you were following me about on the crags,' he bellows after he's sat down.

'I intended to surprise you, not creep up and frighten you half to death.'

'You didn't frighten me. I was a bit taken aback, that's all.'

He opens the lid of the casserole dish and slops some of its contents onto my plate. A couple of peas and a piece of carrot bounce onto the tablecloth. I wait politely until he's served himself, then I demolish most of mine in about two minutes flat. Many hours have passed since I ate those Wotsits in Leeds Station and I'm ravenous after all that fell running. The casserole is delicious and I manage to chew the chicken without any problems. When I look up he's gaping at me in amazement.

'What?' I ask.

He doesn't reply.

There isn't enough space in his mum's kitchen for a dishwasher, so he does the washing up and I pick up a tea towel with a map of Airedale on it, and do the drying. Neither of us says a word. When we go back into the living room, we sit at either end of the massive seating unit. I make several attempts to start a conversation, but each time, he responds by waving his hands about as though I'm a small mosquito and he's trying to waft me away. At first I find it quite funny, but soon becomes tedious and then soul destroying. I think about the little box I've carried so carefully in my inside pocket from one part of Yorkshire to another. What a failure today has been. It started out so brightly, too.

I drag myself out of my chair and go to fetch my jacket and my backpack from the hall.

'If you don't want to talk to me properly, I may as well go. Thank your mum for the casserole. It was great.'

'Where do you think you'll get to at this time of night, round here?'

'That pub on the little square near the tree probably has rooms. Otherwise I'll call a cab to take me back into Skipton. There must be a hotel somewhere.'

He leans forward on the sofa, with his arms resting on his thighs and his hands clasped, and he stares at the beige swirls in the carpet as though they're way more interesting than I could ever be.

'Right,' I say in a brisk, let's-get-on-with-it tone.

He looks up at me.

'That's it then?'

'I don't know. You tell me.'

'Tell you what?'

'Oh, for God's sake, Bartosz! I'm getting fed up of this game.'

'What game?'

'The one where you refuse to engage with me.'

'Well how would you feel if it was the other way round?'

'Erm, I don't know. Pleased to see you, perhaps. Once I'd got over the shock.'

'Why do you think I'd be pleased to see you? I thought you were meant to be clever. Surely you can see that coming here and doing it in front of my mum is out of order.' He looks down at his hands. 'It's cruel, Gawain,' he says quietly.

'I'm not doing anything in front of your mum. She's line dancing in Gargoyle.'

'Gargrave.'

I know that. I was just trying to make him lighten up a little. Trying and failing.

He stands up and walks over to the mantelpiece above the electric fire. Turning his back to me, he picks up a Spanish flamenco doll mounted on a metal stand, tips it upside down and idly looks up its skirt. Apart from the crisp rustle of the stiff material between his fingers, silence emanates from him in waves. I gaze hopelessly at the rigid set of his shoulders.

Then, with a lurch that feels like a kick in the small of my back, I realise I've completely failed to read the room and the only other person in it, even though it's Bartosz, a person who's body language and patterns of speech I can usually translate as easily as if they're my own.

I'm such an idiot.

'Why do you think I'm here?' I ask his back.

He remains silent, but he puts the doll down and turns to face me. He's still looking down at the carpet, though.

'Bartosz?'

He folds his arms. I understand now. He's not being stubborn or difficult. He's bracing himself to hear what I have to say. I go over to him, dig my both my hands into his beard and pull his face down as close to mine as it will go. He lets me, but he slams his eyes shut.

'If you don't open your eyes I'll pull your eyelids up with my fingers,' I say.

His eyes open to narrow slits.

'I haven't come to tell it's over, you prize lemon. Look at me, I'm wearing my best olive green shirt, for God's sake.'

'Eh?'

'I've come to claim you.'

'Claim me?'

'Do you want me to go or not?'

'Not,' he mumbles reluctantly.

'You're such a tit, Bartosz.'

'So are you.' His arms creep round my waist and he rests his chin on the top of my head. I remember how sweaty and generally filthy I am.

'Can I have a bath?'

He leads me upstairs and shows me where the bathroom is. Then he fusses about in the airing cupboard finding fresh towels.

'Come in with me.'

'I've just showered.'

'Not with me.'

I sit with my back to him in the steam. H pulls me close to him and pinches my belly.

'You've put on weight!'

I explain about the gravel in my mouth and how I don't mind about things touching my teeth, now that I know why it bothered me so much before. To prove my point, I climb out of the bath and drip over the bathroom carpet and down the stairs to the hall to fetch the Maltesers I bought in Leeds. I get back in, put one in his ear and then extract it with my mouth. I make him watch as I munch one, then we share the rest of the pack while we're still in submerged in the hot water.

'Can you do other things with your teeth, now?'

'Probably. What did you have in mind?'

When his mum gets back from her line dancing, Bartosz makes a pot of tea and we settle ourselves in the living room with a tin of Teatime Assortment. I tell them about my newly discovered family, and Bartosz slips bits of gypsy creams and ginger snaps into my mouth so he can listen to my gnashing.

'Do you remember Paddy?' He asks his mum.

'The shire horse in the field next to the glove factory?'

'The noise his teeth used to make when we fed him Polos and little apples? Here you are, Paddy.'

He feeds me half a party ring and his mum laughs.

'Will your mum mind me sleeping in your room?' I ask as we make our way upstairs for the night.

'What century do you think she's living in?'

I shrug. I don't know much about how things work with mothers in situations like this.

He only has a single bed. He gets in first, then I carefully insinuate myself into the narrow space, partly on top of him and partly around his edges. We re-familiarise ourselves with the feel and scent of each other's skin and I whisper cheesy nothings into his ear about home, how for me it's just him, wherever he is, and that I'd follow him anywhere, even if he decided to go and live in a yurt in Outer Mongolia. The soles of my feet shrivel slightly as the words come out of my mouth, but I've finally realised that sometimes you have to verbalise things to be absolutely certain the other person gets it. He says I'd never cope with life under canvas, which is probably true, but I can tell he approves of my declaration by the way he nudges his nose into my hair while I'm making it.

I'm still not sure he really understands that I've finally grown into myself and become the person I'm meant to be, though, and that the new me is prepared to be lot bolder than the old version. Time to show him. I proceed with a quiet, workmanlike confidence and it doesn't take him long to realise what I'm up to.

'Are you sure you know what you're doing?'

'I'm a doctor. I've seen diagrams.'

'This is weird,' he mumbles, after I've tentatively got things started.

I ignore him. When two of my fingers find what they're searching for, he gasps.

'Want me to stop?'

'I didn't say that, did I?'

Carefully, I proceed to the next stage of the endeavour. I have to pause to accustom myself to the unfamiliar sensation, which is as strange for me as it is for him. Strange in a good way, though.

'Have you nodded off?' He asks.

Tacked onto end of his bed is a headboard made from shiny black plastic, which is quilted and pierced by black buttons at regular intervals, and stuffed with something soft that has separated itself into a collection of small lumps. The word *kapok* enters my head. It must be one of the least romantic words in the universe, and it almost derails me. But somehow, I manage to get back on track and soon this tacky relic from the seventies begins to tap out a muffled and tentative, but incredibly cheerful and optimistic beat against the wall. Gradually it picks up speed. Squish-bump, squish-bump it goes and Bartosz adds a pleasing accompaniment in the form of quiet little yelps. I've never heard him make noises like this before and I'm beyond proud that I'm the one forcing them out of him.

'Jesus, I'm going to die,' he says eventually, between groans. Then he says it again, twice.

Afterwards, I'm exhausted, but I've never felt so victorious. Bartosz, completely pole axed, whimpers into his pillow.

But the little box is still sitting in the pocket of my jacket waiting for me to do and say the other thing.

31. Gawain

When I wake up, sunlight is streaming onto the bed through a gap in the curtains. Bartosz stirs in his sleep. I prod him until he opens his eyes.

'What's your mum doing today?'
'She usually goes to the market in Skipton on Saturday mornings.'
"So we could go out then? It wouldn't be rude?'
'Where do you want to go?'
'How far is it to Howarth?'
'It's just down the road, but…'
'But what?'
'Nothing.'

By the time we're half way there, the sky is full of grey clouds and when we reach the big parking area between the parsonage and a row of weavers' cottages, rain is gushing from sky in torrents. We sit in his car, peering out at sheets of water blowing over the concrete surface of the car park, uncertain what to do next. My intention was for us to walk up to Top Withens and for me to get my little box out and go down on one knee up there on the wild, windy moors, under those iconic trees. But I hadn't bargained for this abrupt change in the weather.

'We could go into the parsonage.' I've longed to go to the Bronte home for years, but it's always been too far away and too difficult to get to in the time available. I know the layout, though, from the internet, and I can think of a couple of places inside that might be suitable for my purposes. Emily's little bedroom, for instance, the room once occupied and possibly still haunted by the mind that created Heathcliff.

'I'm not bloody well going in there again,' Bartosz declares gruffly.

'Why not? What's wrong with it?'

'If you knew the number of times I've been forced to go round that place on school trips, yawning my head off, you wouldn't ask. One time, I was so fed up I started mucking about and got sent out. I had to spend an hour in the graveyard on my own. In the snow.'

'What did you do?'

'Sat on a gravestone and nearly froze my bollocks off.'

'I meant what did you get chucked out for?'

'I hid behind a door and jumped out roaring my head off to frighten Juliet Bethell coming through the door. Only it wasn't Juliet Bethell, it was poor old Mrs Winstone, who had a heart condition. She had to go and sit on a stool near the entrance for a bit. My parents got a letter from the school about it. They banned me from playing football for a month.'

'You're so badass.'

'Yeah well. I'll keep my bad arse in the car this time. You trot off. It won't take you long. There's nowt much to see. Just a few little shoes in a glass case. And some boring rooms full of old furniture.'

'I don't want to go on my own.'

'You'll be better off without me there, dogging your heels. When you're done, we can go look round the shops if you want and get a coffee or something.'

'It's time for your football show on the radio, isn't it?'

'You know me too well. Bugger off and leave me in peace.'

He hunches himself up in his seat, fluffs himself out and half-closes his eyes like a wood pigeon perched in a tree on a cold day, and I go off and spend about forty minutes in the parsonage on my own. Loads of other people have decided to do the same thing because of the rain, so there wouldn't have been enough floor space for me to go down on one knee. And anyway, it would be too public in there, particularly if the only answer I'm going to get is one of his abrupt put downs. Nevertheless, I enjoy looking around and on the way out I go into the bookshop and buy a chunky biography of Emily, a new one I haven't come across before.

'When are you going to find time to read that?' Bartosz scoffs when I get back to the car. 'Never mind, it'll make a good doorstop.'

'I'm a quick reader. I'll find time.'

We wander down to the steep, cobbled street where most of the shops are situated. The heavy rain has dwindled to a vicious, cold drizzle that feels like an aerial attack by a mass of rapidly descending sharp pins. He trudges along and I hop about beside him.

'You seem a bit on edge. Do you need the toilet? There was one in the car park. You should have gone then,' he says.

'I'm skittish. Like Bertha Mason.'

'Eh?'

'Never mind.'

I look in a few shop windows, pretending to scan the merchandise on display for potential Christmas gift ideas, but what I'm really doing is attempting to see what kind of spaces and hidden corners there might be inside. He doesn't even bother trying to show an interest in second-hand books or tourist trinkets or Bronte fudge. Instead, he puts his hands in his pockets, stares bleakly down at the cobbles and kicks the kerb with his right boot. Gradually, the drizzle gets to us both. A lot of it has ended up down the back of my neck inside my jacket. I accidentally shiver, which is annoying, because he notices.

'Come on, let's go and get a hot drink,' he says.

I almost give in. Maybe it would be ok to do it across the table in a café or even in the car before we head back to his mum's house. It's not what I had in mind, though. I wanted the setting to be a bit unusual, dramatic even. Something to tell our kids about, if we have any. We end up outside an establishment that calls itself the *Bronte Christmas Emporium*. Its Georgian bow window glitters with fairy lights that make blurry reflections on the wet paving stones outside and chocolate snowmen surrounded by tiny Christmas trees made out of green glass stare out at us. I peek through the door and see immediately that the space inside is dimly lit and full of odd little nooks and crannies. And at the back, I spot a staircase, leading to another area of possibilities on the upper floor. I grab Bartosz by the sleeve of his jacket and start to pull him through the door. A bell tinkles.

'I'll wait for you out here,' he says, removing my hand from his sleeve and stepping niftily backwards out of the doorway.

'No you won't.'

I dodge behind him and manage to shove him inside before the door swings shut again. This creates a small commotion and makes him very cross. Several customers turn their heads to gawp at us.

'Five minutes.' I say. 'Then we can go find a café.'

He grunts.

The ground floor is full of people in rainwear, shaking out their umbrellas and tripping over a pair of couple of small and very soggy dogs, which are running amok, sniffing everybody's shoes and boots. I head straight for the stairs and Bartosz traipses up behind me, tutting under his breath. The second floor is much quieter, more of a grotto really, with delicate ornaments in the shape of fairies and elves dangling from the ceiling between floral garlands and swags of fake, but reasonably tasteful, holly and ivy. At the back of the room, I notice a deep and relatively private little alcove that houses a collection of festive babywear illuminated by a string of golden pinpricks of light, which slowly switch between the on and the off position. Four seconds off and four seconds on. The timing is slightly too slow. When the lights are off, the alcove is plunged into darkness for what seems like ages, and when they come on again, their sudden brightness is dazzling.

It suits my purposes perfectly.

The only other people in this upstairs space are a young American couple. As I wait for them to leave, I examine a range of different festive wreaths and end up putting several of them on head and looking at myself in a little silver framed mirror. My favourite is mostly fake yew and ivy but it also has little, pale green, bell-shaped flowers on stalks which make little dangling shadows on my forehead. I think it looks very fetching and I decide to leave it on. The American couple are and shaking and commenting on a series of snow globes. There are loads of the things in different sizes and shapes. They could be at it for ages if they decide to inspect them all. The danger is that they will stay up here for longer than the very short amount of time it will take for Bartosz to get fed up of this glittering space, or that more people will come up the stairs and we'll never be alone.

Next, they spend what seems like an eternity looking at a cuckoo clock in which the bird's head has been replaced by that of Father Christmas. It suddenly shoots out and bellows a robotic *ho-ho-ho* at high volume. The entire effect is peculiarly jarring and unpleasant, and it gives me a nasty shock. It annoys the hell out of Bartosz.

'I've never seen so much crap in all my life,' he shouts in a voice that makes the baubles rattle. Then he notices my wreath. 'What have you got that thing on your head for?'

The American couple swing round, to see what he's talking about. One glimpse of me is enough to send them scurrying out. Quick as a flash, I dash across the floor and push the door shut behind them. I can't believe my luck when I see it has a lock with a key in it. I turn the key. Nobody can disturb us now. This is it, I think. It's taken long enough, but the stars have finally aligned in my favour.

'What's going on?' Bartosz says.

I plonk another of the wreaths on his head. Its main features are pine cones and a sprinkling of fake snow. It's less camp than the one I'm wearing and it makes him look like the Ghost of Christmas Present. I push him into the alcove. When we first go in, the fairy lights are off. But by the time they come on again I'm on one knee in front of him. He looks down at me.

'We can't do that here!'

'Why not?'

'They've got security cameras. We'll be arrested.'

Since last night he thinks I've turned into some kind of sex pest.

'You're such an idiot, sometimes, Bartosz.'

'What *are* you doing, then?'

'Shut up for a minute, will you.'

Everything is starting to unravel. The miserable sod is doing his best to ruin it, but I'm way too far in to let that happen. I reach into the inside pocket of my jacket and bring out the box. I open it, get the ring out and take a couple of seconds to prepare myself. But stage fright kicks in and the little speech I've rehearsed in my head comes out all mangled.

'I was devastated when you suggested it, but now I think it was the right thing to do because it's thrown everything up into the air and made it fall back to earth into more of the right kind of heap, so it makes more sense. Or it will do. Hopefully.'

'What was?'

'What was what?'

'The right thing to do?'

'Being apart for two weeks.'

When the lighting permits, I look up at him. He's staring down at me with an expression of mulish stupidity on his face, not his best look. I really hope he's doing it deliberately to wind me up, because I don't want to marry a man who's happy to pass himself off as an oaf in public.

'I just wanted you to give it some thought,' he says.

'I have. You know that.'

'Yes, but what has crawling about on your hands and knees in a shop got to do with anything?'

'Are you winding me up? Either way, I'm going to get really angry in a minute.'

'What are you going to do? Bite me?'

He laughs at his little joke, shuffles backwards a bit and puts his hands into the pockets of his jeans. I'm beginning to think I should abandon this endeavour, but I remind myself of what Jacob said, about being more dominant, and I keep going.

'Look, Bartosz, I don't want to be your boyfriend or your partner.' I hold the ring out towards him. 'My granddad made this out of an old sixpence and a bit of wire or something when he was a prisoner of war, and he gave it to my grandmother. When she died, they kept it for me. He's put a kind of sliding mechanism into it so it fits any finger. I'm not sure how long it will last before it falls to bits, but we can get proper bands, too.'

He looks down at the ring, but he keeps his hands in his pockets and doesn't take it from me. 'I've heard about prisoners of war doing stuff like that," he says. 'They made all kinds of things, like ash trays and decorative wall plaques and buckets out of elephant's feet. Although I can't think where they got *them* from. Unless someone brought a lorry load back from Burma.'

This irritating and irrelevant soliloquy is interrupted by a frantic knocking at the door. A man's voice on the other side says *hello* and asks if everything's alright. I thrust the ring at Bartosz and I gear myself up to say the words that usually accompany this gesture. But he's distracted by the knocking and shouting, and he turns away from me, marches over to the door and unlocks it, leaving me kneeling in the alcove alone. I spring to my feet, put the ring on one of my own fingers and quickly hide my bejewelled hand in my back pocket.

'What in heaven's name is going on? You can't just lock the door.' A smartly dressed older gentleman wearing prissy looking, wire-framed spectacles, trips into the room on small, dainty feet, encased in highly polished brogues. He stands in the middle of the floor with his hands on his hips. 'It's a shop, is this,' he says.

Bartosz apologises to the man and accompanies this expression of regret with the same half bow thing he did to my sister when he first met her. Then he grabs my other hand, hurries me down the stairs and removes the wreaths from our respective heads so the girl behind the counter can put them through the till. He puts them back on our heads when we leave the shop, and he grabs my hand and leads me across the street and down an alleyway at a run. When we reach the graveyard, he hoists me up into the air then sits me on the top of one of the table-like tombstones. The seat of my trousers becomes immediately soaked with rainwater. Not a nice feeling.

He stands in front of me, looking a bit gothic, like Mr Rochester might do if he had leaves and pine cones on his head. 'What have you done with that ring?' He yells.

I bring my hand out of my pocket and slide it off my finger. I hold it out and look at it.

'What's the matter with you?' He shouts. 'Lost your bottle?'

I get up and stand on the tombstone so I'm looking down at him. That's better. My inner balloon reinflates again. I hold out the ring towards him. Sod it, I think. If he laughs or turns me down, at least I'll be able to tell Jacob I tried. I roar at Bartosz through the rain, in the loudest voice I can manage. 'Bartosz, will you marry me?'

A handful of crows flutter into the air from the tops of the gloomy trees and clatter about. But the small group of tourists braving the weather at the far end of the graveyard, close to the parsonage don't even notice.

For a few seconds Bartosz stares up at me, blinking rainwater away from his eyelashes. He has a fake bewildered look on his face, not as though he's thinking about my proposal, but as if he's wondering who I am exactly. He's enjoying this, I can tell. I hold his gaze and force my eyes as wide open as they'll go, so I'm not doing my peering thing. Eventually, he reaches out and takes the ring from me and puts it on the appropriate finger. He plays with the mechanism, making the circumference of the ring bigger and then tightening it again. "It's clever, this," he says, quietly, as though he's talking to himself.

Then he looks up at me again.

'Do you love me, then?' He asks, casually, as though it's a matter of vague interest to him, nothing more.

'Of course I do, you stupid sod.'

'Say it.'

'I love you, Bartosz.'

I don't say the words. I scream them. But the sky doesn't fall in and I don't shatter into a thousand pieces. He scrambles up onto the tomb and pulls me towards him by the edges of my leather jacket. At first, he seems deadly serious and I think he's going to kiss me, all passionate and Heathcliff-like, but it doesn't happen because, suddenly, neither of us can stop laughing. He climbs down again, holds out his arms and tells me to jump. I do, without a moment's hesitation, and he catches me and carries me up and down the paths between the gravestones. My legs grip him round his waist for a while and then I slide to the ground. After that we prance about like crazy people beneath the trees and the crows, making a spectacle of ourselves until we're dizzy. I wonder if Emily's ghost is watching us. Or Charlotte's.

I hope so.

We finally manage to spin our way out of the churchyard and we go into a café with steamed up windows. The place is packed, but the stars have aligned for us again, because squeezed into a corner at the back is a single empty table with two chairs. We buy two gingerbread men with shiny little pink and blue buttons made out of icing. He opts for an Americano and I choose a hot chocolate with marshmallows and whipped cream. We prop the gingerbread men against the sugar bowl so their hands are touching. Then we take a photo of them and send it to Bartosz's mum, Amanda and of course, Jacob.

Thank you!

Thank you so much for reading *Gawain and the Green Man*. I really hope you enjoyed the story of Gawain's quest for happiness.

If so, please consider leaving a review on your favourite social media site.

If you'd like to hear more about Gawain and his family, please look out for the next book in the series, *Aunty Susan and the Fabric of Time*, in which Gawain's Aunty Susan attempts to unravel a mystery from long ago, with the help of her nephew, Jacob.

Thanks once again!

Kate

About the Author

Kate Laxen grew up in the North of England, but now lives in the South, in an area not too far from London, where footpaths wind their way between industrial estates and stretches of woodland, and canals form liminal spaces that separate rows of houses from green fields. Perhaps because of this, she prefers characters who don't live in the mainstream, but tend to occupy the borderlands and make their own way through life as individuals, not members of a crowd.

Printed in Great Britain
by Amazon